Right Off the Map by C. E. Montague

"One of the finest novels I have read. For all the epic grandeur of its religious blend of austerity and homeliness, Right Off the Map is, as a novel, engrossingly good."—Punch.

"Mr. Montague's power of telling a story is almost unequalled. He makes every page live, he is a master of irony and satire, and has brilliant wit. No one will put down this book without feeling that they have listened to a magic story told by a master spinner of words."—Westminster Gazette.

"We are proud of Mr. Montague as one of the finest writers of his time."—The Manchester Guardian.

Charles Edward Montague was born in London on New Year's Day, 1867 and educated at the City of London School and then Balliol College, Oxford.

At university, Montague, a keen writer, wrote several literary reviews for the Manchester Guardian and was then invited for a month's trial and, after impressing, to work there.

Montague and the editor, C. P. Scott shared the same political views and between them they turned the Manchester Guardian into a vibrant and campaigning newspaper. They were for Irish Home Rule and against the Boer War and the First World War.

But now that the war had begun. Montague believed that it was important to give full and unequivocal support to the British government. Despite his age, 47, he was determined to serve.

Montague was soon promoted to the rank of second lieutenant and with it a transfer to Military Intelligence. The war also brought about a crisis in his faith and it was resolved by Montague temporarily putting it to one side and carrying on with the fighting.

In November 1918 the war was over and Montague could now return home to his wife and family and also to the Manchester Guardian where he would continue to work until retirement in 1925.

For Montague the war had been corrosive but it had given him much to write about both for the paper but also for his books which he now hoped to also spend more time on. Among those to flow from his pen are the novels A Hind Let Loose and Rough Justice as well as collections of short stories, other essays and a travel book.

He finally retired in 1925, and settled down to become a full-time writer in the last years of his life. Charles Edward Montague died in Manchester on May 28th, 1928 at the age of 61.

Index of Contents

BOOK ONE

CHAPTER I

A GOODLY PLACE

I

The old Republic of Goya could not have chosen a more convenient moment for tumbling to pieces. All the English in the place were ready to act. Perhaps the fine political sense of the race had smelt what was coming. Or Bishop Case, the doyen of Goya's small bevy of Anglican parsons, may have been right in seeing, as he said, a Hand in the timing of the smash.

Most of the well-to-do Britons in Goya had settled in Ria. It is the most temperate province; it stands well away from the scorched Equatorial deserts of the North and also from the chronic gales of the far South. In Ria the hedges are made of geraniums and fuchsias. The streets are not literally paved with gold, but under some of them there lie a great many useful coins of silver and copper—still in the rough, but only needing a little mining and minting. Englishmen owned nearly all the mines that were at work already; they held a good half of the farmed land; they ran the banks and ruled the best clubs. A few of the leading people might be Jews, Germans and other sufferers from the disability of non-Englishness. But the language of Britain prevailed; so did her sports; so did comfortable middle-class Albion's ideas of what is best worth having in this life.

II

So the new Republic of Ria had an easy birth. Only a little tact was needed to make political power hand itself over and to detach the one desirable province of Goya, the prime joint of the animal, from the boiling pieces and the offal. The ease with which a sort of Rome could be built in a day, or little more, surprised the architects themselves.

They would certainly rather have had it not a Republic. In England, in old days, some of their wives had been presented at Court. Some of themselves had come out to this remote part of the earth, as Coriolanus went to Antium, in disgust at the excesses of democracy at home. Republicanism was no ideal of theirs. But a king who can be anointed without looking foolish is not to be got by just looking round. It did occur to a few people of the right sort that Cyril Burnage might have done, with credit, the ceremonial duties of a monarch. He was the best speaker in Ria, and had the most regal figure to be seen in the English Club. It crossed a few other minds that Andrew Bute, a prodigious hand at finance, might have made a neat job of the business side of kingship. And yet a vision of either Cyril or Andrew hedged with a mystic divinity would not quite present itself to the imagination—not though Zadok the priest and Nathan the prophet should descend from Heaven to assist in the hedging. So a Republic it had to be.

There was consolation for that. There was the reflection that forms, thank God, are not everything. Poor old besotted England herself was now a veiled republic really, though still a kingdom in form. In Ria there would be Hone of that nonsense. Republicanism in Ria would be the veil, not the face, much less the heart. There the right men would keep hold of the reins—the men with solid stakes in the country, the men of position, brains and the gift of command. As to this there was only one mind among men so various as Bute, the chief captain of business in all Goya; Dr. Browell, the head of Ria's new and palatially housed University; Burnage, the eloquent editor of her chief journal the Voice, and Bishop Case, her managing man in the affairs of the spirit.

III

The Constitution of the new State was the fine fruit of much sagacious thinking on all hands, and particularly pf much caution. Everybody was to have a vote if he could read in two languages, one of them being English. To some of you readers this franchise may seem dangerously wide. But its perils could be diminished, in practice, by a judicious choice of a second language wherein to examine any particular applicant for a vote. One well-thumbed page of Icelandic verse is said to have repelled from the roll of electors the whole of a great rush of immigrant trade-union workmen from Lancashire, who might otherwise have absolutely flooded out the old and choice electorate.

When that first hour of peril was past, some additional dams were thrown up, to guard against other inundations of mud. The teaching bestowed by the State upon the children of the poorer whites and half-castes was thoughtfully amended. As Burnage said in the Voice, it was "brought into a saner relation with the needs of life—the needs of the body, the mind, the soul and the country." Much of a child's time at school would now be spent in imbibing the ever-living truths of the Bible and Prayer-Book about the importance and beauty of being lowly and meek and of remembering one's station in life and of not being pert to the wise and the great. Much was spent, too, on simple technical studies and exercises suitable to the child's age, such as the gathering of currants, the scavenging of roads or the scaring of birds away from the crops of some estate lent by its owner for this educative purpose. Mere "verbal studies," such as advanced reading, grammar and history, were almost abandoned in the State schools. "A good riddance, too!" the Bishop used to say, in his sturdy common-sense tone. "What use is a bellyful of East wind to the vitals of honest labouring folk?"

As an educational expert Dr. Browell agreed warmly. The moral grandeur of unsophisticated manual toil was ever present to both these instructed minds. When the Bishop preached to the schoolboys of Ria City, the capital, his text was that much study is a weariness of the flesh and when Dr. Browell distributed prizes to the girls the burden of his address was, "Be good, sweet maid, and let who will be clever."

IV

It is known that the Devil may enter into the mind of man and dwell there, even if his educators have done their best to make the quarters unattractive to a fiend. So there were times when that one per cent, of the population of Ria whom God had presumably directed to govern the rest felt as the owner of an excellent sheep walk might feel if the flock began to look as though they might bite him; all together, and derange the whole of his thoughtful plan for their conversion into marketable mutton. Good sharp teeth, too, might be inserted by the Rian flock if they should ever be so wicked as to attempt an assault upon their pastors. Twenty-five per cent of them were British—tough, dark tin-miners from Cornwall, dour little factory hands from Lanark and Oldham who wouldn't say "Sir" to Jehovah, Anaks inexplicably reared on potatoes and Indian meal in mud cabins in the County Cork, and perky human sparrows from the London gutters, with wits as sharp and as indelicate as a pin. The rest of the available labour was neither black nor yellow, nor a good brown, nor yet irreproachably white. It was a mixed breed of short men, dark-haired, black-eyed, working like mules for the price of three platefuls of beans to the day and a heavy drink at the week-end: In their cups they would knife their friends with an unreserve which gave the statesmen of the new Ria material for thought and discussion.

Some of the statesmen were for simply "putting down" this vigorous trait and for "standing no nonsense." Murder Was murder, they said, with a thin lucidity. Others said No to all this. They were humanists. Not to get rid of a troublesome thing, but to discover the right use for it—this, they said, was the true wisdom of life. The best plush was made of silk waste: why not turn the choler of these poor fellows into a knightly grace and a military asset? Let Ria double her insufficient army and make everyone serve who could not read the two languages. Then the irascible braves might, some day, win a better frontier for the country. Anyhow, if fight they must, it was better to let their minds run on fighting the right people, foreigners. So this "native policy" was adopted.

Thought was taken, too, for plebeians of British origin. Whatever their faults, they came of the blood; there must reside in them somewhere the spirit of empire. They only had to see the native Rians aright—as a Heaven-sent breed of stout coolies for British foremen to keep to a job; or else as large, fierce and possibly faithful dogs for the servants of a British household to let loose at burglars or tramps. So all the gangers in the mines, the stewards of farms and the non-commissioned officers in the army were presently British, and pains were taken to nourish in this class the just pride of a caste that will not deign to league itself with the castless untouchables below it. This plan provided against any native disloyalty. And, if ever the Socialist plague should infect this picked, and almost petted, upper working-class, there would still be, as a last defence, a rank and file of the same blood as the traitors, nor too good friends with them.

V

When the re-makers of Ria had seen to these matters, they rested for some time and perceived the beauty of the first chapter of their Bibles. They saw what they had made, and behold! it was very good. They had their cares, of course. Who hasn't? Even the whole world's Creator is said to have had His. There was some printed chatter about native rights and a close ruling clique and about an attempt to replant in new soil the uprooted old England of feudal days. Even now there was a strike at Bute's great steel and armament works. But philosophers bear with such rubs. "My dear Bishop," Dr. Browell would say to his friend, "we mustn't expect to have Eden without the reptilia."

"No," Case replied with quite a light sigh. "I suppose Ireland is an exception." And they would agree, for the twentieth time or more, that when all was said and done the new Ria was indeed an Eden, an England undecayed and uncorrupted—what England might have been now if she could only have found again, after the Great War, the talisman of her old greatness in the spacious days.

Certainly the meadows round Ria City were rather like those of Sussex or Hants, but enriched by some miracle, so that the backs of grazing cows only just rose above the grass. England had iron, but Ria had silver—even gold, it was rumoured, in the sands of her one patch of frontier desert in the North, now in dispute with her unreasonable neighbours the Portans. England was a green and pleasant land, but all central Ria was one glorious terraced garden. Its verdure stepped down a continuous staircase, called the Big Slope, through half the world's climates, almost from Arctic to tropic. In the suburb of Bel Alp, hung high on the hillside above the capital, you were in the temperate zone. From it you looked down a many-ledged slant of ten miles to the level shine of the gayest of the oceans, almost a mile below you in vertical height, with the line of its lazy surf creaming under big palms. But if you looked inland, up the Slope, you saw, far off, hoisted incredibly high above the earth and all ordinary clouds, a row of snowy spires that looked fit to serve as a garden railing for Paradise.

The Bishop liked the old saying that all claret would be port if it could. And all countries, he had no doubt, would have been England if they could, at any rate until lately. But what would port be if it could? And what about England? Surely, he said, something like Ria; so much was sound here which at home had gone to the dogs. Here the natural leaders led; a man was master in his own house, or his mine, or his mill; and he could invest what he saved—no Radical moth could corrupt his treasure, nor Communist break in and steal; nobody of any note played the mischievous game of drafting new earths and new heavens, with all the old valleys exalted by Act of Parliament, and all the hills of God's making flattened out. A goodly and a godly place: take it for all in all, Bishop Case had no serious fault to find with it.

CHAPTER II

A LEADER OF MEN

I

The office of the Voice was at the centre of Ria City. But its editor, Burnage, was not always there when the evening's work was humming most loudly. On stuffy days he would not descend from the cool of Bel Alp; he would mould public opinion from his home, among his roses, fountains and objects of art.

This he was doing on one of the hottest of afternoons, towards the end of a truly golden summer. The room he sat in was large, lofty and furnished with expensive simplicity. The table he wrote at was choice Chippendale, rather severe. Round it there stretched a shiny expanse of blond parquet, perfectly laid. It was diversified only by one Oriental rug, but this one was a beauty. On the walls there hung nothing except one Rembrandt etching.

Burnage was bent over his work and writing absorbedly. What you would have seen of him, if you came in at the door, was chiefly the curly crown of a head of pleasant brown hair and the toes of a pair of exemplary boots sticking out towards you from under the table. Now and again these delicate toes would flick or twitch, so far as the best leather can express outwardly these movements within it; then they would quiesce again, like the hands of a dreaming child. Tides of happy fluency were evidently rising and falling and rising again in the preoccupied writer's mind. Many persons used to get pleasure from the eloquence that came into Burnage's head when, once he was launched into one of his leading articles in the Voice. But none got more pleasure than he did. And now he was well launched. At every sentence he grew more earnest and enjoyed it more. He was entreating Ria to think at least twice before going to war with Porto, her unlovable neighbour, as she was somewhat minded to do.

This creative rapture may have endured for half an hour when someone knocked at the door and was not noticed by the rapt writer. To a second knock, also ignored, there succeeded a purposeful rattling of the door handle. The charm remaining unbroken by this tactful violence, a scraggy shoulder, followed by one of the gravest faces conceivable, edged itself into the room. This face was a young man's, but its colour was that of soiled parchment; the whole forehead was strongly cross-hatched with vertical and horizontal wrinkles; the shoulders were bent; the man was a modernist statue of Care. He was the Voice's musical critic.

The editor, being in Heaven, did not look up, even now. And at this the visitor's air of sombre thought was slightly qualified with a wintry gleam—apparently of amused compassion for a creature so absurdly possessed by concerns that must be relatively trivial. "Have you a moment to spare?" the visitor asked. He spoke like one who recalls a loose, indolent mind to things that matter.

Burnage raised from his writing a pair of brown eyes kindly patient under this interruption, though they were still vague with such dreams as eloquence is made of. "You, Hendie? Rather. So glad you've come round."

All the features of the face thus raised were modelled as if some large committee of popular sculptors had had the making of it. An austere connoisseur of masculine beauty might, perhaps, have said as much with an ironic or caustic note in his voice. But most of us would be jubilant if nature had served us no worse. And at least one thing about the face was uncommon—the high development of the muscles of expression round the mouth and eyes, the places where orators and comedians amass all sorts of little aids to the grand operations that they execute on our souls.

"About that performance—" Hendie began.

Performance? What could the fellow mean? "When's this it is?" Burnage asked gently. Burnage had moved only from the neck upward; his shoulders were still bent down over his blotter; his pen had risen only a short inch from the paper.

"Friday. This coming Friday." Hendie spoke almost severely. People really ought to know what is going on in the world, or at least the big things.

But Burnage said, "What is the performance, exactly? I fear I have forgotten."'

"Why, 'Parsifal'! At the Opera House. The first performance ever given in Ria."

"Oh, ho!" The editor, in his good nature, simulated an interest in the event.

"I fear," Hendie pursued, "it may prove unfortunate for the Voice if I don't write our notice."

"Well, won't you?"

"Neroni sings at the Lyceum, that very night. I must notice Neroni."

"Have we no deputy critic?"

Hendie groaned, "We have Schill."

"Well, if you do Neroni, Schill will do 'Parsifal,' won't he?"

Hendie's solemnity deepened. "I fear," he said, "there will be much disappointment among intelligent people if anyone but myself writes on the 'Parsifal.'"

"Suppose you swop, if it's so bad as that. Let Schill do Neroni, and you go to 'Parsifal.'"

Hendie's gloom was unrelieved. "I'm afraid it would make a painful impression on our readers to see Neroni noticed by a stopgap."

At last the trouble was manifest. Space was space, time was time, and Hendie could not be in two places at once. Yet Burnage suffered him mildly, if not gladly. Well, choose which you prefer, my dear fellow, and send Schill to the other. Good-night. I know you'll arrange for the best." Burnage lowered his eyes and his pen.

Hendie retreated slowly, bowed down by his undissipated cares. He was muttering still, "A most frightful misfortune," when he reached the door. Thence he looked back, but by that time Burnage was writing. Hendie sighed and went out.

III

Twenty minutes passed, with no sound but the scrawl of the pen. The glare behind the creamy blind of a tall window at Burnage's back was becoming less fierce. Then the door opened again—no knock this time—and Crisp, the "commercial editor" of the Voice, came in, hatless and in slippers.

Burnage had cultivated the feeling that he and his staff were a band of brothers. Most of them lived at Bel Alp—Crisp nearest—and Burnage made them free of his house: they were to come straight in to his study when they liked. Crisp had just done it. He held his unfolded spectacles in one hand; from the other hung a copy of the Voice gingerly held by a corner of a page, like some unclean thing on its way to the dust-hole.

Crisp was fifty years old; he was grizzled, scanty-haired, restless and parched. On the muddy white of his cheeks the dark hairs of several moles showed up more clearly than the leaden pupils did on the dull whites of his eyes. Each end of his thin-lipped mouth twisted down like the tail of a Q and helped to perfect a general air of glum moroseness. "This is a dreadful business," he began sternly, before Burnage had time to put on his editorial expression of long-suffering geniality.

"You, Crisp? Jolly to see you," said Burnage.

"A dreadful business," Crisp repeated, scornfully shaking the polluted page that he held.

"You mean," said Burnage, "this clamour for war?"

"War? War! No! This! On the commercial page!"

"Something wrong?"

"Mean you've not seen?" Crisp didn't hide his amazement. Did editors never look at their own papers? He pointed tragic-ally at the dishevelled sheet in his hand. "The entire last paragraph of my monthly review of the wool trade! Printed upside down! The thing that every soul on 'Change would turn to, first, in the paper to-day! Upside down!"

The editor inspected the offence. Only six lines were inverted. Still, they did stand on their heads. "Yes, it's deplorable; very," he murmured soothingly. Are we not to mourn with them that mourn?

There was another knock on the door at that moment. Hendie, Fate's other victim, re-entered. He had forgotten a glove. As he took it up he glowered at Crisp. No doubt he grieved for Crisp. Crisp might write on commerce, for bread; still, even he was one of the poor dumb multitude who must suffer when music is not criticised as well as it should be. Hendie went away, bowed. Crisp watched him sombrely till he was out. Then Crisp made a tragic gesture towards the door. "There!" he said, "You can see it in everyone's face."

The touch of comedy drew no sign of amusement from Burnage. He only said, "No doubt, no doubt."

Crisp had a planted look, as if he might stay there, demanding consolation and rejecting it, as long as the supply of it lasted. "Well, good-night, my dear fellow," said Burnage. "I think I won't come to the office to-night, but I shall send down a leader." He drew his chair in to his table and dipped his pen.

Crisp went out, too much occupied with his wrongs to think of closing the door.

In a second Burnage was writing again. Presently the sun-shine, filtered through the creamy blind, ceased to play melodies of vari-coloured lustre on his brown hair. But the coming-on of evening was lost on him. He was entranced with the pleasure of writing things that were sure to stir people's hearts. And yet, even now, there were sounds that Burnage could detect more quickly than you or I could have done it in his place. He suddenly stopped writing; his head lifted; it turned to one side sharply, as a terrier's does when the first dim wisp of a new and exciting scent drifts his way. 'then the pen fell clean out of his hand; he jumped up and gazed at the half-open door with the eagerness of an expectant child. He had beauty beyond question then, with his standardised features all lit and ennobled with a glow of self-forgetful affection and joy.

Even you or I might have heard by this time a faint whine as of silk rubbing on silk; surely the rustle of a fine dress against some fine under-garment, as their wearer walked. Burnage's mouth fell fairly agape, like a naif young lover's, though he was now thirty-six. He knew it was his wife.

CHAPTER III

A LEADER OF LEADERS

I

Rose Burnage was a fragile, womanish woman, disturbing to male tranquility. Wherever she went you had an enhanced sense of sex; it travelled about with her as the atmosphere does with the earth. She came into rooms like a censer alight, shaking out round her a mysterious fume of subtle provocation and disquiet.

She wore clothes with a kind of elegant witchery, especially if they were costly and freakish ones, of an orchid-like beauty, like those she had on now; she lived herself into them so intensely that their fantasies seemed to have blossomed out from what was rare and daring in her own loveliness; she carried them off with an air, as some handsome women give a triumphant grace to wild acts of rudeness or unreason, by making them immensely their own.

Some nervous force, I fear, has to go to the winning of these victories; and at this moment the lady's spirits were at a stage of depression that verged on collapse.

Burnage ran to embrace her as if she had come back from the Arctic Circle, long overdue. "Wait!" she said tartly, waving him off while she undid the bows of ribbon that fastened a charmful dust-cloak. The last of the bows would not give way at a touch; so she fell out with it, pulled it still tighter and then dragged angrily at the ribbons till one of them tore away from its side of the cloak and so set her free. She gave a pouting scowl at the ruins, flung her paragon of a sunshade on to a chair whence it slid to the floor, dropped wearily into the chair her husband had vacated and began to draw off her fair gloves with every sign of lassitude and displeasure.

Burnage drew nearer. He wanted a hand to kiss.

He did not get it. "Wait, wait! I can't be touched yet." His Rose was prickly. She tugged at a glove that clung to a hot hand. It came off at last, leaving white prints of its seams on the pink skin.

Rose was thirty-six. Of all her grievances that one was the chief. She was growing hideous, so she had said often of late.

Of course she wasn't. Possibly you might say of the pink hands that their most perfect beauty of contour was just beginning to show that some day it might pass. If, with that in your mind, you turned to her face, and yet were capable of judging it coldly, you might perhaps think of midsummer still radiant but shaken with its own fear of the yellowing hand; not stricken, but presentient.

With her hands bare she seemed better able to breathe. She threw her head back, with closed eyes; she dangled one dove-coloured glove from two slack finger-tips hanging over an arm of her chair; she fanned herself with the first thing to hand—it was the half-filled last page of Burnage's writing. "A garden party!" she groaned. "On a day like this! Monstrous!"

"Perhaps, dear," he said humbly, "the Butes didn't know how hot it would be, when they sent out their cards."

Her head started up, as if her sudden vexation had levered it up with a jerk. "Oh, there you go! There you go. One can't say a word but you take it in that literal, reasonable way that drives me distracted." Shutting her eyes, she let her head fall back again; she withdrew into some inner chamber of her dissatisfaction.

Burnage knelt beside her, murmuring, "Dear, dear one, you're tired." He stroked her dangling hand, took the weight of the glove away from it, and kissed it in several places, which he picked out with much care. She seemed too indifferent even to resist.

There was a full minute's silence: then her eyes opened on him. "Cyril," she said, "do say something. Do make things a little amusing for me."

"Yes, darling," he said, and tried his best to be witty. It was not his line. And who can sparkle on demand?

"Can't you imagine," she said with the laboured patience of people forced to explain simple things to a very dull child, "what it must be for me to come in, tired to death with being civil for hours to that horde at the Butes'—all the world's worst bores and dowds and roughs and flashy little bloods—and find you here, all cool and quiet and happy, playing with your toys—and no egoistic noodles or frumps or prosers to put up with?"

He did not mention Hendie or Crisp—did not even think of them: there was no wish for a repartee in his heart. He caressed her limp hand ruefully. "It is dull for you, Rosekin," he said.

She sighed and sat up, with a gesture that seemed to give him up for good as a talker. Failing better entertainment at his hands, she surveyed the paper-strewn table before her. "What were you writing when I came in and disturbed?" she asked languidly "A leader," he said.

"I thought you dictated those things."

"I do, as a rule. But my typewriter man is away. I was scraping along."

"And never asked me to help!"

"You—my poor tired one!"

"Cyril, does it never occur to you that a wife might enjoy comradeship with her husband?"

"My kind darling!" He glowed at the sight of this novel tint in his opalesque lady.

II

"Where were you? Let's see. Is this it?" She ruffled the little pile of written sheets on the table. "Oh, it's that?" He had given her back the sheet that she had used as a fan and had then dropped on the floor.

She viewed with disfavour its presumable dustiness. She shook it and held it far off, to read, as if it might soil her at closer quarters: "'But far,'" she read aloud, with no trace of relish, "'beyond and above these minor considerations—national strength, national prosperity, national security—there stands, paramount and indefeasible, the loftier consideration of national—' national what is it?" She boggled and frowned at the word that had dared to hold her up. "Can't be 'righteousness,' can it?"

"Yes, dear; 'righteousness'; 'national righteousness,'" His voice began on a note of weak self-defence; it ended like a mere appeal for quarter. Rose had bedevilled the stuff, just by reading it out. It had seemed so good while he wrote it: he had felt noble thoughts filling his mind like a trumpeter's cheeks, and trumpet notes coming out of him too, full and silver. Now the whole thing had gone false; the trumpet was cracked; the sonorous period sounded like some tired cheapjack's effort to belly out his bombast to the full measure of rotundity required by his trade.

"Oh, I see," said Rose slowly—by no means as if she much liked what she saw. "'National righteousness'!" Then she tried shifting the stress: "'National righteousness.'" She made the phrase seem like some queer little beast, to be stared at, behind and before. "Well, well—" It was as if she let the poor little beast creep off at last, half dead with the rigour of her inspection.

She read on, aloud. But she seemed aloof and only faintly inquisitive, and quite uncompassionate, like an entomologist who has no love for his beetles: "For, surely, it should be a patriot's aim not only to do all he can to keep inviolate the frontier of his country and to make her whole soil one impregnable citadel, but—'" Rose shifted her seat a little, lowered the page while she did so, and muttered, "'pregnable citadel but.'" No doubt she only wanted to keep her place, and yet it was indolently insolent—as though what she read were a mere string of sounds, all alike without meaning or value, so that the string might be cut and re-tied at any syllable equally well.

She re-settled herself and went on: "'but to win, by strenuous right-doing and heroic self-control, such honour in the minds of all the nations of the world as an honest, generous and inoffensive man wins in the minds of his neighbours. So the question we all have to ask of ourselves is—Have we ground to believe that, if we should now go to war—?'"

She let the page drop. "War!" she exclaimed, with the first gleam of vivacity that had shone in her eyes. "War? Why, we never have wars in this hole. War with whom?"

"The Portans."

"The people who grab all the rooms in the mountain hotels. And eat with a knife. Are you sure there shouldn't be war?"

III

He smiled feebly. "To make them be nicer at table?"

She withered up such frivolity. "Really, my dear, I suppose you are not all children, you that run these unlucky new countries. Isn't there anything serious to squabble about?"

"Yes. Quite a big patch of sand."

"Who cares about that?"

"A big Syndicate does. It owns all the sand."

"Well, why doesn't it play castles and be happy? What more does it want?"

"It wants to own it in Ria—not Porto."

"Why?"

"This sand is full of gold. And the Syndicate knows—or its boss does. That's Bute."

"My little red host at that horrible party?"

"Yes. Nobody else knows, as yet."

She brightened a little. "You seem to," she said.

He looked a little ill-at-ease. "You remember Jenkin?" he said. "A boy I got into the orphanage? Well, he has grown up. He's Bute's right-hand man. But he still tells me—well, a good deal."

Her face lit up more, at this gleam of intrigue. "Bread that you cast on the waters? And now it comes back? Oh! you children of light! You always out-dodge the poor babes of this world. But still I can't see. What makes the little vulgarian care?"

"It's like this. If you find gold in Porto, you have to go halves with the State. If it's in Ria, the State lets you stick to three-quarters. Now, there are some sixty million pounds' worth of gold in that sand. If the sand is in Ria, that's forty-five millions for Bute and his gang."

"And only thirty if it's in Porto?"

"That's right."

For a moment she mused, with growing zest, on this peep into the fascinating machinery of unpresentable motives behind the dull, correct facade of politics. "Which is it in?" she presently asked.

"Neither." He tried to make his revelations slowly, just to lengthen out the joy of having something to say which she did not find dull.

But she said imperiously, "Cyril, enlighten me, please," to press him on. However much his common platitudes grated upon her, anything like paradox or enigma sat at least equally ill on him in her sight.

"I mean, no one knows," he said quickly.

"Why? Isn't there a map, with a black line, to show the frontier?"

"No. Only a faint dotted line. It was drawn with a lead pencil and ruler, just for the time, when Ria and Porto were setting up house for themselves. A Commission—half Rians, half Portans—were sent to peg out the frontier. Most of the work they did well enough. But then they came to this flat sandy part. No one dreamt, at the time, there was any gold there. And their horses were sick, and the wine had run out; there was bad water and a little fever. They were all old friends by that time. So one night after dinner they got out their big map and just drew a straight line of dots across the piece they had not ridden, and marked it 'Provisional Frontier' and said it must do. Who'd ever want to go near such a beast of a desert, they said—much less to quarrel over it?"

"So that's the way they do these things!" As Rose spoke she gave almost a sigh of relief, or of elated discovery. The conduct of public affairs had always seemed so lifelessly, dingily regular, humdrum and drab. Here was a raw human touch, anyway.

"Sometimes, I fear," he said gravely. "And now"—the magniloquent public man was swelling in him again—"two great communities are grievously endangered by those men's neglect of an imperative duty."

She gave a little shudder of distaste, and his magniloquence stopped. He spoke plainly again for the moment: "You see, a mere line drawn like that is no use. To make it any good you must ride every yard, with a map in your hand, and see how all the little streams go, and tiny ridges, and mark it by them—

almost rail it. Well, Bute's lot of sand is just on that useless pro-visional line. That's why we, and not only we, but the Portans, who, after all, are our fellow creatures, are menaced with—"

"Oh, don't drop into public speaking again," she cut in. "I see what Bute wants. But how's he to get it, poor thing?

"By making lots of other people want it too."

"What other people?"

"Public opinion. The people, you know. The credulous crowd."

"Make them want it enough to turn out and fight for it? How can he make them?"

"Oh! by telling them they do already. See—if I looked in a glass and saw myself foam at the mouth and get purple, shouldn't I think I was angry?"

"Cyril, you're talking quite pointedly. Go on. Interpret. 'The glass' is—?"

"The 'mirror of public opinion,' you know. The Press. Bute has bought up half the papers in Ria—more— all, in fact, except the dear old Voice."

At last she laughed quite gaily. "That little red man!" It tickled her to find that the little guy had such mettle.

"He buys up the mirrors and then paints what he likes on the glass," said her husband indignantly. "I should never have thought it was in him," she said with gusto.

He looked at her, rather aghastly. "You see what he paints?"

"Just don't I?" She rose and walked about, with all her silks swishing and whining. She chuckled over the daring knavery of the man. "Don't I see the gallant Rian got up to look like St. George, pinking the fell Portan dragon! And all that little prespiring man!" Suddenly her pacing stopped. "It takes two, though," she said, "to get up a fight."

He looked graver than ever. "Two countries. But only one Bute."

"Cyril! You don't mean to say that—?" '

"Not quite directly. But there's a company 'allied' to Bute's, as they call it. It owns half the papers in Porto."

"And it paints on them!" she exclaimed. "Paints the Portan knight-at-arms, seven feet high quelling the dastard Rian! Well, of all little, red, perspiring men—!" She paced about freely again, a tall sailing figure of wayward enjoyment and dazzling unreason. Her risen spirits had straightened her frame as water erects a cut tulip.

Burnage adored her like that. He would have had her be always like that. But oh! how the sight and sound of her at such moments changed the proportions of things and deranged all perspectives.

"Rose," he petitioned fondly and ruefully, "aren't you just a little proud of our old Voice? It's all that stands between poor Ria and war."

"Oh, yes—very noble and all that." She spoke half-absently, as a busy elder will .do when he praises a child's vaunted toy without looking at it. Next moment she halted abruptly in her magnificent walk, and scowled at the tiny watch on her wrist. "Seven-thirty! And those wretched people coming to dinner!" She snatched up her delicate paraphernalia as if they were dusters too dirty to use, and marched out augustly, offended by Time.

He went back to his table, just to fit a tail on to his leader before dressing. He made much the same scratching sound with his pen as before. But the old rapture had wilted. The toy that, when left to himself, he had been making with so much delight, looked poor and ramshackle now that the unenjoying eyes of the elder—the mentally elder—child whom he worshipped had fallen upon it and blasted it.

CHAPTER IV

THEY PEER INTO THE PIT

I

After dinner Cyril and Rose and the four "wretched people," their guests, sat out on the wide drawing-room balcony, under the stars, and let the night touch their faces with its cool fingers.

The Bishop had come with his wife—a mild, faint penumbra he carried about with him. The long-widowed Dr. Browell had brought his one daughter, Clare, a large, silent girl whom no one minded. All but Rose sat well back in long, low, comfortable chairs.

Nowhere round them was there so much as one hard, straight line to be seen. Every visible edge of woodwork or masonry was rounded out with the soft swell of clustering creepers or fringed fantastically with their tassels, tendrils and festoons. Much labour had gone to the making of all this freakish or curvilinear luxuriance. For Nature has given to Ria only one half of what is required to plump a peach or redden a rose. Light and warmth seldom fail, from sunrise to sunset. But Ria is almost rainless, except in the mountains along her east border. Down the Big Slope, at every few miles, a granite-grey torrent of glacier water tumbles in a rocky trough and pours out to waste in the sea the other half of the makings of perfect verdure. Wherever man has forced a part of one of these torrents to spread itself over a patch of the Slope, perfect verdure is splashed out on the earth like a spill of bright green paint. Only by grace of much hose and many watering-cans had the Burnages' garden remained beautiful during this torrid summer. Now that the gardeners were gone for the night, peace and a good smell were exhaled, like a grace after meat, from the grateful wet earth. There was a tiny plopping sound of water sucked down contentedly by cracks in the baked soil. And yet there was not perfect peace on the Burnages' balcony.

Rose was there: that was one reason; Rose, unrestfully sitting up on the edge of her chair. Her elbows on the balustrade, her chin leaning on both hands, she gazed downhill at the twinkle and turbid glow of Ria City, two thousand feet lower. The attitude was that of a notorious stone demon that stares down from a tower of Notre Dame, gloating over the broil and bale of Paris. But Rose did not gloat. Her look was one of loveless curiosity only. "How that town growls!" she said, with a slight frown.

"To-night in particular?" Dr. Browell inquired in a light tone of virile allowance for the engaging petulance of lovely woman.

Burnage knew how that tone grated and jarred upon Rose. "Yes," he intervened. "Louder each night now—louder every hour. Listen!"

II

They became silent, to listen. The only near sound was the fussing of some small bird late to bed and nervous about it. As foreground daisies stand out against a distant Mont Blanc, this clear little rustle was planted upon a vast and vague background of sound—an immense murmur that dinned and dinned on. You might have fancied you saw the huge hum rise from the city like a thin column of smoke and roll up to tarnish the stars with its fumes.

"They won't stay at home," Burnage said. "They walk about in the streets half the night, singing and shouting. They're going wild. Listen!"

Clare Browell was not yet old enough to be blind, incurious, or incapable of wonder. She looked down, rather awed, at the enigmatic monster fidgeting obscurely in its pit of darkness.

The Bishop was perfectly easy. "A world-wide unrest, I imagine," he said. "'This strange disease of modern life,' you know. The craving for pleasure, excitement." The Bishop's voice was as manifestly born to co-operate with a' cathedral organ as his legs were predestined to wear gaiters. But no real alarm appeared in him.

A light breath of air lifted into momentary clearness the grinding clang of a tune played by a steam roundabout. Such were the joys of the ants that swarmed over each other in the hot (ant-hill below. The thought touched Burnage—a little. "I suppose," he said, with dulcet melancholy, "it is we, in a way, that have made these poor creatures whatever they are." He really felt it, just then, in a light, an almost voluptuous way—that the drone of the great saucepan seething away in the darkness down-hill had been tuned to its pitch of to-night by all the things the rulers of Ria had done and left undone. "A man's character is his Fate"—and the Fate of other men too; the grave old reflection regaled him like a tragic play, sombrely, yet not alarmingly nor painfully.

"Won't you leave the Creator some credit?" the Bishop said cheerfully.

"What harm," Browell said, "if they do come out and stretch their legs and make a little noise?" The learned man's voice was robust. Most of us hug in our hearts some secret, swaggering vision of ourselves. The learned Browell's, I fancy, was that of a rude man of action, unlettered perhaps but a most terrible fellow, versed in carnage, a great cutter of knots with his sword and thrower of swords into scales.

"Hear, hear," the Bishop applauded. "Young men will be stirring, God bless them. Better let off steam in the open than brew bad blood on the sly, like this treacherous strike of the gun-makers. Now of all times, to strike! With Porto getting flatly insolent."

"Insolent? Oh, oh," Burnage deprecated gently.

"There, there, my dear man." The Bishop was soothing. "Of course you guides of public opinion do well to go slow when war's in the wind. But you and I know well enough that there are many worse things." The Bishop declaimed:

"And, as I note how nobly natures form
Under the war's red rain, I deem it true
That He who made the earthquake and the storm
Perchance made battles too."

The Bishop's voice was melodious. And, like much, other music, it probably quickened in each hearer's mind whatever secret reverie had possessed it before—deepened Burnage's dream of a Rose grown kind or of multitudes hanging on his lips, and Browell's of the gallant desperado that had been lost to the world, and Heaven knows what shy maiden meditation of Clare's, and Rose's harsh and witty sense of the dull absurdities of them all.

The Bishop alone entertained her a little. To Rose's palate there was some saltness about the snubs the Bishop gave to the meek Gospel which employed and tried to control him; they were so pat and crushing. How funny a Bible and Prayer Book frankly revised and edited by the Bishop would be! "War give I unto you"; "Jesus, the Prince of War"; "Seek War arid ensue it"; "Blessed are the war-makers." Oh! there was some sport in the Bishop.

But Cyril, Cyril! There he was again, the poor savourless good soul, maundering away at his weary old standard figures of speech—"They come out like bees growing angry, buzzing ever louder and louder. Before we know what, they may be stinging."

"Stinging the proper persons, I trust," said the Bishop.

Cyril shrugged his shoulders. He did it quite effectively; but then—how well his wife knew that shrug!— had seen it on scores of platforms—could tell when it was coming! "Who knows?" said Cyril. "The Portans? Perhaps. Their own employers and rulers? Perhaps. War fever, strike fever—which may prove stronger?"

But Case was cheerily paternal. "Tut, man, have faith in your kind. You don't seriously doubt whether these honest fellows would rather put forth their strength for the cause of right, of country and of God, or for the cause of wickedness and wrong, to ruin their best friends and natural leaders—just for a handful of silver to add to a wage already amply sufficient for everything short of bestial indulgence."

A minute's silence followed. It often did, in all sorts of gatherings, when Case had just been sonorous. You wanted to hear out, to the last vibration, so fine a wind instrument.

As they sat silent the brassy bray of the merry-go-round ascended to their ears for a second or two, borne on a sort of rising sign of wind. That ended the spell cast by audible beauty. Browell could speak: "You say 'employers.' Shouldn't the noun be in the singular?"

He paused a moment, to raise expectation of what he should say. The old don was happy. He had a piece of the world's news to give to these men of the world. "I hear," he went on, "our friend Bute has bought—only to-day—a controlling share in the whole federation of gun-making firms."

III

The hostess had dropped out of the talk. It was her way to practise an insolent inattention to guests who failed to entertain her. But at Bute's name she half turned her head.

Clare had been waiting for that. For as long as she could remember, Clare had adored secretly, almost guiltily, the beauty of Mrs. Burnage. For many minutes now she had been watching for the averted face to come round into profile. It came, with all the suave curves of cheek, chin and neck interplaying at the turn; to Clare's senses they sang themselves like a song—with that rhythmic rightness and unity; every line lived, as if it had not been drawn once for all and then left, but were always drawing itself; the face seemed to Clare, in the lyric warmth of her worship, to have the super-animation that fine drawings have while the glowing mind of the artist is still calling them into existence. Indistinctly she heard Burnage saying, "War!—with Bute finding the guns—at a price!"

"Well, you know, somebody must," said Browell. Browell held a standing brief, you see, for the sturdy common sense that soon sweeps away cobwebs.

"But—Bute!" Burnage murmured.

"Does it really matter," the Bishop asked, "what shop we go to for guns—or for boot-laces? Don't you think wars are won in men's hearts more than in any ordnance workshops? Our gunsmiths will do well enough if our people's spirit is sound and if all of us use our strength with a will, as members one of another."

"What is our war strength—I wonder?" Burnage mildly speculated.

"Shall we say," said the Bishop, "about ten times what it would have been if our hearts were not pure and our consciences void of offence? But don't let us bring a point of national honour down to a question of how many men equipped with Mr. Smith's rifles are likely to beat a hundred men armed with the rifles of Messrs. Jones."

This exalted line of thought stirred Browell so deeply that he had to interject the quotation:

"High Heaven rejects the lore

Of nicely calculated less or more."

"Exactly," the divine agreed. He waxed nobler and nobler under this stimulation. "It isn't really by living for safety that nations live safe. It's by enduring hardness, by steeling their metal in more and more fiery furnaces, welcoming burdens almost too great for their strength, courting the discipline, it may be, of momentary failure—"

Roused to a very ecstasy of concurrence, Browell broke in to quote the lines so dear to people who live sheltered lives—

"Then welcome each rebuff That turn earth's smoothness rough."

"Precisely," said Case.

IV

Rose had been listening since the mention of Bute. Nobody now present could excite her; not even Case. At best they were mildly amusing grotesques, gargoyles occupying their several places to more or less good comic effect—Browell, the bluff pantaloon, with his virilist posturings; Case with his droll skill in dodging all the kill-joy side of the religion he lived on. But this little, red, unsightly Bute, whom she had been snubbing to-day for his ugliness and his impudent compliments—Bute might be a live red spark among all these white ashes of dullness. Wherever you turned, there was this mole of a Bute working away underground and throwing up, here, there and everywhere, shameless signs of himself. Bute must, at least, be no nullity.

Rose's spirits, as you know, were apt to leap about, from zero up to boiling point, according to the weather or any of a hundred local causes of momentary heat or chill. And now, for the second time, the idea of this vivid rogue, Bute, was elating her fast. Why, there might be lots of men like that—men who dared do things and stir the dust of the world. It might be such a man who was due to arrive at the house at any time now—a friend of Cyril's youth, one whom she had never seen and whom Cyril had not seen for twelve years—a professional soldier, just brought out from England to give the right stamp to the Adjutant-General's branch of the inexpert Rian army.

Cyril had spoken warmly of this Major John Willan. That had led Rose to expect a dull man, but now she was growing almost sure he must be a live wire. She almost said that he was, to her guests. "You'd love Major Willan," she told Dr Browell. "He's one of you men of action." She trusted gaily to her beauty and the vanity of the poor pedant to blind him to her contemptuous irony.

"A soldier?" Browell asked eagerly. The coffee-cup he was holding rattled in its saucer; his-feeble hand shook with nervous joy at the thought of this possible brother-in-arms for the slashing dragoon or tarry sailor of his own fond dreams.

"The soldier," she said. "The only modern Major Dalgetty, who never stops fighting. A soldier of fortune, you know."

"The fortune first and the soldiering after?" the Bishop said, and then laughed, or crowed, like the hen that has just laid an egg.

"Not much of the fortune left now, I'm afraid," Burnage said.

"Too many good causes about." He knew how Rose's teeth were set on edge by Case's poor attempts at wit; she had winced, and he came in to save her the painful effort of making some forbearing reply. But if Rose relished anything else still less than the episcopal sallies, it was the notion of being rescued from conversational perils or fixes by so innocent a champion as Cyril. So the sub-acid look the Bishop had brought to her face remained there; but some incalculable gust diverted the jet of her sarcasm, so that it suddenly played on neither the Bishop nor Cyril but on the absent and innocent cause of their offences. She rattled on wildly: "An amateur of lost causes, you know. A March rat, with a bee in its bonnet; He boards the worst coffin-ship he can find, and the coffin-ship sinks in due time and the virtuous rat swims away to another as soon as he's quite satisfied that the new one is rotten."

"Not one of our own officers, I gather." The Bishop spoke rather dryly. Martial valour was a virtue, but it should be practised in the right quarter.

Rose almost derided the notion. "Ours! No!—at least, not till now. Everyone else's! Of course he'll touch nothing that's naughty. Whenever he feels like setting another Andromeda free he writes to ask Cyril if she's respectable. He's Don Quixote revised and corrected—consults his spiritual father first and then charges a windmill. You see, he fagged for Cyril at school; so of course Cyril's the wisest and best of mankind."

CHAPTER V

A MERE SOLDIER

I

From Burnage's house you could see by day the straight groove of a cable railway mounting the long slant from the City to Bel Alp: What you saw at night, when a train was drawn up the slant or let down it, was only a needle of light silently darning its way in and out of a ground fabric of darkness, as bridges, shrubberies, or mounds obscured for an instant the train's moving lamps. An exhibition of this luminous weaving was now going on.

One of the passengers in the ascending train was a tall, erect, broad-shouldered man of about thirty-four, with mild eyes and a willing expression. The effect of docile strength was heightened by spectacles. He was got up, outside, like most well-to-do Englishmen. But he looked, more essentially, like some very strong, but benign, wild animal, not broken in spirit but highly tractable by its natural disposition, and kept out of mischief by its intense enjoyment of every quite ordinary thing that happened to it. Just now he was looking from window to window in quick succession, lest he should miss any of the delights that were half-visible on both sides of the railway.

On each side a low bank of earth sloped up from the line, and these banks were a market-garden crowded with all kinds and tints of roses. Among them the strong lights of the train struck lively and fugitive notes of white, crimson, scarlet and pink, as they passed, and this gay melody of colour seemed to induce in the large man a state of happiness that was almost shame-faced.

For nobody else noticed the show. Some of the other passengers were searching wearily through evening papers, as if their hope of finding a piquant divorce case had fallen very low. Others sat motionless, or only blinking, like horses too tired to graze. Some stared at one another's faces with lassitude or distaste, and some stared with dull surprise at the news, the bulk and big assemblance of the sunburnt man who was so irrationally enjoying a world quite charmless to themselves.

At Bel Alp, in the small station yard—an arbour embosomed in flowering creepers—a large car that glittered in the starlight was waiting to take the big man some three hundred yards along a gravel ledge cut level out of a slope that was nappy here with dense, continuous garden shrubbery. He was visited by a youthful wish to take a running header off the lower edge of the gravel drive into the soft slope of verdure below. It looked as if it would sustain any bulk that dived into it fairly flat. But he gave up the sweet thought: one mustn't spoil people's shrubberies.

Would he like to go to his room, he was asked at Burnage's door? Or straight through the house? "They," he was told, were "all out on the verandah."

They? All? People to dinner, then? For he knew Burnage was childless. Yes, he would go straight through to the verandah.

II

To all but the most intrepid social expert it is somewhat daunting to join a company that has sat long before you arrive. It seems as if by that time they must surely have coalesced into a sort of league—they will have reached mutual understandings; anyhow, you will be fumbling blindly among the intricacies of their latest relations with one another.

Even the unsuspicious Willan felt this now, when he had shaken, with furtive violence, the hand of the friend in whom he had chosen a Mentor for himself. And, as he felt "out of it," he was not at his best. And even his best was not the brilliance of any major star in the social heavens.

Burnage had always liked Willan quite sincerely. And now he had hoped that this friend of his youth might cut a good figure before the supreme tribunal of Rose's critical mind, as men hope to see their brides shine in any larger world to which marriage may have admitted these ladies. So a twinge of disappointment had to hide itself under the kind protectorate that Burnage exercised over his ineffective admirer. Why on earth should the old dear—he was really two years younger than Burnage—never do himself justice? With his magnificent body, his healthy boy face, his great record of soldiering, John might so easily have stepped into their midst like a Greek God of War with sheathed sword. But no, Cyril could only remember one moment at which John had not only been the right thing, but looked it too—in a lost race at Henley Regatta, with John at number six in the school boat, holding his beaten crew together as if the frown of fortune on the good cause had only turned his huge strength and steady will into something twice as strong and composed as themselves. He had been beautiful then, with the serenity of supreme and happy effort seated in his face. But oh! why could he not come trailing a few clouds of glory now, with Rose watching and listening and all the visible world a-thrill with tense starlight above and the casting of momentous dice in the dim city below?

"Mostly loafing around, I'm afraid." Willan was answering Rose's command: "Now tell us everything you've done. We know all about the Great War. That was splendid. But everything else, since you left the poor old British army. Everything. Now, begin."

Rose had said it with a kind of cruel brightness. She knew well enough the paralysing effect of an invitation to a decent man to make himself a bore.

Burnage could never quite believe that his idol absolutely liked to torment people. So he came blundering in with his own hobby of trying to put everyone at his ease and at home. "I know," he said to Willan, "you've made me a stamp-collector again. Gosh! the rare war 'supercharges' that came on your letters! from Turkey, Morocco, China—"

"In fact," Mrs. Burnage persisted, "wherever any engaging carnage has been, all over the world."

"They will do it, you know," Willan said ruefully. He spoke like a man suspected of abetting mischief and not very sure that he has a defence.

"And you too, nest ce pas?" said Rose.

"I did hang round a little." Willan's was the dismal candour of a boy who has been caught too near the jam. "Never quite the real thing, though."

"And what, may we ask," said Browell, "was the special form taken by this unreality?"

"Foreign legioning—that sort of thing."

Burnage laughed. "Quite real death, I suppose, if you're hit?"

His voice was clement and Willan turned to him gratefully.

"Well, being hit is not what you're after, you know."

"You risk it, I suppose?" Rose spoke almost pettishly now. Willan became a trifle more fluent; "Oh, you risk it," he said, "at every soft job in the world—hunting, tobogganing, climbing—every game that is more fun than work is."

"Yes, yes"—the Bishop's voice showed signs of a strain on his power of putting up with nonsense—"but in war men face death, I presume, for what they feel to be right."

What with the stars and the lamps, Willan could see distinctly that Case wore gaiters. And could gaiters err. On a question of conduct especially? Easier to suppose that he, Willan, a heathenish layman, must have misread the plain facts which he thought he had seen. Still, one's own little footling bit of experience was all that there was to go by. So he took heart to stick to such lights as he had! "You see, sir, that's just where the jar comes. You go on the side that seems right, or looks weak, or something, and try to feel fine about having done it. No good. Everyone sees what you're after, as soon as you get near a front."

"Honour? Why not?" said the Bishop, now quite the austere father in God.

But Willan was slowly working things clear in his mind. "Not honour, exactly. Just—fighting."

"Shall we say—fighting for honour? To win it?" said Burnage, the tireless softener of conversational jolts and absorber of conversational shocks.

But Willan was getting it off his chest, now. "No," he said. "Fighting to fight. There's no game like it, nor sport. It's like all the great games there are, put together. And everyone's game. Every animal's, even. Just look at dogs, cocks, robins, all of 'em. And every savage is out for it, just like a white."

Browell and Case were shifting uneasily in their long chairs. Such talk profaned things they held sacred. In a grave, friendly tone of remonstrance the Bishop recalled to sanity the wayward dabbler in unreason. "Is not there something," he said, "a little bigger than sport—mind, I don't say a word against sport, but isn't there something a shade or two nobler about the nice sense of personal honour that makes a whole nation draw itself up like one rightly sensitive man, to resent a foul insult?" As Case went on, the good round phrases warmed him, and his voice gained in grandeur.

Undoubtedly Willan was shaken. Ten to one, he reflected, the Bishop was right. A Bishop would be sure to know. All that Willan could do was to go on fumbling about among his own coarse blocks of personal experience. "Sort of man," he said humbly, "would hit you over the nose directly you did a thing he didn't like?"

The Bishop gave the slightest possible snort. Oh! the befouling mind of this man! Like a slug, crawling and smearing. He vulgarised everything.

Before Burnage could pour in emollient oil, Browell had tackled the offender in his high-pitched, donnish voice: "Aren't you putting the case just a little—shall I say?—baldly?"

"Sorry," said Willan. "Seems, somehow, the only way I can get hold of the thing."

"Through the concrete case, you mean?" said Burnage soothingly. "The individual instance?"

"That sort of thing," said Willan. "Some fellow I've met, you know. Something I've seen. Of course, it don't come to much."

Browell's remonstrative voice shrilled up higher than ever towards the treble. "No doubt it's an excellent method to visualise one's conceptions, so far as one can. How would it be, then, to try to see before us a whole nation fused simply solid in a single furnace of generous passion—all of it springing up, like one man, from its office stools and shop counters—aye, and its lecture-rooms too—in a burst of proud scorn for its old sheltered, soulless, materialist life—its money-grubbing and its cabbage-gardening and all its poring over books and intellectualities?"

During the earlier part of this burst of eloquence Willan's face had expressed little more than a strong, but baffled, desire to receive light and leading. Among its last words, however, his intellect seemed to espy something that it could clutch. "About cabbage-gardening—" he said. I did see that sort of thing once—in India. I had gone out to see Trask—you remember old Trask at school, Cyril? Trask had a mission out there—had a tribe all to himself. Real old primitives, too: they had been living in trees till Trask came along—hadn't quite done being monkeys, you know."

A slight sound of disrelish came from the Bishop.

"Not on all fours, you know, but pretty hairy. Trask had coaxed them down off the trees and got them to sow corn and cabbages. 'This other Eden' he called the place when he felt happy. They seemed to like it, all right. So Trask set them building a church and a jail and a whole lot of improvements. They were just roofing a school when I came. It went on all right till early one morning we heard no end of a row in the clearing."

Willan paused, rather aghast. Why, he was doing the talking—a queer job for him. But Mrs. Burnage would not let him off.

"Oh, pray go on," she said sweetly. "From 'row in the clearing.'" Willan obeyed. "They had on their war-paint, every man Jack. They'd lit a bonfire and they were doing a war-dance round it, and screeching like good 'uns. Old Trask charged out in his pyjamas and slippers to make them stop playing the goat and put out the fire and get down to weeding the cabbages. No bonn: they said weeding was low—you might weed for whole years and it wouldn't make half a man of you. 'What about Adam?' yelled Trask. 'Isn't Eden itself good enough for you?' No bonn that, either. One man had a drum that he'd kept hidden under the thatch of his house. He told Trask a proper god of their own had turned up in the night to ask why the deuce they had not got a fight on with somebody. Seemed it was one of the old lot of gods that Trask thought he'd quite got 'em out of.

'D'you mean to say,' said Trask, 'you'd be wicked enough to chuck building the school?' 'Wicked yourself,' said the man. Wasn't it measly, the man said, to think about weeding and schools while such rotten scrubs as the Ooraons—that was the tribe next door to Trask's crowd—were crawling about on the earth and not stamped on? 'Why, what harm have they done?' said old Trask, 'Done!' said the man with the drum. 'Ain't they liars and thieves and covered with lice, and not half our size, and their women all sluts, and all their dogs mangy? You listen!' And off he went, banging the drum and making 'em all dance and sing a song about how the right sort of Gods wanted to see the Ooraon well jumped on. That's how they mobilise in those parts. The end of it was that they let a whopping good yell, all together, and pushed off for the woods."

Again Willan paused, a little horrified at his own loquacity.

Two hundred yards down the hillside a large French window was thrown open in a house that had been bulging with festal light. Through the luminous gap thus opened there spurted a little jet of confused pleasant sound, the low, jolly din of a successful party at its climax. Then the audible gaiety sank and, in the stillness that followed, a good tenor voice began to shed into the listening night the evocative spell of its passionate virility.

The song was martial, of an immemorial kind—God with us, away with counsels of meekness and weakness, be the men your fathers were, and smite the dastards low. But the charm of the round, ringing notes seemed to make the whole visible world abet the use that they were put to. The dark dome with its pulse of thrilled stars, the mild outspread plain of calm, shimmering sea and the real spires of more distant snow—all became ministers to one emotion and helped to feed the same flame.

Willan murmured, "A topping good song!" when it ended. Yet he saw, at least dimly, that, in a way, it had answered him and defeated him. He had talked of war as he had seen and known it; he had only said what was true; and yet what could be more true than the self-attesting veracity of whatever was sung with that divine beauty and power? Certainly war at close quarters, the war of trenches and charges, raids and retreats, had not been, to his senses, what one might think it to be, with that voice in one's ears, singing that song. But perhaps there was some higher order of truth than the common one which he knew; somebody else's way of taking in an experience might be more authentic than his. Perhaps one might see a fine thing as a cruel or mean one through one's own want of a natural gift. He might have done that. If so, what must all these people be thinking of him?

All their faces were in shadow at the moment, except the big, silent girl's. He found hers turned upon him, not with any look of condemnation, nor yet of assent, but with a kind of uncommitted openness or neutrality. He felt a great wish to explain to her, she looked so good a person to have on one's side—or, at any rate, not to be condemned by. It was a handsome, large-featured face, not a highly expressive one yet, but a splendid vehicle for expression if a deep feeling should ever require it. She looked as Surrey or Devonshire might have looked in the Ice Age, with the beauty waiting to thaw and awake. Willan viewed the unwarmed young planet with awe.

"A topping good song," he repeated, almost to himself. But Mrs Burnage heard. "Oh! you mustn't force yourself," she said, with bright, frosty irony, "to be uncritical, on our account. Do call it 'screeching' if you like or; 'no end of a row in the clearing.'"

A quick burst of applause had come from the lighted house after the song. Now came a silence in which a single speaking voice might just be made out by good ears, though the words could not be followed. Then this ended, in turn, in a fierce salvo of cheers from many mouths. Rose looked at Willan mockingly. "A good whopping yell all together," she said. She seemed to be daring him to go on, to make out his case, whereas he had no case he wished to make out—had only tried to have something to say, so as not to sit mum in the midst of them all when everyone else was saying his bit, to keep the talk going. Cyril came to his rescue. "By Jove, I'm forgetting," he said; "you've not seen your room."

Rose disdained every such bourgeois virtue as civil reserve. As Willan and Burnage passed into the house, she threw the Bishop a look that made him shrug his shoulders with a glance at the retreating figure of the Major. "We are what we are, my dear lady," he said. "Body or soul, it's all one—we can't add that cubit."

IV

While Burnage escorted his parting guests to their cars a telephone raised its lonely little thrill of sound in his distant study. It rang on unappeasably till the last guest was gone. Then he went to quiet it.

Ten minutes after, he went out again to the balcony. Rose was still there. She had collapsed into a chair with her spirits reacting darkly after the labours of hospitality. "There's news," he said, rather portentously.

Much too portentously, Rose thought. It was one of his orator tricks, this super-significant modulating of gestures and tones to fit what he said. It had jarred on her often before. She had derisively called it "overdressing the right key." "No, really?" she drawled, with a disinclination to find that there was anything in it.

Cyril amended his tone. "It's from Jenkin," he said, un-portentously now.

"Who's Jenkin? Oh, I remember—your convenient bedes man. Well?" A little flicker of curiosity had risen in her voice.

"Bute is buying the paper—over my head."

"The Voice. But isn't it yours?"

"Less than half of it is. Old Platt's executors hold 51 per cent of the shares. And now they have sold them to Bute."

"What vipers! Can you be turned out?"

"Yes, at any moment."

She thought for a minute or so. Then she broke out crossly, "Well, I really can't sorrow to-night. I'm too tired," and threw herself back in her chair, boring her head wearily into the cushions.

Lights on the quiet hill-side, as well as in the city, were going out rapidly now. She lay for a while, drearily viewing the process of their extinction. Then she said, "So, in a week, you may be—nobody."

"Yes," he said.

"And here am I who have not once seen you throned in your glory at your own office. Hadn't I better come quick, lest they dethrone you?" There was a kind of cheerless sympathy in her tone.

"Oh, my dear one!" he broke out in joy. What loss or abasement would not be gain if it gave him and his doings any interest in her sight?

"To-morrow?" she asked.

He closed with her eagerly. "Rather! To-morrow!" She never had shown the slightest desire before to visit the chief scene of his labours.

CHAPTER VI

ROSE OPENS A SLUICE

I

In the Voice office the editor's room is on the first floor, and the stairs leading to it are steep. "Oh, do open some window or other," cried Rose, as she and her husband arrived. She dropped, exhausted, into the editor's chair. She spoke as if he had long been insisting on keeping the air out, in spite of her prayers.

He obeyed, with solicitous zeal. The wide bay window faced westward; through its side lights you looked along the street, south and north, up and down. He opened all three, and a kindly freshness came in, just stirring the drawn blinds—all blinds are drawn in Ria, to keep out the middle-day heat.

Sunset was over; invisible fans were moving the air. From the earth, even in that mid-city place, there had begun to escape its happy evening sigh of release from the day's glare of the furnace that forges the rickety candelabra of the Rian cactus and fuses the queer splashes of gaudy enamel on to the Rian orchids. Little jocund noises were reviving in the street—a livelier shuffling of feet, a few bars of whistling, a tinkle of laughter; a fountain began to play somewhere in hearing.

Rose was a little softened by the charm of the cooling twilight. "This is a good little bower of yours," she said. "It seems a pity to. lose it."

"Not quite lost yet," he said. "Who knows? Bute may grow a conscience, even now. He may come to see that, whatever the other papers may be, the Voice is really a public institution—not a mere megaphone to be bought and sold in the mart and—"

"Oh, yes, yes." Rose hurriedly turned off that tap. What she meant was as plain as if she had said, "Oh, do stop this babble. Be serious." She went on: "Of course, he's by way of being a friend."

He shrugged. "Of a kind—yes."

"No tiff as yet, is there?" she asked. "No noble bristling of manes?"

"No."

"Of course not." But Rose checked any fuller expression of scorn for Cyril's "insipid habit of inoffensiveness all round. "Then he might want you to hang on here—but for this war that he requires?"

"But for this war he wouldn't be buying the Voice."

"Would there be war if the Voice said there ought to be?"

"Yes. In a week. We're the only obstacle left."

"Then, in a week you'll be a stainless nonentity? Rather indigent, too?"

"I shall have you?"

"You'd have me anyhow. Oh, bother!"

II

Willan, untimely again, was the cause of this frank interjection. Released for an hour or two from the work of one of his first days in the Rian War Office, Willan had just been making the round, for the first time in his life, of the sights of newspaper production. He now came in, almost deaf with the clang and roar of printing-machines and almost dumb with respect for this vociferous expression of the personality of Burnage.

The sight of this irrational devotion of Willan's seemed to irritate the fastidious Rose too much to let her sit still. She sprang up and walked to the window, leaving Cyril to his friend. First she glanced out through a thin slit of space between the central window's frame and its blind. While doing this she fingered restlessly the string of the blind till by some thoughtless movement she let off the catch. The blind flew up instantly, rolled by a spring.

Through the large opening so suddenly made, the life of the street came in like a puff of blown smoke. The voices under the window were much more numerous now. They were all fused together into a level nondescript buzz like that of a full ballroom or banquet-hall. This made a kind of ground colour of sound, with a vague neutral texture of tone of its own, nothing more; it was just a low wash of audible life. But now and again some separate and salient sound would plant itself on this indefinite background and show up against it. A snatch of a song chorus would break out into clearness. Or some lull would come; the background would pale down, as it were, to a fainter shade of itself, and a single voice would stand out for a little while undulating in oratorical rises and falls, and so maintain a precarious distinctness till at some burst of laughter or cheers it was re-immersed in the general multitudinous hum.

Rose turned from the window at last. "The animals," she said, "are simply howling."

The superfluous Willan was taking his leave; he had to go back to his War Office, over the way. He had just been speaking low to Burnage. "You're absolutely right. You public men have got to keep this country quiet for at least five years, or there'll be a smash. I've had a first look round, and nearly everything seems rusty or rotten—the training obsolete; shoddy equipment; all the wrong guns; no checking of contracts; General Staff at sixes and sevens. There'll be five years hard work to get the whole show fit for war. Hullo! Smoke? Nothing alight in this place of yours?" Willan sniffed expertly. "It's torches," said Rose. "Only torches, out in the street. We don't run to bonfires here, like your friend's friends in India." Yes, they smelt the burning pitch; they could see turbid streaks of flame and smoke reaching up into the dusky air above the layer of lamplight.

Rose's smile was such as to hurry the visitor's exit.

III

The moment the door had closed behind Willan, Rose said: "You're accusing me, Cyril. You're thinking me rude to your friend."

He had sat down and did not immediately speak, nor look up. He could find nothing worth saying about his friend's unsuccess in her sight.

She came towards him, away from the window. "Look up," she said, standing in front of his chair. He obeyed. He found her not queenly only, but animated, as she used to be before they were engaged. With the last of a deep russet glow dying down behind her in the sky, her eyes and her smile had mystery as well as fire. "I'm sorry," she said, almost tenderly, "but I had to get rid of him, Cyril. He's nice, but I had to get rid of him."

He looked at her dazedly. Some sudden exaltation of her spirits had brought back to the early afternoon of her beauty the brilliancy of its morning, a radiance to worship and to revel in, not to parley with. She began, "Cyril—and then came to sit on the broad arm of his chair, her face above his head and a little behind it. She kept on stroking his hair with both hands while she breathed half-formed, audible thoughts; they fell about him like petals from that most desired rose, her adorable mouth: "We two together—in great wild days—tempest and trouble and venture and sudden resolve—and the grasped chance, and triumph and rest and all our old love young again."

Power poured through the fingers she pressed on his hair; her unwonted kindness bemused him; the values of many things changed; it became the aim of all existence, theirs and everyone else's, that they two should be just as they were at that moment; other times, other actions and joys were only the husks and dressings of life; here was its glowing heart.

"What a night!" she murmured. "Don't speak. Don't move. Only listen." She held her breath, and he his, in passionate accord with the breast that pressed his shoulder; they listened like one creature. Below the window the deep, level hum was swelling; it boomed; it was beginning to undulate too, with tong rollers like an Atlantic's.

They let their breath go, together, at last. She whispered "Look!" and lifted both her hands clear of his head.

He rose and went straight to the window, as though he had become a part of her body and moved only by her will. He leant out of the window a little. He fancied, but only dimly, that even in that moment the great roar surged louder than ever. He turned to her, to say so.

"No! Look! Only look!" she said quickly. So he stood where he was, half looking out, half looking at her, draining the drug of her beauty. He did not choose what he did; he could do nothing else; it was the nobleness of life, the climax of everything.

"Tell me what there is—out there," she asked him, with a sort of mystic simplicity.

"Oh; crowds," he murmured, gazing at her still. "Black crowds." He was leaving the window, to draw to her lips.

"No, no!" She waved him back. "Look carefully—for me. Is any space clear on the pavement—just under the window?"

While he looked out, she glanced round the room, now growing dark, espied the electric-light switch near the door, and turned it. A fierce pallor of light filled the room: Cyril blinked when he turned to report: "I see some pavement clear just below, but not much. The crowd almost covers it."

"Will it, quite—I wonder. Watch for me, Cyril."

He looked out and down, till the longing to see her made him half turn again. She said instantly, "Doesn't a miracle happen to crowds?"

He said, "Miracle?" absently, thinking only of the miracle of exaltation, shining in her white face. Absently he stood at the window, rooted there by her will.

"Yes," she said, almost exultantly, "when the bodies all touch one another, and the sparks come, and everything rushes together—what drops of rain do on a window—make little swerves in at each other, and soon they're not drops any more: they're a stream—and then they're a river. What is the pavement like, Cyril?"

Again he looked down at the street. "Much blacker," he said. "Oh! Very much blacker."

"Ah!" she exclaimed. She was excited. But she held herself in and spoke almost quietly. "What was I saying? Oh yes, how the little weak things in the street swarm and swarm till they all touch at last, and then they're not thousands of little weak separate things any longer, but' one enormous thing—an animal, a magical horse of a million horse power, waiting for anybody to ride it who dares." Her excitement was rising again. "Now!" she cried eagerly. "Look! Any clear pavement now?"

He leant out and looked down. "None, they're packed tight."

"To the right!" she cried. "Look—to the right!—up the street. Is there any room there?"

"Some. Yes; far off, a good deal."

"To the left?" She came nearer him. "Look!"

"Yes. A little way off there's—why, there is nobody. Why—my God!" he cried, starting back into the room; "the whole crowd is under this window!"

For that second the lover besotted with love was all but roused from his opiate ecstasy of subjection. The medicine-woman saw her drug failing, and somehow she drew up into one irresistible onset all the sweetness and strength of her lure, as if she could borrow at will, for her momentary purpose, the whole mysterious force that turns woods into choirs in spring and enamels jungle and. swamp with heavenly freaks of wild colour. Never in all his recollection of her had she shed on Cyril a look so tenderly arch. "Darling," she murmured, "how could there not be a crowd?—when a famous speaker stands at a window—opens it—lights it? Haven't you almost been calling for silence? Listen!"

Articulate calls could be heard above the formless bellow of the crowd: "Speech!" "Good old Burnage!" "Spit it out!" "Speech!" He stood back in the room, out of the mob's sight, immobilised still by the first shock of being confronted with the expectation which now was so evident. But the shock was passing away already. Rose's instinct had known how to mix with the potion of sex a special simple for the rhetorician. How could that artist refrain for long from sniffing up the intoxicant scent of the feast dished up for his use—the great audience primed with expectancy, all its feelers out, all its pores opened by holiday companionship in the kind summer night, its wits alive with the stir of momentous events, a great choice to be made by them all, and a parting of road? When he murmured "You planned it!" to Rose, there was no bitterness in his voice—only a sort of voluptuous chiding of arts that could lift him above earth so ravishingly.

She replied with gay shamelessness: "What if I did?" She put a hand on one of his and it seemed to him as if an assurance of all that rarest vintage of love which she had always withheld from him were flowing into him where their hands touched. "I've brought the magical horse," she cooed softly. "Won't you take it from me—ride into safety and triumph—and carry me with you?"

She lifted the hand of his that she had touched. She laid a long kiss on it; still holding it in her own hand she led him straight to the window; there she bowed, as if presenting him to the immense white-spotted stretch of upturned faces. Then, with a last pressure of his hand, to bind him over to do her whole will, she fell back from his side and he held up the hand she had pressed, to ask for silence.

IV

Before Burnage opened his mouth there were many cheers from the crowd, some hisses; also a few angry cries of "Pro-Portan!" and "Traitor!" One little Cockney voice squealed "Portan gowld! 'E's been pide for it!" But calls' of "Sh!" soon procured dead silence.

He glanced round at Rose. Would she look pleased with him? Not yet. Or, at most, her pleasure was provisional, conditional. So far he had done as she wished—let him go on and keep up to the mark. But what mark? He could not be sure, even now. She had drawn a chair in on his right. She sat there, out of sight from the street, but near enough to rain influence upon Cyril.

He spoke, at first, with an engaging Quakerish simplicity. "My friends," he began. He knew his job; he was a craftsman; his voice, his face, and his arms would still do the right things if half his mind were somewhere else and quite out of action.

A nasty interjection gave him the chance to add, with winning humility, "At least, I hope I may still call some of you so."

There were mixed shouts of "Yes!" "Blimy, no," "Git on an' we'll see," "Give 'im a chance!" But they all wanted to hear; soon the silence was so deep that the faint flickering sound of a torch burning quietly in the street came in clear at the window.

"At least," the finely managed—or managing—voice continued, "many of you know me. You know me as one who has never, from the first to last, said or written one word that would help to force you, or coax you, up to the verge of the high precipice of war. You know how minutely the journal which I have controlled has counted the cost of that plunge; how persistently it has pointed to this and that weakness in our defences; how—"

A few yells of "Yuss, ya crabbed yer country," "Naggin' skunk!" and "Sneerin' trytor f" gave way in a moment before renewed shouts of "Give 'im a chance." Meanwhile the orator stood like a Genius of Patience—his sentence suspended, his gesture arrested—a statuesque symbol of faith in his countrymen's sense of fair play. When silence returned, he resumed: "—how the Voice has striven to pierce to the very core of the dispute, to bring out what it is about, to show it in all the simplicity that it admits of, to help men here—yes, and elsewhere—to see how easily, how nobly and how soon it could be settled by the tribunals of reason and conscience alone."

There was another brief scuffle of voices below, shouts of "You did!" "Thot's reet," and "Good ol' iron!" contending amain with "Y'elped the enemy" and "Portan gowld—thet done it!"

During the moment's rest thus afforded, Burnage glanced down at Rose on his right. The glance was an entreaty of some sort—either for guidance or for release—"Tell me, quickly, what to do, and what to say," or "Let me off, even now."

No express answer was given. Rose offered only a vague, enigmatic, intense stimulation. Her face was kindled but not legible, she sat like a vivacious Sphinx or riddling Egeria—Delphic, chimaeric, possessed of some God but not making his ways plain to man. Man still had to guess and to fumble.

Burnage did so. "Of all," he went on, "that I have thus said I have not one word to unsay."

There were murmurs below and a faint cheer was smothered by groans. The momentary interruption gave him just time to peer down once more at his wife's face. It frightened him. The light in it seemed to be sinking. The whole illumination of his world was threatened. Behind the orator's set mask his mind rushed hither and thither in panic search for some means, any means, to keep that sun from failing him. And then, suddenly, the means appeared, or it seemed so. He plunged at it.

No sign of his agitation appeared on him. Such is the gift of these artists, as of the comedians who set the whole house in a roar, just the same, though their mothers have died in the after-noon, or their wives gone off with handsomer men. All the change, if any, was that his periods gathered, as they rolled on, a more rhythmic swell and rotundity. "For I believe, from the depths of my heart, that, when the lives of thousands are at stake, a public man, if err he must, should err upon the side of caution, of moderation, and of peace. But there may come a point when some of us—nay, when all of us, are strangely touched to finer issues than we have yet known, by a something within us which is not ourselves. There comes a moment when all the early arithmetic of prudence, all the nice calculations of statecraft, are swept—and rightly swept—away by an underlying passion of love for our country and our people."

In the crowd the silence had grown more profound. They all wanted to know what was coming. A recantation?

"For me," said Burnage slowly—"mind, I can only speak for myself—but, for me, that point has now been reached. That tremendous moment has come. Whatever it costs me or mine, however it may injure me in your esteem, I cannot and I will not close my eyes to the fact that the rulers of Porto have thrown down a gage of battle—"

A cheer broke out, but Burnage held up a hand and there were many peremptory or imploring cries of "Sh!" Perfect silence was re-established almost at once. He went on—"a gage of battle which honour compels us to take up."

The cheers that came now were as sudden and loud as the sharp-edged crack of near thunder. At last the din lessened and single shouts could emerge—"Sense at last!" "Good ol Burnage!" "Wot's wrong wi' Cyril!" "Nuffink!" "Three cheers for the war!" A lusty voice started "For he's a jolly good fellow" and in a second some thousands of voices were roaring the tune.

His eyes sought Rose's face while the hubbub endured. Was she pleased with him now? That was all he 'could care about. In no doing of her will was there anything difficult or anything shameful; to do it was the only peace, and to see her face satisfied with him was the one supreme joy. If she cared for the smell of the incense smoking up now from the street, he was glad he had set it alight, whatever it cost.

Damn its cost. Honour, duty, conviction, the fortitude that withstands a multitude to its face, for its good—these were pale names, mere tepid abstractions, compared with the warm life in Rose. Let her lead.

But would she? What was she thinking? She smiled—a little; clapped her hands—slightly. "Quite good, dear," she said, in a cool, measured way, as if some higher praise were withheld—as if there were something or other about his oratorical feat which she. could not quite do with. Was it the rhetorician's trade tools and staple banalities—booming and unction and fair round-bellied periods that cried out to be parodied? Or was she feeling herself to be cheated again by the old second-rateness of life—wishing that she could be moved as the crowd was by Cyril—wishing that the salt could have its savour back and she be as easily stirred as the vulgar and the dull? All that her worshipper saw was that she still had her outworks of irony and reserve; the gods still kept men at a distance.

But he had to tighten the orator's mask on his face and go trumpeting on, for the uproar that had let him rest had now subsided. Almost in absence of mind he picked out the appropriate tools from his bag—the tone of genial, confidential seriousness, the winning air of studied moderation, the pose of the good, easy man reluctantly forced to struggle for life and liberty. It was win now or go under for ever, and so on, and so on.

Buzz-uzz-uzz—I fear it fell on Rose's ears more dully at each moment since the single piquant one of Cyril's boxing of the compass. Could nothing ever seem exciting again for more than one moment? Like an invalid teased by a bee that fumes and bangs against a window, she drearily followed now the technics of the performance—the orator's parade of meekness and boast of modesty, the putting on of rueful faces and the dabbling in of smears of heavy jocosity, the hackneyed figuration about closing ranks and keeping powder dry and standing shoulder to shoulder. The little straw fire of Rose's moment of exaltation had died down.

What remained, I suppose, was the usual desolation of those who carry about them, wherever they go, a sufficient plant for manufacturing a private desert of their own. But, as yet, she clung feebly, without real hope, to the notion that from this old dreariness of hers some deliverance might come through this speech that she had caused her servant to make. While she went on there was a sort of desperate relic of hope. But, good Heavens!—he was ending? His voice was taking on the peroratorical note; the cadenza was almost in sight. During a momentary pause for cheering she called his name in an imperious whisper.

He looked down bewilderedly, with his nervous force nearly spent.

"Cyril," she repeated almost angrily, "you must go on. You've said hardly anything yet—nothing at all about Christ and 'duty to God and man' and all that sort of thing."

He looked as if he would ask humbly that this cup might pass from him—but not if she really wanted it drained to the end.

She obviously did. "Quick!" she said. "Quick!—before you lose hold of them."

So he pulled himself together and went on, and she listened, craving for some stir in her heart. She longed, like everyone else, to have a noble life of it. But all she could get was an impression of a machine still running well. Cyril was shying, with all the proper resonance and gusto, "To any tender consciences—and of those I would speak with the utmost respect—whom the idea of war afflicts by its seeming contrast with the Christian ideal of peace on earth and good-will towards men—to these I would not be content merely to cite the divine example of One who came to our earth not to bring peace but a sword. I would also beg every sincerely religious man to ask his own heart, simply and honestly, this question—Is it really possible to doubt that in no long time the spread of that Gospel of peace and mercy, justice and truth, must be vastly, immeasurably advanced by the triumph of our arms? Remember—and this is no idle boast—that ours is a God fearing people. Its sense of duty is intense. With no outward professions of uncommon godliness, but none the less truly for that, its life is ruled from hour to hour by obedience to God's will. We have no human king. It is the Bible that reigns."

"What a ghastly false note!" may have been the first thought of the fastidious Rose. But the cheering was great: Cyril knew his own job. He had to pause before going on. "And now I seem to feel thrilling through us, through our whole race, at this moment of quickened insight and deepened devotion, the stir of a new impulse to carry beyond our own borders this moral standard of ours, this rule of willing duty and sane obedience to the highest law—to carry this secret of happiness across our frontiers and to make its blessings known to peoples now less fortunate—so to widen our borders as to widen yet more the liberty and happiness of those whom we may bring under our sway; to win new lands—in name, perhaps, for ourselves and our children, but also, in a truer and a higher sense, for truth and righteousness and God. In that inspiration let us now forget party, forget self, forget everything but our country and our loyalty. We stand, as a nation, alone in the world. We have no foreign allies. Let us, then, be the truest allies one to another, unswerving in our purpose, unshakable in our patriotism, each man resting his own fortitude on the sure knowledge that every one of his fellows is steeled like himself to face any danger or hardship, endure any test and overcome any temptation or weakness—'faithful unto death.'"

CHAPTER VII

ROSE PUTS IT ALL AWAY FROM HER

I

That was the end. But for a minute or two the spent orator had to stand at the open window, meekly accepting the due ovation, before he could back out of sight of the public, drop down on a chair and look appealingly to Rose for her more precious approval. Cyril was quite haggard with hunger for that. He even asked, like a child, "Are you pleased with me?"

"Y-yes," she said. Her voice hung on the word, as though the question had to be weighed. "I thought you spoke—oh! quite well." She said it like one trying to make the best of a thing that might well have been better.

"But the substance—the line that I took?" he pressed eagerly.

"Well—" She had again that balancing tone.

He sat up in dismay. "Why, was it not the thing you wanted?"

"Oh! yes—one of them."

"Them?"

"Are there not always two possible courses?"

"Why, what was the other?"

"My dear Cyril!" She chid his obtuseness. "Why, naturellement, to tell dear King Mob about the bad Trust and how it buys papers, and how it mines for the root of all evil, and goes up and down making mischief."

He was startled. "My darling! I only heard it in confidence."

"And couldn't soil your hands to save your country from war profiteers and axe-grinders and up as trees, Minotaurs, spiders and powers of darkness?" A glint of animation was lit in her disappointed face as she worked up her ironic list of rhetorical labels that might have been tied on to Bute.

He stared at her, aghast. "So that was the line you'd have liked!"

"I don't say so."

"You did want the other?" he almost entreated.

She gave a little joyless and elusive laugh. "I can't say that, either," she said.

He gaped at her. "Was there—another line open?"

"I can't see it. Can you?"

"Then—surely—one of those two?"

"But which? Don't you see? That's the point—which?" She had the air of an elder making a confidant of a child in some trivial and cheerless perplexity. "Which? Of course, either is good enough, in a way."

"Either! Dear, they're opposites. If one of them's right, the other's just devilish. They have got nothing in common."

"Yes—clearness—if they're run hard, for all that they're worth. Both are bold—they're straight lines— they don't go wiggle-waggle the way people do when they're fussing over their poor darling consciences." She broke off to listen to something.

"Oh, my God! There's the Bishop's impossible clarion voice on your stairs. You must entertain him—I really can't stand any Bishop just now."

Many previous calls on the editor, to cadge this, that or the other scrap of publicity in the Voice, had taught the Bishop all the topography of its office. So he made his way straight to the editor's door, unannounced, and entered the room like a triumphal process—head high, tread elastic, eyes sparkling, all his fine high vitality at its highest.

At sight of Mrs. Burnage in that place he gave a gesture of joyous surprise. Would she forgive so rude an intrusion? he had happened to be passing in the street—"the merest chance, but what a chance! It gave me what I shall never lose as long as I live—your good man's noble speech."

He turned to Burnage; he threw back his own head as if the better to inspect so choice a specimen of mankind. "I simply want," he said, with the appropriate action, "to shake your hand and to thank you, as I have thanked God already." Case was quite flurried with desire to rally at once round the hero of the hour.

Burnage feebly demurred, but the sturdy divine bore down all resistance. At no time could other people say much when Case had golden words minted and ready for issue. And just now he evidently felt a more than ordinary need to be audibly virile and sane and, where two or three conquering forces were gathered, together, to be in their midst. "Don't ever dream," he said, "of us parsons as standing aloof from our country's aspirations. No, no! It's no less as a patriot than as a humble follower of Christ that I say a most heart-felt Amen to your rousing words." He turned again to Mrs. Burnage, as if to give her a proper share in this distribution of laurels and bays.

"Thank you so much," she said fascinatingly. Mechanically she had turned up the lights in her face, to meet social requirements.

For Cyril was not meeting them. He was listening blankly to the roar outside. His speech must have quite doubled that volume of sound. Nothing could stop it now, curse it! It rose and fell like a chant; at some moments it rushed up almost into a shriek. And the fisherman who had let out this genie cowered under the voice of the monster whom nothing could now force or wheedle back into the pot.

But the Bishop was charmed. The Bishop edged towards the window, like one irresistibly drawn, till the crowd caught a glimpse of him, cheered him and shouted his name. He drew nearer still, beamed out over the white faces and torches, extended his hands as if in benediction; then he fell back slowly, reluctantly, as a boy takes a sweet out of his mouth. "Well," he said, taking up his hat, "I know how busy you must be."

While Burnage was seeing Case out, Rose stood up and stole towards the window. She had seen the Bishop inhaling the cheers, sucking them up as if they were a good joy-giving drink, with a lingering and voluptuous suck. A new stimulant? Yes, she would just taste the cup of that drunkenness. She sidled furtively up to the window and leaned out a little. A cheer rose at once, and she bowed and smiled regally, drawing more cheers while she stood thus, trying to imbibe them well, waiting for some great lift of the heart to befall her—vision, illusion, delusion, any mood that might be passionate, any escape from her own vapid shortage of relish for the contents of life.

I suppose the strong waters had no strength for her: she had drawn back, looking sour, even before she heard Cyril's returning feet in the passage, and others besides. He came in, bringing Willan.

III

Whenever this goodly frame, the earth, seemed to Rose to be a more than usually sterile promontory, it was her way, as you know, to wreak her disgust on the first human being to hand. It was Willan's turn now. If looks could kill, he might well have perished before he was half through the door.

"You here again!" she exclaimed with a frankness so brutal that Cyril could not but wince.

He had to take the edge off such harshness. "Yes," he said, putting his arm through Willan's, "John has come back, like a brick, and is saying kind things."

"Oh?" said Rose, with so signal a lack of cordiality that Willan had to make some excuse for his presence.

"You see," he said, "my War Office room is just opposite. So your old speech made a mess of my work."

Willan looked affectionately at his hero. How could warmer praise pass, face to face, between men who had been friends at school?

"Well?" said Rose, coldly.

But Willan was looking at Burnage. Willan was wholly absorbed "and carried away with admiration of Burnage's performance. Whips and scorpions are nothing to a man wholly absorbed in anything: he is unwoundable. And Willan was very handsome now, because there was transpiring from him the ardour of faith and veneration which does not just evaporate, but forms a kind of transfiguring aura, almost physical, round the face of the possessed person. "Just wash out," he said in a low voice, "what I said about not being ready. We must be. Only don't expect very much at first. We may get knocked a bit, at first."

"Knocked!" Burnage blankly repeated the word.

"The Portans may push us back a few miles," said Willan cheerfully, "if they're ready for war. We're not. But then no British country ever was, when a war started. We'll just have to play the old game again—learn war while fighting."

"You think we shall be invaded?" Burnage asked.

"Well, one or t'other must do a bit of invading. And rushing is no game for us. Too like the French in T4, when they butted bang into Alsace and got a sore head."

"A long war, then?"

"Oh, we'll stick it out, as you said—all stick together, you know. I only hope we sojer-men may do our job half as well as you have just done yours. It's my very last war—I turn good after this. But I've never known one where I felt so dead sure that it couldn't be helped—thanks to you!"

Burnage was growing numb. A certain very cold shadow is apt to cast itself on these capable orators now and again. They will offer, any day, to mould the career of a nation. Such offers are part of the ordinary practice of their charming art. But sometimes, to the artist's consternation, the offer is flatly accepted. He finds, to his astonishment and distress, that resonant words do really count for something, apart from the first pleasure they give and the first cheers they bring in—that words may be dynamic and send hundreds of thousands of men to be killed for a bad cause or for nothing at all, and stunt as many babies by cutting of part of their food. Burnage had certainly not been self-complacent, before Willan came in, about his feat at the window. Still, he had only felt rather dirty and sick—he had taken a kind of bribe from his wife to do something shabby, and then had been bilked. But it was not till now that he felt, in any vivid way, that he had been sending the trustful friend of his youth, with a good many others, to fight a doubtful battle for higher dividends on shares of the Bute group of companies. Ripe public man as he was, it came to him as a horrible revelation that, in some cases, a man cannot try to brighten things for his wife without setting forces to work that may wreck a good deal of his and her world while he looks helplessly on.

Perhaps a sense of something dramatic in the contact of the two men at that moment led Rose to eye them with a faint and momentary revival of interest. However displeased and disappointed with life she might be, still she scrutinised it with an acid equity; she gave it its chance of retrieving past failures. Wearily and peevishly, yet pertinaciously, she searched people's faces for signals of authentic passion or tragic intensity. When Willan and Burnage went out arm-in-arm, Rose pushed the door a little wider open behind them, to hear what she might of their talk. She half heard a desperate attempt by Willan, on the stairs, to splutter out thanks to Cyril for showing him what a clean business this coming war was.

"It makes simply everything different," Willan was saying joyfully, and "It makes an honest man of me at last."

After this prodigy of effusiveness Rose's ear caught no more till Cyril's step could again be heard in the passage. As it approached, a telephone bell rang in a little room next the editor's, with one door opening into his. There must have been another door opening into the passage outside, for the bell stopped the next moment and Cyril's voice could be heard saying, "Yes. Yes. Burnage speaking," and then, "Oh; it's you, Jenkin? Yes?"

She pricked her ears, but she heard nothing more till the final, "Good-night."

Cyril came in to her slowly. His face appeared to have sunk in; it looked smaller; his voice was dull. "All a mistake!" he said. "Bute is not buying the Voice. A mistake of Jenkin's. He simply misheard."

"Oh, these key-holes!" said Rose, with a hard, bitter bright-ness. "They are no good. I've just tried."

"It's some other paper he's buying, of the same name. A little paper—in Porto."

Rose threw her head back in a loud, joyous laugh. "So the great play is a farce, after all! And Faust sold his soul just by accident! Oh, Cyril! we'd better give up. We try to be epic and tragic and sup with the Devil and ride on the whirlwind, and all that we get is a neat little fool's cap for each of us. Well, we'll talk of it later; I can't go into it now. I'm too tired."

IV

As he took her down to her car they met Hendie. He looked strangely cordial and gay. Another cursed admirer, fresh from the street? Burnage shrank from him.

But Hendie would not be put off. "You've heard?" he asked briskly.

"What's that?" Burnage inquired, in fright. Could war have been declared already? Could Hendie, of all men, have heard of it first?

"All's safe!" said Hendie. "Neroni's concert is off—for a fortnight. I can do both the things now. Good-night!" It was clear he felt glad to be able to give complete peace to his editor's mind. He bounded on up the stairs. He had grown nimble.

Rose shuddered. "Whose was that vellum-bound face?"

She did not listen to his answer. When he had made it he put his palm under her elbow and clasped the joint tenderly. "Don't grieve about all this old tangle," he began kindly and timidly.

"No!" she announced, with no responsive softness. "I'm simply going to put it all away from me." It was a formula she often used, when she specially wished to cut herself clear of the plaguy way that effects have of following causes, when once you set causes in motion, although you may only have done it for fun, or just to kill time. And somehow Cyril was always a part of that which she put away from her thus. It was as if he were implicated somehow in the frowardness of this causation-ridden world.

So nothing came of his attempt at consolation. Rose was out of reach by now, remote in her own misty island of separate and superior gloom. He went back to his room and sat down to the ticklish literary job of squaring all that he had said from his window to-night, with all that he had written in the Voice a few hours before, while the unapproachable lady drove home in the blues through the streets which her doings had helped to set in a roar with high spirits, desire and hope.

BOOK TWO

CHAPTER VIII

A CITY ON TIPTOE

I

From Ria City you can see, on a clear day, the east frontier of Ria, the State, though it is some eighty miles off. It is quite a model frontier. If you were appointed to make a new world you would probably put some such fence between each country and the next, to prevent any naughty-boy country from jumping over too easily.

As seen from Ria City, this barrier between Ria and Porto looks like a rather irregularly spiked garden railing, painted dead white. The height of the tips of these spikes, above the sea level, ranges between twelve and fifteen thousand feet, and none of the dips between spike and spike sinks lower than ten thousand feet. The fence is white because all its upper part is always covered with snow. Towards the end of fine summers, like that in which Ria declared war on Porto, the sun is just able to melt the winter snow off the two or three lowest of the dips between the peaks of this mountain range.

You cannot see from the City the actual sky-line of any of these dips. Something gets in the way. It is as if a broad screen, with a level top, had been placed in front of the whole range, with only the upper three thousand feet of the range sticking up above the fop of the screen. This is because the Big Slope of Ria rises more steeply for the first fifty miles East of the City than do the beds of the deep mountain valleys above—each about thirty miles long—which lead up to those dips, nicks or passes. These relatively flat-bottomed valleys are as completely out of our sight as is the upper surface of a shelf eight feet high when you stand on the floor. For working purposes your horizon line is the level of the ground at the lower end of these valleys, where they debouch upon the Big Slope, though behind the horizon you do see that chain of white spires. These look so ethereally lifted above all human concerns that they seem to count among curious and beautiful shapes of cloud rather than as solid items of the ordinary inhabited globe.

There is nearly always a clear sky, of rather hard blue, over the City; the mountains are much hugged by clouds, mostly of the cumulus, or cauliflower, form, their tops presenting billowy white bulges to the sun, while their dark under-sides often seem to rest or fidget in the beds of those invisible valleys, like huge beasts wallowing in troughs. When the wind is uneasy, and much cloud about, the mouth of one of these valleys, seen from below, will appear to be constantly sucking in or disgorging soft bulks of a vaporous blackness that shifts, mantles, seethes, wreathes and makes you wonder indolently what the inside of the valley is like. And somehow these almost unvisited cauldrons are not made less mysterious, but rather more so, by your seeing how wholly they must lie under the observation of watchers so supremely unrevealing as the great iced peaks which overlook them. Like the slow blink in the eyes of some magnificent cat, drugged with hours of sun and of proud private dreams, those august recluses seem only to shed an additional vesture of enigma on every object of their pensive survey. Quivering in hazes of remoteness, winking through depth behind depth of the frustrating clarity of sunburnt air, their downward gaze upon a mystery only sets it off the better; they prompt you to reverie and to wonder.

II

For several days this mystificatory drug had been working to some effect on the people of Ria City. All day and every day the sun burnished intensely the light upper edges of pillow-like clouds that pressed their black bellies heavily down into the mountain valleys. Through this layer of darkness the musing snow peaks rose into dazzling sunshine above; the wriggling clouds were impaled on white spears. Towards the mouth of one of these valleys, due East of the City, nearly everyone's eyes had been turning for a whole week. It was known as Scout Valley. As war had begun, ho true news could be published. But everyone knew pretty well that just below the mouth of that cloudy defile the Rian main army was massing for the invasion of Porto; unless, indeed, it were already pushing on, up the dark trough itself, to gain Scout Pass at its head—the one point where any sort of track crossed the main frontier ridge.

From the City, of course, you could make out no actual movement of troops. You could tell where Scout Valley was if you identified two tall white peaks on the main ridge behind. Between these two, as it seemed—only, thirty miles nearer to your eye—was the valley's mouth. You might see, too, with a good tele-scope that, as the wind shifted about, sombre masses of cloud were belched out of this orifice, to tumble down the uppermost part of the Big Slope below it, or were sucked up from the Slope and gorged by Scout Valley. But as to military movements, all that most Rians knew was that for seven days past the railway running from the City, straight up the Big Slope, had been thronged, day arid night, with troop trains bound for the little terminus outside the entrance to Scout Valley.

So the common man, to whom secrets of State were not told, looked solely towards Scout Valley, felt that great things were doing up there, was sure that the army would give a good account of itself, and said he pitied any Portans that got in its way. Those who lived nearer the heart of the rose turned their telescopes still more intently upon the narrower entrance of Boat Valley, the parallel valley next to the Scout, upon its south side. Cyril and Rose and perhaps a hundred other persons in the City knew that the really exciting move of the campaign was to be made by way of Boat Valley.

While the main army marched up to Scout Pass, a small force of picked men, all British by birth, was to push up Boat Valley at top speed, find its way across the summit ridge and then work northward and establish itself on the heights overlooking the Portan approach to Scout Pass, on the East of the main ridge. Once this was done, without the enemy's knowledge, it would be all the better if the Portans did try the bold thing and come out to meet the Rian army at the frontier ridge. For the Portans would then be exposed to two fires, from two higher points, as they approached Scout Pass—from the top of the Pass itself in their front, and from the heights on their left—the latter an enfilade fire.

That the Portans might be the first to reach the top of Scout Pass no one seriously feared. The Portan capital was three hundred miles from the Pass. There were known to be no defences on the Pass; no Portan railway approached it; there was no appreciable Portan garrison, or military depot within two hundred miles, a war between the two infant States having never been dreamt of until the last month. So it was not in Porto's power to win a race to the frontier.

But neither was it in the nature of Portans to do any such thing—so any fluent person in Ria would have told you. The Portan notion of national defence was to let the enemy's army plunge deep into Porto and drown there—spend itself for nothing, like a bullet fired into deep sand—or like Napoleon's army in Russia. Everyone whom you were likely to meet at dinner parties in Ria City knew all about it. They all pooh-poohed the Russian comparison. Porto, they said with some force, was not Russia. Still, they allowed that the Portan plan was, no doubt, the best the Portans could adopt, they being what they were—a scratch crew of mongrels, British, Australian, American, mixed dagoes, Germans and Dutch, with the English tongue mainly in use but the Teutonic phlegm uppermost in the character of the crowd, if you could say that it had one. Every country must make its strategy fit its own temperament, and no doubt the passive resistance stunt was the best thing to be done with a collection of natural sluggards with no initiative or fire.

So the Portans were not to be at the frontier. And yet, like a good cautious soldier, the Rian Commander-in-Chief, General Miln, would not omit so brilliant a stroke of prudence as this rapid march of a single brigade of infantry, along with a few mountain guns, with orders to cut in on the Portans' left flank if by any miracle they should acquire the wit and boldness to do what they certainly wouldn't.

"In my trade," General Miln explained to Burnage, with honest professional pride, "the duds provide only against what is possible. A man who knows his job heads off the impossible too."

Miln, you see, told Burnage everything—the only way to get the right things kept dark in the press, wherever the press is run by men of honour.

III

At the end of the week's waiting the physical clouds of suspended moisture, though not the subtler cloud of mystery, lifted completely; for the next three days no fleck could be detected in the staring, aching blue of the sky that canopied all Ria from the warm surf to the topmost pinnacle of ice; all the Big Slope seemed to swim in a quiver of sultry haze.

This made the Scout Valley enigma more piquant than ever. That a whole army should disappear into a giant trench full of mist was striking enough; but it tantalised curiosity more that the army should vanish into a landscape searchingly illuminated—that by day it should count for no more in the visible scene than as many ants in the next field but one, and that by night no spark should be seen of all the bivouac fires that must be burning brightly up there in the keen air of the heights.

This period of waiting in front of a winking and twinkling Sphinx worked in divers ways upon the minds and nerves of divers persons. Cyril Burnage lost his sleep. Browell recovered his: he was happy; he felt he was "living dangerously"—an ideal much in vogue at the time among middle-aged men of sedentary employment. The gunmakers' union had instantly called off the strike; they cursed the war, but most of the men had some friend in the haze up above, and nothing that might lessen his chance of pulling through was to be thought of. So the furnaces roared more than ever and the foundations of some, at least, of Bute's next dividends were well and truly laid. Larger and larger crowds walked or loitered all night in the streets of the City, staring up at the place where a very bright star flashed and winked over the unseen Scout Pass.

Demand creates supply, and everybody longed for news so intensely that spirited traders began to invent and sell it in spite of all difficulties. No lie was too crude to sell: a Portan spy had been caught, bomb in hand, beside the Ria Town Hall; the Portan army had mutinied; Marx, the Portan Minister of War, had taken prussic acid. But what sold best were good practical reasons for hating every Portan alive; evening papers had it on the best authority that a Rian living in Porto had been shot in a market-place for refusing to fight against his own country; that Portan troops had derailed a train-load of Rian women and children fleeing to the frontier; and that Portan soldiers had been told off to visit all wells and streams which the invading Rians might use and to poison them with cyanide of potassium sewn up in one-pound bags.

A few days of active commerce in these grounds of offence sufficed to purge the popular mind of any belief that this was to be a war between two nations of the ordinary human type, like the other wars of history. It was soon settled that the Portans were a race apart and were disentitled, because of their vices, to count among civilised beings; they were semi-savages or bloodthirsty hounds. Lively Rian writers described the shifty eyes and foxy faces of the Portan General Staff, the clod-hopping boors who commanded battalions and companies, the thieving and cheating of quartermasters and sergeants and the poltroonery of the rank and file, who could only be forced to the front with the lash and would shoot their officers if they dared. For a penny you could buy the most positive assurances that it was a regular part of Portan field tactics to raise the white flag and then fire from under it, and that a Portan colonel had boasted in an eating-house of the large number of white flags that his battalion carried into action for this purpose.

But how could it be otherwise?—so the Rian Press asked next. For Portan officers were not gentlemen: one Portan general had been a pig-dealer; another had dealt in potatoes—not very wholesale either—in his youth; one battalion commander was an old money-lender and fleeced his own mess; another looked like an orang-outang, and smelt so, too.

So, with tropical swiftness, there grew before the minds of Rian readers of the newspapers a mental image of the typical or normal Portan. It was an ugly figure, but not daunting; huge, but misshapen and flabby; a cowardly giant and doddering bully; cruel and mean, but unable, for lack of daring and wit, to betray and murder as freely as he desired.

Up and down the streets of Ria City the thronging non-combatants drifted, day and night, feeding their souls on these ample bellyfuls of East wind. They hugged a doubly pleasant conviction—that they were Jack confronting Giant Blunderbore, and that Blunderbore was a dropsical lout and would crumple up at a touch. Heroism and good business too, a gallant enterprise and a dead cert—what more could anyone want?

IV

Dr. Browell proved with the greatest ease that this was an extraordinarily noble state of the public mind. He knew it could not last for ever; still, he said that the war had lifted the nation off the dull flat earth of its common peace-time morality and mentality; it was living now, so to speak, on a sunny table-land and breathing a purer and more bracing air. Even to be old in this air was, he said, Heaven; what must it be to be young?

If anyone objected that this or that expression of the patriotic temper was not exactly the thing, Browell would rebuke him for self-will and pride. The nation, Browell explained, was a higher organism than any of the human units composing it. Was not a man a higher organism than his little finger or big toe? Let the objector reflect that in him the relatively low was criticising the relatively high, and the less spiritual being was finding fault with the more spiritual. Would it not be wiser, as well as more seemly, to assume that this superior incarnation of himself and everybody else had got hold of some deep truth too difficult for his own poor brain to grasp single-handed? Let him have faith and merge his own frail judgment and will in the more exalted will and judgment of a finely inspired community.

A few rejected this comfortable doctrine. One of them was Crisp, a born kicker and jibber. He said he doubted whether anyone need be taught to shout with the crowd, either in war or in peace, so much of this virtuous habit was born in us all. Browell smiled on hearing of this. No doubt poor Crisp, he said, was soured a little by the momentary check the war had put upon trade; still, as the poet said, "we are not cotton-spinners all"; probably even the poor cantankerous Crisp would toe the line like a man and stop talking nonsense, if the call came to him.

Another recusant was Hendie. He went about pooh-poohing all the good reasons currently given for the war. Oh, it had to come, of course, but only because there was a great find of gold in the case, so he had heard, and a great find of gold must always play the devil with everyone who had to do with it. Did nobody know his Wagner well enough to see that? Hendie jeered, too, at "that funny little anti-deist," as he called the Bishop, from whom it was generally felt that nothing but holy desire, good counsels and just works was proceeding at the time. But Hendie was a known crank, wilfully blind to the decent distinctions of race, religion, domicile—every distinction, indeed, except between having and not having a sense of the right thing in music. Even the incessant singing of Ria's patriotic songs was said to be only hardening him in this fad.

In these spacious days on the table-land Burnage's breath was taken away more than once by things that he read in his Voice. He had tried a little, at first, to stem the flow of fairy tales about fantastic enemy doings. But a shriek of suspicion rose from the Voice's readers at once. Why was the Voice hushing up the facts fearlessly printed elsewhere, about the female aborigine whom a Portan general had once sawn in two because she could not work any faster? How could the Voice hope to be trusted, about anything else, when it suppressed that shocking business of the poisoned wells? Was Burnage wobbling back into "pro-Portanism" after having seemed to clamber out of the ditch?

He threw up his hands; he gave in. Within a week of the declaration of war there was no Rian paper that painted the Portan ogre in colours more horrific than the Voice's. Then all went well and the Voice was acclaimed as a faithful spokesman of its country.

CHAPTER IX

ANOTHER ADVENTURER

I

As a veteran who, in the Great War, had put in a year on the Staff, besides three years fighting, Willan was now Brigade-Major of Colonel Main's highly reputed brigade, engaged in the Boat Valley movement. So he had gone to the Northern Station alone and had travelled up the Big Slope in the aristocratic seclusion of a Staff train, which is an excellent thing. He had thus escaped the jubilant send-off which the City was giving to regimental officers and men as they marched through the streets to the station—the mobbing, the pelting with roses, the kisses from surprising, hot-lipped women, perfectly respectable, the little flasks of whisky and Cognac from many good-natured men.

Willan had seen one of these Rian ecstasies. It troubled him a little. He knew there was always pretty good bursts at such times, in all countries. Still, this one had certainly troubled him a little. Somehow it seemed, in a way, over-pitched; rather too many of the marching men were drunk; the women who kissed the drunk and the sober were somehow more Maenadic, to Willan's thinking, than need quite be: it seemed like a bit of the older England oddly gone wrong, hecticised and tropicalised like an English plant over-stimulated, over-grown, flaunting out into a garish and dishevelled burlesque of itself. Still, he had felt rather hot in the face when he found he was thinking these things. Was he turning prig as he grew older? Of course it was only a few duds and shriekers who overdid things; nine out of ten of these people must be as sound as bells: think of that girl at Burnage's house with the game, reticent strength in her face and the serene equity of it! Come to that—think of Burnage. Willan had kicked himself, in his thoughts, for crabbing a lot of people of whom he knew little or nothing. And yet he felt curiously sure that some such discomforting reflections as his own had been visiting the Captain who sat opposite to him in the Staff train, and whose face seemed not wholly strange, though Willan could not give him a name. There was no one else in their compartment.

"Decent country,'.' Willan said, with a little jerk of his head towards the landscape visible from the window. The train had by now clanked its way over all the steel plates and junction points of the suburbs and past the bespangled brilliance of the outer zone of villa gardens.

"Yes. Know it well, sir?" asked the other man.

"First saw it ten days ago."

"Old inhabitant, compared with me. My seniority in Ria is eight days."

After a pause the stranger who was not quite strange had jerked his head towards the landscape and asked the absurd but useful question: "Seem to you at all like Asia Minor, sir?"

"Hullo!" said Willan. "So that's where I saw you?"

"That's right. In that mucky retreat with the Greeks."

Then they smoked for a time, while Willan recalled the place and time of his former meeting with Merrick; the hustled retreat, almost flight, of a second-rate forte that was half Greek irregulars, half foreign legion; the rain and the blanketing darkness, the troops and the civilian fugitives plodding along, jumbled together, through the deep mud of the road, the silly shots loosed in panic, and then the shrieks of women as they plunged away into the fields or marshes on each side of the road—anywhere to get away from the imagined sabres of pursuing Turkish cavalry. Plodding along near the rear, Willan had struck up with two or three other men of the nation that can retreat with more credit and less agitation than any other. Each had fancied himself alone with his pipe and the too emotional dagoes and was enormously glad of the gruff company of the others.

"Are any more of that lot in this business, sir?" Merrick asked.

"There's Gish. Remember Gish? The pacifist—the man who led anti-war riots till war was declared and then rushed off to get at the fun—simply couldn't keep off it."

"Yes, the ruffian—and he an old married man! He's here?" "Yes. In charge of a rum little beast of a gun that goes on a mule. I say, though—"

"Sir?"

"You needn't talk about Gish. I've heard about you—propaganding all over the place for the League and universal disarmament—till a scrap starts somewhere, out at the ends of the earth, and there you are, next train."

Merrick began, "Well, it is rather in-and-out running, I know—!" but Willan stopped him with "Oh! don't explain.

We're all in much the same hole. All war is a beast, but each particular war that turns up is a dear."

"Yes, it seems to be the only war you ever loved. But this is my last."

"Same here," said Willan.

II

The train had gathered pace by that time. It was running level across one of the broad ledges that give the Big Slope of Ria more likeness to an immensely wide, shallow staircase than to a smooth inclined plane. So the torrential rivers, that are grey with granite-dust scoured off mountains by glaciers, descend the Big Slope as a spiff of milk descends a flight of stone steps. They gad about and almost loiter on the flat tread of each step; then they find its outer edge and fling themselves hurriedly down to the next level.

A train mounting the Slope has just the converse succession of experiences. At each rise of the stairs the engine's voice loses its expression of confident power; the engine strains and grunts obliquely up a steep slant, calms down at the top and slides along, happy and purring, for the next eight or ten miles: then its groans of remonstrance recommence.

Contemplating this rhythmic alternation of serene and agitated effort, Willan and Merrick sat back in their several corners and said very little, but doubtless liked well to have each other there. For they were both of the sort to whom you can say anything in reason, and also of the sort to whom you can say nothing, for quite a Jong time, without any risk of being thought unsociable.

To men of their kind the place to which they were going was at that moment, of all places in the world, the best one to be in. They were in for a bout of the great sport to which all the delicious sports of the field lead up, and for which they serve as practice games, so that in war, at its best, all the separate joys and stir's of them all, the delights masked by some little hardship, the sharp-flavoured raptures called danger and toil, are fused into one supreme ecstasy. Of course, there was no doubt it was one of the world's curses too; but Merrick's mind had peace; he had done all he could to expel from the earth this plague which carried with it such strange delights. And Willan's mind had peace, because Burnage had swept every doubt out of it; no other war had ever been so clear a case as this of right against wrong—of an ill-armed, ill-trained and ill-provided David going forth against a probably well-founded Goliath who was a pretty bad lot. So they sat back happy in their several corners.

They travelled much in those fifty miles. Each ledge of the Slope was like a new country; it had a different climate and a verdure of its own. Willan viewed these changes with extreme enjoyment and little knowledge. A public school, an army crammer and Sandhurst had given him no skill as a spectator of the world. At the end of a day he could not have named a dozen out of the hundreds of exciting flowers which had shaken their pendant tassels of daring colour in the wind of the passing train. But all this rich confusion of loveliness helped his thoughts towards clearness. Who on earth, he thought—who, that had ever tried it, could easily give up this soldiering life—the busy, healthy, changeful life of the body? It gave you all that men sought in a holiday—the open air, the jolly exercise, the rested mind, the changing scene, the companionship of countless good fellows—fellows like Merrick; and, to give still more taste to it all, the salt of a little risk, the tingle of a good gamble? Praise and kindness from everyone, too, as if your magnificent game were work of some sort more exalted than that of people who use themselves up in dreariness, dust and foul air, putting together again the little stock of human belongings that the last war has scattered or smashed. Willan had not the habit of throwing the word God about, even within his own mind. But he thanked with a will whatever it was that had caused such a person as Burnage to exist and to have power in Ria.

He was so busy doing this, or simply thinking how well off he was and into what a good thing he had got, that it was with a start of surprise he found the train had pulled up under an almost perpendicular wall of bare rock, several hundred feet high. "Looks," he said to Merrick, "as if we were there."

Evening was falling, and evening falls chilly six thousand feet up, even in semi-tropical Ria. The station was five miles short of the terminus under the mouth of Scout Valley. It was, in fact, a little below the much narrower mouth, or drainage spout, of Boat Valley, and no one got out here except the Staff and a few specially employed officers of Main's brigade. Willan rejoiced to find that Merrick was one of them.

III

There was happiness that night in the little headquarters mess of the brigade. The Staff tents had been pitched in the jaws of Boat Valley, where it narrows to a gut two hundred yards wide, between nearly vertical walls of smooth stone. Outside the tents the valley torrent flowed almost silently down the level bed of the gut before making its three-hundred-foot jump from a stone sill, or take-off, down to the upper edge of the Big Slope below. The place was idyllic; the clover and thyme in the short turf round the tents were sheer pastoral poetry; so were the tiny plash and prattle of the stream as it crossed this lawn-like sward.

Just within this gate of Boat Valley the brigade was in bivouac for the night. From it there came the pleasant low murmur that usually rises from a bivouac where things are all going well. The men knew that they were a picked lot and that their job was important; all were animated with the first exhilaration of being on active service; officers and men were on the best of terms with themselves, one another and all the non-Portan world. From the whole bivouac this general contentment seemed to exhale like a perfume.

At the head-quarters mess there was the emotional satisfaction of eating a slightly plainer dinner than there would have been at the club; also the earthlier happiness of finding that, thanks to a fine mess-president, some champagne had accrued; also, in due time, a little good port. It was explained, with a cheerful twinkle, that these blessings had reached the camp by mistake, instead of some cases of castor oil. Everyone laughed happily.

Everyone laughed happily at everything. Everyone's spirits were kindled by the notion of swooping down upon a sluggish enemy from the skyey mountain-tops. Dix, the Brigade's Staff-Captain, a wonderfully well-read fellow, quoted some verses about a mountain eagle perched on the tip of a mountain, right up close to the sun, watching till he spots his prey, and then dropping plump down on its back like a thunderbolt. Queer to think a poet should get at anything so like real life.

The mess, who had not known one another two days ago, were now thawing fast. An amazingly good lot of fellows, they found. Willan and Merrick—who turned out to be there as a sort of extra Staff-Captain—were politely tempted to tell yarns about the Great War, which they, alone had been in; and they politely resisted the temptation and were the better thought of for that. What was any old war, long dead and buried, compared with this live one?

Having that which was needed, the mess toasted one another, and due praise flowed free. Never had troops had such a chief as the acting Brigadier, Colonel Main; in his reply even that cold man spoke warmly—seldom, he said, could a commander have had a more distinguished Staff; as to the regimental officers of the brigade, the N.C.O.'s, the men, every speaker glowed with the conscious generosity of his eulogies.

After all this handsomeness Willan ached to be alone with his large-scale map of Boat Valley, to read and re-read it, to soak himself in it till he could shut his eyes and see each mile of the valley as it would strike the eye when the march brought him up to it. But first of all, before people began to turn in, he wanted to find out what these Portans really were like—because knowing your man is, in any old contest, the first step to licking him. So he questioned such of the mess as said they knew Porto as well as the backs of their hands.

Their testimony agreed. They said, quite independently, almost precisely the same two or three things. One was that a Portan hated two things more than any others—cold steel and a surprise attack: Portans could shoot pretty straight and they could use cover like beetles, but would never wait for the bayonet if you went at them hard when they weren't expecting you. Another point of agreement was that the Portan was cunning enough, in a way—in fact, he was full of dog's tricks—but had no horse sense—"no what we call gumption."

Willan wondered. All his life he seemed to have been hearing about people like these. The Boers had been like this when he was a boy. The Germans had been like this in the Great War; Was every enemy like that? Had we been like that to the Germans? Were Portan officers saying to-night that this was what Rians were like? Willan went and revelled in the big-scale map, which had no distorting emotions.

Just before turning in for the night, the Brigadier, over the last pipe of the day, took his Staff into his confidence. Masters of war, he explained, like masters of anything else, moved in a world of quite simple ideas. They "saw large." "As to minute calculations," the Brigadier said, "tactical niceties, and so on, don't you believe it. That's shop-window stuff for civilians, There's only one rule in actual war, and it's this: the way to do the blighters down is just to go in at 'em straight."

"In fact, sir," Dix enthusiastically quoted:—'If you want to win your battles, take and work your blooming guns.'"

"That's right," said the Colonel. "War's like cricket: 'You just put your bat to the ball' as old Grace used to say." Willan thought that this, too, he had heard somewhere else.

IV

He and Merrick walked away together under the stars to their several tents when the Colonel's pipe was out and verbal inspiration had failed him. "Useful lot of tips flying round in this place," said the Captain to the Major. He said it with decorous seriousness, but an undercurrent of humour might be suspected.

"Fine flow of words to the mouth altogether," the other young veteran grunted, less reticently.

"Well, I suppose," said Merrick, "you get it in every H.Q. in Creation, the night before business begins."

"That's right," Willan allowed. "I suppose they'll be bucking a little bit over there, too." He nodded towards the East, where a very bright star was shining over the little rounded black nick that was made by Scout Pass in the snow wall of the frontier. "Well, good-night." They had come to the door of Merrick's bell tent.

Willan walked on to his. He stood for a minute or two before going in, and looked up the valley and down at the Big Slope. Ahead, towards the Pass, it was awesomely silent and black under the starlight; Boat Valley looked as if it were brimming with a kind of enigmatic solemnity. It seemed odd that anyone should square up to a serious job, and a place such as that, in a mood of pertness or swank. And yet it was probably only a "pi" fairytale, got up by preachers and prigs, that bluster was apt to bring down on the blusterer some grand smash of retributive justice. Willan had seen enough fighting to know that some braggarts are very stout fellows indeed, and that pride has often gone before rises. Good fellow, this Merrick—he had the decent working charity that comes of knowing many common men well—he accepted us all as we were, in our incorrigible "halfness," our Crooked attempts to go straight and our incomplete failures.

He turned to look down the fifty-mile stretch of terraced incline towards the city. There, too, was a look of enigma, grave and beautiful; not like the other enigma of blackness brooded over by one bright particular star. Below, the dimness was white; it was that of delicate mists shifting and hovering, as though with some vague tenderness, over the uneasy sleep of the hot earth and the excited city in the distance. Somehow it brought again to his mind the face of the large, still girl at the Burnages', with its look of vacancy that was not mere feckless emptiness but a calm readiness to receive something unknown. Not but that she was redoubtable, too, like every great question unanswered or judgment reserved. He felt that it mattered to him tremendously—even more now than at the time, whether she had condemned him that night. It would not be easy for a man to bear if she thought him a poor sort of beast.

He tried to call up and to scrutinise her face, as he remembered it. He tried to make out that it gave him some chance of acquittal, that hers was only a listening and balancing look, not a summing-up or condemning one. But the fifty miles of white mist and black landscape between him and her seemed to try to estrange them. Across it he put in such pleas as passionate resolution and hope can enter that her unuttered judgment might still be suspended till he had tried this time to make a less poor thing of his innings on the earth.

CHAPTER X

IN THE MOUNTAINS

I

The ground plan of Boat Valley resembled a horizontal section of a string of sausages. At every three or four miles the valley narrowed to a strait—a mere rocky gateway between unscaleable precipices on each side. At each gut of this kind there was just room for the valley torrent and the road to find their way through. Between each gut and the next the valley expanded to a width of anything from half a mile to a mile. Just before, or at, each gut the ground rose sharply, the torrent became a waterfall, and the road had to mount in zigzags; even then it was about as steep as a laden mule could walk. The wider stretches of valley between' these steep rises were almost as level as lakes. You might say the valley was built in nine or ten storeys.

When Main's brigade, in column of route, had gained the third of these storeys, they lost the sun and did not see it again on that day. The sides of the valley thenceforth were steep rock, and now they ran up out of sight into perturbed, blackish-blue clouds. The next rise in the road, some three miles ahead, could be-seen climbing up into dark cloud like a ladder leading to an unlighted loft.

That night it rained—not heavily, but enough to soak every man, all his clothes and his blanket. It also thundered—not with violence, but still the mountains made the most of what thunder there was: the sound of each peal went banging about from crag to crag, cannoning and rebounding so long as to leave no silent gap between each peal and the next. At last the long, muffled grumble sank into a discontinuous series of low barks or growls, like the final remarks of a watch-dog when he feels that perhaps his worst suspicions have been mistaken, but still is a little uneasy.

During the first part of the night the valley torrent, a few yards away from the Staff's quarters, kept up a loud, droning roar, with an occasional crash as the stream succeeded in overturning some unstable boulder in its bed. Then the roar diminished as the frost immobilised, for the rest of the night, the torrent's head streams and feeders, higher up.

Willan had gone to sleep quickly, drugged with the keen air, the day's sun and the happy tiredness of a strong man well exercised. He was awakened by a multitudinous coughing. So?—it had begun—that everlasting cough of armies in the field, not mentioned by martial poets. But everybody made the best of everything in the morning, although somehow the breakfast tea ran short for the men: these things happen at picnics, and war was still a picnic of a rough, jolly kind. The men who went tealess lay on their stomachs beside some sheeny, streaky pools, like tarnished mirrors, that lay handy: the men lapped up the stagnant water—it saved them five minutes' walk to the clean torrent, and regimental officers did not like to bother the men about trifles.

II

The road up the valley grew rougher that day as they marched. After six miles it came to an abrupt end at the ruins of two cheese-makers' log huts. At one time a fair bridle track had gone on from here to a few goatherds' huts at the head of the valley. But the valley's English owner had found that its pastoral use impaired its value for the stalking of wild goats: so he had made it derelict six years before, and floods and storms had abolished all trace of the track. No word of all this seemed to have reached the Rian War Office. Its Staff map was seven years old, and Willan had noted on his copy that a good track for horses and men was marked as running up almost to Boat Pass.

The valley itself was growing rougher, all that day. The torrent had ravaged it brutally and capriciously: now it would eat out a new bed for itself through a starveling wood of pine and walnut; then, when the wood was laid waste, the torrent would dam itself off again from the mess of naked roots and rotting timber that it had made: it would throw a wild stockade of bleached boulders across its last bed while it turned aside to tear a new channel somewhere else for its boiling flood of melted ice mixed with grey granules of granite.

There was a kind of beastly grandeur about the scene of these gadding devastations. From now onward almost the whole level width of the valley was strewn with stones of all sizes and shapes, from pebbles to thousand-ton blocks. The place was like one monster tip; for millions of years the peaks higher up had shot their rubbish here, after carting it down on the endless bands of moraines. Then the torrent had played the deuce with this refuse; like a wild boar in a temper, it had rooted up furrows this way and that with the vast wanton strength of its tusks.

On any rough ground the worst of roads is luxury, compared with roadlessness. Even a rude track gives direction. Where the road ended, the pace of the little army came down by about three-quarters. No regular order of march was possible now. Over the waste of rocks, boulders and scree the men and mules scrambled and stumbled as best they could, each man picking the easiest way he could find, while keeping as near as he might to the general stream of his company or platoon. He was not always very near it.

For half an hour or so the men would be jumping from boulder to boulder, high above the ground; then they would have to wade ankle-deep in loose granular shale. On whichever side of the main torrent they were, it would look as if the better going were on the other. So they crossed and re-crossed the stream many times, partly fording it and partly using chance stepping-stones. Each time they waded the stream then soaked boots became softer, and so did the soles of their feet; thus any hard and sharp stone under a foot could batter or punch it to much greater advantage.

Some of the officers fretted sadly about the inevitable remission of march discipline. They felt that troops not marching in fours or in file could scarcely be called troops at all. But the men pushed on stoutly, and did not abuse their accidental liberty. At every fresh crossing of the stream they larked and splashed one another, but did not loiter seriously. They sang and chaffed in all the dialects of the original Britain and of the ones overseas.

That day the sun came back: it beat down on the heads of the men from a sky of hot tin, and it beat up at their eyes from the rain-washed and sun-bleached stones underfoot, most of them too hot to hold. Also it swiftly dried, and more than dried, their often-soaked boots. Willan could so interpret his job as to make it call upon him to pervade the whole of the moving column. About four in the afternoon he noticed, with concern, that some of the men's, boots were beginning to go. They were turning mulberry-colour, diversified with a white bloom, rather like mildew. They seemed to be tightening over the instep; after a fresh soaking the water would ooze from the uppers as if they were many-layered pads of good blotting-paper. The stitching was still holding out, but some of the threads, now bleached white and clearly visible, were beginning to cut through the stuff that they sewed; a few of the needle-holes had thus run into each other and were turning seams into continuous slits in the material.

At half-past four an hour's halt was ordered. Many of the men took off their boots, having just crossed the torrent again, and put them out to dry on the stones. Some of them laughingly compared the leaks at their respective seams. A few had to shuffle along, with their soles on the ground, to keep their foot-gear on at all, so completely was it breaking up. At the end of the hour some of the sun-dried boots had baked hard and brittle, like pastry; they broke at the wrinkles sooner than smooth out again. Willan had to report to the brigade commander that many men would soon be too footsore to walk.

The Colonel growled and made a show of being the hard and exacting commander, the merciless user-up of his men. But he wasn't. Perhaps his favourite dream of himself was of a chieftain gruff and short in speech, but adored by all his followers—these would easily see through his harsh outer crust to the heart of gold and the master mind. So he halted the column five, miles short of the point it should have reached that day.

III

It was a pity. In war time the time-table may be everything. The brigade's loss of pace would delay the main army too, for both movements were timed to fit into each other. And there was no reason to hope that the men's boots would be any better at this time to-morrow. Rather the opposite. Still, no chief adored by his men could leave a thick trail of them behind him to nurse bleeding feet in the wilderness.

War, he told his Staff that night, was always like that; you always had to expect some unpredictable rub of the green; if you brought off one half of your plan you would do pretty well—it was long odds the enemy would have brought off only a quarter of his. So most of the Staff were nearly as jolly that night as the night before. All comradeship grows closer in the aweing company of great mountains. They cleanse your bosom, but they also make you gladder than ever to have a friend near.

The way the N.C.O.s and men kept up their spirits was splendid; the Staff felt sure of that, when from their own quarters, a little apart, they listened at night to the men's choruses—some of them jolly and some sentimental, but all sung with a go that made the valley ring from one black side wall to the other. The force was to keep its buglers till it topped the crest of the frontier ridge. There it was considered that furtiveness ought to begin, at any rate by way of practice. Willan could not quite square his own notions of war with this plan of sending a secret force to steal up on an enemy, bugle in hand, and blowing for all it was worth. But the Colonel had pooh-poohed Willan's caution as fantastic. Willan, he said, was an old pedant; he was Fluellen; he was obsessed with the disciplines of the ancients. So there Was nothing for Willan to do but enjoy the calls, and certainly they were divinely beautiful that night, with their brave and poignant melodies thrown slowly from echo to echo, up among the challenged heights.

They had risen two thousand feet in the day; the snow-line was now not far off, and the cold that night was astonishing. Clearly the Rian War Office had not expected this when planning field service kit for its soldiers. Most of the men were too cold to sleep, though tired enough. Willan had gone to sleep early: he lay in the open, but had a cunning way of swaddling himself in a blanket so as to have two thicknesses all round him. Even then the sharpening frost woke him, after midnight. At once he had a sense of an immense incompleteness in the quiet of the night. The camp, he could tell, was not sleeping, or else it tossed in its sleep. He rose and walked softly round a part of the men's lines. Nearly all the thousands of larva-like shapes muffled in shoddy blankets were silent, but many heads were raised a little, or bodies turned over, as he passed, and many eyes were shining wide in the dark.

The younger officers were less silent. One group of subalterns had quite given up trying to sleep. They were talking hard; the innocent boyish attempt at soldierly fewness of words was giving way, as usual, before the equally innocent longing of the boyish heart to unpack itself aloud. A few ardent souls were arguing, under their breath, about containing forces and re-entering angles and box barrages and enfilade fires, but more had for their themes some wonderful run with the Mid-Ria hounds, or some tremendous amour, or the magnificent way that someone, somewhere, had led his men straight up to a nest of machine-guns—presumably for some military purpose. These spoke rather more loudly: in some mysterious way the knowledge had spread through the force that its commander had no use for bookish young Moltkes as officers: all he wanted was guts and high spirits and natural gumption; damn all theorisers and pundits.

As Willan came back to his blanket, he noticed a very slight movement in Merrick's adjacent one. "No shut-eye yet?" Willan asked, low.

Merrick's voice was that of the most wide-awake. "It's those damned boots," he said. "Are they all made by one robber?" "I fancy so," said Willan.

"Gosh! That old game not dead!" Merrick's voice was, somehow, very likeable. Even in things that worried or angered him he could see some humorous side, some farcical touch of jaunty shamelessness or quaint effrontery that amused him.

"Bute is the name of this daisy, isn't it?" Merrick said, presently. "Ever meet him, by any chance?"

"No. I guess he must be decent, in a way. I know a man who doesn't bar him, anyhow—has had him to the house and so on. Perhaps we've just struck a bad patch of leather by some beastly fluke—a few mangy cows—or a bit of bad tanning."

"Your friend—? Is he—particular?"

"I was at school with him."

"Oh! Of course that's rather conclusive. What I hear a wicked world saying is that this fellow, Bute, has too many early Italian Madonnas and Children—very high prices. Seems he collects Christian Art."

"Well, how's it worse than postage stamps?"

"It costs a bit more. To get a top-hole Raphael you have to sell a lot of boots and make a lot on each pair. Much might be done with a little cardboard, you know, and brown paper." Willan was swaddling himself in his blanket. "Well," he said, "here's for a sleep."

IV

So far it had looked as if the valley might have an end somewhere. But next day—the third of the march—it looked endless. The sky was clear, and the two dreamy peaks of snow flanking Boat Pass seemed scarcely to be in the same world as the horrible troughful of glare and scorched scrub and hot stones in which the men and mules floundered along at a pace of about half a mile to the hour.

Wherever they were, all that day, the view ahead was the same. From the top of each side wall of the valley many ridges slanted down to the torrent. They saw one ridge behind another in profile, like noses of men standing in line, but the lower part of each ridge on each side struck in between the lower parts of two ridges on the other, each set of ridges intersecting the other set, like each of two crossed hair-combs, tooth between tooth. Some of these ridges were bare rock, either smooth or jagged with rocky splinters and flakes; others were meagrely fledged with a few scraggy, long-suffering trees. The base of every one of these ridges had to be rounded. And all the time the two basking steeples of snow, the goal of this pilgrimage, maintained or deepened their air of aloofness by day; at night they became as spectrally cold and remote as if Nature herself had decided to have no relations between them and any mere human sweat and hope and endeavour.

However, this third sunset of the march brought the blessing of letters and newspapers, carried up from the rail-head on fast going mules. The town-bred Englishry of the brigade had been fairly starving for newspapers—for news of sport, of war atrocities, of murders and divorces, of all the great interests. Most exciting of all, at the moment, there might be news of the enemy beast crouching or slinking about in his jungle beyond the mystic white paling. And news there was, sure enough, true or false; and a special plenty of news about what was said to be happening in Porto.

The news was fairly devoured. Each man to whom a news-paper had come was at once like a hen who has found a large worm in a populous fowl-run—the wormless fowls give her no peace wherein to do justice to the dainty. Private rights had to give way, as in other famine-stricken communities; papers were commandeered and little congregations formed themselves round each of these wells of pleasure, while some leather-lunged reader would give out at the top of his voice the war news and the racing. It seemed that some futile attempt at military secrecy was being made in Porto. Private telegraphing and telephoning had been stopped, and all letters were censored. "Eavesdropping curs!" exclaimed Dix, the Staff-Captain, when this news was read at the headquarters mess.

"I wonder how the news got through," Merrick said, musing and smiling.

"Hope we do the gagging better," Willan grunted.

Certainly a curiously large amount of news seemed to be arriving still from the locked and sealed enemy country. All of it, too, was just such news as the rulers of Porto would most wish to hush up—that the hearts of most Portans were not in the war; that Portan reservists were not rejoining the colours in anything like their full strength; that there were few war volunteers and that these would go home when it rained; that half the shells in stock would not burst, and that the only officers up to their jobs were a few hired Germans.

All the early part of the night the bivouac was humming with echoes of this heartening news. Everywhere Willan and Merrick heard fragments of excited talk when they made their round, now customary, of part of the lines.

"'ear that bit about the quitters?"

"Ah! Desertin' in 'ordes. Goin' strite 'ome."

"Let's 'ope all the Weedin' outfit won't ha' done a bunk afore we can git across an' set abaht them."

"I doan't blaame 'em. Nowt to eat, nobbut offal. A felly can't feight wi'out victuals."

"T'ynt the grub, Geordie. They're sof '—that's wot they are. Sof'! Not gime, sime's Englishmen. On'y gotta tap 'em on the conk, an' they'll curl up. Sime as a nytive."

"Most all on 'em is nytives."

"They can't 'andle nytives,—Portans can't. Nowbody can't 'andle nytives, on'y Englishmen."

So the bivouac buzzed, as it went off to sleep. Great, after all, is the power of the Press, if not for men's good, at least for their enfeeblement.

V

A wind rose towards midnight. It whined among the crags surrounding the head of the valley and overlooking it on both sides. The big rock basin just under the Pass, and still ten miles away, was a boiling potful of cloud, stirred round and round by the wind. For a moment or two, now and then, the actual Pass would come into sight, as a low black nick in the white eastern sky-line.

"Good!" said Willan, on getting one of these glimpses. "No snow on it yet!"

Merrick, half asleep, gave an appreciative grunt. Bute's boots were certainly not built for use on snow. But the passage over the main ridge was only just Clear; a hundred feet above it on each side the rocks were powdered white, as though with a sugar-castor. The two peaks that stood like gate-posts, each side of the Pass, had been re-whitened with fresh snow; they tapered up to incredible heights into strata of air with different lights of their own; a moon invisible to Willan and Merrick was evidently shining straight on the tips of those two unearthly spires. One of them had, lance-like, a pennon—a slim streamer of white cloud attached at one end to the top of the peak, while the other end floated out far on the air, horizontally: all round it now was clear sky.

"That old mountain is smoking his pipe," Merrick grunted, now more fully awake. "Rotten sign."

The old Alpine phrase recalled to Willan delectable things—Zermatt on a warm August night, coffee and pipes on the little tables set out in the village street, and low voices and laughter, quick and quiet and free like the summer lightning leaping about overhead, with the shining snows looking down.

"Mountaineer?" he asked Merrick.

"I've dabbled in it a bit. In some other games too. I've stuck my thumb in quite a lot of jam-pots."

"None like this, though, is there?" Willan indicated slightly the bivouacked men, the wild openness of night, and the high, strange events waiting beyond the dark beauty of the Pass.'

"No," said Merrick. "All the good old joys. The air, and no puzzles to solve; no old social fussing and grind: and a jolly good sweat every day, but the sun and the wind chiefly. And no one to call you a loafer for grabbing it all—one may even start thinking, oneself, that one's pulling one's weight—that things will be better, all round, if we bring off a win."

"This time they will," Willan said with decision. "This is a war in a thousand."

"It always is," said Merrick, with a smile, but no sneer; somehow he could be a sceptic without belittling the glamour of True Crosses and Saints' bones for their less critical adorers.

The Pass was hidden now by a whirl of wild cloud tom to tatters and then huddled together again. Round the peaks and over the ridges the rising wind was fairly raving; it wailed, hallooed and screamed with the fantastic urgency of tormented animals or men. Willan was reminded how easily on any rough night in a high Alpine hut you Can hear the most desperate cries for help, howls of rage and moans of despair coming from the wastes of ice and stone above you—all wind, only wind. He asked Merrick, did he remember?

"Rather!" said Merrick. "Lights too—signals; lanterns swinging in men's hands, all sorts. Why, I can see 'em now. Look there."

Yes, it was easy to fancy that fitful sparks and flashes were blinking and glimmering on the steep final ascent to the Pass, a little lower than the clouds. Only a slightly larger stock of nervousness than Merrick and Willan could muster, between them—and perhaps a little more imagination, too—were needed to suggest that malign eyes were up there in the frozen wilds, watching and gleaming.

CHAPTER XI

UPLIFT IN RIA

I

"Fust blood drawn! The Star of Eve! Fus' blood drawn. Extra speshul. Star of Eve.'"

This rousing news was cried in Ria City on the afternoon of the third day after Willan and Merrick had looked up at the hubbub in the heavens over Boat Pass. In the main street the police had just opened out a central lane or gangway through a crowd, that another battalion of volunteers for the war might march along it to the railway station. The crowd on each side of the gangway was now eight or nine deep. Along the open space under some cherry trees, in the rear of the crowd on one side, a newsboy was hawking an evening paper.

His stock-in-trade was of an edition a good hour old by this time; so its appeal to the public had lost its first sting. The boy's own sense of this falling-off in the quality of his wares was impairing his vivacity as a salesman. He vociferated without assurance or fire. Still, when anything like a purchasing face came into sight, hope would return and the breathless haste of a courier just arrived with astonishing tidings would be simulated once more as he broke out in factitious frenzy: "Fus' blood drawn."

A strong, ruddy, pleasant-faced workman of forty or so, who stood at the rear of the crowd, and looked like a steady old slowcoach, turned round and beckoned to the boy.

"Wot's that you got?" he asked.

"Fus' blood drawn! En'my killin' our wounded! Strite, guv'nor."

The holder of obsolete stock affected reluctance to keep the general public waiting. "'Urry up, guv'nor," he said. And then, as though to remind the whole street that he would be free in another moment to supply its needs, "Fus' blood drawn! En'my's inoomanity to wounded! Fus' blood drawn!"

The cautious customer paid his penny and fell back a little to read the paper, dropping his tool-bag on a seat and standing over it. The boy sauntered on. Probably most of the crowd were happy enough. There was a spectacle on. There was excitement, and nothing to pay. Some others looked grave, like the reading workman. A few were visibly in torment. One of them, a middle-aged woman shabbily dressed, appealed to him:

"Beggy pardon. Is this the way the soldiers go?"

"That's it, mum," he said, with an impulse of respect for such unconcealable sorrow.

She groaned, as if his answer had quenched some flicker of hope that there might be no road to the station at all. She shuffled closer to the crowd and eyed hopelessly the dense mass of human backs. The workman folded his paper, took up his bag, and tapped with a finger the nearest back in front of her, saying—"Mister—"

A hard face was turned round. The workman indicated the woman's woe-begone face with a slight lurch of his head. The hard face did not look less hard, but its owner spoke low to a man in front of himself, and he to another, and they all pushed hard to one side till a cleft opened through the whole crowd, and the dusty mater dolorosa walked through it, un-jostled, to the front row.

Her first helper, still at the rear, seemed to spy friends in the approaching figures of an old man, past work, with a resigned face, and a girl of twenty or so, whose good looks were half bleared and scalded away with much crying.

"Wot, oldard!" said the younger man. "Come to see the boys push off?"

"One of 'em," said the elder. "Our Joe's in this lot." The girl looked away.

"And 'e in a good job and all!" The workman glanced at the girl as he spoke. Clearly, she was the "all."

"I sent 'im, John," said the old man. "I didn't mean to, but I done it."

"Why, 'ow'd that be?" said John.

"We was settin' at 'ome, Monday night, an' Mary come in to see us. Mary was readin' us bits in the paper. Weren't ee, Mary?"

"Wot O, Mary," said John to the girl, in repair of any previous shortage of salutation on his part.

The girl's "Good evening, Mr. Brench," was just audible.

The old man continued: "I said to her, 'Ain't there no news o' this war?' I said. 'Not so very much,' she says. Didn't ee Mary? 'Oldin' orf of it, like?'"

She assented ruefully. What good had she got by her tactics?

The aged man went on: "'There's just a great war speech,' she says. 'That's wot they call it 'ere,' she says, 'gev by a Mr. Burnage.'"

"I picked that bit," Mary owned now. "I thought no one minded them speeches."

The old man resumed: "'Let's 'ave it,' I said, an' she read it all out. Eh, but 'e knows 'ow to go it, does Burnage." Even now the recollected fumes of those strong waters of rhetoric could work almost visibly on this ancient. "'It isn't 'ere I'd stay,' I said, 'if the legs would march under me.' And then Joe set very quiet, movin' 'is pipe about in 'is 'ands, till 'e says of a sudden, 'I'm off out o' this,' an' 'e offed it, an' when 'e come back 'e was quite the old soljer."

Far up the street a rising burst of cheers came into hearing. The crowd stood on tiptoe, craning that way. "It's them coming," said Brench. He looked at Mary carefully. "You'll 'ave to mind 'er, oldard," he whispered.

In a lull in the cheers the newsboy's voice rose once more: "Fus' blood! Revoltin' outrige! En'my killin' all our wounded!"

Mary looked at the boy as if he bit. "Oh, let's get away," she begged, wailing.

But the old Spartan said, "'Old up, Mary girl. 'Elp 'im to do it 'ead up, the way a lad oughter."

She pulled herself together hard, and Brench's knowledge of mankind gained for them, too, a place in the front row of the crowd.

II

Facing them, across the street, was a fine building of new stone with "Voice of Ria," in big gilt capitals, across its facade. Over the sill of an open bay window on the first floor a red rug had been laid, and two ladies sat leaning their arms upon this, and beaming down on the street with the resolute benignity of good-natured cynosures for vulgar eyes. They wore radiant garden-party clothes, and each had a big basket of cut flowers ready to hand. The window looked a little like an opera box when a diva is to be pelted with roses.

The cheering came on: it seemed to ride in the air, above the heads of the crowd, with a quick rising rhythm, like an approach of cantering hoofs. And then the troops appeared, with a band at their head to play them off to the war with a jovial dance tune. The two ladies waved handkerchiefs and little Rian flags, smiled freely, and threw down the flowers from their baskets to the marching men.

Volunteers, only trained for a week, the men had no march discipline to spoil. Their amateur officers were quite content to get them entrained anyhow. Many men had wives or sweet-hearts hanging on one arm, with hands locked round it. Some of the men caught the thrown flowers and put them in their caps, or stuck their caps on their bayonets to wave up at the radiant flower-throwers. Many of the men were noisily tipsy; even a few of the officers were.

Nearly all the leading company had passed when there came a break in the run of the on-coming cheers from the rear. Something or other, it seemed, in that part of the column must be checking the crowd's shouts rather than evoking them. This approaching gap of silence had all but reached the old man and the girl when a loud single guffaw broke into it. As if this sound had touched a spring, or broken a spell, there arose an instant hubbub of facetious cheers and laughter. The object of this ovation was' clearly a certain trio of soldiers.

The middle man of the three was helplessly and grotesquely drunk. He was held up and lugged along by an abashed comrade on his left, and by a leering and winking one on his right. His feet shuffled and trailed, his head hung forward loosely. A grinning comrade carried his rifle. A heavier lurch than usual made his cap fall off, almost at Mary's feet; so his face could be seen.

The old man called out "Joe! It's good-bye, lad. Mary's 'ere." But Joe was past hearing or looking.

A slatternly harlot with a fat, paint-sodden face shrilled out, "Crahyst!—it's 'is father!" and then looked away, sparing the smitten ancient. Up at the open window the face of a tall girl, standing behind the two seated ladies, fell suddenly back out of sight, as if on the same impulse of mercy. The two ladies' set, affable smile became a little uncertain.

From farther up the column an officer came back to see what the check was. "March along there, men," he ordered cheer-' fully. The cap was picked up and jammed on awry, and the trio reeled on, up the street. A boozy-faced giant, who towered among the crowd, roared, "Onward, Chrisjin sowljers!" and then roared with laughter at his own wit.

The father and the lover flinched away. They struggled back out of the crowd to a big seat under the trees, and sat there, battered sick with misery, a foot or two apart, each of their hearts locked up fiercely alone with its own pain. Up the street the band was playing again and the rollicking tune came in wafts to their ears, mixed with the running salute of sociable jeers and horse laughs that escorted the well-beloved to the slaughter.

III

In a few minutes more the rear of the column had passed; the crowd had broken up; it was filling more loosely the whole street and the gravelled and tree-shaded space on one side of it, under the War Office windows and opposite those of the Voice.

It was autumn, but editions of the evening papers blew in and raged and then vanished as often and as quickly during those tumultuous days as the showers of the traditional April. The next yell to arise at a distance and come swiftly nearer and louder. was "Speshul! Grite vict'ry speshul! Rian lancers at work! Grite pig-stickin' speshul."

The arriving newsboys shouted breathlessly while they ran, only stopping here and there to transfer their thick bundles of papers to the grasp of elbow and ribs while with both hands they dealt out papers and change to knots of eager buyers. The tides of the sea are said to come and go at the bidding of the moon. But these flow and ebb only twice in the day: in the spirits of Ria City a fine spring tide of exultation would rise five or six times in one afternoon, as the hour arrived for the Star of Eve and Evening Mail to put some new consignment of moonshine on the market.

"'Ere y' are, Tommy," roared the author of the "Chrisjin sowljers" sally, as one of the boys ran near him. The huge varlet must have been a fine figure as nature made him. Even now he had a gross sort of good looks, although growing bulbous in stomach and Bardolphian in nose. A vast consumer, you would say, of his country's beef, corn, dairy stuff, tobacco, beer and spirits, and a producer of nothing at all. Somehow the war seemed to be warming and cheering that breed.

This specimen had about him a starveling satellite, dressed in close imitation of his gaudy principal, like a cash bookmaker's clerk, and apparently primed to do odd jobs for that magnate.

"Spit it out, Ikey," the lion said to the jackal, handing him the purchased newspaper. The lion sat down on the same seat as the old man and Mary, lit a cigar with a figure resembling his own, and disposed himself to listen.

"Righto, Mr. Sprott," said Ikey. "Begins, 'The litest.' Dited 'The Firin' line.' 'Ere y'are. The Star of Eve's War Correspondent writes: 'The campine 'as opened brilliantly. As I write, an entire brigade is gowin' into action, movin' as stiddily as on paride. A squadron of Lancers, flung out on our right, 'as drawn fus' blood, 'avin' cut up an outpost of enemy riflemen. The en'my fired till ridden dahn, an' then rised the white flag. No quarter was give 'em, the feelin.' in the service bein' that to grant it in such kises would be to forgow the mor'l advantage of the lance as a weppin,"

"Bit o' sense, thet is," Sprott commented. "Wojjer 'ave a lance for? Jus' to mike the en'my like it?" He spoke loudly and firmly, as though he were stemming a rush of contrary opinion from somebody else. Ikey coincided. "Naow, nor yit yer.bynet."

"War's war—thet's wot I sye," urged Sprott. "W'y, wot's to mike these Portans chuck it if it yn't mide dingerous for 'em to gow on?"

"Thet's right," assented Ikey.

A little group of loiterers gathered round the loud voices and Sprott raised his voice rather higher.

"Seems to me as it's all 'Kamerad' an' 'Downcher see me w'ite flag up?' an' 'Min' me feelin's, please, and tike me to th' orspital.' Mikin' war in kid gloves—thet's wot these 'ere Portans wawnt. Well, I've 'ad enough o' thet gime, so I tell yer, strite."

Sprott paused, and glanced up at the opposite window, where Mrs. Burnage and Mrs. Case had just been joined by the Bishop.

"Well!" said Sprott, "if thet yn't Bishop Kise! Good ol' Bishop."

Everyone who heard him stared up. In the last few days the Bishop had strengthened his hold on public respect by publishing a cheap and readable pamphlet based on a month's holiday in Porto, and showing, beyond reasonable doubt, that the Portans combined in themselves all the special vices of the Canaanites, Midianites, Amalekites and other bad lots commemorated in the Old Testament. The success of this feat, followed by the moment's tidings of victory, was now filling Sprott and many others with the racing man's instinctive reverence for anyone who has backed a winner in good time and heavily. There were murmurs of hearty assent when Sprott added—"'E knew a bit, th' ol' pawson did. It was 'e gev us the 'orfice to tike this war on."

"'Im an' Burnage," a bystander said. He pointed to the open window with his pipe. "Thet's where 'e done it. I 'eard 'im." Sprott almost snatched the name off the bystander's lips. "Ah!—Burnage, too. Talk abaht stitesmanship! Wot I sye's this. S'posin' one of these stitesmen, wot's in the know, gits 'old of a sof' thing, wot I sye's ' Let 'im put 'is country on to it.' Reel pytrotism, thet is. Ah! an' Burnage done it." There were cheers at this, and more staring up at the window, as if something of interest might happen. Mrs. Burnage's public occasion smile, which had taken a short rest, came on duty again.

IV

The street was growing fuller than ever. People had come out like bees to enjoy this sunshine news. Many single voices grew louder and wilder, and, then seemed to be merged' in a kind of general voice—

a shrill, continuous din compounded of yells, articulate and inarticulate, cat-calls, whistles, blasts on little tin or cardboard trumpets, and impromptus of his instruments of percussion or of deflation. There were endless cheers for the war, for the army, for General Miln, the Commander-in-Chief, for all sorts of heroes.

Wavy lines of factory-girls, arm-in-arm, some of them half-drunk, swayed along amidst the crowd, jostling men and squealing pert coquetries. About these Bacchantes there hovered sundry lecherous-looking males, much attracted by this throwing down of the outer earthworks of sex. Arms were thrown round strange necks in riggish embraces. Girls shrieked endearments, immodesties, or abuse, like cats at their amorous crises on the roofs. Men fanned these erotic fires with jests and buffooneries less shrill and more purposeful. The famous conjunction of Mars and Venus had found its old strength again. On these coming-on humours the two ladies at the window looked down with the amused tolerance of the great, who feel that you must let. the common people have their fling now and then, and not expect too much of them, so long as their hearts are in the right place.

Sprott, too, was marvellously worked upon. He suddenly became unable to endure any longer the sight of these vast resources of public emotion going unexploited by the talents of man. He leapt up on a public seat, took off his hat, and, with a large gesture, demanded a hearing. In Ria City such commencements of speech were common in those days. In streets, restaurants and theatres, fluent patriots would suddenly feel themselves to be burdened with some momentous message, and would jump up and be eloquent without formality, like birds.

"One mowment, lydies and gentlemen," Sprott bellowed enormously. A pool of silence formed itself round him at once, in the midst of a whole continent of din. "The mos' important war, I think I mye sye, in all 'ist'ry," Sprott went on with unction, "'as reached to-dye the beginning of a 'appy end. For the 'ole nytion a baptism o' fire; for our 'eroic army an' sagycious stitesmen an everlasting crown o' glory. I might sye much. But stye! At yonder owpen window, on the orf side o' th' crowd, I see standin', with 'is grycious wife and a lidy friend, a fytheful minister of tfiet Gawd o' Battles before 'om we 'ave 'umbly lide our cause, an' 'oo 'as jus' annahnced in trumpet townes as 'ow thet cause is just. My Lord Bishop, will you fyvour your countrymen with a few words.?"

With the noble gesture of a chairman who has practised self-sacrificed brevity in introducing the chief-speaker at a meeting, Sprott sat down on the back of the seat he had stood on. The crowd cheered amain, called for the Bishop and stared up invitingly at the window.

The Bishop shook his head—but very gently. Like a rising divine to whom a bishopric is offered, he deprecated, but did not utterly refuse. To him, as to Sprott, all this public passion was a kind of asset, not to be allowed to go to waste. With a smile of gracious self-surrender, he came forward a little more, leant out and spoke low, as it seemed; but everyone heard.

"My friends," he said, "my heart is full. If my lips should speak all that is in it, I fear that I should weary you sadly. Only this will I say—that I thank God for this hour. First, for its tremendous vindication of the truth that as a nation sows, so shall it reap, and that in this country of ours a righteous and religious life, public and private, has not been lived in vain. And, secondly, I thank God from my heart for using us all to show to mankind how much a just war can do for a nation—how it moulds and disciplines men's characters, how it sifts and purifies and steels them for all noble purposes. All I dare say to you is—" the Bishop clasped his hands and looked reverently upwards—" I thank God, I thank God for all that He, and He alone, hath done this day."

The devout elocution was perfect. Several earnest voices among the crowd said "Amen." One workman said to a friend "'Ere, let's git aht of it, mite. No better 'n bein' in a bloody church." The old man and the girl, on their seat, scarcely noticed: they went on numbly enduring. The Bishop and the two ladies bowed and beamed themselves back out of sight, to go home to dinner. Sprott jumped up again, before the audience could dissolve.

"Fella-countrymen," he said, "if I consulted jus' the dictytes of me own 'eart, I should arsk you to sye grice along o' me, for the sustynin' feast of pytrotism an' of moral elevytion we 'ave just enjyed. But, frien's, we gotta think of others. Grice arter meat—Oh! yuss. But grite before bein' mide cat's-meat of—thet's wot the Portans orter sye," Loud laughter greeted this sally. "An' we oughter 'elp 'em sye it," Sprott pursued. "I propowse, lydies an' gentlemen, if I 'ave your approval, to sen' to the Pres'dent'of Porto the follerin' message, an' I will spare no expense to see that it is convyed: 'For wot you're abaht to receive mye the Lord mike you truly thankful.'"

There was great laughter at this stroke of wit. Nearly everybody was primed to make merry. Throughout the great boulevardish street the revel of nymphs and satyrs went on famously, many of the nymphs being now drunk and far, far from inexorable. Policemen made allowances—was this day of days a time to be fussy? The old man and Mary had got up and stolen away, sick and stiff with pain, deaf and blind with it, almost limping. But they were kill-joys too unimportant to do any harm to the carnival. It roared away round them.

It roafed so loud that at first a new flight of newsboys could scarcely make themselves heard crying a later edition. "War speshul, piper. Slight reverse, piper! Grite War, speshul! Colonel killed, speshul!"

CHAPTER XII

TEMPERAMENTAL

I

You might have imagined, five minutes before, that there was scarcely a self-possessed person, except yourself and the police-men, in all that crowded street. But now you would have seen that, wherever the boys penetrated, there seemed to be two or three sober-faced men holding qut pennies for the papers. One of them was Brench. He looked up from the print, after reading, and met the eyes of another man like him, a stranger.

"Please God it's temp'rary," said Brench.

"It's gotta be," the other answered quietly.

Another flight of boys arrived, red and spluttering. They brought the Evening Mail, the rival paper. It seemed to practise less reserve than the other. The boys were bawling: "Grive reverse, speshul! 'Eavy losses, speshul! Rian retreat, speshul'!"

A lady hurried past with a white face of torment. She looked wildly at one of the boys; she seemed like a beaten child begging not to be hit any more.

The boy caught sight of her. "'Ere y'are, lidy. 'Ard fightin'. 'Eavy losses!"

Another boy was slouching past, still laden with some copies of the previous edition, now dead stock. He was making shamefaced attempts to market his obsolete news, shouting halfheartedly, "Vict'ry! Grite Vict'ry! Lancers at work, vict'ry!"

The lady turned, as it were to a rescuer. But the first boy snarled scathingly round on the impostor. "Garn 'ome wi' yer rotten curl-pipers. It's a old piper, lidy. 'Eavy losses, lidy. Speshul."

The lady fled on, while the boy damned her eyes for delaying him.

The street was emptying fast; the sun had set, and the blast of chilly news was driving into their hives the bees that had made such a buzz. In half an hour all that was left of the carnival noise was a few sottish voices droning tags of sentimental songs, with many stoppages to hiccup and tailings off into gibberish. The only figures left in sight were four raffish hobbledehoys, coaxing or dragging two drunken girls of fifteen into a little side street.

With the sunset a light wind had come, almost cold. It capered about the vacated street and sported fantastically with the eddying dust, bits of paper, portraits of General Miln, and one or two early-withered leaves that had just fallen with a dry rustle on the seat from which Sprott had spoken acceptably.

II

Lights were coming out in the windows of the Voice; from the cheerlessly darkening street the office looked brilliant. But the stairs were patchy with shadows when Burnage came in from a call at the War Office and met the Bishop coming down.

In newspaper offices Case had always shown his warmest geniality. Like a good public man, he had liked to stand well with the Press. But there was none of that now. His very tread seemed heavier with wrath. Like a shaft of physical light, dis-pleasure emitted itself from his eyes; it traversed the tangled lights and glooms of the stairway as a great ray from a covered sun strikes across clear sky and cloudy. Burnage instinctively flattened himself a little against the wall: he had done it at school when the terrific head-master came by: he had wished he were wall-coloured then.

"May I ask, is this news true?" the Bishop asked, sternly. It was the voice of a wronged man, and of a man not used to being wronged: the success of enterprises fraught with a portion of his personal prestige had always come in as simply his due.

"It's not the whole truth," Burnage said, almost humbly.

"I beg to hear the whole truth," said Case, in no beggar's voice. It was clear that he would go near to make an example of somebody shortly.

Burnage raised his hands a little, and then let them fall. "It's defeat," he said. "A rout. The Boat Valley column surprised and cut up—all its mountain guns lost—the whole brigade destroyed or in flight."

The Bishop's voice rose, blustering: "I refuse to believe it."

Burnage went drearily on: "The main army driven in, too, in Scout Valley to-day. I've just seen the War Office people. Of course we won't publish all that we know. The War Office tries to call it a 'retreat.' What's the use? Whole battalions—brigades, running—throwing away packs and rifles and running!"

"My countrymen cowards!" The Bishop blustered still, but with diminished confidence. Assurance, a fine presence, a dominant voice had carried the day so often—could there be days that they could not carry? "I shall believe that when I see it," he said, as firmly as he could.

"We shall see them,'" Burnage groaned.

"Them!"

"Yes—the fugitives—here."

"And then—?" The Bishop's anger was manifestly growing again: charge after charge was adding itself to the blasting-powder that would presently explode.

"They will be—followed—of course." Even the mild Burnage was growing a little restive under this interrogation which was almost an arraignment.

But the interrogation was ruthless. "And then?" he demanded.

"Then? A siege, I suppose."

This detonated all the husbanded anger of the Bishop. "A siege!" he exclaimed. "Of Ria City! The capital! Monstrous! The mere idea is monstrous!" He turned to look upstairs and call to his wife, who could be heard still taking leave of Mrs. Burnage on the first floor. "My dear! Are you ready!"

While this most obedient of his subjects was coming down-stairs, Case turned to Burnage again. He spoke in a low, severe voice. "I am bound to say, before any worse harm is done, that at the proper time the country will insist on a stern reckoning with all who have exposed it to so appalling a danger as insufficient preparation renders a war."

A rustling system of fine textile stuffs, with Mrs. Case the frail engine that propelled it, had come down to them now. Burnage strove feebly to abate the gloom of the farewell. "Of course," he said, "there may not be a siege."

"I trust not," said the Bishop austerely. "Good-night."

It was not what the Bishop might do that troubled Burnage. It was what he might indicate to be coming; His pompously accusing voice might be sounding only the first note in a full symphony of public denunciation. But now he heard Rose calling down to him impatiently. Would Rose turn from him too? He ran up the stairs.

No; the various and incalculable woman was elate. Her eyes had black shadows of fatigue under them, but her mind was alight: quite little things had become, to her, vivid and brilliant. She spoke of candied rose-leaves for dessert to-morrow, when people were to dine with them; Cyril must take care to order red leaves and not white: a table with no dab of clear red upon it was not a table at all; and this time they must have everything right. "Think how we'll see it all still, when we're old!" she said, kindling. "How a fern lay on the cloth, or a flower hung over the lip of a vase on the night that the world came to life."

"Or died," he murmured, not meaning it—nor anything else, at the moment—knowing only that she was adorable now, just as she was, possessed with a vision of life no longer trite and stale but fired with a terrible and magnificent thrill. Doting on her with his eyes, he said gently: "In a week we'll be besieged."

She only sparkled the more. "Like Paris! Like Troy! Imagine!" Oh! she was right off the ground, quite disengaged from any sense of the hard conditions on which the dark rapture of tragic life is to be had. "'A day shall come,'" he murmured dreamily, with his eyes fixed on her, "'when ancient Troy shall perish and Priam and his people shall be slain.'"

"Why not," she exclaimed, with an almost wild animation, "so long as we go down with spirit? Oh! we'll be Caesars; we'll fall with an air." She was walking swiftly up and down the room again, quickening the rush of the mind and wearing down its poor friend the body. "I can't go horde yet," she broke out. "I must go out and walk. I must see what a city is like in its hour of fate. You—surely you can spare half an hour. Send the car home—I'll take a taxi when I'm tired."

III

As they were leaving the editor's room, an office messenger brought a sheaf of crinkled sheets of paper. Burnage took them, glanced down the pages, seemed to be going to speak, but then stopped; he gave the sheets back to the boy.

From the wide, empty street, between the great War Office and the office of the Voice, they turned into a street rather less empty. To this street, too, the War Office presented a florid Renaissance facade. At its centre a wide recess, a kind of blind porch, was approached by a fine flight of steps. On the back-wall of this elevated recess, where a door might have been, there hung a large green baize-covered board, to pin notices on. No notice was pinned there as yet; but, as the Burnages passed, a gloriously uniformed War Office porter came up and carefully affixed five large sheets of paper to the board with drawing-pins.

The moment the man appeared, there had begun a sudden convergence of people upon him from every part of the street from which he could be seen. It was as if these people had all been balls of dried pith and the porter had charged the green board with electricity. Some of them ran. A frail veiled lady, about middle-aged, was one of the first up the steps; she went at a little run, half-stumbling with eagerness. Arrived at the board, she ran her eye swiftly down the first sheet, up again and down the second, then half down the third, and then it looked as if some heavy, concealed fist had suddenly shot out through the paper and baize and struck her hard in the face. A man standing behind caught her as she fell backwards: he carried, rather than supported, her down the steps to the street. There he looked puzzled what to do next, till a dusty charwoman, who had been sweeping a block of offices over the way, ran across the street with a glass of water and took charge, crooning incoherent sounds of understanding and compassion.

Rose looked at her husband enquiringly. "Yes," he answered. "The first list of casualties. Darling, don't stay here."

"Ah!" she said. "The relatives!" She was absorbed. With a hand laid on his arm she detained him; she gazed at the high recess with its pallid death-rolls grisly under the arc lamps' cold moonlight. Life and death, there they were; war's most bitter part was being fought at the head of those steps: people went up who had husbands, brothers and sons, and came down bereaved of them: and the carnage went on under no anodyne of hot blood and high spirits.

Rose could savour drama. She saw them all in their tragic entanglement as they mounted to this high altar of pain and withdrew from it, smitten or spared—no longer mere common masks carried about on legs and making streets look crowded; they were inexhaustibly various now, and immensely individual. One man ran his finger quickly down the list, stopped short at a name and went away jealously upright, on guard against pity. Of one married couple the man, of another the woman, was clearly accepted by both as fate's special victim, the other as merely a minister in the temple of that superior grief. Another pair went up the steps in obvious comradeship, and came down frozen apart, each shut away in a separate prison of misery. A woman, widowed already, looked as if the name she feared to find had called out to her that it was there, before she could see, so far away was she still when she sank down on a pale ash-wood bench that had now been brought out for the many needing it: she rocked herself feebly, wailing "My little son!" as if it were still the time when he dinted her breast with miniature fingers in firelight nursery nights. Rose could see a man feasting on grief and drunk with self-pity, and also a man who looked right through the list but found no torment assigned to himself, and then looked quickly round at the people nearest; his face fell, and he went away with his eyes on the ground and his upper lip trembling, as if he had stolen his happiness' from those others.

With a reckless integrity Rose recognised that she was feeling no grief. Moved—yes, as one is moved by the involvement of Desdemona and Lear in their fates, but not grieved. The forest gloom and sunset splendour of tragedy touched and possessed her as the poignancy of summer dawns and the singing voices of boys had done in her youth, before the world went dull. Was all the wonder and glory coming back—event and passion and the enigmatic ache of the delighted spirit at the rare moments when life had seemed as if it might open out to her in the next minute all its glowing core of sadness dyed with beauty?

Cyril was pressing her arm to draw her away. She had for-gotten him. But she yielded. She knew one must never quite drain the whole cup of any enchantment. They moved away, she trying to hold her sudden consciousness of a vapid water turning itself into wine, he waiting to speak till she should seem ready to listen. Under a lamp he looked at her eagerly. "There's a name in the list," he said.

"List?" she repeated, vaguely at first. Her thoughts had gone far beyond that. Then she remembered. "You've read it?" she asked.

"It was what came as WQ were leaving the office." He spoke rather pleadingly. Would she not give him a little credit for not crying out under his own little loss? But not unless she cared to.

Of course she saw all that; she saw every move of his plain mind as you see every wave of the tail of a fish slowly travelling about a glass tank. And she was vexed. He was disappointing again. It was like him to drag some harsh little "reality" in, just when she had the greatest thing in the whole world to attend to. It was as if she were being carried away, mind and heart, by some mighty play, and he nudged her to say one of the actors had just lost his mother. Still, she bore with him. His mind lived in valleys; no use to try to explain what one saw from the heights. "Colonel Main?" she asked, patiently.

"Oh! he's missing, too, and believed to be dead. But I didn't mean him."

"Is it Mr. . . . you know—your school friend with the quaint views?"

"Willan—yes."

"I'm really very sorry. Only wounded, I hope?" Still Missing—believed to be killed. So are Dix, Lovel-Waters, young Seaton—a whole crowd of them—nearly a thousand. Nobody knows what it means, unless the Portans have got them, dead or alive. They've simply vanished."

They were walking along the west side of a large treeless square. Over the roofs to the East there gleamed the cold tips of the mountains into which the army had gone which was now broken. So? All those men, those infinitesimal granules of purpose and will, were blowing about like spilt dust over that desert of stone and snow, close to the sky. Or could some have regained already the captaincy of their fate—have made fast and be lying up close in crannies of that wall of wonder, biding their time, and nursing their strength?

"Missing—believed to be killed"—wonderful words! There might yet be mystery, fire, distinction left in the world.

BOOK THREE

CHAPTER XIII

BOAT VALLEY HAS A DEVIL

I

For the fourth night of its advance up the valley Main's force had bivouacked in full sight of Boat Pass. The Pass was some four miles away, but it looked scarcely two in the morbid clearness of the air next morning. That glaring transparency boded no good.

Just behind the brigade lay the last of the valley's many constrictions. At this one a dam of living rock, nine hundred feet high, must in old times have made a deep lake of all the last four miles of valley from the dam right up to the sharp final rise to the Pass. Through this dam the lake must have cut a sluice for itself by degrees and so flowed dear away. Through the bed of the sluice the valley torrent now hustled down: beside the torrent there was just room—though no sort of track—for Main's column to squeeze through: during hour after hour of yesterday a thin file of men and mules had scrambled up into the open valley above, like a crowd slowly filtering into a football ground by one pay-gate.

This last reach of the valley was flat for more than three miles ahead. Then would begin the rise to the actual Pass. From the bivouac this rise looked like the back of a theatre's auditorium, seen from the back of the stage—round, hollow and steep. All the flat part of the valley in front was strewn with fragments of rock, of all sizes, poured down from the heights on both sides like the refuse sent tumbling downhill from a high mountain quarry.

On both sides of the valley its bounding walls looked unclimbably steep. From the top of each wall, about where the valley was widest, there spouted a waterfall. The water shot out into the air, as though drained off the roof of a church by a gargoyle: in mid-air it turned to blown mist, so that none of it seemed to reach the floor of the valley below; yet a stream came into existence again under each of these two wispy and wavy columns of spray, and hurried on, helter-skelter, to join the main valley torrent.

From this last reach of the valley the Pass and the whole valley had taken their name. For it was shaped like a rather short flat-bottomed dinghy, with very high gunwales. Even the Pass, with its neat little dip cut in the sky-line, resembled the small semi-circular groove that is used for working a scull over a dinghy's stern.

II

In the pride and joy of his first command in the field, the Colonel would leave undone none of those things which, in face of an enemy, ought to be done—however completely the presence of anything hostile was out of the question as yet. So the column's outfit of advanced guard, flank guards and rear guard, on the fifth morning of the advance, was a study in war. The whole breadth of the valley, besides, was investigated by scouts, thrown out well in advance of the march. The scouts had started before dawn, and by nine o'clock the rear of the column was in motion: its head was already far up the valley. There had been frost in the night, so high were they here, and the shivering troops had slept badly. But now the stones were too hot to hold with bare hands; the whole valley swam in a glass-coloured shimmer of haze; a rock half a mile off would not stay still for the eye; it quaked elusively. With a good glass the scouts, thrown out fanwise in front, could at times be descried crawling like beetles among and over the bleached rocks and boulders.

If only the rain would come, which that skim-milky sky had predicted at sunrise! How the scorched men would have bared their chests to it, to let it soak in! By noon they were feeling like worms lost on a hot sandy path, their vital moisture drying up, their eyes vexed and cowed by the brutal upward glare of the fiery stones that felt hot through the remains of their boots. It seemed enormously long since dawn, , when the first rim seen of the sun had looked spiky and cool—anyone could have stared at it then; enormously long, too, till any evening coolness could come—if indeed it ever should come, for the hope of it seemed rather fond, like hopes of good things after death. Perhaps the earth was really falling into the sun, after all.

When the men were almost too thoroughly dazed and quelled with the heat to mind anything else, queerness, a new brand of queerness, began to infest this accursed troughful of burnt, trembling air. From somewhere far out on the left, to their front, a good mile away, there came slowly winging, muted and sleepy, the solitary report of a Rian scout's rifle, and then nothing more. The one report went slowly rebounding about from precipice to precipice, all round the valley, drowsily.

All the scouts had been out of sight at the moment, making their way among the great stones. Almost all of them now came into sight instantly. They popped up everywhere ahead, perched on big stones like so many notes of interrogation. None of them signalled any explanation to the column; so none of them could have fired the shot or known why it was fired.

The column was halted. A corporal was sent with a small party to find what had happened. The other men waited listlessly, making poor jokes and surmises—had some blighter shot himself?—got a touch of sun and thought he'd chuck it? One officer said he had known a man killed by his own rabbit-gun while he was crossing a stile, and every two stones made a stile in this blasted place. The brigadier said it was good for all ranks. "All war," he said, "is just rum things turning up—all sorts of rum things, all the time. They've got to get used to it. Let 'em be jumpy for nothing now—they won't be gun-shy long." The corporal's party came back with the corpse of a scout, eyes open, face scowling, fists clenched. There was no bullet wound; just one adequate stab in the heart region. The man's unfixed bayonet, found beside his right hand, was shown to Colonel Main.

"Stow the damned thing away," he said quickly to Willan. The bayonet had bent grossly, grotesquely. It must not get about that a Rian bayonet would bend on a rib. "Mad, I suppose?" he asked the brigade surgeon.

The surgeon gave him the answer desired. "Sunstroke, no doubt. Or some sudden mania."

"Hefty jab, sir," Willan said, "to give oneself. Odd he should waste the shot, too."

"Thought he'd do a bit of firing over his own grave, perhaps," the brigadier said lightly. "Or some brilliant notion."

They left it at that.

III

Another purgatorial hour crept round the face of the clock as the column crawled on, up the torrid bed of that airless valley. Its pace was a, snail's; its scouts, probing ahead on both sides, were the snail's reconnoitring horns. And then, exactly as before, the familiar crack of a Rian army rifle was heard, but now far out on the right, well ahead of the column.

Again the many scouts bobbed up, tiptoe on high stones, rather like hares up on their hind legs, perturbed and peering over the tops of long grass. Again the column was halted. The men looked at each other. A spasm of uneasy jocularity twisted some of their faces. Again research was carried out, and another dead scout was found stabbed, once but sufficiently, in the vitals.

The brigadier was angry. "These fellows," he said to Merrick, "are all a damn suicide club. I'm not going to have any more of it." So all the scouts were called in, and the snail crawled on again, now without any feelers.

Willan, always moving about on his job, was near the head of the column just then. He noticed a growing disquiet in the men's faces. Their songs had stopped for some time past, and now the chaff, too, was subsiding. He could see they were puzzling it out. What was this imp or angel of death that pervaded an empty valley and laid stiff and silent a man who three hours ago had been munching cheese and small button-like biscuits along with oneself? Overhead a hawk was busy, hunting mountain choughs. Willan chanced to see it hover enormously high above one terrified chough, and then let itself drop like a big stone, right on to the prey. The chough gave the shriek of a thrush when the cat's claws go in, and Willan saw several men start at the cry. "My God! What's that?" one of them shouted, and then bit his lip and reddened with anger at not having kept a shut mouth. A bit nervy, thought Willan. Hawks were having great hunting that day. They drew the choughs' coverts, drove the yelling wretches into the open, and put them to death at leisure, as stoats hold their grim battles of rabbits; Many men's eyes were up in the air half the time, watching the massacre. So it was not one man, but hundreds, whose eyes caught a singular gleam at the very head of the valley, some two miles away and only a few hundred feet below the dipping sky-line of Boat Pass. The gleam lasted not more than a second. It had a kind of circular swing, Willan fancied; the flash of it seemed to him to wheel round a pretty large arc of a circle before going out. Dix said it was like the refracted ray of sunlight you throw on the ceiling from the round back of a spoon, to amuse children. Merrick found it to be like a half-turn of the revolving lamp of a lighthouse.

Merrick had noted another oddity. It was not at all distinct, so baffling was the heat haze in the air. It was a thing like an uncut lead pencil sticking up obliquely into the air from behind, as it seemed, the rough rocks strewing the top of the Pass. A stake, perhaps; possibly a flag-staff in a cairn, left by one of the two or three exploring parties who were said to have crossed the great range long ago by this trackless route. Still, he showed it to Willan, and then reported it to the Colonel.

The Colonel looked through his glass and saw nothing. So Merrick looked again, and saw nothing either. This made Merrick graver, but Main was amused. No doubt he felt his officers were getting rattled by spook fancies and ought to be laughed out of such nonsense. Was it an Irish round tower, he asked, or just a blow-hole of a Portan tunnel, for invading Ria by excursion train? Or the post of a Portan notice-board on the frontier, to say that trespassers would be prosecuted? Had Willan seen it? Willan was the safety-first man. What did Willan say? the brigadier had grown a little disdainful about the humdrum wariness of his veteran Brigade-Major.

"If it were not impossible, sir," said Willan, "I should say it was a high-velocity gun running in and out on rails."

"That fellow's nerve is going," the Colonel said to the brigade's Medical Officer, ten minut.es later, glancing at Willan. "You may have him upon your hands yet."

IV

During the luncheon rest on that day, the Staff and a few regimental officers who were invited to join them were laughing and chaffing harder than ever. One man chaffed because his spirits had risen in presence of things queer, perhaps boding, possibly the raw material of great adventure; another because he enjoyed human converse, and chaff was the only mode of converse he knew; another because he felt a little lonely, with these eerie things going on, and liked to have the jolly din of voices kept up; another to prove to himself that he was nonchalant in face of the creepy symptoms—as athletes of small experience plume themselves upon their many yawns before a big race, fancying this effect of nervousness to be a sign of robust unconcern. The Colonel chaffed because he felt that a leader of men must lead all the time, as a rider must ride all the time, sometimes sobering, sometimes enlivening, always keeping up a flow of right guidance and of stimulation, if only by means so humble as chaff. "Old gun still there?" he asked Willan jovially, as the meal ended.

Willan took a long look through the glass, and then said: "It is and it isn't, sir. Still running backwards and forwards. Testing the rails—it looks like."

The Colonel stared at him. Was Willan's brain going? Or only his eye? Good thing that this force should have a commander who—well, who wasn't a regular Moltke, perhaps, but at least a man that you couldn't stampede with any number of candles inside hollow turnips. Moltke? What would old Moltke have done here and now? Got uneasy? Not he. But taken extra precautions—without getting uneasy? Perhaps.

The Colonel badly wanted to get on with the job. And here was another day slipping away; past noon now, and only a mile or two done. Would the War Office people be saying, "Why on earth don't the fellow get a move on?" Beastly way people had of judging generals by results and not by their difficulties! Yes, but a sound fellow like Haig, wouldn't let himself be ruled by that; he wouldn't take blind risks for his men; he'd say, "If I don't know all's clear ahead, I'll act as if I did know there was trouble waiting." The Colonel wanted immensely to be a good soldier and do the right thing.

So he mastered his longing to move in column straight up the mile and a half to the top of the Pass. Instead, he would provide against the impossible; he would have a field-day of it—make believe that the Pass was held by an enemy army and "take" it in due form. He would deploy his whole brigade as it came up, except a small reserve. Using his mountain guns, those smart little fellows, he would first sprinkle the objective and its rear with all the best brands of vermin-killers, especially gas. And up the slope which would thus be warranted harmless he would advance the finest infantry in the world, moving steadily in open order, to destroy the imaginary enemy.

CHAPTER XIV

THE SMASH

I

That ceremonial approach to the Pass was quite nicely done—for commanders and troops who had never had a hard brigade field-day to teach them their alphabet.

Not that it resembled war. War is furtive, and the Brigadier could not forgo the delight of seeing every arm of his command doing its part in the little manoeuvre. So each of his darling mountain guns was perched on one of a group of old moraine mounds that diversified the floor of the valley. And on the highest and most central mound of all the Brigadier posted him-self and his Staff. As there was no enemy fire in question, he could acquit himself of the amateurish bravado of flouting it.

Under his all-seeing eye the infantry deployed and scrambled forward in pretty good order, widening their front as they went, till it stretched right across the bed of the valley to its precipitous side walls. The flanks were then to advance a little faster than the centre; also to close on the centre gradually;

thus, as the valley's side walls converged towards the Pass, the front line would mount the final slope in the form of a crescent, horns forward, till it re-formed into a column to cross the actual Pass.

The Colonel was the best company for his Staff while this fascinating movement proceeded. In his delight he could even forget the men's boots. The little guns put down a little barrage, thin but exhilarating, in front of the advancing troops. The Colonel fancied the steep final slope up to the Pass had somehow got on the men's nerves—that they vaguely felt it to be sinister or tainted. Well, this fumigation would take the malign prestige out of it; no one could mind a ghost who had had a horsewhipping under his own eyes.

The men were very willing, certainly. They wanted to get at that Pass and look over. Everyone wants to look over a pass. Still, heat, fatigue, sore feet and dry throats did not cease to exist. When the centre had to halt for a while, that the flanks might get on, the men in the centre did not curse the flank men for sloth, as some ardent generals fancy that troops do at such times: the men were glad enough of the breather; they mopped the sweat out of their eyes, sang "Nobody knows how dry we are, dry we are," and said devoutly, "Roll on, sunset." But the Staff, of course, heard nothing of that from their mound.

II

What the Staff saw of the infantry now, in mid-afternoon, was rather like a movement of ants on a rough gravel path, a few feet away. The men were visible discontinuously. However little they tried to use cover, the rock-strewn ground absorbed and half hid them as the stony bed of a torrent swallows up and conceals the thin trickle of water left during a drought. Sometimes, at some part of the line, hot a man would be visible; then one or more tiny figures would come into sight, stepping or jumping from rock to rock, or poised for a minute as on a pedestal—some subaltern or N.C.O., no doubt, getting the right direction for his men.

The Brigadier, with his glass to his eyes, was in Heaven; he was God, for the moment—he saw all that he had brought about, and he approved it; in this jubilant state he told Willan, whose glass was up also, to look at a fine figure of a young officer balanced on one of those stone plinths" Like Michael Angelo's David, isn't he?"

Willan did not know that celebrated work. There were quite a lot of celebrated works of art that Willan, with his public-school and Sandhurst education, did not know. But he looked. Yes, it was a splendid figure of a man—there for another moment and then gone. For, while Willan was still looking, the figure was suddenly sheared off the top of the stone, razed clean away like a golf ball swept off a tee by an invisible driver.

The miracle was silent. But a moment later there followed a slow, pensive sound that was more like a dreamy recollection of a rifle-shot than the report itself. At the same moment two other uplifted figures of Rian officers in the distance were mown as swiftly and completely off their pedestals, and then again two of those drowsed and softened explosions came, almost together, and joined the first one in echoing slowly about from side to side of the valley. In another minute every upstanding figure along the whole of the Rian front line had been polished off the stone it had stood on; and the air over and round the Brigadier's pulpit-like post of observation and command had begun to whistle or sing in a way that roused in Willan and Merrick the liveliest recollections.

There immediately followed, in the centre of the Rian front, a desolating spectacle of heroism poured out to waste like liquid gold spilt upon sand. A patch of ground there, in advance of the Rian front line, was less cumbered with large rocks than most of the valley. A little body of Rian troops—about a platoon—emerged from the protecting crevices among the rocks, formed a line in close order and ran forward, with a little officer waving a cane in front of them as he ran, to find and assail the invisible angel of death that had begun to breathe from the opposite slope. Somehow, God knows how, these men, ignorant of war, led by a child as ignorant, kept their dressing almost perfectly as they ran, fifty of them running and jumping over the stony ground abreast, like a huge field of hurdle-racers running level. For fifty yards or so they made this offer of themselves to death and then, in one second, as it seemed, death looked up and stretched out one hand and accepted them all. There ran along the little line a kind of travelling wave of collapse, as the next line of standing grass gives progressively to the scythe when it sweeps round from the mower's right to his left.

Willan recognised at once the not quite, but nearly, simultaneous deletion of a line of fleshen creatures sprayed from right to left with the continuous jet of bullets as a machine-gun's muzzle plays across their front. He recognised it even before the type-writer tapping of the gun reached his ears. He did not like the cool deliberation which had let the charging men cover so much ground before wiping them out with one gun and no more. This enemy must be beastly sure of himself. That crafty, quiet killing of the two scouts, almost before they could fire a shot, that masterly stowage of a mobile waiting force among such meagre cover as the rubbish of an almost naked valley, and now this cool taking of time before putting headlong attackers to death—these Portans were playing like men who felt they had the game in hand. This was going to be a war and no mistake.

Willan made the reflection with the curious supernormal clearness and precision which, at moments disturbing to other people, descend like the Holy Ghost on men of a useful soldiering temperament. Observation, inference, deduction, all the modes and means of putting two and two together had suddenly become strangely easy, satisfying and restful. In one and the same moment he watched all that happened, kept eye and ear cocked on the Colonel for orders, thought what he would do now if he were in command of the whole force, what he would do if he were a company commander yonder, what he would do if he were the Portan commander, thought about his youth, about Burn age, about that unforgettable young woman who was Judgment Day and had Paradise in her gift—he was sure of that now—but who might think you rather a worm—though she wouldn't tread on you hard, even then. All these faculties and thoughts went on without hustling or muddling one another, and there was time for them all in each moment. It was heavenly. Like a God, too, he could now have emotions without any disablement, see pitiful tilings with an unexhausting compassion, and witness tragic mistakes with sorrow but no wear and tear.

"That damned gallantry, again!" he grunted to himself. For all across the valley in front there now flowered out into calamity and frustration the seed sown by generations of sentimentalising about mere willingness to be killed, as if it were the end and acme of all soldiership as well as the beginning of it. The battle was out of the Colonel's hands now; indeed, it was out of the hands of his battalion commanders. Platoon and company commanders were doing whatever seemed to them good; and what seemed to almost all of them good was no more than that which seems good to the plucky small boy who has taken a hit on the nose. All thought for themselves and their men, all calculation of ultimate loss and advantage, all they had learnt, if they had learnt anything, about the relation of means to ends in war, were swallowed up in a passion of longing to get home on the other boy's nose; damn everything else! This virtue of the private soldier was all that the average Rian officer had to bring into battle, and Willan watched the result.

At point after point along the Rian front line small bodies of Rians rose into sight, clearly without any understanding between them and not in execution of any one plan; they just relinquished cover, hoisted themselves aloft like targets on a range, and plunged forward, anyhow, against the unseen power that could sprinkle death like water from a gardener's hose. Nowhere was there the slightest sign that the enemy was flurried, hurt or over-tasked by the duty of extinguishing all this prodigal valour. Not an enemy head had bobbed up; there was no smoke and Willan detected no flash. He saw the effects, but no cause, line after line of Rian troops going down, as if, life had suddenly failed them from within, before they could reach, or even locate, the concealed nozzles which spat these infallible jets of destruction. It was as though the opposite slope had been empty throughout and the mere earth had taken offence at the Rians' approach and was killing them out, a platoon at a time, by some mysterious emission of venom from itself.

III

In the next half-hour some Rian officers who escaped the fate of the rest learned how to be soldiers. Hitherto they had only been heroes, which is different and may be less useful. They had begun by treating their own lives and their men's as a lawful stake wherewith to gamble for certain very personal distinctions. They had now begun to see that these lives were humble tools belonging to their country, to be used for its ends alone, and made the most of, and not played the fool with.

In twenty minutes the whole jerry-built edifice of egoistic martialism in which they had grown up was tumbled about their ears and they had learnt to economise with passionate cunning their country's diminishing means of defence. They kept what was left of their men well crouched behind big stones; they almost bit the nose off any fool who popped up his, head for bravado; they dropped the last infirmity of subalterns and did not run useless risks for their men to see them run them; they made the biggest sacrifice of all and accepted whole-heartedly the lowly and noble fate of insects that build coral reefs and of men that build nations—the taking of infinitesimal means to great ends that may seem very distant.

Were they in time, though? Could anything pull the game round? Here they were, helpless, nailed to the ground. Nothing to do but to grovel warily, hope for something to perturb the enemy, and then fight like dervishes in support of the perturber. And the perturber, if any, must be the Rian mountain guns. Let the little guns but worry the Portan riflemen in their confounded shelters, and the Rian infantry might try again and might have a chance of doing some good.

No doubt these Rian infantry officers had not seen all that had happened. They had been too busy. When the affray had begun, the Rian guns had ceased fire. To keep up their review-day sprinkling of all the slope in rear of the enemy would now have seemed childish. Also, the Portan front line was invisible, and the advanced Rians, for all that could be made out, were so closely in contact with it that the guns might kill as many Rians as Portans. So the gunners held their fire while the Brigadier, on his mound, was alternately muttering "Oh; great fellows!" when some little unit of Rian infantry went headlong to complete destruction, and "Rotten!" "Dead rotten!" when some company commander preserved half his company by making them take cover as soon as the futility of doing anything was manifest.

In twenty minutes from the start not a man of either side's infantry was in sight, except some hundreds of Rian casualties, motionless or wriggling, in the open places. Still, the Brigadier felt pretty sure where the enemy front line must be. "It's time we murdered them a bit," he said to Willan, "with our guns."

In a couple of minutes the Rian guns, throned on their mounds, got to work, and bespattered the conjectured enemy front. There were even some signs of early success. For the first time that day a Portan was seen. Like rabbits bolted from their burrows, a man in a rock-coloured uniform could be seen here and there to bob up from some much-peppered place, scamper a few yards, leaping from stone to stone, and then flop instantaneously down into some invisible crevice.

The Brigadier's spirits rose. Here, at any rate, were mortal men to let fly at, not a mere damned mountain-side. For quite three minutes the Brigadier had this felicity to enjoy before a new instrument came in to take a hand in the concert. Willan recognised its hollow serial rap as the voice of the latest make of quick-firing gun. Somebody was playing its stream of little shells as a fireman probes about a burning building with his hard-pumped jet of water. The falling stream wavered and groped, about over the ground till it pitched on one of the Rian mountain guns. There it steadied itself and poured down till the gun's activity was utterly quenched. Then the jet felt its way to the next Rian gun, always keeping up its own revolting stutter while it moved, and in two minutes more that gun was stilled too, with bodies lying pell-mell round it. So the hidden engine went methodically On from gun to gun, putting them out like a row of lit candles.

Now that all their short-range targets were used up, the enemy's riflemen had time to grow busy on fancy marks such as Main and his staff on their mound. Dix was carried off, groaning in spite of himself, with his intestines perforated. Willan found himself bubbling with an irrational but joyous excitement—the joy of a child when the snowballs are coming in thick, the joy of a boy when a grand stone-fight gets hottish. Quite a lawful pleasure, too, for him: he was there in attendance, awaiting orders. But clearly not the place for any commander whose continued existence must be assumed to be useful.

"Ought you to be here, sir?" Willan presently ventured to ask.

Anyone versed in war would have seen that for Main to stay there was not business; he would also have seen in Willan's words one of the harmless liberties which good-humoured veterans will permit their subordinates to take with them, during the common exhilaration of being under fire together. But Main was not a veteran; only an inexperienced brave man burning to do the fine thing on his first day of battle. Fearless for himself, but overwrought, worried, unable to feel sure of others or to post himself behind their eyes, all that he saw, or fancied he saw, at that moment was one of his Staff uneasy under fire. "I'm all right, if you are," he growled.

Willan swallowed the snub. He had done what he could and now gave himself up to enjoyment of the thrilled air and his own aerated thoughts. None of this joy appeared in his face, and Main eyed him askance—perhaps thought he was cracking and must be bucked up with something immediate to do. Another Rian gun fell silent at that moment, away on the right. The gun looked uninjured, though every man round it was down. "Willan," the Brigadier called. He pointed to the gun, "Like to' get that thing into shelter?"

"Very good, sir," said Willan. He made off at once. He knew that breed of gun, and its anatomy,' and he liked it.

Ten minutes after, the Brigadier's eye was caught by a large figure bent over the derelict gun and labouring steadily to dis-joint it. Others had seen the bent figure too, for little fountains of dry dust began to jump up round it, near and far off, where Portan rifle bullets took the ground, more and more of them each minute. But the anatomist of the gun laboured on with an air of deliberation that must have looked insane to anyone who did not know the weight of each of the five pieces of that gun.

"Merrick," the Brigadier said, "he's a stout fellow, Willan. I was mistaken." At that moment the Brigadier was shot through the liver and spine. He had only a moment of clear consciousness left. "Tell him," he said to Merrick, "I'm sorry," and rolled over, dying like a gentleman, although as a soldier he had had his deficiencies.

"I will, sir," said Merrick. When he looked up from the dead he saw Willan staggering down the lee side of the gun's moraine mound, with both arms hugging to his chest and stomach the biggest piece of the gun.

IV

Probably half the Rians who were crouching among the stones did not know, even now, that they had lost a battle. They just waited and wondered—what next? Was it some sort of a draw? Would there be a truce now, and the armies exchange cigarettes and pick up their wounded, as in the film stories? Or had the Portans had a bellyful? Had the Rian guns bundled them out of it, over the Pass? From the midst of a battle you seldom see how it goes.

To puzzle them the more, the flow of brigade orders had stopped altogether. No one knew why. No one hidden down among the stones could tell that the Brigadier and Dix were dead, that Willan had been sent off to do a freak job, and that Merrick, the only other Staff officer left, was running to join the Brigade-Major where he toiled to salvage the mountain gun. For the moment no brigade command could function, if any existed.

So the whole force, which had been an organism, was now dissolving into a great many constituent parts. And each of these parts was, in turn, becoming a rude new organism, with its own measure of cohesion and strength and fitness or unfitness to survive. At one place a Captain who had his wits about him would cannily draw together the sorry remains of his company, hearten them up with his own cheerful firmness, and teach them how to shift cover and keep well in touch—till, in the eagerness of his activity, he forgot himself for a second, stood up six inches too high and was shot through the head. Another company commander, with Main's doctrines still working yeastily in his head, would suddenly make up his mind that now was the time to rush the blighters with the bayonet; he would give the word and break cover, followed perhaps by three or four men, and rush forward, uphill, to be expeditiously executed. And then some cool-headed Sergeant would take over command and would start on the slow job of nursing the remaining men back into a fit state for use later on.

On the minds of many N.C.O.s and privates new lights were breaking. Some were noticing, with silent fury, how much of an officer's fighting reputation may come from merely holding the lives of his men extremely cheap. Others were dourly thinking how many duties of all kinds this, that and the other of their betters must have neglected, to bring them where they were—almost barefoot, armed with tin bayonets, unfed, unled, shut up like cheap pigeons in traps, to rise and be shot now or to wait and be shot later, as they chose. And some men, as they wriggled among the rocks, with sore eyes and furred mouths and empty bellies that angered them like wrongs, were listening to an inward whisper that all this beastliness was not the real thing, not the authentic test of heroism to which they had wished to submit themselves—it was all a false start, a wash-out, a mess to be got out of, anyhow, on any terms, so as to be alive when the veritable trumpet sounded for them to ride the proper ring.

So decomposition began, and it went on fast. Far out on the left a subaltern lying half-mad with the pain of a groin wound raised a white handkerchief on the end of his cane, waved it for some seconds and then put the muzzle of his revolver into his mouth-and blew off the upper half of his head. The white flutter had caught the eye of a big red sergeant in the centre, a man like a figure of Mars to look at. "No bloody use layin' 'ere to be murdered," he said in a blustering way, and began to wave a sheet of newspaper stuck on the point of his bayonet.

One of his men, a scraggy, spent little creature, leapt up, purple with fury. "Chuck it? My God, no!" he yelled. He snatched the paper from the Sergeant's bayonet, climbed to the top of the big rock that was in front of them both and stood there, with every inch of his little length exposed, firing round after round at the invulnerable slope in front till he fell off the rock with half a dozen bullets through him. And so a seeming foulness came into the fight. In place after place one Rian would try to show the white flag and another would fire away to cancel the weaker brother's overture for surrender. In ten minutes the famous symbol had lost, for the time being, the whole of its significance and its sanctity; wherever it showed, it was instantly fired upon, before a burst of fresh fire could come from under it; and two armies of ordinary decent men, such as all white armies are, were thinking each other to be collections of treacherous curs, undeserving of quarter.

That, too, told variously on different men. One Rian, on finding that the enemy seemed to be fiends, would jump up in a frenzy of rage which neither fear nor discipline could control: he would plunge up the opposite slope in mad hunger to get at one of the hell-hounds, in hope to gouge out his eyes or to hammer his nose and jaws into a mess of offal. So he was soon killed. Another would be overtaken by panic at this new vision of the atrocity of war and he would start to run straight back from the front, recklessly and shamelessly—anything to get away, like a sheep when it smells what there is in the butcher's yard.

The first man to run was like the first scream of "Fire" in a crowded theatre. The scream raises a question. Will the public opinion of the audience accept or reject it as the veracious and natural voice of the audience's heart at that moment? Each Rian who bolted now was so much of the veto of public shame removed from the bolting impulse in the minds of the rest. Public opinion may declare with the same speed and firmness in favour of dying like men or in favour of living like rats, and in another ten minutes every staunch and unswerving adherent of public opinion at the Rian front was running, with his head well ducked, and some with their bodies bent double.

There remained the stiff-necked, the faddists, the cranks who would not throw themselves into the general movement of their world. Of these mulish individualists there were at least several hundreds. Many were left quite alone, for the time, clinging to their solitary posts among the stones with the deep-seated mysterious unreason which dares to persevere in a set purpose, even without hope.

V

Soon the bed of Boat Valley, behind the wrecked Rian guns, began to be speckled pretty thickly with fugitive dots. They drew in from both flanks as they fled; all took the shortest route to the high and narrow Western gateway by which the brigade had entered the boat-shaped final section of the valley the night before.

And now a striking addition was made to the unexpected sounds of the day. It came from the place which had interested Willan more than it interested the Brigadier in that distant and irreconstructible time when the battle had not yet been lost. Now, as then, the pencil-like object was sticking up from just behind the crest of Boat Pass, but its top was more depressed now; it pointed more distinctly down the valley, and the new sound was preceded by a violent splash of flame from the tip, as it seemed, of the pencil. This appeared to start a long whirring, wafting noise which travelled along an arch-shaped course high above the heads of such Rians as had not fled.

The great shell burst where the fleeing Rians were thickest, its burst throwing up a geyser of smoke, dust, rocks, men and bits of men; the turbid murk was shot for an instant with a central flame against which these solid objects showed curiously clear and black. The unwounded fled on, all the faster, huddling together like sheep when the sheep-dog runs in at them from behind.

The pencil's tip withdrew, reappeared, flamed again and dropped its second bale of explosive, not in the midst of the rout but among the foremost of the fugitives. It was as though the sheep-dog had run round one flank of the flock, to head it back from in front. The flock checked for an instant, then huddled again and tore on more frantically than ever.

Down the whole final stretch of the valley the gun shepherded these fond lovers of life. It barked and bit at them everywhere in turn—at their rear, their front and both their flanks. They swayed and faltered all ways, flinching away from wherever the last shell had pitched, though the next would always pitch somewhere else.

The last shell of all pitched right in the thick of the rabble as they plunged and fought to get through the four-mile valley's back gate. Twilight had come by that time. In the failing light the dregs of the rout could just be seen by the friends whom they had deserted. It looked like the last swirl of soiled water you let out of a basin when you have finished washing your hands and have pulled out the plug.

CHAPTER XV

AN EMERGENCY EXIT

I

The little mountain gun gave Willan plenty to do, merely to disjoint it. And then it took all his big body's strength to carry it off, bit by bit, and stow it under a rock that overhung westward—a regular hood of safety for the treasure. He was well pelted the whole time, but every moment that he remained un-hit brought its dram of glee, like a boy's flukily long escape from being caught at hide-and-seek. He could have capered with joy, and he did grin and shiver with it. Life was enlivened; safety was rescued from the dull tastelessness that afflicts it when it is cheap—a mere glamourless prolongation of life as a matter of course: safety was now a new triumph at each instant, it was a win, a leap that came off.

Where such ecstasies are to be had, more men than one will come for a share. As Willan staggered down the mound, with his second load hugged to his chest with both arms, two men ran up, out of nowhere, to help. One was a tall subaltern, with carroty hair; the other a stretcher-bearer whom the Rian War Office had recruited at the last moment and sent into the field with no fuller uniform than a Red Cross armlet. He was a shambling, rabbit-faced man, clad in an odd assemblage of other men's cast-off things. He had a greasy black frock-coat, with shiny elbows and frayed sleeves, grey flannel trousers, yellow boots and a rotten sun-helmet of pith.

"Hullo! Hullo!" said Willan, laying a friendly hand on this ally's armlet, in rebuke of his offer of combatant service.

The rabbit-faced man tore off the red cross which was his only hope of life if caught soldiering without a uniform. He threw it away, rushed up the mound, and was tumbled down with a bullet in his entrails before he could seize a piece of the gun. "Down't wyste no time on me," he said, when Willan picked him up and laid him easy, as soon as all the gun was safe. In a few seconds the rabbit-faced man was dead, and the crude yellow of his boots and the greasy stains on his frock-coat had acquired a curious dignity.

"He was a good man, sir," the subaltern said, almost fiercely, as if he defied Willan or the world to sneer at the boots or the grease stains—whatever he, the subaltern, might have had to say to them half an hour ago.

"He was," said Willan. "You'll do, too." The senior had just time to utter this commendation before an effusion of shrapnel overhead rendered the subaltern as secure against cancer, phthisis and all the most horrible deaths as the frock-coated man had been for two minutes.

Willan went up the mound again and brought down a stock of the little gun's ammunition, which had been lying behind it.

II

The long Portan gun on the Pass had now finished its abattoir job and turned in for the night. Twilight was thickening to darkness. It seemed almost unfair to have come through like that—to be breathing air that was like a cool drink when for those two stout-hearted fellows beside him there was no evening freshness to feel, nor little winds beginning to scamper about in the dark. Still, no time to think. No trace of Main or the rest of the Staff remained on their mound. But lots of good men must be still hanging on in the front line, ready for anything. Just give them a lead and they would make a great try to pull the thing straight. He must see to it.

Two or three times, as he went forward, stooping and groping, he drew a shot from a Portan sniper. But it was no light for fancy shooting; nothing came too near, and he took passionate care to run no silly risks; the tail of the team had the match to save now; it must not throw a single wicket away for a lark. He stopped only once on his way—at a small tarn lost in the desert of stones. He was drawn to it by a mixed noise of low groans and a lapping sound as of dogs. Nearly all wounded men who are still conscious want one thing; the wounded from all the near part of the Rian front line must have somehow smelt this water and crawled to it like rats dying of poison. Their bodies fringed the shaly beach of the tarn; some were on all fours, with their heads down, drinking like cattle, some flat on their chests and sucking feebly. Many had died as they lay, face down in the water and some may have thus drowned, being too weak to move. A few others were making ground slowly towards the water; Willan spotted a man who was still thirty yards from the tarn's edge; he would lie quite still for some seconds, as though dead, and when he had thus collected a little strength he would squirm a few feet nearer to the water with the frantic wrigglings of either half of a snake just cut in two, and then rest again, before another effort.

Willan picked up the twisting bundle of torn flesh and broken bone and laid it with its face touching the water, near another man who seemed, in the bad light, to have no face—only a face shaped mask of little stones or shale, like the roughcast on a house: cheeks, forehead, eyeballs, the mucous insides of the lips were all thickly studded with sharp pebbles. No doubt something had burst near his feet and driven a blast of grit and scree into his skin and flesh till it was like half-finished asphalt, with blood soaking inertly round the pebbles instead of tar.

There was work there for a score of surgeons, if only to make the deaths of many men more endurable. But for soldiers to hang back and attend to the wounded while there is combatant work to be done is a capital crime. Willan left them to lap water and ooze blood and went on to seek the whole men, the lucky and game dogs who must still be crouching among the stones, ready to bite.

Soon he did see a man. It was a young Rian officer. Thirty yards ahead of Willan he popped up, almost full length, like a startled hare, stared round and made a wild bolt back towards Willan, whom he seemed not to have seen. He was fairly frenzied with terror, blind and deaf with it. Near Willan he stumbled and fell on his face.

Willan put out a hand. "Lost your bearings?" he asked cheerfully. "Not that way. The fun's up here. I'm going there." He spoke as if he were telling a puzzled huntsman the line of a fox that has given everybody else the slip.

The boy gaped at this unknown senior who couldn't see that a fellow was cutting it. He had turned cur; he had done for him-self, and now a stranger's absurd faith in his manhood had done the miracle and raised his lost manhood from the dead. He saw his chance and jumped at it. "Thank you, sir," he spluttered thickly, his mouth all furry with viscous foam, and at that moment Merrick somehow slipped into their company, asking the boy in tranquil and humorous voice that no mischances perturbed, "Are you lost, too? Damned institution—twilight, isn't it?"

The boy gasped, "Thank, you, sir," again; then he rushed back, along the way he had come, and dropped out of sight where he had popped up. "You did that very well," said Willan, when Merrick and he were alone. "You damned old humbug," he added.

"I somehow thought," said Merrick with quaint gravity, "I'd heard some soul-cure business going on while I was stealing up on you two."

Willan left it at that. "Well," he said platitudinously, "this is a pretty kettle of fish. Wants a blessed Ministry of Reconstruction."

"I've got one tip," said Merrick. "It seems there's a level bit, clear of all these stones and muck, close under the rocks on the south. It runs right along down the valley."

"Good work," said Willan. "We'll pull out all that's left on this front—tell 'em to sneak off, the best way they can, to the right flank, three hundred yards to the rear, and assemble there. Got it? Then we'll know what strength we have and we can rig up a new front or else slink off in good order, during the night. Got it?"

"Right, sir."

"I'll go along to the left and give 'em the word. You tell the right and then take charge at the point of assembly till I come. They'll be striking matches if nobody's there. And—I say—"

"Sir?"

"We've got a little gun."

"World conquest, sir—that's what we're out for. There's nothing can hold us."

They set out on their errands.

III

Where a lesion occurs in a bodily tissue Nature gets to work without talking, tries hard to draw the torn, edges together and tasks herself to build up reparatory cells. This work of repair had already begun in the big gash which had been made in the flesh of the Rian army and nation. Along the stricken front a new nerve system was forming; joint action and concentrated purpose were in the first stage of restoration. The visit of Willan, now in acting command of the force, to the survivors ensconced by ones, twos and threes along the left half of the Rian front organised all these reviving activities into an attempt to execute a single manoeuvre.

The men had been a picked force to begin with. Now they had been much more stringently sifted by ordeal of battle. They knew it and they respected themselves and one another; the way they now carried out Willan's orders would have done credit to veterans, which they were not.

Of course a night withdrawal was a gamble.' But then nothing but gambling was left to be done. When the Portans advanced at dawn the next day the tattered rags of the brigade would be consumed at leisure by the enemy's guns. As it was, the Portans would only need to fire a few rocket lights now, in order to see whatever the Rians were doing, inspect their assembly under the valley's southern wall and massacre them with a few machine-guns. But the Portans, so far as they were a race at all, were a phlegmatic race. They were rather like the old Boers. After a win they had seemed, in their older wars, to have an impulse to sit down on the field of battle and think and not presume. No Portan general was known to have ever improved an advantage as much as he might.

All the daylight was gone now. There was no moon as yet. For the men to assemble from all parts of that wilderness of great and little stones in pitchy darkness was a shin-breaking and ankle twisting business. But all ranks were thankful enough to have no moon telling tales for the next hour or two, and also to have a wind rising: it whistled and whined and went pretty far to drown such noise as they could not help making—the rasping grind of boot-nails on the stones, the jarring of rifles against big rocks and the loud whispers of men bewildered and asking the way or damning the blocks that they struck with their shins;

They certainly had much to thank the Portans for. Not a sound or a gleam came from the victorious enemy's lines. At any moment the withdrawing Rians might become like cock-roaches caught promenading the kitchen floor in force when cook has apparently gone off to bed and has then reappeared with a baleful flash lamp and hearth-brush, to sweep them up and throw them into the fire. But the Portan tradition held good. The rough slope they infested went on being as black as the pit, and dead still, from minute to minute, for two solid hours. And then the Rian officers who were left came together under the valley's beetling South wall to concert the next move.

There were nine of them, and Willan found, to his deep contentment, that there were at least nine hundred N.C.O.s and men. He called the eight surviving sergeants into council too. Then he put the alternatives as he saw them. Should they choose the best cover they could, under the wall where they were, and delay the Portan advance to-morrow by enfilade fire as long as they could hold out? Or retreat altogether, report to General Miln, and ask for fresh orders? Or fall back to the narrow gate of the valley and make a stand there? Of course, he explained, the decision would have to be his; but first let them say what they thought and how much their men would be up to.

When he had finished, a voice that he had heard somewhere before was raised, with an obvious effort. "You know, sir? there's a way out of the valley on this side—three hundred yards from here."

Why, of course he knew the voice—and why it spoke with an effort. It was the voice of the boy that had lost his head, and that Merrick and Willan had headed back in the dusk. "The deuce there is!" said Willan. "It looks like the wall of a house. Away fit for troops?"

"It is a bit steep, sir. An old goat-herd's track. Well engineered, though—it zigzags all over the crag." "Could you give a lead up, in the dark?"

The boy said, "Yes, sir," very low—rather like a decent man in the dock when he says "Guilty."

Somehow Willan understood. So that was where the poor kid had been bolting to. Just now the kid was well within reach of Willan's left arm; Willan extended it, took hold of the back of the kid's upper arm and kneaded or massaged it in a friendly and meditative manner.

Merrick asked, "What does this ladder lead to? Some loft?"

"A sort of flat shelf, sir—kind of platform—a thousand feet up from here. It must be half a mile square. Quite good observation over this valley."

They all meditated, Willan giving them time for it. Then he said, "Seems to me to be good enough, gentlemen—eh? We ought to be able to rake the enemy all day to-morrow, if he's for going down the valley. Perhaps we might then go along on the top of this side ridge and hit him again the next day. Any snag to it, Merrick?"

"Can't see one, sir, unless it's the moon." Merrick looked towards the Pass. Behind it a strong radiance was rising to suffuse more and more of the sky above. But that sky was wild and billowy with heavy lumps and rags of cloud hustled roughly by an increasing wind.

Willan summed up. "If the night is shiny," he said, "fewer of our fellows will fall off this bit of crag. If it isn't, the enemy won't see us so well. So, we'll try. We'll start now. Every man, please, must be up, and well in cover, before the first scrap of grey shows in the sky."

All were manifestly glad. It felt like making a break with the past and all its misfortunes and blunders—at any rate with this, hellish valley.

CHAPTER XVI

RIGHT OFF THE MAP

I

In a few minutes the little force was stringing out into single file, like thread unwound from a reel—and looking, like the thread, as if it were going to be infinite. Young Seaton, the ex-runaway, led it along the base of the cliff, peering up all the while, till he spotted the place he wanted, checked for a moment, made sure he was there, and then halted the men, and addressed himself with a will to the climb. There was a slight recess cut or worn out of the granite wall of the valley. Down a smooth groove in the middle of the recess a small torrent half slid and half fell the whole thousand feet from the top of the wall. The groove was quite unclimbable. But, forty feet beyond it, there was a very small exception to the general sheerness of the crag.

Mountain rubbish—waste stone of all sizes, split off and sent tumbling down by the quarrying action of rain, frost and sun—must at this point have been falling for many centuries down the vertical face of the precipice. So it had formed a great heap leaning against that vertical face and presenting on its outer side a slope of loose scree about a hundred feet high and rising at the steepest angle at which loose scree can come to rest, even for the moment.

Up this slope the leader drove his way by digging his boot-toes deeply in. The shifting stuff gave under every step; but it did not slip down quite so much as the step had lifted the foot; with much labour and puffing, the first hundred feet of the ascent were duly achieved. But then came a crisis.

The scree slope was ending. The loose stuff grew palpably thinner underfoot; a few yards farther on, its uppermost stones could be seen lying up against a granite wall which rose bald and perpendicular above them. The rude natural ladder had served its turn. It had to be quitted.

Seaton knew that to do this was just possible. To his left, as he stood near the top of the scree shoot, the face of the main crag was much more diversified with ledges, cracks and incidents of all kinds than could have been imagined on viewing it from below, even by day. And the whole crag, at this part, began to recede from the vertical. Block was piled on block, the upper block often lying back a foot or two behind the outer edge of the lower, on the side facing the valley, so as to leave a narrow ledge of standing-room on top of each block and at the foot of the next. Kicking a firm step for himself in the scree, Seaton reached up with both arms, laid hold of the upper edge of a block and hauled himself up till he could sit on its top. Then he helped the next man up, putting the man's hands in the right places, and showing him the proper movements. The man proved handy, so Seaton left him there with orders to get the rest up, man by man, in the same way, while Seaton scrambled on, up a sort of rough and gigantic natural staircase, with each step from three to six feet high in the rise, but the treads not wide in due proportion. The men struggled up manfully in his wake.

A hundred and fifty feet higher up the general angle of the wall became gentler, occasional growths of grasses and stunted wild plants could be felt by the scramblers' hands; some fifty feet higher again, their feet began to feel beneath them an unmistakable path which, in spite of its tininess, knew its own mind about the way to go: it wriggled about in countless minute and purposeful twists and zigzags, gadding cunningly hither and thither over the great bulge—still redoubtably steep—of rock and clinging soil which formed here the upper part of the valley's containing wall. As the long file of men coiled cautiously upward, each man always had some eighteen inches of width to stand on, but his body almost rubbed along the rock at his side and he felt as if he walked on a system of zigzagging footboards up the black side of a ship.

So long as the track can be made out at all, such walking may be easier by night than by day, for in the dark you may not see that if you stepped over the outer edge of the path you would fall some hundreds of feet, almost clear through the air. So you walk in a natural way, and you are all right. The light of the risen moon was now all that could have been longed for. Filtered through fast-moving clouds, it was enough to show up the track, but not enough to betray the column to anyone watching below, nor enough to make the drop below look giddily sheer. Only one man in nine hundred made a bad slip and fell off the ledge. He fell on top of two men who were on the opposite tack, just below him, and these good fellows saw him coming, braced themselves taut, and fielded him grandly, catching him with their four hands and dragging him in to the gangway.

But all of this took time; only an hour was left before the first grey of dawn when the last man of the force scrambled up from the top of the slithery scree to the bottom step of the granite staircase above. He did it with difficulty. Every man who had kicked his way up the scree had sent a little more of it streaming, downward. By now its upper extremity had been lowered by several feet, a fid helping arms stretched down from above were needed for the last few men to get a lodgment on the solid rock. The force had verily kicked down the ladder by which it. had mounted. No pursuit of it was possible now. But in the joy of his heart at having everybody up in time, and just to make a real good job of it, Willan could not forbear to go back at the last with a small party of hefty fatigue-men, to fetch the little mountain-gun and its ammunition to the foot of the shoot, and sling them up the face of the rock with a long coil of rope that he had seen near the gun on its mound. It was heavy work and it could not be hurried: each piece of the gun had to be wrapped about with many dead men's tunics to keep it from banging noisily against the rocks. But the gun and every man of the force were at the top of the crag, a little back from its edge and quite out of sight from the valley, a thousand feet below them, before the face of the night sky had begun to grow sick over the top of Boat Pass.

"One trick to us," said Willan cheerfully.

Merrick chuckled too. "Odd trick?" he said. "Damned odd one, too."

"We'll make the men get a sleep if they can," said Willan. "Let 'em eat their iron rations too, if they're hungry. Condition's simply everything in these freak stunts."

Willan could not see the smile of affectionate amusement on Merrick's face on hearing his matter-of-fact commander enunciate an abstract general principle—even one so practical.

They went off to see to it.

II

That dawn was even more dreary than sunless dawns commonly are. The whites of its eyes were muddy; the black opaqueness of night only gave way to another sort of opaqueness, more turbid though more pallid. First this thicker curtain blotted out the two white sentinel peaks on each side of Boat Pass; then it settled downwards till the actual nidi of the Pass, visible in silhouette all through the night, disappeared altogether.

The little group of Rian officers peered out cautiously into this dimness, over the edge of the crag by which they had reached this high platform. Soon there was no need for caution. Like the Pious Aeneas in times of risk, they were hidden in a cloud.

"Damn," said Willan tranquilly, after some thought. "And blast!" he subjoined, equally without rancour, after a further silent review of what could be done with a mist, and what couldn't. "Where," he asked, "is the Oldest Inhabitant of these mountains?"

Seaton came forward out of the mist: he had learned during the night to answer to this brilliant nickname, of Willan's invention.

"Well, O.I.," said Willan, "what does this mess mean?"

"Snow, sir," said the youthful authority on the place.

When once it was said, everybody could see it. The dull, white hangings were drawing in round them; soon grey, fly-like spots began to stand out almost dark on this paler background; the spots moved waywardly, some dropping headlong, some dawdling about in mid-air, a few flitting upwards capriciously.

In a few minutes more the visible world had shrunk into a few cubic yards of space: within this chamber the tiny white mats fell softly and soberly; outside it they seemed to whirl any way in confusion. "We'll let the men carry on resting," said Willan.

Some hours passed; the sun must have risen: now and then a pane of yellower pallor would open in the muffling wall of woolly grey; presumably the sun was there. But then the pane vanished again. Few of the men could sleep long for the cold, though all were dead tired. The rest sat about, shivering and yawning. No officer had slept at all; none except Willan had wound up his watch last night; he gave them the time now, and they were amazed—only three hours since dawn, and they had felt as if mid-day were past. And still it snowed on.

At ten the fall was denser than ever and much straighter; it seemed to be muffling all the stir and the sounds of the world. But it didn't. About ten-thirty there jarred in on the stillness a noise of stones scrunching against other stones, and then of steel or iron grating on stone. While the Rian officers listened and peered with all their souls, striving to drive sight and hearing like gimlets into the wall of grey dimness that confined them, the sounds grew louder and more numerous: they were unmistakably nearer. Clearly the Portans were moving—straight, perhaps, to the destruction of Ria.

Willan had feared it. Here was he with nine hundred rifles—and even a miniature cannon—impregnably ambushed, commanding the whole valley below without risking a man, as marksmen on roofs command the street below them; and there were the Portans advancing in safety, right under his blinded riflemen's muzzles. Would this infernal snow never cease?

"Le bon Dieu Boche again?" said Merrick, tickled still by recollections of rueful French humour on mornings when rain had messed up an Allied attack.

"There's one thing to it," Willan said. "If they slip us, we've slipped them too. You twig what has happened downstairs—to us, I mean? To our tracks?"

No; Merrick hadn't thought of that. "By Jove, yes!" he said now.

"Four inches of snow," Willan reckoned, "over every jack trace of us. And a foot or two more if it lasts."

Both were silent awhile, working out what it might mean. The process was impeded by Captain Lovel-Waters, now in acting command of a battalion of the brigade. "Incalculable swine!" he grumbled. "

Sitting on their lead all night, and then going on blind in a fog at ten in the morning!"

"I 'spec' they only work from ten to six,' said Merrick, gravely. "Soldiers' Union, probably. Charges double for over-time and night work."

Lovel-Waters scowled. "Damn your old good-humour, Merrick. Can't you help curse, like a Christian?" He turned to Willan. "How'd it be, sir, to loose a blind shot or two at 'em?"

Merrick chaffed on, undisturbed. "Some Bible precedent, ain't there? 'Bow drawn at a venture,' was it? Lot of first-class scientific fighting in the bible."

"Well, it might stampede 'em a bit," Lovel-Waters contended.

"I'm afraid they're too beastly rational," Willan decided, though now the grating and grinding noises below were louder than ever—heartrending proofs of the excellence of the targets which the perversity of Nature was wasting.

III

Many hundreds, if not a few thousands of iron-clad boots must have scrunched and slipped on the snow-covered stones of the valley during the next two hours. Then the clatter and squeal of these contacts began to diminish, and certain lesser sounds contrived to make themselves heard in the relative stillness below.

One of them seemed to be that of spade and pick used on stones and hard ground. Another was unquestionably voices. No words could be made out, the distance was too great; but there were scraps of loud speech that had the harsh rasp of orders, and then—more surprisingly—there was a sudden and absolute cessation of all sounds of voice or tools. This silence lasted a minute or two, and then it was invaded by a single voice, loud, slow and sonorous, like a grave speech or a recitation.

The voice had gone on, resonant and level, for some minutes when a sudden rent was torn in the white cocoon that enveloped the Rian officers on their perch. The ragged-edged hole gaped wider and wider, till Willan saw through it the small tarn where Hell had been on show the evening before: his soldier habit of noting whatever place he was in made him remember the tarn by its triangular shape. But the ground was white round it now; no visible bodies of wounded men fringed it, but near it a long open trench looked black against the snow. And here at last were visible enemies. A line of men in uniform stood round the trench, bare-headed and motionless, their heads bent down a little, while some sort of chaplain, it seemed, stood at the head of the trench, book in hand: he must be reading aloud. Then the voice stopped, the men round the trench moved, put on their caps and got busy, filling the trench with their spades.

Next moment some freak of the wind ripped a new gap in the frayed edge of the vaporous frame round the picture.,

"Oh, damn!" Lovel-Waters was growling. "Why can't we see the men we want to nit? They're the Johnnies. What's the use to tis of nice good Portans, burying our dead?"

No luck: the new hole in the curtain showed little more than two uniformed Potrans stooping low over some bundle that lay on the ground, half covered with snow. Willan gazed at the group through his glass, and saw the bundle wriggle feebly. The two men slightly lifted one end of the bundle, and brushed the snow off it. The end looked like the head of a man, but where the face should have been there was only a black mask when the snow was brushed off.

Willan remembered: why, of course, 'the man with the asphalted face, tarred with blood. One of the stooping men Tolled up the left sleeve of this effigy. The arm showed white underneath—real flesh, not tarmac. The other man, bending lower, fingered the arm. The defaced creature gave a slight start and then ceased to wriggle.

"Morphia!" Willan let the word go with a breath as if a pain had suddenly stopped in himself.

Lovel-Waters lowered his glass. He, too, had been watching. His look was almost one of consternation. So they're decent!" he said. An honest man, he would re-arrange his ideas if fairness demanded it. Still, it did cause discomfort.

"The confounded old enemy's always like that," Merrick said quaintly. "It's one of the disappointments of life."

IV

The edges of that irregular window in the clouds had rushed together again. The more multitudinous sound of hobnailed boots scraping on stone had passed quite out of hearing. The wind had dropped, and the snow was falling with a slowness almost pensive, a deprecatory hover, a look of gentle reluctance to alight unmasked on the earth. So it snowed for another hour, as if it had infinite time for the job, and then it ended abruptly. The whole dome of obscurity, round and above the Rians, split open, the relics of it were whisked away into the sky like the bits of a dividing and lifting stage curtain. All the four-mile stretch of Boat Valley below was empty, except its extreme lower end. There, through the gut where the dregs of the rout had been swilled down last night, the tip of the tail of a well-ordered force was just disappearing—some baggage mules and an obvious ambulance section.

"My God! Is there nothing to hit?" exclaimed poor Lovel-Waters in agony.

"Only the morphia merchant," said Willan, "and we may be needing him later on. All the world before us, Lovel. We're a lost legion, my boy."

"'We've done the impossible, Lovel," said Merrick. "With some slight assistance from Nature, we're clean off the Intelligence map.   We're an unmarked force; we're x, the unknown quantity; we don't exist, till we see fit to cut in."

Lovel-Waters began to perceive, and to exult. "Why, when we chip in, we'll be like a damned meteorite—knobby thing dropping clean out of the sky."

"We want a bit to eat, though, first," said Willan.

"A boot or two would come in useful, too," said Merrick. No more than Willan had Merrick failed to see scores of the great fellows who followed their lead digging almost naked feet into that abominable shoot of bruising and cutting scree. Scores of them now were standing about on the snow with only rags tied round their feet.

"That's right," said Willan. "Now, then Inhabitant, miracle wanted. Isn't there some way you chivied the goats that will lead to a first-class hotel and a boot-shop? What about this valley next on the South—the one that's marked 'Lost Valley (no information) on these inexpressibly bloody Staff maps?"

Seaton glowed visibly with pleasure under Willan's chaff. It seemed, more than anything else, to certify the ex-coward a man among men. One does not chaff those whom one would blackball. "There's a way to Lost Valley, sir," Seaton said eagerly. "Rather a beast, though. It goes over there." He pointed behind them, away from Boat Valley, up to a dip in the snowy crest of the ridge, on a lower shelf of which they were standing—a lateral ridge running out to the West from the mightier main chain that ran North and South. It looked a good place for a well-found Swiss Alpine Corps to manoeuvre in; less good for born townsmen without any boots to speak of.

"Why 'Lost' Valley? Willan asked the Oldest Inhabitant. "Only because it's a little tricky to get in or out of. So nobody tries, if he can help it."

"Lamentable spirit. What like, when you're in?"

"A real top-hole place. You see, sir, it's wonderful deep—a thousand foot less above the sea level than Boat Valley is. Wide, too, and that way it gets lots of sun and ain't covered all over with stones. So it's fertile—its chockful of cows, and the people grow oats and potatoes and all sorts of greenstuff."

"Do they grow any shoes?" Merrick asked.

"It's their game," Seaton said, "all the winter. They should' be just about starting it now. When the snow comes they bring down the cows from the pastures high up, where the cheese is made all the summer. Then there's most, of their time on their hands, so half of 'em carve wooden cows, and the others make boots, all the time till the spring."

"My young friend," said Merrick, "you'll go pretty far in this world if you always have aces like this up your sleeve." He turned to Willan. "March off, sir?" he asked.

"One moment," said Willan. "How long is this trek?" he asked Seaton. "I don't mean for you. How long d'you say for troops, driven hard?"

"Eight hours, sir. That's to the highest grass in Lost Valley. Four hours more to the village."

Willan reflected. "Twelve to the grub. Right, Merrick, we'll push off. Nearly two o'clock now. Nothing to eat till we're there. And we'll have half the men down with frost-bite unless we're over that beastly pass before dark. Lead away, Seaton." The men streamed away in the sunshine, over slushy snow. The platform they stood on had seemed high till now. It felt abysmally low as they gazed up at the white wall that still intervened between them and the fodder and litter which were now becoming, for the time, the goal of ambition, the ultimate good, life's aim and crown.

CHAPTER XVII

LOST VALLEY

I

In every mountain country you will find some legend of A lost valley, having in it a tiny world that is better than our big one. Its pastures are deeper and its waters clearer, and its trees are heavier with fruit. To lock it in, safe from such thieves as men have been since the Fall, there are usually hanging glaciers and tiers of unclimbable precipice.

There may be people in the lost valley of myth and there may not. According to most of the local legends there lingers in it a choice morsel of the Golden Age which vanished everywhere else some time ago. Even Shakespeare could only partly resuscitate it in the Forest of Arden. Perhaps a ripe apple, bitten by a child's teeth, has been found in a mountain torrent into which the stream that drains the lost valley must have made its way by some underground channel that cannot now be traced. And there may be other proofs of man's presence there, equally cogent. The valley of other legends has no human possessors; only the wild goats, the white hares and the chamois of all the surrounding mountains flock to it in winter to live out the evil months in this patch of mild fruitfulness left over from Eden; the valley stream is never quite frozen, nor its grass buried deep under snow.

No doubt the pretty myth tells the truth in a way. Some hunter astray in the upper wilds may have gained a brief glimpse, through a fugitive loop-hole in a cloud, of a sunlit pasture on some mountain shoulder below. With his own bearings lost and with no expectation in him of any such contrast to the sunless barrenness and desolation all round him, the legend may not do much more than express the man's ecstatic sense of the unearthly beauty and goodness of that un-recognised emerald cup brimming with radiance and warmth, and tinkling like the Heaven of Alpine children, with the bells of happy cows. Soon the man's true report turns to myth; rumour spreads that he vowed he would come back next summer to search for the valley, but died in the spring; and then it is said that whoever sees the lost valley will die within the year, like the men in the Bible who looked at God's private and personal things. But the hunter's own vision was real.

That was how Ria's Lost Valley had come by the name. No maker of maps had ever been in it and very few other people except the members of the village commune that possessed it. For one thing, you had to be agile to get in at all. Its lower end, where it debouched on the Big Slope of Ria, was very narrow, and access to it could only be gained by climbing, hand and foot, up a hundred feet of steep rock, with a waterfall wetting you while you climbed. No cart could enter; and how the first cattle were hoisted into the valley no one can remember.

Everywhere else the valley was fenced round with precipices, broken only at one point on the North side, where the goat-herd's path known to Seaton found a steep and rough way<down a deeply cut and slightly receding gully. The precipice that closed the head of the valley was one of the highest sheer crags in the world. Almost from the top of the main frontier range it dropped, all but straight, the two vertical miles to the valley meadow beneath. At the top of this wall the snow never melted, though corn grew brown at its foot; bits of ice broken off from glaciers that hung near the crest of the ridge would fall upon growing cherries and poppies.

You see how some famished stranger, with a humble cast of mind, lost in foul weather among the upper snows, might sight the fat cows wading deep in beflowered grass among sunny orchards and say to himself that surely those cosy houses of brown timber, mellowly weathered and jolly with gay window-boxes, must be the veritable mansions of the blest.

Certainly those, who lived there had been saved from some of the ills of this life, in our days. Their parents, English and Irish factory hands, had emigrated from Lancashire. Some "epoch-making improvement in manufacturing "machinery" from which great blessings were expected for the world, had begun its benign operations by throwing these adventurers out of employment. In the unmapped and almost unexplored recesses of Eastern Ria the little band of young men and women who had become superfluous, but remained hungry, had knocked up a little new world for themselves. They had gone back to their face's beginnings—had squatted on the virgin soil and wrung out of it food, clothes and houses.

Their first year's produce they had simply shared out with arithmetical justice, being all friends, good-natured, and rather awed by the aspect of the naked earth,' the grim angel with whom they now wrestled for a living. Presently they had found that even to go shares fairly may become quite an intricate business as civilisation goes on. So they had got their heads down to it and planned out a mixed system of private belongings and common belongings; everyone wanted a house or room of his own, but nobody wanted to fence off a separate feed for his one cow. They had read neither Mill nor Ruskin nor Marx, and none of them wanted to make out a case for any "broad principle" in particular. Mother-wit, good-humour and comrade-like fairness roughed out the plan, and it did pretty well. It may have been unsymmetrical, unprogressive, uneconomic and all sorts of bad things for three hundred people to live on milk, butter, cheese, oatmeal and a little meat, all of their own raising, to make their own clothes out of stuff that they wove from yarn they had spun from the wool of their own sheep, and their boots of leather from the hides of their own cows. And yet the perverse creatures, without a policeman, a bank, a jail or so much as one self-conscious class, were substantially decent and happy.

II

These innocents nicknamed themselves the Lost Tribe. They must have been even more at a loss when they looked up from the morning's business of threshing oats and attending to cows and saw that a long black thread had thrust itself over the snowy crest of the valley's Northern wall and was slowly twisting forward, down the white slope below. Would the worm-like thing, never broken and nowhere thicker than anywhere else, never cease to come crawling wavily over that shining skyline?

It was men, sure enough. Men in hundreds, all in single file and all walking carefully, as in the fear of God, in the footsteps of a leader who serpentined this way and that, cannily picking his way round the ends of the many crevasses that split up the snow-covered glacier.

It was strange enough that a seemingly endless runlet of men should be trickling into Lost Valley at all; stranger that they should come by a way never used by anyone but a few nimble hunters and goat-herds. But that was not all; the men were soon seen to be soldiers carrying arms.

The first surmise was appalling. News of a danger of war with Porto, though not of its declaration, had reached the Lost Tribe. This, then, must be a Portan army stealing down upon Ria by a back stair.

The tip of the black thread had now reached the lower edge of the snow. There it paused and began to form a black lump on the bleached scree as the thread behind paid itself in. When all the black thread had wound itself into this ball, a small fragment detached itself from the ball and made for the village. Being few and unarmed, the Lost Tribe simply did nothing but go on with their work, in great misery, abiding their fate. At the end of two hours the approaching forerunners of the foul portent above began to show signs of separate individual action; one of them had a deuce of a stride; another jumped from stone to stone in a quite personal way. In half an hour more each of them had a face of his own, and in ten more minutes all terror suddenly ended and deep, peaceful bliss filled the world. The uniforms were Rian.

To their enormous sense of relief the Tribe gave no expression at all. They went on working with an air, if possible, of even deeper absorption. They were like children on whose beloved secret game a party of strange adults have broken in. Your humble soul finds it quite hard to believe that what he has faced and won is the real, the hard and glorious battle of existence. Misgivings assail him. Has he, perhaps, been only loitering, all the time, in some lazy back-water, far out of the great stream? The sight of strangers, persons of different experience, is apt to confound him—these, doubtless, are the real swimmers, dominators of the authentic flood. No longer afraid, but desperately shy, the Tribe scarcely look up at their visitants. Half-raised heads and stolid greetings of "Mornin'" were all that might have passed, on the villagers' side, if Merrick, commanding the military mission, had not accosted the possessor of a pair of twinkling blue eyes that were much to his liking. "Who's the head man, brother, in this burg?" Merrick enquired.

"A head man is ut?" the tribesman replied in the speech of Kildare, which Merrick had loved in early days at the Curragh.

By a kind of sympathetic assimilation Merrick began to speak something a little like it himself. "Is there no sort of mayor or a foreman you have, will speak for the people?"

The man with the fun in his eyes looked a little perplexed. "There's wan man does wan thing, and wan does another, but divil a foreman is there in ut at all." He spoke rather humbly, as if he now saw that rulers, like trousers, are things that you ought to have about you.

"Anyway," Merrick pressed, "whom do I go to, for quarters and rations for nine hundred men?"

"Won't I tell the people myself in a minnut?"

"The food's to be had?" Merrick asked, rather astonished.

"Is ut food? If that doesn't beat all! An' the place bulgin' with food, to put by for the winter!"
"Any to spare?"

"How wouldn't we spare it, the way Governmints pay, an' they jingling with money."

"Good," said Merrick. "Then about quarters?"

The man's face collapsed. "I'm that sorry," he said, "but the divil a bed has there ever been in ut."

Merrick laughed. "We're not tourists," he said. "Is there straw for nine hundred?"

The man was elate. "Aye, an' for millions. An' all the sweet hay in the barns. Ye've only to bid them step down, while I speak to the people."

He went about it. Merrick called up his couple of signallers. In a minute the two brisk little flags were flapping crisply. In ten minutes more the dark ball of thread at the edge of the snows had begun to unwind and the tip of the thread was crawling down upon the village.

III

Willan's men were in Heaven that night. The year's harvest of hay was still its full depth in the barns where they lay. To perfect the joy of warm rest they could spy through the cracks in the timber walls of the barns a skyful of stars flashing with frost. It was ecstasy just to have every muscle go slack, and to feel the hay moulding itself into circumstantial imbedments for elbow, hip, ankle, for every fretful projection of the sore body. No more ice on the eyelashes now, no burning pain in frozen feet, no long-drawn agonies of abstention from just sinking down on the snow to rest and have peace and let the world go hang. They had it now, peace passing all understanding, and they had kept their pride too. Has the world any tiredness like the soldier's, or any rest quite so grateful as his?

To top all, their Paradise was not to suffer abridgement. No Revelly to-morrow: every man was to sleep his sleep out—all the next day if he chose'; and the thought of this was the deepest repose of all; it immersed the men in a sense of tranquil and endless fruition, a conscious eternity of unpalling beatitude.

The long night was Willan's idea. The trudge and climb over the-pass had finished all the men's boots; some scores of feet were slightly frost-bitten; hundreds of others were bleeding from cuts made by sharp stones; burst blisters were general. Many men's nerves were so frayed that they jumped if some one spoke loudly behind them: they had got on each other's nerves at the end and begun to bicker and nag like cross children, picked men as they were. What reached Lost Valley was not a force fit for the field. It was only what could, in a short time, be made such a force, and a magnifcent one—not a single man arrived without his rifle, his ammunition pouches and his bandolier of extra cartridges. In one sense there was not a minute to lose; already the country's danger might be extreme. In another sense, slow going was just as imperative: till they were rested and shod the force could do nothing likely to count. But Willan had had to insist. Some of the regimental officers hated the notion of letting anyone sleep a long time at a crisis so fateful. Lovel-Waters hated it most. He would have liked to rush at the enemy naked and fasting. That would have satisfied his craving for unheard-of and impracticable heroism. Though he did not know it, he was deeply in love with gallant failure, fruitless devotion, noble catastrophe, and his vision of tragic beauty in these was dearer to his innermost heart than any taking of mere humdrum means to a military end. Willan and Merrick liked the romantic enthusiast, and they had taken some trouble to argue the case with, him before Willan issued the order.

The only thing that had told on their side Was that Lovel-Waters' own boots, being no production of Bute's, had stood the rough work perfectly. Had they dissolved along with the boots of the men, Lovel-Waters would have begged even more urgently than he did to bf suffered to lead his battalion down Lost Valley at daybreak, search out the enemy and fight to the last man in defence of the country. "How could I die better?" Lovel-Waters had asked.

But Willan and Merrick meant business, and not a romantic progress to martyrdom at a high expense to the country in man-power.

CHAPTER XVIII

"A GOOD PLOT: EXCELLENT FRIENDS"

I

Whatever their cares, the bodies of Willan and Merrick were in Heaven, like other people's, that night. Also they had a little hayloft to themselves. So they could feast their practical minds on the sordid details for which they had both been hungering during an hour of Love'-Waters' noblest tall talk.

"I suppose there is time to refit, for another go in," said Merrick. When keen on a project, he liked to put its chance of success at the lowest, always in a very cheerful voice.

"Time?" said Willan. "Heaps. I tell you we hold the strongest hand ever dealt. Just a sleep or two and a wash or two and one or two little things to be got, and then we'll nip in like a fourteenth trump."

"Well," the genial pessimist allowed, "it may do for a film, anyhow. 'The Hidden Hand, or Little Willan's Casting Vote.'" "How many pairs of boots was it the lads of the village said they could turn out in a day? Wasn't it forty?"

"That was the maximum."

"Well," said Willan, "maximums are things that you beat when you have to. Forty a day, and nine hundred wanted. We'll have the lot in three weeks."

"And who's to hold Lovel the Fiery down for three weeks? He's breaking his heart. You know, you've robbed that man. You've done him out of a vision fulfilled."

"Vision?"

"Yes—the hopeless dawn—the gaunt troops mustering in the grisly light to-morrow."

"Oh! blow grisly dawns."

"With all respect, sir, you're a heathen. All damn vulgar practicality. You're merely out to win the war. Lovel's after the things of the spirit. He wants the joys of the lost battle—the fall of the unsullied plume in the last ditch—not these materialist dodges for getting men into condition and buying them boots." Willan did not answer at once. Merrick's chaff suggested ideas that were new to Willan, perhaps, a little baffling, but interesting and curious. While he thought, Merrick eyed him with much satisfaction. A't last Merrick asked, "Quite sure there'll be any war left in three weeks? Who's to hold the Portans that long—even if we do hold Lovel?"

"There's almost all the Rian army."

"All except the only bit of it that's any good. We had the picked stuff, to start with. The best quarter of that is up here, out of action. The other three-quarters are dead or have run for it. What's left?"

"Well, suppose they do slip up—the main army, I mean. Suppose they fall right back on the city. The enemy could not be there, at the worst, in much less than a week. And any old town could hold out for a fortnight. Besides—"

"Yes?"

"We've only just started this war—and started exactly the way that British troops always do. Look at Mons, Isandula, Colenso. Licked every time. It's the only way we get going."

"Cheerful doctrine."

"I don't say I want to slip up, by way of a start. Still, there you are. The breed seems to need a good wipe in the eye before it will get down to business."

"Good old traditional theory, that. I suppose the reserve fund of guts in the breed has held out. Will it, though, in this flash Rian outfit—all gold-bugs and jaw and flag-wagging?" Willan considered the question. Then he said, more positively than he usually said things, "They'll stick it." He thought again and then added: "You see, they're well led."

"The civilians?"

"Yes."

"Who on earth could lead civilians?"

"One of 'em."

"Hum, as they say." Merrick was not derisive—only genially sceptical.

II

Willan had taken a liking to Merrick. But Merrick had -now unknowingly pricked a raw place. It spurred Willan to one of his rare attempts to stick up, in talk, for one of his private notions. To start on this venture at all he had to force a tone of gruff vehemence. "Look here," he began, "isn't that line rather rot, when you come to think of it?"

"Line?" Merrick queried, with perfect good humour.

"Sneering, you know, at civilians—as if no one ever did anything that's baulking except in a war! As if war were not more fun than peace is!"

Merrick considered the matter temperately. He had the open mind, not much obstructed either by principle or by prejudice. "Winning," he said, "is a beano all through. What about lickings, though?—yesterday's, say."

"Ain't all sport," Willan argued, "part wins and part losses—games, shooting, anything? It's the doing the thing that is the fun, seems to me—win or lose. It's What makes you half drunk with the rippingness of it. Yesterday, even—squinting over the edge of that crag at the Portans. I had to make faces with joy at being just there and not missing it—simply the huge lark of it all—the hide-and-seek business. Who'd be a civilian at that sort of time—stuck up at home in a town, doing sums, making—"

"Boots?" Merrick playfully asked.

"Oh! there's an odd thief or two everywhere. Think of some sergeant-cooks that you've known. But civvies are decent, take 'em all round, just like other people. Only they're out of the most topping game in the world. And then we sneer at 'em. Oh, I've done it, all right—more than you, very likely."

"They do it themselves," Merrick said. "That's the trouble. 'Oh, Tommy, Tommy Atkins, what a noble heart you are!'—it isn't soldiers write that bilge."

"That's right enough," Willan admitted. "Wonderful the things they'll say. And they themselves pukka heroes and martyrs and all, sticking it out, till they die, in poison-gas places in towns,—offices, factories, all sorts of Black Holes of Calcutta. Or these people here, that have done pretty near the whole of humanity's job on the earth, you might say, right from the start—come to this place just as it had been left the day after Creation and finished it off. And then we come down like a million white ants to eat up all their grub, on tick, and make a muck of their hay—bring the Portans down on them too, perhaps—and they respect us, good Lord!—the innocent saints! They talk of our 'sacrificing ourselves for the country!' I rather wonder all these people, who really do keep the world going round, don't go on strike every time there's a war and say we shan't have any grub unless we come home and work."

"Well," said Merrick, turning over in the perfumed hay luxuriously, "it certainly would be a deprivation."

III

Willan luxuriated too. Snuggling deep in the warm, scented bedding, his boots off, his feet washed and happy, his tunic laid under his face to keep off the tickling hay, he had nothing more to ask, in the bodily way. To his great body and sane nerves and vitals, in their rude health and hardihood, vicissitudes of utter tiredness and deep rest, of iced winds and blistering sunshine, brought raptures that were almost spiritual. Like bread and wine used for a sacrament, these alternations of stress and ease did more than satisfy a few elementary needs of the flesh. They set the whole soul astir; life was raised to a higher power of itself, and the delighted spirit felt such a lift of release that it seemed to look back at its own ordinary state as a kind of captivity now ended.

Some crevices among the great logs of the barn wall were whitening now with the rise of an unclouded moon. It was freezing, and a clean, shrill whistle blew, off and on, round the bam as some austere wind wept about its business among the shivering stars. Inside the barn there was heat, glorious heat, a little block of it, a tiny island of it, moored out there in an ocean of such cold as stuns and quells. No, he couldn't sleep yet; it was too excitingly good. Wriggling round in the hay, so that Merrick might hear, he said: "Mind you, I don't think the Quakers are right altogether. There can be such a thing as a war that you simply must fight."

"Every war's that when it starts," said Merrick. "It's only after it's over that they find out it was silly or caddish."

"It is, nine times out of ten. Even the good old Great War they don't seem quite so sure about now. But one time in ten—in a huddred, perhaps—you've simply got to fight it out. It's like fighting a rough to keep him from raping your sister. You may love the fighting itself, just as a dog does. Still, the fact that it gives you a good time don't, in itself, make it wrong. And, I tell you, we've got the right thing this time. It's a war in a hundred."

"Every war is, at this stage," Merrick said cheerfully.

"But this one's just. It's absolutely just."

"They always are, till later."

"Old, stiff-necked scoffer! I scoffed too:—till just the other day. I felt pretty cynical—sceptical—what d'you call it—about our old trade. Just after I came out to Ria to take my job over I went to stay with a man I've known always. I wanted to talk this thing out. He's the only man going that ever could make things run clear in my head."

"Is this the Heaven-sent leader?"

"No ribaldry, now. When I got to his house there were a few people there, dining—clever people—highbrows, you know. They talked a lot about war—how noble it was, and all that. I couldn't keep in step with 'em at all. I said my own little bit—gas, you know—about the whole fighting game as I'd seen it. They didn't want that—had no use for it. They all set upon me—all but Burnage himself—"

"Burnage, the orator man?"

"The man for me. The rest—all but a beautiful girl who was there and said nothing—sprang up and choked me. Gosh! they were brilliant! I was half-dead when they'd done. I couldn't get any talk then with my man. But the next night I heard him.

He made a great speech to a crowd, from a window—"

"That's he."

"He's it, I can tell you. I was just over the way, in my little room at the W.O. It was hot and I had my window wide open, so I heard every word. I could feel that whacking crowd change while he spoke. They grew; they became twice the men that they were; fineness seemed to go out of him, into that crowd. Into me, too. I saw all my cynical sort of suspicions were rot. Anyhow, I had got it at last—a war that wasn't like others—the one you let yourself go at, without any beast of a fear that some day you might feel sick and sorry for having ever been in it."

IV

It was quite dark in the barn, so Merrick could safely give way to a rather rueful as well as affectionate smile while Willan made this protracted sortie from the citadel of reticence. Though their years were almost the same, Merrick must have been a good deal older in mind than his new friend. For Merrick was quite past the best age for believing in miracles; also past the best age for having his soul searched and upheaved by the positive assurances of public men face to face with fine audiences. What was truth, after all? It was a very sensible question of Pilate's. Perhaps there was no truth, nor falsehood either, in any actual set of words arranged in a certain order. Perhaps they were only a neutral surface over which truth or falsehood could be cast by different minds or tongues, as a blue or an amber light is projected by turns on a colourless piece of stage canvas. Merrick's time was over for fancying that the amber light was really the blessed sun, or the blue light the chaste moon, like this strapping innocent, his commander.

But Merrick had grown fond of Willan. Fie would not think of questioning further the plenary-inspiration of Willan's friend as a revealer of saving truths. That might hurt Willan sorely. Besides, even the good-natured Merrick had at least one little affair of his own to think of. "What day," he asked, "was this agreeable dinner—where they hacked your shins?"

"A Thursday. The Thursday before the war started."

"Was an old boy there who talked blood and fire and wanted to hew Agag to pieces and so forth?"

"There were two of 'em."

"Had one a fair daughter?"

"Yes. It was she shied no bricks at me."

"Oh, my prophetic soul! My uncle! And my cousin Clare. No, Clare wouldn't jump on you. Clare would be wanting to hear what you'd say. She's like that. She wants to find out for herself and not just to say what everyone's saying. Men don't think a beautiful girl is ever like that, with a real live mind of her own, like a man's. But Clare is."

Merrick, the most lightly flitting of sceptical wits, was talking with a remarkable earnestness. Willan marvelled at first, then thought to himself, "Why, of course—" and said with friendly simplicity: "You're engaged to the lady?"

"N-no." But Merrick's voice hung on the word. Clearly the one word did not say all. But it was for Merrick to say something more or to leave it at that. Willan could only wait and listen intensely, for Merrick to speak if he would. Infinitesimal noises became almost loud, Willan listened so hard. A loose stone was blown over the edge of a crag, far away, and fell rattling; the oarage of the wings of a single great bird, flying high over the valley on some lonely night quest of its own, was distinct. The taut silence strained on, from minute to minute.

Then Merrick broke it suddenly, quietly as though the two had talked about his chances hundreds of times. "I seem to get on pretty well for a bit, and then I say something that makes her look at me as if— oh! not nastily, you know, but as if she were trying her best to make but to herself that I'm not such a beast, as I sound. Ever feel you get looked at like that?"

"Why, I catch it all over the place. Poor old Main gave me tons of it. So did your very respectable uncle. As to the Bishop man!—Gummy!"

"That's different," Merrick assured him. "They're both the sort that jabber away by rote all the time. They got everything jammed into place in their heads long ago; they don't really look at anything now. Whatever you say to them only touches some wheezy old bell in their minds and out pops an old phrase that's supposed to be right for occasions like that. And then you come in, like a wise child just dropped out of Mars, with no bells and phrases about you. You only just say how things strike you, right out, as if there were no sacred bell-and-phrase system to think of. It puts the wind up them. But that's not my trouble with Clare. Mine is the other way round. I don't talk like you.

I can't. I'm not green enough, in a way. No offence, you know: Christ was the limit in greenness about the ways of the crowd I know best, and you too—the 'nice people' crowd, English country house crowd, the crowd that say things by numbers, like drill. I've always talked their way, it's so easy. In fact, I can't talk any other way now. But at times, when I do it to Clare, she just looks at me and wonders—not snubbing or superior—quite friendly and kind—but still she just wonders: and then I get a sort of wind up; I feel 'Oh good Lord! she's found me out now—she's gone and seen I don't mean that at all, and that I'm only saying it because it's the done thing among a lot of fools who think it's the done thing among other fools.' She has that sort of smashing honesty, you know. To talk to her is pretty well like looking at the sun, full face. It almost dazzles you—the awful straightness of the way she sees a thing."

"I wish you luck, old boy." Willan rather wished he could have had a little practice with his voice, before saying this. He found it needed some elocution. Still, it came out pretty well. So his was to be only the confidant's part: he was cast for it now, almost before he had found out that the part he would have liked to play was the lover's. He had to hold his peace for ever now; he had bound himself over by letting old Merrick run on as he had, about his hope and his fears. Of course, she would not disdain Merrick, that happy genius of wit and charm, courage and honour. What woman could? Well, he would go to their wedding. "Good night. You bet it comes all right," he said to Merrick. "Good day to-morrow. Good work on those boots."

I

Many willing minds have offered to show why the Portans were able to crumple up the Rian main army in Scout Valley so easily and so cheaply as they did. Some say it was because the religious instruction in Portan schools had always been more firmly dogmatic; some say, because for several years the Rians had spent less, per head, on beer, and more on spirits, than the Portans; others, because the Rians had not bought enough high-explosive shells from Bute and his friends. But I doubt whether any one of these causes accounts for it all. The actual treading out of the grapes of wrath may have looked a rough and fluky affair. Still, the wine probably came out pretty much as the directors of the vineyard had made it. By their modes of planting, manuring and pruning they had, at any rate, flavoured the cup that had to be drunk by Ria's unfortunate troops.

Perhaps the Portans were still more surprised by the ease of their victory than the Rians. Like the housemaid who breaks your finest china, while dusting it without exceptional violence, the Portans might have said, "They came to pieces in our hands"—first Main's brigade in Boat Valley and then the Rian main army near Scout Pass two days after. The Portans had merely made war diligently as the text-books of the trade directed. They had kept their heads. Quite early in the great Scout Valley rout the Portan Commander-in-Chief had given orders to cease firing into the thick of the retreating Rians. "We must not waste them," he said, "they will help to eat up any food there is in the City."

In the same spirit of strict attention to business, the Portans flatly refused to take any non-wounded prisoners. Any whole Rian who put up his hands was told to be off after his friends. He was, they told him, on the ration strength of Ria, not of Porto. So the poor wretch had to catch up the rest of the rout and to show it, still more afflictingly than before, how little a Rian soldier on his native, or adoptive, heath had come to be feared. It did not improve the moral of the beaten army.

Down the Big Slope the enemy moved steadily in the wake of the Rian stampede, shepherding it on, and keeping it in a convenient state of disorder, for four days. At the end. of that time the City was duly besieged. Of course, it had no walls or forts, for it had no antiquity. All that happened was that a few Portan shells came in every day, just to remind the population that a siege was going on. If anyone tried to go out and live somewhere else he could walk quite a mile from the City in perfect freedom. But then he was always met by armed Portans and was directed to return and to go on eating.

As the capital of a State justly proud of its highly modern organisation, the City could live almost as healthy a life as is lived by a very young child so long as its nurse appears every four hours with warm milk in a bottle. Morning, noon and night, the City had always been wholesomely and punctually fed by the surrounding country. After a single day's siege the City began to betray, on an enormous scale, the consternation of your wife when the milkman has forgotten to call two times running. Within three days it dawned upon countless highly civilised minds that fresh, and even tinned, meat does not originate in the shop.

For some days more the Portans were content to let these facts sink into the mind, only adding just an extra shell or two each day, lest the Rians should forget, even between meal-times, that life is real, life is serious. The shells did not kill, on an average, more than one person apiece, but they disturbed far more than one mind. They led many Rians to think, with some heat, about the imperfections of ruling persons. Their wrath was not cooled when they learnt that two of the Portan high-velocity guns, which kept them in mind of their end, had a range four miles longer than the range of any gun possessed by Ria. Long John and Long John's Pal, as the Rian gunners christened these remembrancers, were idyllically emplaced at New Arden, a patch of woodland lawn full of wild flowers, with a clear spring, high on the Big Slope above the Burnages' house. There did they see no enemy but autumn and rough weather. For heavy gunners the pastoral life is much improved by being four miles out of the other fellow's range.

II

From the sylvan peace of Bel Alp Cyril and Rose had had to descend into the zone of short rations below, to Rose's un-affected disgust. "But surely—surely—" she had begun, more than once, to her husband, when confronted with this inconvenience. She wore her beautiful tragic scowl as she said it, and once she gave a quick little stamp of a foot. Could mismanagement go further?—the question blazed in her eyes.

At the end of a week the rations of all, or nearly all, the besieged were cut down by a half. Somehow the very best hotels were still able to serve enough of the very best things to the very best people. But the well-dressed part of the population made, on the whole, quite noble gestures. After a gallant offer to resign, if anyone cared to take on its job, the Ministry took to its bosom the leaders of the Opposition and a few "representative men Burnage and two or three captains of Big Business who were believed to have done extraordinarily well for themselves in their illustrious lives: let them now, it was implied, evince the same genius in the service of their country.

This constellation of bright particular stars was hailed as a truly National Government. It was adjured by the Press to shine with a candle-power equal to the aggregate candle-powers of all its individually dazzling ingredients. The Cabinet responded by vowing, on all possible occasions, to hold out against the enemy for ever, and by referring other matters to sub-committees of itself. It assured the Commander-in-Chief (every member standing up in his place) that he possessed the absolute confidence of every soul in the City; and in reply the Commander-in-Chief said that the spirit of the City was magnificent. So if transports of mutual stimulation, among august persons, could save the country, the country looked pretty safe.

The second week of the siege was certainly more tedious than the first. As the week went on, the tedium increased with remarkable velocity. The daily rations were now given out at the City's elementary schools, the supply of food for the young mind being suspended until happier times. A notice was put' up on the school doors at the end of this second week, that each day's ration was to be cut down again, this time by one-third. How would "every soul in the City" take it? The great and wise asked each other and wondered. But, like good practical men, they did not merely sit still and wonder.

They resolved to go out and see. Each was to take a ward of the City; he was to visit its ration-distributing stations, see that all was done properly, hear any complaints from the people, and feel carefully the pulse of the great common heart; he would be affable, breezy and brotherly; he would buck up the moral of the poor and lowly and he would try to find out what the poor and lowly had at the backs of their heads.

III

Promptly at seven o'clock on the seventeenth morning of the siege Burnage reached the infant-school where he was to do his bit as one of these hearteners and observers.

It was a gaunt room, with all the paint dirty. A sight of it must have taught infants that life is no joke, if their slum had left them in any doubt on the point. Across and across it ran rows of continuous desks of rough wood and rough iron. A central gangway intersected these at right angles. A second gangway ran along one side of the room, between the ends of the desks and the grease-stained green wall. At one end of the room a chair and desk for a teacher were hoisted on a little platform, leaving just room on the platform for a second chair beside the first. At the opposite end of the room a door led to a lobby and through it to the street.

The rations for issue were piled, in many little packets, on tables right and left of the platform. An armed soldier guarded each table. A civilian clerk was on duty, to dole out the packets.

A Major Ladelle, middle-aged and retired but serving again in this time of need, took the teacher's chair. Burnage sat down on the chair on his right. Burnage had the obliging and cheerful air of the politician on parade, Ladelle the air of some officers also on parade—no active and immediate wrath but much of it in reserve. He looked round to see that the soldiers on duty were shaved, and then said "Carry on," sharply.

Even with the street door closed, the simmering buzz of the long queue chafing outside was audible. The moment the door was opened by the two sentries guarding it a harsher din burst into the room as though it had been corked up in a bottle before and now the cork had come out. On the crest of this big wave of massed sound a few shrill individual cries rode like clear, sharply curled foam: "'Oo're you a-shovin'?" "I yn't shovin'. It's them be'ind shovin'." "Well, keep yerself to yerself." "'Ow, shut yer grite mouf, mikin' a draught down me back." "Gam, funny!"

The twelve most efficient hustlers or dodgers near the head of the ill-kept queue were let in by the two guards. Then the door was forced to, in the face of the rest. In single file the twelve champions were suffered to trickle along the side gangway, re-polishing the greasy wall with greasy shoulders, for each to give his name and address to a middle-aged Corporal clerk, the Brench whom you know; he sat at the upper end of the side gangway, with a big account-book before him. As he verified each name and address in the book he sang out "All correct, Sir," and the applicant stepped up to one of the tables, received his four little separate packets of victuals under the Major's menacing eye and passed on down the central gangway and so out by a minor door to the street.

The winner of the first helping was a large and slatternly virago. Taking her packet of bread from the clerk she weighed it scornfully in one hand and then held it up to the Major. "Nine ounces!" she squealed. "Call them nine ounces?"

"No. Six. You should read notices. Pass on," said the Major.

The termagant shuffled slowly down the centre gangway. She was opening her packet of meat, gloomily. At sight of the meat her gloom turned to fury. She held it out for the later comers to see from their parallel gangway. "Meat!" she snarled. "Gawd! Bloody offal! Orf an of moke!"

"Turn that woman out," the Major ordered. Two soldiers, standing by in case of need, propelled her gently to the exit. "Any applicant," the Major said, with colourless grimness, "who is disorderly here will forfeit his or her rations. Carry on."

The applicants held their peace anxiously.

IV

It took two hours to teach the last dozen of the queue. Brench looked long at the face of one of them. He had plenty of time to do this, for the Major and Burnage had left the room, to speak to some momentous caller, just as the man, a fat, malodorous fellow, came up to Brench and his register of the rations. Brench knew the bulbous face well enough—had seen it swelling and ogling, winking and leering, under the windows of the Voice, while the man gabbed to the crowd, and the oldard and Mary sat agonising under the trees. Brench had seen the face much more recently too.

When he had made quite sure, Brench said in a very low but quite firm voice, "Won't do. Your name ain't Mace. It's Sprott. And you been here before."

The man tried cajolery. "Mitey," he whispered, "down't you gow an' be spiteful. 'Ave a sense of honour."

"It won't do," Brench repeated.

The man changed his tactics. "Shut yer fice, will yer, or I'll mike yer sorry," he said in a venomous undertone.

"I've told you," said Brench.

Sprott certainly had boldness. Nudging the man next behind him in the queue he indicated Brench with a lurch of his own head. "See 'im, Mister?" he said. "A trytor. A imissary. Crep' into a plice o' trust. Caught red-'anded, attemp'in' to do us out of our grub—you an' me, Mister."

The wildest assertion, if made with assurance enough, can at least stagger a simple-minded hearer. The man who had been addressed gaped at the Corporal.

Brench was no public man. So he had had little practice in hearing public abuse of himself. But he kept a hold on his temper. "I've warned you," he said.

Sprott assumed the air of a superior dismissing an underling's unsatisfactory attempt at self-defiance. "Too lite, me man," Sprott bluffed. "It's too lite now. They'll know the sort o' lot you are, soon's I git near the Myjor." He added in a lower voice, "if ya down't mind wot y'are about."

Ladelle and Burnage returned at that moment. "Carry on," the Major ordered.

Brench rose and stretched out an arm like a toll-bar across the cheat's front. "This man, sir," he said, "has received a ration already to-day, under a different name."

The Major scrutinised Sprott. "He has," the Major certified. He turned to the soldiers waiting in reserve. "Arrest that man," he said, with no sign of personal interest in the affair.

A soldier fell-in on each side of Sprott. "I presume," said the prisoner, "I 'ave a right to be 'eard in me own defence." His voice was half bluster, half whine.

"Not now," the Major said. "Carry on rationing."

"I mus' reelly pynt out—" Sprott began.

"Take the prisoner away," said the Major.

As Sprott was marched off to the guard-room he passed close under Burnage's eyes and gave Burnage a purposeful look of recognition and entreaty. It was both obsequious and insolent—the look of a cringing dun—and Burnage wondered. Where had he seen that Bardolphian face, and heard blatant and unctuous words flowing out of it? Then he remembered.

In three minutes the issue of rations was over. Clerks and orderlies totted up figures and put away the few rations un-claimed. The Major sat motionless, staring as straight at his front as any sentry guarding a palace.

"That's all, then?" Burnage said, almost in awe before the Major's vast, blank impassivity. It was like the sea's or a mountain's.

"There is that charge of personation," the Major said; then he left a long silence; then he resumed: "Do you wish us to deal with it here? We have summary powers, you know; especially you civil magistrates."

"Certainly, certainly," Burnage replied. Then he added, "I've seen this fellow before. I fancy he needs to be somewhat—somewhat searchingly interrogated—more so, perhaps, than is quite easy in public." The Major slowly turned upon Burnage a look of faint and cold curiosity. "You want to question him in private?"

"I believe it might be of advantage."

"As you choose." The passing flicker of curiosity in the Major's mind was clearly extinct. "Sergeant, show Mr. Burnage to the guard-room."

V

"So it's you?" Burnage said to the captive when they were alone. His voice had a fine mournful severity.

Sprott promptly rejected this opening of the conversation and substituted another. "Now, guv'nor, you know me. You know as I'm a pytriot, at least."

"Is it patriotic," Burnage upbraided, "to steal your country-men's food?"

"Down't ya see?" Sprott asked reproachfully. "Wot, down't ya see?" He waited a few seconds, as if to give time for a fuller sense of the true state of things to dawn in Burnage's mind. Then he went on: "Simply forcin' a crisis—thet's wot I'm at. Down't ya tumble to it? Forcin' on a crisis. Wot! y'nt a crisis gotta come? Yn't we gotta be much worse afore we're better? An yn't a man to 'ave the guts to force a crisis?"

Burnage stared at the fellow. What was he driving at? Was it all the mere impudent farce that it seemed? Or might there be—possibly—something to learn through this rascal—no doubt indirectly? You see, Burnage did not know the Sprotts of this world. Indeed he knew no one outside his own little set. That was his world. "Well?" he said, as sternly as he could, to hide his perplexity.

Sprott did know mankind—to a point: he knew all that you learn if you live by your wits in racing men's clubs and on courses. He could nose out with demoniac quickness a fear or a hidden desire in anybody from whom he had something to get. No doubt he scented at once in Burnage the common fear of well-to-do men that they are only amateurs at living, and that the real professional livers are men who touch caps and say "Sir" to them, as a champion sculler or a Test cricketer used to do when they were boys fumbling and bungling at this master's craft. So Sprott's tone now was that of the experienced and devoted N.C.O. who respectfully pulls a young officer through the job he has never learned how to do. "Why, you, sir, know as well as me—an' if ya down't, 'oo does?—the wye it tries the bes' man's mor'l fibre to stan' up an' fice a grite Rian aujience—I mye sye, the most testin' aujience a speaker can find in the 'ole modern world."

"Well, well, what of it?" said Burnage.

"You 'ave, I think, sir, 'ad occysion to observe"—Sprott's proud humility was immense—"the wye that I 'ave stood that test?"

"I have heard you speak once, I believe. What about it?"

"Well, is it likely, now, as a man wiv a record like me is a-gowin' to turn 'is back on 'isself so fur as—?"

He broke off, and then, with an expression of hearty human appeal to the kin-ship of all first-rate persons, he said, "Ow! Mr. Burnage! Sir! Need I sye more? Cawn't ya see I did if fer me country's sike?"

Rubbish! Rubbish, of course. Burnage saw through it—with one mental eye out of two. And yet, strangely, he wanted the rogue to go on. A hateful rogue, a foul fungoid growth on the mob—and yet, on that very account, he might serve as an inlet into the dim, mysterious, momentous mind of the mob at this moment. "How so?" Burnage asked.

"Be forcin' a crisis. See 'ere, sir; it's no shame to you, wiv' all the preoccipytions you 'ave, to be jest a bit out o' touch wiv' the popilar mind. Me, now, thet's diff rent. Cawn't 'elp keepin' in touch wiv 'em, I cawnt. Movin' among 'em; me 'and on then pulse, like; me'eart up agen their'n. An'thet's the wye," Sprott said impressively, "as I can tell yer wot they're syin'."

"Well?" said Burnage again. Even a scoundrel trying to talk himself out of a scrape might give incidentally some indica-tion worth notice.

"They're syin'; 'This war yn't wot was advertised.' 'We been put on to a loser'—thet's wot they're syin'. They're syin', 'Are we to set 'ere an' be murdered?' Gobblessyer, in their 'eart they've chucked it already, sime's a boxer 'as when 'e stawts lookin' around fer a chawnce to gow down to escipe punishment."

"I cannot believe it," said Burnage. But he had begun to.

Sprott's fine scent for anything rotten possibly brought him the grateful smell of a lie. For he went on with even fuller assurance: "Ah! if you knew wot I know. An' now I arsk ya. Seein' as 'ow the gime's up—
—" Burnage shook his head, but Sprott went on audaciously—"Yn't it the truest kind o' public service to shorten the pine o' this grite popilytion? Why, all thet food"—he waved an arm towards the school-room—"it's nothin' better'n a curse—keepin' 'em up an' keepin' 'em up, jes' to suffer. Nothink else, on'y to suffer. An' the end of it all jest the sime."

Sprott paused for a moment, and then went on more slowly and gravely, as many orators do when they are about to say something particularly silly or vicious, and do not wish it to be recognised as such. "Speakin' on'y for meself, I tike it as a simple pytriotic dooty to mike awye wiv this deloosive grub. No good to anyone, it yn't. Jes' shuts the people's eyes agen the fac's. We're beat—thet's wot it is. We gotta fice the fac' like men—we're beat. Our nashn'al dest'ny—thet's wot it is, an' we yn't gotta funk it like we're doin'—spinnin' out the grub to mike it larst. Better shove it in the fire, sime as I'd ha' done if I'd ha' brought it off jes' now. On'y wye to sive the people from their mis'ry."

VI

Oh! no! Burnage was not taken in. The lie was too gross' too farcical. But, he reflected hastily, everything has some meaning or other. Even this thief was the expression of his experiences; his very lies took their colour from his surroundings. And then again the timid educated man was moved by that involuntary deference to the senses and instincts of the ignorant. His whole life had been sheltered from rude, elementary hardships and risks: the first rough emergency sent him to hang round such oracles as the supposed horse-sense and mother-wit of the illiterate and poor, their rat-like sense of unsoundness in a craft that may strike a shipping director as fit for the sea.

There was a knock at the door. An orderly brought in Major Ladelle's compliments and did Mr. Burnage desire the Major to wait any longer?

No, no. Mr. Burnage was sorry. He would come instantly. And he did.

"I rather think I should vote for letting the poor devil off," he said to the Major. "He seems to have acted under some idiotic delusion." "Let us be dissipated"—so Burnage's tone indirectly suggested; "let us indulge our good-nature for once, you and me."

But Ladelle would have no active part in any debauch of lenity. "You wish the prisoner dismissed?" he asked coldly.

Burnage nodded. "Sergeant," the Major ordered, "turn the prisoner into the street." It was done. To Burnage a frigid relation with anyone seemed unendurable. He had to try to be friends. "I fear we must walk cannily," he said in an apologetic way.

The Major grunted. Burnage went on: "I fear the state of things in the City is becoming critical. Have you noticed no signs of weakening?"

"I don't know," Ladelle said, "that the army is any worse now than it was when it bolted." Perhaps he thought, "Oh. damn this blundering civilian! Need he go rubbing it in."

"It isn't the army," said Burnage. "They're splendid, of course. It's the mass of the people I mean."

"Can't say. Don't come across 'em." The Major had picked up his stick and his gloves. The two parted uncordially.

Both were hurt. Everyone seemed to be hurt, in these days, by the touch of anyone else. There was the cold rage of these crestfallen soldiers; cruel fellows, Burnage felt; they itched to retrieve the army's recent loss of caste; all they cared for was some little splash of success in the field, to salve their wounded self-love, no matter what it cost anyone else, no matter how little real good it might do. Were they not as selfish, in their own way, as the poor slinking mice of the slums, whose defeatism Sprott had, no doubt, expressed correctly enough? Was not everybody being selfish, whether he wanted to throw up the sponge, lest he be hit, or to perish with all eyes upon him, and plenty of limelight, and lots of his countrymen perishing, too, round that superb central figure, himself?

Bute, that God of Battles, was said to be in central Italy, seeking yet more masterpieces of religious art to buy with his profits on shells, rifles, and boots. Browell, poor pedant, was wallowing in a mushy Heaven of sentiment, seeing visions of embattled Ria as living dangerously, epically, hoisted on the Sunny tableland of a heroism high above her common self. And then the poor brute crowd, ranging the streets with a pain in its belly, and eyeing the shops and banks and good houses and wondering which would be the best to loot first. And all these forms of baseness, naked and unashamed, or dressed up as virtues, would go on increasing till the siege came to its inevitable end; and then the ordered life of Ria would probably be blotted out by some lapse into murderous chaos, and Rose herself would not be safe in the street.

As the terror of that thought grew he hurried more and more to reach the first-rate hotel in which Rose and he had found shelter.

CHAPTER XX

I

It was almost the hour for Rose to be at her work in one of the improvised city hospitals for the wounded. Nurses with a training had run short immediately after the routs in Boat and Scout Valleys. All the women of fashion in Ria were nurses now—had taken first-aid courses and trusted to temperament and zeal for the rest of the skill required.

Rose had been one of the last to take to this work. She had the habit of lateness—had almost taken a pride in it, she was always so thoroughly able to carry it off. And now, with any luck, Cyril might just be in time to see her before she left the hotel. He longed to see her after his depressing morning; he longed for it as a man wet through and tired longs to lie in the sun. Inside the hotel's big swing door he met Browell coming from the lift. Browell's face was all a-beam with a peculiar radiance that it had whenever Browell felt that he had been shining in conversation. It lingered on, like the after-glow of Alpine sunsets. He wrung Burnage's hand—he really must felicitate Burnage on his dear wife's devotion and charm. "A nurse—such a womanly occupation!" He maundered on about the brave and the fair till the lift snatched Burnage aloft.

He found Rose in their sitting-room, in the fair out-door kit of a nurse, dragging on her second glove with indignant violence. Manifestly the world had been offending her. "You met that rag-bag of old cliches?" she demanded.

"Browell?"

"Of course. Do you know what he called me just now? Think. What would he call me?"

"What?"

"Can't you tell? Oh! my poor Cyril, there's only one thing that every bore calls me now. Why, of course, 'a ministering angel'. I've met nine dull men—signally dull men—since I put on these sentimental clothes. Six of them—two devastating thirds—have lugged in that musty old tag. They let fly at sight. Oh! if I'd known what it would mean when I took to this overcrowded line of beneficence!"

Cyril, with all his own troubles forgotten in the contemplation of hers, looked at her with a kind of dumb-stricken tenderness. That always fretted her. It seemed so stupid! It had sometimes made her say in despair, "Oh! can't you say something to make life more bearable?" She might have said it now, but a knock at the door forestalled her.

It was Crisp. He came in too heavily laden, as usual, with his own cares to say "How do you do?"

Even in these evil days Burnage had tried to keep open house for his staff. They were to look in whenever they liked. So he broke out effusively, "Crisp! My dear fellow! Dear, you know Mr. Crisp?"

Two of the grimmest salutations possible were exchanged.

Burnage made talk cordially. "Well, and how are the solid interests bearing the strain?"

"They're feeling it," said Crisp portentously. "If only," he added, "because of their work-people."

"Ah! the kind fellows!" said Burnage.

"Yesterday," said Crisp, "the last blast furnace was blown out. Tens of thousands of idle men in the streets. And now they're getting hungry."

"The poor fellows!" said Burnage.

"And that," Crisp pursued, "in a city crammed with portable goods of every description!"

"Then your solid interests do fear for themselves, just a little?" Rose spoke in a tone of ironic relief from the excess of moral beauty that had been overcharging the atmosphere.

But irony was thrown away on Crisp. He looked at Rose as if he were stooping to the level of a little toddling uptaught sex. "Men of business," he told her, "have a habit of bringing everything to the touchstone of sound common sense."

"That's better," said Rose. "I was fearing they might be little lower than seraphs."

Crisp couldn't say about seraphs. Still, he took it that Mrs. Burnage had seen her mistake. He would let her down lightly. He would be courtly and graceful. "But let me assure you," he gallantly said, "that if we City men do abide rather strictly in our own sphere, by a pretty plain, stern code of conduct, we all know how to honour in her proper sphere a geunine—if I may say so—ministering angel."

The poor man visibly plumed himself on the elegance of this effort. "Oh; thank you so much," said Rose. She raked him with her brilliant company smile while her teeth almost chattered with rage. She sent Cyril an all but audible look. It said, "Get the man out, or you'll see murder done."

II

He hurried Crisp off, on some feeble pretext. And then he scarcely dared to come back. You think he might have chaffed Rose—told her that people who call others seraphs must look to have angels thrown at their heads? But he had never been on chaffing terms with Rose. And he had only his plush rhetorical brains—and those smitten silent and helpless by very love of her. So when he came back he was of no use at all to the beautiful shrew who was walking the room, frowning and quivering.

"Now!" she challenged him in wrathful triumph. "Do you see now?"

"The poor man meant no harm, dear love," he interceded timidly, so futile was his notion of the way to pour in oil and balm.

She stopped dead. "Meant no harm!" She flung his words at him like stones. "Who ever did mean harm? Eve didn't. Pilate didn't. Bolshies don't. Do keep these platitudes for your more public speeches, Cyril. Don't desolate me"

A husband" less dull, or less devoted, might perhaps have put up his hands in surrender, gone on his knees, kissed her shoe, to give a playful cast to his subjection. But Cyril had no shifts of the kind. He could only look as well crushed as he was.

She may not have wished that, in her heart—may have wished that he had spirit and wit, to stand up to her. "Well," she said, with a dreary subsidence into relative mildness, "don't be a victim." She recommended her walking. She wearily explained her special crossness of to-day. "If only you could try this nursing! No doubt you think it's all holding dying men's hands, and catching the last words, to send to the wives. Or helping at big operations—the life-or-death touch and all that. I thought so, once. Well, it isn't. It's sitting and sitting and hearing a clock tick three thousand and six hundred times and then start all over again, very slow and loud and dry, in a hot room that's all a faded yellow. You watch a soiled band of sunlight go crawling across an oil clothed floor, sideways, a few inches an hour, for whole afternoons. And nothing—nothing happens at all, ever. And oh! the smell!"

"Ah yes! The blood!" he said tenderly.

"No, no!" she almost hooted. "The foul antiseptics. What can have possessed the man that invented them?" I suppose she craved to shock his dullness, to throw little bombs and see what would happen. "My dear one!" the literal lover protested, "they rob war of half its horrors."

Of course that only quickened her impulse to scandalise such a dunce. "Pass them on, you must mean, to the nurses," she said. She saw him wince at the callousness she affected. Perhaps she thought herself a brute, to be hurting him so much, for such poor sport as it gave her. But who could help sticking pins into a pincushion which asked for them so clearly. She must do some, thing for relief, and she was not one of the women who find it in private crying.

So she ran on from one fantastic show of heartlessness to another more outrageous, and he made little feeble attempts to show her things as they were, till the bell of their telephone rang and a message came up from the hall to say that a lady and gentleman wished to see Mrs. Burnage.

III

"Ask who," Rose ordered him. "Probably another 'ministering angel,'" she groaned as he stood at the 'phone. While they waited she looked at a clock that had been staring at her throughout. She exclaimed, "Horror! I'm late for parade. More than an hour! Why didn't you tell me?"

"The Bishop and Bishopess," he reported. "Now coming up in the lift."

He left the 'phone. They looked at each other. Why the Cases? The Bishop had not frequented them since the war began to go wrong. He had a taste for sitting well in the sun, and there was coming to be a patch of shade where Burnage was.

Rose suddenly said: "They're two of the fussers that manage my hospital—Hon. Sec. and Chairman." She would just greet them, then fly.

She worked up a cold wintry sparkle of liveliness as they entered. So glad to see them. Only a glimpse, though, she feared. Now she must rush away to her work. There was a war on.

Mrs. Case laid a timid hand upon Rose's arm. "I'm so sorry," she said. "I mean—I'm so glad—you needn't hurry now. I mean—" Although she hesitated, the faint, almost obliterated woman was becoming more distinct under pressure of trouble. There were appearing traits of compassion and mercy.

"Oh, but I must," Rose announced overridingly. "You don't know what might happen to one of my patients."

"We do, indeed, I grieve to say," said the Bishop, with a kind of gusto.

For once Mrs. Case took the lead away from her husband. She put the soothing and deprecating hand on Rose's arm again. "When we went in," she began with an effort, "to your ward and found that—that there wasn't a nurse there—of course the night nurse ought to have stayed till you came—we just waked a nurse that was off duty then, and she took your place till—some arrangement—" The speaker was all but in tears.

Rose queried loftily: "Arrangement? Well, I must bolt. Can't you imagine the face of that nurse you waked up?—the look of uncomplaining martyrdom it has by now? It's growing saintlier every second I wait."

"Oh! please, please, don't think about her," Mrs. Case pleaded piteously. "She has been relieved by now, and—Rose stiffened. "Relieved? I don't understand. I'm not there."

"The truth is," said the Bishop, with no outward sign of such pain as it had cost his wife to carry their mission thus far, "the Committee was sitting at the time, and it felt that the wisest and kindest course would be to relieve Mrs. Burnage of routine employment as a nurse."

Burnage jumped up, white. "Dismissed!" he gasped.

"Oh! no, no—don't say that," wailed Mrs. Case. "Don't take it like that. You know, we did want to make Clara Browell do some real nursing—she has been washing the men's shirts and scrubbing the floors, for so long, and—"

The poor kind bungling woman was losing herself and she hesitated and Rose said austerely, "So, that was her qualification for taking my place?"

"Oh, no, no, I didn't mean that." But the poor lady was gravelled. She glanced at her husband and he back at her. Her look was ruthful, dissuasive, imploring. His expressed the sober joy that some men take in making up their minds that they have no right to shirk hurting somebody else very badly. "I see I am compelled to inform you," he said to Burnage incisively, "that in Mrs. Burnage's absence from duty a patient has died of a sudden hemorrhage through being unattended to."

"Oh, my God!" cried Burnage. His consternation was not so much at the news as at the look of pain that it had brought to his wife's face. He had turned to her so instantly that he had seen the sorrow stab into her—simple, quite self-forgetful sorrow, at first, for the poor fellow whom she might have kept from dying. Mrs. Case saw it too.

Rose's face had changed by the time Case turned to her. They say the mouth of a child is clean till the moment of its birth, but that, a moment later, it is already infested with a multifarious horde of microbes. So, perhaps, Rose's grief, which was pure at its birth, was infested within a few seconds with sundry bacilli that turned it into a sour, chagrined murmur against all the muddlesome world of people and things that had rubbed her face in the ashes. Not that even this chagrin was wholly ignoble. I fancy she had longed, in her fashion, to find again in this hospital-work the lost secret of having a noble life of it; she had wished and tried to be one of the great tranquil souls who have peace in their labour, or one of the eager and nobly absorbed who find exhilaration in a perpetual stir of endeavour. Only a new frustration had come of it all.

Mrs. Case said good-bye with a timid affectionateness. "We are friends," she said to Rose, "aren't we?"

She was too frail a thing to wreak vengeance on. "Oh! more than friends," said Rose, mildly enough. She did not even scourge with sarcasm the retreating Bishop.

IV

When the two visitors had escaped, and Cyril came back to Rose, there was a minute in which the whole drift of their lives might perhaps have been changed, if he had had courage, or she humility. They might have met, really met, in the prison of humiliation that now held them both as they had never met in their years of apparent success. But she kept to her separate cell, and his was not the masterful love that breaks in. Nothing passed; the propitious moment went to waste. Only when it was over, and no miracle done, he laid a hand on her forehead with vague nervous tenderness. Had she a headache, he meant to ask; might he try to stroke it away?

But by now she was back in the inmost keep of her cheerless independence; the gates had clanged to. "I can't bear to be touched," she said quickly, withdrawing her head from his palm. The rejected hand of consolation dangled foolishly.

"What did that other man say?" she asked suddenly.

"Crisp? Oh! He said what they're all saying—that people are losing heart now."

"The cowards! I thought they would."

"Many men seem to blame me. The Bishop blamed me the moment the news became bad. Whoever goes under seems to him wicked."

"Wise parson!" said Rose. Her laugh was about as cheerful as a midwinter dawn over fens. "No coquetting with Christ and the weary-and-heavily-laden interest."

"Oh! I don't mind Case. But there are others. They're saying-there wouldn't have been any siege but for me—that there wouldn't have been any war."

"There wouldn't," Rose said with disdain. "They wouldn't have dared—without someone to make them all tipsy with old phrases—froth about finer issues and unbroken fronts. There—don't wince; there was a head on it once. Well, what are they going to do?"

"What is there to do? Surrender at once? Ora week later, when a few thousands more have been killed? That's the choice."

"How'll they choose? Hadn't you better choose for them—again?—make them a speech?—just to say which." Her voice was thrilling up into provocative wildness. She rose. "Shall I open the window?"

He tried to calm her. "Darling," he said, "the thing's Serious."

"Frightfully. So frightfully that you'd better do something." She egged herself on to taunt him brutally—probably hating herself all the time for a brute, and yet as incapable as a drunkard of ruling herself. "And what can you do but make speeches?"

He was so numbed by the pain her jibes gave him that he could think of nothing to say but the old tragic flourish of "Well, at least I can fall."

That touch of the second-rate theatre drove the fastidious creature almost distracted. "Fall!" she exclaimed. "What good is falling? Anybody can fall. Humpty Dumpty could fall.

And you've fallen already. Better do what Humpty Dumpty couldn't, hadn't you?"

"You mean—"

"Oh! get up again, get up again."

He made a common gesture of despair and she treated it as a question. "How? Well, I suppose you can do your work, whatever it is, better or worse. What do you do at these old Cabinet meetings you go to? You never tell me anything."

"We just hang on. We keep things going. We're trying to find if there's any chance of relief from outside—any sort of force left anywhere in the country."

"How can you tell?"

"We can't, so far. We've not got one aeroplane left. We send out spies, to get through, but they never come back. I suppose they're all shot."

"Volunteers! What sort of men offer for that?"

"All sorts. Some pretty odd ones. Hendie is going to-day in a rotten old-fashioned balloon that they're gumming together. You remember Hendie?"

"The music man with the crinkly zinc face? He's one of the heroes?"

"Well—he says it's sure death to stay here, now that there's no decent music. He agrees to give any message we like to anyone in the open, just so that he may get out."

She laughed her mirthless laugh. "A deserter who works out his passage? Quite nice for him, but is it worth while for the country?"

"It might—there's a bare off chance that there may be some kind of push going on—a forlorn hope, you know—a few stout fellows keeping their end up—even Willan conceivably—"

"Ah! the beloved Willan!"

"Just possibly—the merest, flukiest off chance, but still—it would be too frightful to fail them." He made a commonplace gesture of horror, one of those stock oratorical gestures of his that always damaged, in Rose's fretfully critical eyes, any cause in which they were used.

She mused for a minute and then said enigmatically, "Decidement, you're a treasure." Then she mused again.

"Darling, what is it?" he begged.

"I was counting," she said, "the things you would gallantly risk for the 'merest off-chance '—was not that it?—of not dis-appointing a very particular friend. A few thousands of lives—a few weeks of slow torture for this luckless City—a few other things. Happy friend of your youth!"

She mused for a little again. Then she asked suddenly, "Tell me, are all you Cabinet people united?"

"No. There are defeatists—undeclared as yet, but there they are."

"Ha! Dastards in the camp?" said Rose dramatically.

"Grant is ripe to give in, and so is Panmure. And the Bute crowd are working that way."

"But you're game—oh yes!—to the last gasp and ditch and all the last things?"

"Well—" he began, discomforted by her tone.

"Oh! don't mind me," she broke in. "We'll all have a dog's life, of course."

"While the siege lasts? My poor darling, yes."

"No, I mean afterwards—when the Portans have put up the price of a peace, because of their extra weeks' trouble, and when Ria, perhaps, is made a province of Porto—and when your name is down on a Portan black list as the pestilent fellow who set the war going and then spun it out. But never mind me." "You?"

"Oh! I can stick anything now," she said in a tone of dreary fortitude. "I'm not so sure of you, though. You'll feel lost, you know, without your dear old 'opportunities of usefulness.' You've been such a bigwig, you know. There, there—it's time for your Cabinet. Run along now, and be a great hero as usual."

Rose was exhausted, by now, with much standing and walking about, as well as with changeful emotions and manoeuvres. She never could sit still for long when vexed, nor yet when much animated with the excitement of taking means to her ends. But Rose had the artistry to make use of every state of herself, even of her own exhaustion, as a means to those ends: weariness itself became an instrument to work with: she made her lassitude tell.

So it was now. She could not help being tired: her spent voice and sunken spirits, her dead collapse into a chair and the flickering down of her scorn from a tall flame to a spark among ashes—these were quite unfeigned: but when they came in the course of nature she used them as colours to paint the picture she wanted her husband to see.

She did it so well that the picture emerged, for him, with a redoubtable distinctness. It was a kind of moon landscape, showing a world burnt out and gone cold, with all his future and hers to be passed in it now—desolate tracts of years with only the lava of old energies, and perhaps the cinders of used-up love, for both of them to live with; not merely a desert like other deserts, which are only very large patches of waste surrounded by a good world, but a whole charred globe on which the greatest courage and strength might be as null as the best swimmer's powers in the Sahara. The menace was not that of death, which can beckon persuasively to any bold spirit; rather that of an ignoble inanition: it seemed poltroonery to acquiesce in it.

If only that paralysis of every noble family could now be escaped, surely there would come a chance of grander efforts for resolution and pride to put forth than this loathsome business of making slum women and children go on enduring the torments of those days—just for the sake of some phantom, perhaps, of superfine romantic honour.

There is much in the way you put a point, even to yourself. Burnage went off to his Cabinet meeting with quite a resolute air. He would not do anything hasty, but he must certainly keep a free hand.

BOOK FIVE

CHAPTER XXI

S.O.S.

I

During their first four days in Lost Valley, Willan's force received no news from the great world. The day they came they heard a great sound of distant guns, much multiplied and confused by echoes, as thunder is among mountains. The maximum uproar soon quieted down. In an hour the gunfire had ended. So it all sounded as if either one side or the other had been knocked dumb without much ado. But which? "Our fellows have done the trick, I could swear," Lovel-Waters declared, with A face of the deepest anxiety. "You're summing up against the weight of evidence," Merrick replied, with perfect serenity.

Next day but one, the first of the scouts that Willan had sent out, upon his arrival, came back with rumours picked up from peasants living below the valley's precipitous entrance. The main force, it was said, had been smashed in Scout Valley; disordered fragments of it were now tumbling down the Big Slope to the City; the Portan army was moving down too, but it was in steam-roller fashion; slow and enormous, it rolled on in one piece; the Portans were everywhere, and the scout, a good hand, had utterly failed to get into touch with any Rian officer or man.

Were not the country people throughout' the Big Slope rising en masse against the invaders? Lovel-Waters asked the question eagerly. No doubt he had romantic visions of a loyal peasantry arming itself with shot-guns and scythes to protect the sacred soil.

No! the scout had to confess he had seen nothing like that. The country people had seemed to be merely fattening fowls, manuring fields and doing a little early ploughing.

"Materialist curs!" groaned Lovel-Waters.

"Trying to look as if they hadn't noticed anything?" Merrick asked, with the humorous gleam in his eyes.

"There might ha' been a bit o' that, sir." The scout's eyes had a responsive twinkle. "Poor devils!" he may have been thinking, like Merrick, "with their work cut out to keep their houses unburnt and their kiddies unstarved, and their peace to be made, presently, with whoever may win—of course he'll say, whichever he is, that they didn't do those things which they ought to have done in his hour of need." The scout had found at a farm a copy apiece of two Rian papers—one of them The Star of Eve, now three days out of date. An account of the Boat Valley battle, or of its first minutes, was there—wildly, crudely fabricated. "'Lancers thrown out on the left,'" Merrick read aloud, chuckling.

Lovel-Waters was scandalised. "The ruffian!" he exclaimed. "And not a lance nor a horse within thirty miles!"

"But eighty miles off," Merrick said, "there may have been a most healthy demand for cavalry chargers—and so the good trader supplied them."

Lovel-Waters had taken up the other paper. "Good lord!" he said. "Here's filth! 'Enemy poisoning wells'; 'Murdering the wounded.'" Lovel-Waters dropped the Star of Eve on the floor and went out of the little whitewashed parlour as if he had to be sick.

Willan and Merrick looked at each other when he was gone. "Born a bit too late," said Merrick. "Bad times, these, for fellows with the gentleman heresy. They shouldn't read papers in war-time." He looked at Willan rather quizzingly. "I s'pose," he said, "these Portans are all right."

"'Course they are," said Willan. "All whites are all right—when they fight. It's only the looking on' that they can't do like sportsmen. Just the same in big boxing—the crowd keeps on squealing for fouls while the men in the ring are holding their tongues right enough. What's that rag that has the muck? Not the Voice, I bet."

"Sorry to say—" Merrick showed him the title of the paper.

"Oh! Burnage must have been off for the night. Some dud was in charge. That will be it."

"Not a doubt of it," said Merrick gravely.

"There's another thing," said Willan. "All these editor men may have put their heads together and said it's a very special case this, and the best thing to do, just for once, is to dish out this bilge to the crowd, just as a tonic—sort of rum ration, you know—not regular food. You see, the whole City may have to stick shelling now—starving too—and of course they're not trained up to stick that sort of thing as troops are, and the editor people may have a pretty good notion we're somewhere about and they're trying their damnedest to give us the time to refit, and they may honestly think the only plan is to keep the civilians foaming hard at the mouth the whole of the time, lest they crack up if they stop it That will be it."

"Yes," said Merrick, with laudable gravity; "that will be it, sure enough."

II

They had no wireless, no means of using the air; they were almost as utterly cast away and cut off as a legion severed from a Roman army in an Alpine battle and lying up for safety at the head of some recondite valley under the snows of a Weisshorn or Mont Blanc. So one of Willan's first aims was to tell the Commander-in-Chief where they were; and how soon they could chip in again, at his orders. Two or more scouts were sent out every day to try to get through. A few of them came back, baffled by the ubiquity of the enemy and the watchfulness of his pickets. The rest just vanished. No message ever came in; among the country people of the Big Slope there seemed to be no rumour of the survival of any part of Main's force except its runaways; it had to be presumed that all the missing were written off as dead or prisoners. That made it all the more urgent that General Miln should be told that the picked and tried little force, so wonderfully hidden in ambush by a train of accidents, would soon be ready to rush out and help him wherever he bade. To know that this column was being prepared at top speed for his use would warm the General's heart; it would help him to keep up the spirit of everyone.

After one or two attempts to write his own despatches, Willan fell back on the literary genius of Lovel-Waters. For this he had a deep respect. He told Lovel-Waters the mere skeleton of fact which he wished to convey, and Lovel-Waters—added to the Staff pro tem—ennobled the conveyance; he took infinite pains to strike the right note in these compositions—calm, virile, modest, but also ringing and rousing—such as would figure well in a great soldier's biography after his death. When Merrick read one of them, he would sometimes move his lips as if he were saying "Pshaw," but Willan thought them fine, and resolved that Lovel-Waters should get his due when the war had been won. Like many men of the sword, Willan carried pretty far an innocent faith in the mightiness of the pen.

At the same time he had to confess to himself that Lovel-Waters' exalted strain of knightliness was a little difficult to live up to. Every day the muscles of Lovel's handsome regular face were drawn more taut with chivalric determination and his eyes became more restless with impatience. So fiery an ardour for the essentials of self-sacrifice seemed almost to rebuke the cheerful preoccupation of Willan and Merrick with the taking of mere plodding means to concrete ends. Nearly all the talk of these two was about such prosaic affairs as the number of hours and minutes which might be saved on every hundred pairs of boots by omitting the loop at the back of each boot for pulling it on; why not let the men lug on their boots anyhow? They would spend hours, too, in feeling the new boots all over, on the men's feet, to make sure that none of them would blister the skin and make men fall out on the march. The specialist in moral sublimity was visibly chafed by these small practicalities. Bellona, goddess of war, meet bride for hero or king, seemed to be let down a little in his sight by taking into her service such homely handmaidens.

III

There were plenty of false starts for hope—a belated footfall at night on the stones of the village street; or one of the passing aircraft that sent all hands flying to cover would seem for a while to have more of a pulse in its hum, a less continuous and even drone, than the Portan machines; or the telescope that they kept trained by day on the lower end of Lost Valley would show in the morning a black speck slowly traversing a bleached expanse of old moraine near the valley's mouth.

But the step would be only some belated Orderly Sergeant's; the plane, when seen overhead, would be gaudy with the Portan yellow and green; and in the evening the speck would arrive and be only a villager back from the outer world and bringing rustic rumours of a tightening siege of the City—how its people were starving to death and its buildings crumbling away under the ceaseless leisurely fire of two immensely distant and invulnerable Portan guns.

How long could people softened by all the circumstantial comforts and conveniences of city life, as well as its unhealthiness for body and soul, be expected to endure that collar of iron with spikes pointing in on the neck? "No time at all," was the answer visible in Lovel-Waters' face after each dose of agonizing rumour; he almost writhed with his craving to let the boot-making go hang and rush at the enemy bare-footed, ineffectual, hopeless, but an inspiring spectacle for men and gods. On these occasions Willan and Merrick would leave him striding in anguish up and down the little whitewashed room that served as their headquarters; they would go off to wheedle yet another hour of overtime work out of the weary villagers who were making boots against the clock: these all worked together in a big schoolroom, while the village women knitted socks at home for the hundreds of men whose shoddy army socks were now nothing but uppers.

"Gie's a bit song, then," a tired bootmaker had said at one of these times, and since that day Willan and Merrick had sung, in the last hours of each working day in the factory, every comic song, drinking song, school song, war song, love song, ballad or hymn that they could remember. As long as anyone sang, the men would make boots, though bleared almost to blindness with the smoky twilight of rude candles and wood fires that they worked in. Then Merrick searched the whole force for singers, till a shining galaxy of talent was organised to keep the thing going from sunset to the unholy hour when awl and needle were downed for the night.

IV

At the end of a fortnight the longed-for bearer of real, official news walked nonchalantly, although lamely, in. He was one Thorney, a subaltern whom a wound in the Great War had left limping for life and condemned to a War Office career except at such ravishing opportunities as this.

Thorney hobbled in on the morning when Sprott tried to steal food and when Rose let the man die. He had taken one whole night to cut and wriggle his way, foot by foot, through the enemy's cordon of barbed wire round the city, without perturbing the enemy sentries a few yards off on each side of him.

Then it had taken nearly a week of travel and research to find out that Lost Valley held an interesting secret and to make his way into it and up it. A much-travelled Rian pedlar, drunk "find babbling in a rustic wine-shop, had given Thorney the invaluable tip.

Willan knew Thorney so well, and they liked each other so much, that their meeting in the village street had to be a demonstration of British phlegm. They did shake hands, but they both looked rather shamefaced about this excess of emotionalism. "You, is it?" said Willan.

"Some one had to come, it seemed," said Thorney, stiffly on his defence against any imputation of courage.

"Quite a good thing to do," said Willan, as though in acquittal, not praise. Thorney was manifestly reassured.

They entered the little whitewashed room. Thorney was introduced to Merrick and given a meal. Then Willan enquired "How's all below?"

"Stuffy, sir. Glad to be out of it. Stuffy things, sieges."

"Proper siege, is it?"

"In a way—yes. Lots of food when I left. No real shellin'—not to write home about. Sort of a siege."

Willan digested this. He had to reckon the proper discount. It was Thorney spoke next. "So there's a few of you left, sir?"

"A few?" said Merrick. "We're near a cool thousand."

"Prize men, too," Willan said.

"We're the winner of the One Thousand," said Merrick.

"And now we're hot stuff for the Oaks."

"We slipped up in Scout Valley?" Willan enquired.

"We ran. Talk about Derby winners!"

"You? You jobbed yourself into that push?"

"I was sorry I had. I hadn't the turn of speed, with this knee; for retreatin' like that—but the spirit was willin', all right."

"What happened?—to you, I mean."

"I was in luck. Every man that wasn't a rabbit seemed to be somewhere close round me. They all got together—made quite a decent hard lump. The Portans kind of split when they came on it—same as water does at a bridge—flows past on each side of a pier—then they closed in again below. The whole blessed battle went past us, right out of sight, and it never came back. We didn't ask it to. We drew our fellows off to one side of the valley—"

"Same here," Willan said.

"Then we waited till dark and sneaked off, down the south aisle "

"Same here," said Willan.

"We didn't bolt, sir, if you understand. It was too dark. But we were good free movers."

"Same here," Willan repeated.

"We had such a burst of speed," said Thorney, "that we slipped clean past the Portans that night and never knew it till next morning. They must have stretched down for a sleep in the fairway without a jack-light to show where they were."

"Seems to be their habit. While they did it, after our scrap, we got over a bit of a wall, into this place."

"We scuttled along under our wall, and out by the way we came in. We'd have done better time if our boots had been leather and not blotting-paper."

"Blot was the only wear in this army," said Merrick. "That's why we're stuck up here. We came in on the bare hoof, but now we're shoeing 'em fast."

"How long d'you think they'll stick it out, down there? A week?" Willan asked.

"A lot more, sir, than that."

"Then we'll raise that siege," said Willan tranquilly.

Thorney looked surprised. "There are a lot of Portans, sir," he said.

"How many," Willan asked, "besieging?"

"Fifty thousand, we guessed."

"That's evens, then, exactly. We've shed our 98 per cent of rabbits. They've got theirs; so you have to deduct 'em."

"Seems logical," said Thorney dubiously. "Any artillery, sir?"

"One nice little cannon," said Merrick, "just to hang on our watch-chain. What have they got?"

"Only two that matter. Two high-velocity beasts—miles out of our range."

Willan turned to Merrick. "As you thought. We'll have to rush those first. It ought to be easy enough, with them trusting us not to exist." He turned to Thorney again, "Did none of my runners ever get through?"

"Devil a man, sir, up to when I left. Of course, that was a whole week ago. Hullo! Hullo!"

As Thorney uttered the exclamation, his face came about as near as his habits and ideals permitted to a look of downright amazement. He walked towards the window, stooping and looking upward as he went, evidently trying to keep in view some Unexpected object high in the air.

The eyes of Willan and Merrick turned instinctively in the same direction as Thorney's. What they saw was a thoroughly old-fashioned balloon of the era before the Great War and the whole modern history of warfare in the air.

The wind had just veered from North-West to due West. It had also freshened; and now it was hurrying the helpless pear-shaped bladder along a course directly over Lost Valley—hustling it with pettish little pushes that left the car swinging out to the rear of the shambling gas-bag above.

"Golly!" said Willan. "The thing's coming down!"

"'Well, 'ere's a element crep' in,'" Merrick quoted from some old play seen in London.

V

Coming down the thing certainly was, in a sense—or the earth was coming up to it. For it had clearly reached the full height that it could rise above the sea's level. Equally clearly, this height was less than that of the central mountain chain towards which it was being so truculently driven. If the balloon pursued its career its only prospect in life was a grand smash against the head of Lost Valley.

A few seconds more made it plain that this smiling future was sufficiently understood by the pilot. He was trying his best to get down. Even at the risk of a bad landing the balloon was now sloping earthward still more steeply than the earth sloped up to meet the balloon, and already a rope with a grappling iron at its lower end was lengthening out briskly under the car. On a flatfish stretch of meadow, half a mile below the village, the car took the ground with little ceremony; two men jumped out on the grass or were poured forth upon it; the great booby gasbag, relieved of their weight, tried to soar again, and the two men clung hard to its cordage, to hold it down to the earth.

All Willan's men had taken cover, at a whistle from the look-out man, the moment the apparition appeared. The heavily garrisoned village had assumed in a few seconds an air of pastoral innocence. A shot in a rabbit-warren does not produce a more convincing appearance of depopulation. Another whistled signal now assembled the entire force, by way of practice for emergencies, and a platoon was sent off at the double to make the balloon secure and bring the two men up to the Commander.

VI

"Two civilians, sir, from Ria City," was the excited young platoon commander's introduction of these tremendous arrivals to Willan. Merrick, Thorney, and Lovel-Waters were with Willan in the whitewashed room.

"Glad to meet you, gentlemen," said Willan in a way that made the pilot a sworn friend from the first. He looked like a skilled mechanic of the kind that has quick brains, character, natural courtesy, skill at his job, knowledge of the world, the power of getting things done by men and machines—everything but a complete education in youth and a few traits and tricks of gentility.

The other visitor simply superseded the Major's opening of the conversation with one of his own. "My name," he began, "is Hendie. You may remember it as that of the musical critic of the Voice."

Willan could not say that he did. But he would not say that he didn't. So he said, "Roughish journey, I fear."

Hendie eyed him correctively. "I assure you," Hendie said gravely, "it needs some effort even to frame an idea of the roughness of such journeys. First, the abominable sense of the earth's subtraction from under you. Then the jostling, jarring mob of crude sensations for the body. Also, for the mind, the importunate and debasing obsession of the thought of the coarse victory that any random bullet might gain over one's animal life—itself the basic condition of any high achievement of mind or will. And then the brutal abruptness of the descent."

"Well, you're safe now," said Willan. He turned to the pilot. "I congratulate you," he said. "I don't know the air, but it struck me you got your ship and your passenger very neatly out of a hell of a fix."

There were subdued or inarticulate sounds of concurrence from Merrick, Lovel-Waters and Thorney.

Hendie went straight on from the last word that Willan had addressed to himself. "Safe for the moment—yes. But this place, I gather, is not near the frontier of any neutral State."

"You're for the frontier, are you?" Lovel-Waters asked. His eyes had begun to shine with disdain.

"Till civilisation revives on this side of it." Hendie's dour gloom was shot with an answering flash of angry scorn.

"Frankly, it's years since I lost any taste I may ever have had for this insane racket."

Lovel-Waters had to practise self-control. For Willan. wen on: "A private journey? You bring no dispatch, then?"

"Do you command," Hendie asked, "a Rian force of any description?"

"I do."

"Then you are qualified, I suppose, to relieve me of this." Hendie searched his pockets till he found a dirty little ball of rolled-up paper. "My carrying this," he said, with some distaste, "was a condition of my having leave to depart. You know what these officials are." He handed the grimy object to Willan. "It was dirtied, I gathered, to disarm suspicion if I fell into the enemy's hands. A transparent subterfuge."

Willan had smoothed out the paper. "A new cipher, to me," he said, almost at once. "Was any verbal message given you? Anything about a key?"

Hendie seemed to rummage half-heartedly among recollections of little interest. "There was something," he said, "that I was to tell you."

Lovel-Waters could bear it no longer. "Good God, sir," he exclaimed. "A message your country's life may depend on!"

Hendie eyed him loftily. Lovel-Waters was clearly negligible in his sight. And yet Lovel-Waters' contemned intervention distracted Hendie in some little degree: it made his faint attempt to remember even more hopeless.

"Never mind," said Willan. "No ciphered message takes half an hour to read, key or no key. Will you excuse us," he said to the pilot and Hendie, "for leaving you for a little? Sorry we've nothing to drink or to smoke, but I hope you'll take luncheon, such as it is." He indicated a modest provision of bread, cheese, butter and milk set out on the bare end of the big kitchen table and told an orderly to bring a second plate and knife.

Hendie bowed coldly in acceptance, and the three soldiers went out to do their work in peace. When they were gone, Hendie sat down to the offered creature comforts without more ado.

The pilot watched him in wonder. Only when Hendie was unmistakably addressing himself to the cheese did the man find words. "You mean,", he said, "to wolf his rations!"

"Do you really hope," said Hendie, "to find any entertainment more to your mind?"

"I do," the pilot said, and went out to try to buy bread from some peasant.

Hendie ate on pensively. When satisfied he took a cigarette-case from his pocket, and began to smoke and to retire still further into the intelligent gloom of his thoughts.

VII

Lovel-Waters did little more than paw the ground with spirited impatience, like a noble horse, while Willan, Merrick and Thorney deciphered the dispatch. It was not a difficult feat. The letters of the alphabet occur, in every language, in a certain order of relative frequency. So you have only to count the number of times that each letter of the cipher appears in a cipher dispatch, and then a little elementary arithmetic will give you the dispatch in plain English. But the low cunning of ciphers had never interested Lovel-Waters; nor was plodding arithmetic his strong suit. So he only radiated martial virility of the best quality while Willan and Merrick minded the P's, Q's and other letters, and Thorney put down figures at their dictation.

The product of half an hour of humdrum mathematics was an urgent appeal from General Miln to the officer in command of any Rian troops still in the field. Written only three hours before, it said that during the past week the situation in Ria City had changed for the worse.

"About since Thorney left," said Merrick.

"That's right," said Willan. "That's how Thorney's so chirpy."

The dispatch requested that any force still in arms should make the earliest possible push to raise the siege of the City. Any attempt would be seconded, with the utmost vigour, by the whole force of the garrison. The prospect of success for any such simultaneous movements would, of course, be much increased if previous word could be sent to General Miln of some unmistakable signal, not intelligible to the enemy, by which the moment of the relieving force's attack on the enemy's lines would be announced to the Commander-in-Chief. The moral of the troops in the city was excellent. But in other respects the situation was critical. That closed the dispatch. Willan read it aloud to his Staff.

"That means the civilians are cracking," said Thorney.

"Not certain," Willan mildly demurred. "Anyhow, we'll soon know."

Lovel-Waters jumped up, with his eyes all alight. "Are we starting to-day?" he asked eagerly.

Willan turned to Merrick. "Think we can push off," he asked, "by daylight to-morrow?"

Merrick reckoned aloud. "The boot men started work at six this morning, with two and a half days' work to be done. That's counting ten hours' work to the day."

Willan considered it. "If they'd work twenty-four hours on end," he then said, "and spurt all the last lap, we could do it. Think you could drive 'em that hard?"

Merrick turned to Thorney, smiling. "I hope you sing a good song?" he enquired.

Thorney stared.

"The boot men will work just as long as they're sung to," Willan explained.

"I can't sing for nuts," Thorney said, "but I'll raise some old wheeze."

"That's four hours' overtime, sir, as I figure it," Merrick reported to the commander. "Now then, Lovel, out with that concertina you're hiding. It's new talent we want."

Lovel-Waters looked embarrassed. "I used," he said, "to caw a few little French things, ages ago." He owned it as truthful men own, when put on their oath, the secret sins of their youth.

"Four hours more, sir," Merrick reported. Willan and he turned on Lovel-Waters the kind of looks that seal friendships.

Thorney nodded towards the room they had left. "What about that beauty," he asked, "that's pouching your grub, sir? Didn't he say he was messed up with music in some way?" Merrick had apparently forgotten Hendie. "That's good enough, sir," he made final report to the commander. "We'll find him a job. Ready to march out at six in the morning, sir."

CHAPTER XXII

ORPHEUS WITH HIS LUTE MADE BOOTS

I

So the musical part of the plan of campaign was assured. And now about that signal. No known mode of signalling in war would do: the enemy would see at once that there were Rian soldiers where, by their calculations, no Rian soldiers should be. Here was a perplexity for the council of war.

For some minutes they racked their brains silently. Then Willan somehow perceived or divined that nothing but diffidence was keeping Seaton from speech. "Any brain wave from the Universal Provider?" Willan asked him invitingly.

"There's a thing, sir," said Seaton, "that might be of use. A thing people do—peasant people, you know—on the Big Slope, on the evenings of a few Saints' days each year. When it's dark they put up a big crucifix, thirty or forty feet high—kind of a sky sign, worked out in lamps, for people down in the City to see, miles away. Some rustic Catholic notion, I fancy—saving the souls, you know, of the godless townspeople. They show the thing for a while, and screen it; then they show it again. They go on like that for an hour. Nobody takes any notice, it's such an old stunt—and the Portans would notice less than the Rians, because the thing is done even more in Porto than here. I know where they keep all the plant. And there's no light-up day for a fortnight to come. How'd it be, sir, to rig up the thing for a signal this week?"

Willan had listened carefully, with an encouraging nod now and then. "I only see one possible jar," he said when Seaton had done. "Mightn't the enemy know that the real thing isn't due for a fortnight?"

No. Seaton felt sure of that. Pretty well every day of the year was some Saint's special day. The choice among them varied each year, according to a sort of rota. Seaton let out shyly, by degrees, that just before the war he got from a village, priest the list for this year: he had a private hobby, he owned, of studying the native Rian customs.

"You're sure," Merrick asked, "the lads of the village won't keep the holy things from us."

"The old priest will see us through that," Seaton assured them. "He'll let us have all the tackle as soon as he knows what it's for. He's a good Rian all right."

"That's good enough," Willan decided.

II

The next thing was how to get word through to General Miln in the City. Willan had never ceased trying for this: now it had to be done; for only a simultaneous rally from the City could give the attack a fair chance.

As to the proper dodge Merrick was found to have the strongest opinion. All his few days of peace-time in Ria he had lived at a place on the Big Slope a few miles out of the City, close to where the Portan line now ran and also close to the river that came down from Scout Valley and flowed right across the Portan lines and through the City. Merrick had bathed, he declared, in every square yard of the stream, in those parts; he asserted that it was rubbish to call it a torrent; it only went a bit fast; and he was sure he could get down it under the noses of the Portan sentries, floating and swimming with his head done up in a big ragged bundle of drift grass or weed. "Easy as anything," Merrick affirmed.

Willan demurred. First, he couldn't have his Chief of Staff off duty, bathing, during active operations. Merrick was ready for that. Here was Thorney, he said, game to take over at once—"most top-hole Brass Hat since Hannibal; man who won the World War by sheer Staff-work."

"Besides," Willan resumed, "you'd not have an earthly. The head-in-the-bundle-of-hay trick is the oldest in civilised warfare. Every sentry on the globe is watching for bundles of hay. You'd be gaffed like a salmon, at sight—they'd land you with a boat-hook through your ear."

Merrick had lots of good answers ready. The river, he argued, wasn't the sort of one the enemy would suspect very much. Not a bathing river really, in the morning early, when its little head streams had been frozen all night, it wasn't much more than a lot of dry stones in a ravine; and in the afternoon there was a bit of spate from the day's melt of snow. So the Portans wouldn't think the game was on.

"In other words—it isn't," Willan said.

"Just a matter of choosing your time, sir," Merrick persisted.

Willan was silent for a little. Merrick persuasively added a last plea; "I'll be no loss to the singing strength, sir. My voice has gone phut."

Willan went on thinking. Merrick would be killed: five to one, the torrent of melted snow and ice would drown him or bash his head against a big stone, if he were not shot first. But Merrick said he knew the place—that meant he did know it; and no other chance of getting the plan through to Miln was in sight. To send other men to a pretty well assured death is the every-day work of commanders in war. Few of them like it. They like it none the better when the man they send to the abattoir is a friend whom they are coming to love; nor does it help when the man's life seems to stand between the commander himself and a woman who keeps him passionately in mind of every look and movement of hers that he has seen. But Miln must be told. And Merrick's going was the only visible hope! Willan could not see it otherwise. "How soon," he asked Merrick in a rough voice, "can you start?"

"Will twenty minutes do, sir?"

"Good." Willan began to write his answer to the appeal of the beleaguered garrison. This time he did not trouble Lovel-Waters. He wanted the thing short and plain—just to say what strength he commanded; that all ranks were in great health and spirits, and also had boots; that he was starting at six the next morning and ought to be outside the enemy's lines within five days, and that he would put up the fiery cross exactly two hours before he attacked. Willan did not put the dispatch into cipher: ciphers were childish; any one could read them; Merrick would eat the dispatch and chew it small too, if death or capture were imminent.

In the whole of Lost Valley there was but one horse, and he no great thing, though he bore the name of Ladas, so honoured on the windy plains of Epsom and of Troy. In infancy Ladas had been slung up with infinite trouble into the valley, in a large canvas bag, and the effort had not been thought worth repeating. But Ladas went down the valley to-day bearing not Merrick alone, in his peasant clothes, but all the hopes of Willan's force for support in their audacious venture. Ladas would save Merrick four of the nine hours he would have taken to walk down to the valley's mouth. Four hours—it might be the making of victory.

III

Merrick was just gone, and everything was seeming surprisingly flat, when Willan went back to the room where Hendie was still smoking and brooding dourly over a spitting fire of damp logs. Willan got down to business. Hendie must have information to give, and information wins more wars than musketry. Would Hendie, he asked, mind telling him—just from Hendie's own point of view—how the City was standing the siege?

Hendie looked up from the fire, his eyes alight with a flame of their own; it shone through gloom. Perhaps the question had hit on the very thought that was filling him then. "It's tragic," he said. "Stale word, of course, but there is no other word for it all. Perhaps you know the look of life in that city, in summer. A ripple used to break out at twilight, all over it. People rested and played; they came to be their human selves again. You remember the voices under the trees where the lamps swing among the acacias?"

"Yes," said Willan.

"Other voices and fresh little noises coming up from the lake—little noises plashing and tinkling like fountains—they could have almost laid dust—they must have been cool on the faces of women stooping and flitting across the pavement from cars to the theatre doors."

The queer fellow spoke tenderly, as men surprised by the sudden coming on of age think of their lost youth. Willan was rather softened. "Not many theatres now, I suppose?" he said, a little ruefully. "How could there be?" Hendie said bitterly. "You know how a lot of minds work—my country is in danger; so I must starve my brain and my heart and everyone else's. The enemy is at the gate; so let us live like brute beasts. The siege-had not lasted a week before half the theatres dosed."

"Oh! that's awful," Willan said soothingly. "No big music either, I suppose?"

"If you'll believe me,"—Hendie's voice was morosely incisive—"there has been none worth that"—he snapped his fingers in scorn—"for three weeks."

For some moments Willan considered this horror of war. No, he hadn't thought of that. And there was something in it. Gad! a war must give a hell of a time to a lot of people who get nothing by it—not even a stir in their blood. Lovel-Waters looked in while Willan was thinking. Lovel was turning to go, when Willan called him back, and Lovel sat down to his separate table and map, but could not take his eyes from the abhorred defeatist.

'"And what's the 'general public' saying?" Willan asked. "I don't quite know what it is, but I seem to have heard of it."

"The only branch of the public I know is the civilised one. Its mind, I should say, is made up to put an end to these degrading losses."

Lovel-Waters was staring. "May I ask," he said with grim restraint, "what are the civilian losses, to date?"

"The losses!" Hendie made a gesture suggestive of infinity.

"How many killed?" Lovel-Waters insisted austerely. "How many wounded?"

The austerity of. Hendie's tone outdid that of the romantic's. "Are we not all somewhere prone," Hendie said, "to make too much of the commonplace act of dying—the only thing that absolutely everybody does? The losses I referred to are less common and more ghastly—the mutilation and the stunting of all people's minds."

"Mean to say women go mad, and so on?" Lovel-Waters demanded.

"There again!" said Hendie reprovingly. "What, after all, are a few of the cases of cerebral lesion, etc., that doctors diagnose as insanity, compared with the universal atrophy of mind that sets in as soon as a civilised city is brought to this state of mental starvation?"

"More frightful, no doubt," said Lovel-Waters, with the most scathing frigidity he could muster, "than wearing a nice little, neat, becoming white feather?"

But there was no withering Hendie. He glanced at the badges and ribbons on Lovel-Waters' uniform. "If you bring up questions of plumage," he said, "I must confess that we poor civilians are quite out of court."

Lovel-Waters eyed the alien creature up and down, as if seeking some point on his person at which a sense of shame could be injected with a suitable needle. Hendie waited a few moments in silence, ready to parry any further thrust from that quarter. None coming, he turned to Willan, "The matter I forgot just now—" he began.

Willan pricked his ears eagerly. "The message," he asked, "from the Commander-in-Chief?"

"I gathered so. A man with prominent eyes. A little undistinguished-looking." Perhaps the face of Lovel-Waters showed some distaste for this summary sketch. For Hendie added, "Oh! I've no doubt that he's the most worthy of men."

"But the message?" Willan pressed.

"Yes. It has just come back to my mind. It was by way of a warning—possibly needless, but that is for you to judge. It was a warning against making any attempt to get messengers into the City by a particular route."

"Which route? Speak quickly, please!" Willan's voice had gone off as if Hendie's last words had pressed a trigger.

Even Hendie brisked up. "By swimming or wading down the Scout River."

Willan's cane lay within reach. Almost before Hendie's last word was out, Willan snatched up the cane and gave the rough deal table a violent lash. The supple thing licked along the bare wood with a smashing noise. Hendie jumped in his chair.

"I beg your pardon," said Willan. "My call for an orderly. If you will go on, sir, as fast as you can, you may just save the life of a very fine man."

Hendie rose to it now. The garrison's scouts had found out that the enemy guarded the river and its banks with extraordinary care. Many strands of barbed-wire had been fastened across it, above water and under, besides strings of scythes, tied end to end, with their edges up-stream. "The surest trap ever set—these were the words," Hendie said.

An orderly stood in the door and saluted. "How far has Captain Merrick got?" Willan asked. "Look at once with the telescope."

"Been lookin' all the time, sir. Six mile, good." The man beamed, happy to bring in good news, as he thought. "Seen 'im this moment, sir, toppin' the Wavin' Arm Ridge, sir. 'E won't be seen no more 'enceforward, sir."

"Going fast?"

"Won'erful well. A local Derby 'orse, that little Ladas, sir. Ridden a treat, too, sir."

Willan nodded and the man saluted and went out. No over-taking Merrick now. No hope now, bar miracles, that Miln would know they were approaching, and come out to help. Well, they must go through with it all—the furtive forced march, the attack, the signal of fire—precisely as if old Merrick were sure to get through.

Lovel-Waters was looking at Hendie ferociously. "Feckless, egoistic devil!"—the unuttered comment was in Lovel-Waters' face—"And a brave man must bleed to death under water because of that swine! Had to get his snout into the trough for an hour before he'd remember his errand! "

Seaton looked at Hendie, too, but not ferociously. Probably he had lost, for the time, the power of finding a subtle pleasure in bringing in verdicts of guilty.

Willan was sorry and nothing but sorry—for this poor little army of his, with' its diminished chance—and for Merrick, the friend to be lost almost as soon as gained—and for Clare, so soon to lose her lovable lover—and Burnage, left to stand out unrelieved to the last, as he certainly would. Willan scarcely thought about Hendie at all. People with ways of their own, people who can't remember a message or take a means to an end—these were everywhere: they were part of the order of nature, as rain is. But he was sorry.

They had sat silent since the orderly's exit, each of them entrenched, for the moment, behind his own barbed wire of secret anger repentance or grief. As they sat so, trying to work, there came7from the school-room, not far away, the sound of a good many voices plunging, more or less together, into the dour and sturdy tune:

A safe stronghold our God is still,
A mighty shield and weapon;
He'll guard us free from all the ill
That our days may happen.
Hendie groaned "Good God!"

"Sir!" said Lovel-Waters, bristling up.

"The raggedness of the attack!" said Hendie, in sorrow.

"Could no one show them how?"

"Merrick tried," Willan thought, without saying it. That made the ragged singing lovely and poignant to Willan's ears now. And yet Hendie was probably right, in a way. Queer things, these arts! A bit of music might only seem dreadfully bad to the wise, though it could fill common men with joy and devotion, fire and strength. Oh, everyone was right, it seemed—only in different ways: nothing was wrong that anyone felt or believed with all' his heart. Merrick, the genial sceptic, had said so, and everything Merrick had said was now becoming strangely valid.

IV

"Beggy pardon, sir; I thought I'd better wake you."

"Hullo, Sergeant! What o'clock?" Willan half-rose from the hay, rubbing his sleep-filled eyes. "All correct?"

"It's two a.m., sir, very near. An' all c'rect, sir, only the men that's on the boots is gettin' very tired, sir, an' the civilian gentlemen 'as come in by balloon 'as got the fiddle out, sir, what we found in the cupboard. 'E's makin' 'em cry. I thought I'd better tell you, sir."

Willan jumped up. He had been in the boot-making room until midnight, running the sing-song, with Seaton to help him. Then Lovel-Waters and Thorney had taken over the job, and Wiilan was to be awakened at four, to take charge again during the last two hours' work of all, as it was hoped they might be. By four the boot men would be pretty well dead-beat and might need a bit of riding to the finish. Had that crisis come already? Willan wondered, as he turned out from the barn's warm luxury into the shrewd, hardy cold of the small hours. There was no frost, but the air had the noble astringency of mountains. Few stars could be seen, for many clouds were beating about in the sky: the clouds seemed to be thickening and first one separate drop of rain and then another were flung in Willan's face by a gusty little night-wandering wind. Good! he thought; let it rain furiously, let it flood the river to twice its right depth; then it might conceivably carry Merrick clean over the barbs and the scythes, to safety and honour and happy love, and a triumph for Cyril and fairness and right, and good days for them all.

It was a different air in the school-room. Dwellers in mountains usually look upon warmth as a species of absolute wealth, like coined money or cows: they do not lightly throw it away. Every window was shut; the panes sweated with beads of foul dampness; the used air stank and the flames of the more distant candles bristled with spiky rays that stuck out glisteningly into the fetid mist. Through this fog of old breath Willan could just see a figure in silhouette at the far end of the room. The figure was pedestailed on a wooden box, and it had the ancient and beautiful pose of a fiddler just about to play.

Yes, Hendie, re-tuning the valley's one fiddle, an old and a rather good one. With it one of the valley's first settlers was said to have haled the souls of his fellows almost out of their bodies by playing old tunes of a night, when the day's work of the exiles was over. And then Hendie played: Heaven knows what he played: Willan certainly didn't; it simply was music to him, in his ignorance—not any particular work of an artist turning some special joy or burden of his into beauty, but music, any music, all music, the mystery that, if you can give yourself to it, will lend you powers which never were yours and let your blind heart see and your lame mind run for as long as the fugitive miracle lasts.

Up the long slopes of heavenly sound Willan was drawn, through trances of unwontedly full comprehension. He could understand anything now, anything—all that was worth having and doing and being, for this short outing a man has on the earth, so oddly short as compared with the time all these things have gone on without him and soon will be going on without him again. Old confusions ran themselves clear in his head; life smoothed itself out.

It felt strange at first, that everyone else in the room was so quiet—surely it could only be with an effort that they, like him, held themselves in—that they did not leap up and cheer and shake hands like people moved by a sudden sense of good fortune. Then, almost at once, he knew better. Why, of course, the bent heads and steady hastening hands knew what they were doing—were stirred as deeply as he, but were turning their passion's heat into force; from that rushing blast of high emotion they were drawing a means for their cramped fingers and bleared eyes to endure beyond the common power of men. What fellows they were!

And what a fellow this Hendie! Into the gloomy face of soiled parchment there had come dreamy ecstasy. Through the chin that pressed dotingly down on the violin Hendie seemed to be feeling, as through an umbilical cord, the beat of some greater heart than his own. Cranky, morose, cantankerous, he had the keys of enchanted gardens as well as the run of those queer deserts of salt bitterness— would flout and grouse and sneer at you all day and then stay out of bed all the night to bewitch you into joyous fortitude. Through the forest Willan could see Lovel-Waters listening, framed in a doorway, his eyes a-swim with visions. When the piece ended, Lovel came over, with rather a fine frank abdication of anger, to thank the fiddler, in his own tall, formal way, for "giving us all so noble a pleasure."

Then Willan must sing, to give Hendie a breather. He sang often during the next two hours; he sang almost every song that had ever moved him enough to stick in his head. Most of them were rankly sentimental; so critical people would say. Willan had lived out of doors in the main; most of his exertions had been physical; and it is only indoors that you become a true hanging judge of popular sentiment in the arts. He sang the much-sung boating song of his old school; its commonplace words never failed to bring him an almost physical scent of cut hay lying in wide water meadows under the sun—that and the redolence of tremendous friendship sealed in youth. And then—

Speed, bonnie boat, like a bird on the wing,
Over the sea to Skye,

which had caused him an unforgettable jump in his heart when first he heard it; he had almost wondered how a thing that meant so much to him could have been going about for so long and he not know. And a song that his mother had sung and that he had liked, partly for that and partly because its words had always seemed to him to be sensible as well as moving—unlike a lot of songs in which people made a great fuss about their own death, as if the world ought to stand still from that great date

ONWARD.
WHEN I AM DEAD, MY DEAREST,
SING NO SAD SONGS FOR ME.
BE THE GREEN GRASS ABOVE ME
WITH SHOWERS AND DEW-DROP WET,
AND IF THOU WILT, REMEMBER,
AND IF THOU WILT, FORGET.

Then Lovel-Waters did his endeavour stoutly, in a falsetto voice queerly remote from the robust virile show of the visible man; queerly touching too, seeming like a survival from some past stage of himself— a lost youth of hothouse freaks and delicacies of delight and melancholy, grace and containment, the very filigree carving of artifice in emotion. Probably he was half ashamed of them now, but it was all he had to offer to the cause and he went through with it; he, disinterred his own nonage's fond performance of "Malbrouck s'en va-t'en guerre"; and then it was—

Dormez, dormez, ma belle,
Dormez toujours,

and

Qu'as tu fait, toi que voilk Pleurant sans cesse,
Qu'as tu fait, toi que voila De ta jeunesse?

and

La vie est vaine:
Un peu d'amour, .
Un peu de haine Et puis—bonjour.
La vie est breve Un peu d'espoir,
Un peu de reve Et puis—bonsoir.

Queer words, think you, to hearten up tired cobblers? But, somehow, they served. The toiling men never applauded; their hands were too busy to clap; even their mouths were at work, holding thread, needles or nails. They sang no choruses now, for the same reason. But they worked on, grimly and incessantly; that was their response.

As the night wore through, the rain grew heavy; it pattered hard on the roof; big drops showed as they spilt themselves on the skylight above Willan's head with a low petulant sound. It delighted him: it was hope for Merrick: besides, it cheered the mind somehow, as midwinter gales make fires burn better. The rough outer weather quickened his inner tumult of glee at being in at the heart of a great and secret endeavour, immensely worth making. No more, now, of his old fear lest he be living quite worthlessly, always chasing the most intense pleasure he knew and making out to himself that this was a good enough life for a man.

Hendie was playing again—more wondrously, it seemed to Willan, than ever. Everything was intensifying itself: the foul mist was growing thicker, the rain more furious, the men's white faces more visibly strained and exhausted; and yet the men were working faster and faster, the needles flying and the hammers tapping at an incredible speed while the tender urgency of the music pressed up and up to its summit of beauty as a spire aspires of its tip. But the lovely thing had to end, and it left Hendie, too, almost done; he was nervous and grim and looked morosely out over the room. "Here's yout crisis," he grunted to Willan. "Better tip 'em a hymn—only damn thing they like, really." He spoke as in sombre scorn of so savage a taste.

Willan hastily ran over in his mind such few hymns as he could remember, tune and words. "Well, what's it to be?" Hendie snapped fiercely, holding his fiddle ready to help.

"Righto," said Willan. "'Lead, kindly Light.'"

"For God's sake, then," Hendie entreated, "don't sing as flat as last time, or you'll stretch me a corpse at your feet." He instantly began to play divinely, and Willan began to do his sorry best.

They were half through the hymn when, to Willan's dismay, one or two men began to join in. Were they done up—unable to work any longer, only able now to sit idle and sing? He felt that Hendie was feeling as much and was all out to make the old dope keep its hold on the men; he was playing like Orpheus, and singing too, for all he was worth. But more men joined in, and then more, till the dim room was booming like a church:

So long Thy power hath blest me, sure it still
Will lead me on,
O'er moor and fen, o'er crag and torrent, till
The night is gone.

When those words were reached, every face in the room was raised, dead-white and dead-tired, but very glad, towards the fiddler. Then Willan looked again and he saw that what man after man had let fall from his hands was the finished work, and that the candle-light had paled and a streaming window to the East was blenching with the dawn. The night was gone and the hobbled relief-force was free.

Willan had given his orders last night: their execution began, the next minute, to reel itself off like the chain of an anchor let go. In the bald twilight outside a bugler was blowing the Assembly before the last score-of men to be fitted had laced their new boots.

"Well, you've pulled it off," Hendie said to Willan, as the room emptied. "God help your intonation—still, you sing as if you cared, and that's damn rare."

"If we win by a neck or anything less," Willan said, "it's you will have done it."

In half an hour the rear-guard of the column was a mile away, streaming down the valley in streaming rain. Hendie watched it out of sight before settling to sleep in the mould that the deep, hay had taken of Willan's large body.

BOOK SIX

CHAPTER XXIII

THE HOME FRONT CREAKS

When Hendie's ramshackle balloon rose from the city, cleared the enemy's snipers and sailed away towards the South, there was some faint stir of hope in the minds of the hungry citizens of Ria. Then the heartless wind veered like a flirt, the balloon took a list to the East, like a blown poplar, and made off in' a great hurry towards the frontier range of mountains. That did away with the hope that had stirred. Now the balloon would founder in the snowy desert of the frontiers; or else it would cross the whole range and come down to be captured somewhere or other in the huge expanse of Porto beyond. No help would come by its means.

That day the enemy's gunfire quickened a little. His gunners made a neat round hole in the front of the Home Office and another in the outer wall of the Members' smoking-room at the Parliament-House. They also knocked several small pieces off the handsome War Office and one off Bishop Case's pleasant house. There seemed to be an almost inspired malignity in their choice of targets. Like those subtle spiders which start by sticking a paralysing claw into the chief nerve centres of their prey, so as to keep the meat fresh and unspoiled but not able to move, the Portans picked out and peppered these vital seats of Rian wisdom and courage.

At 6 p.m., to the tick, this battering of Ria's administrative vitals ceased for the day. Then it was remembered that it had begun, in the morning, precisely at ten. This exact eight-hour day had a methodical look which did no good to the spirits of the besieged. It gave to the process of vivisection an air of fixity and of probably immense duration, like that of a respectable bank. The citizens had perfect peace, wherein to indulge this reflection, till ten the next morning. To most of them, perhaps, the future began to look like an extremely long, straight, dusty, shadeless road down which they would have to walk for ever and then find themselves walking it still. No one really likes such roads.

At ten the first shell came whistling punctually in, and chipped a richly carved corner off the Ministry of Mines. An impressive number of other fragments of good stonework came off during the day; the popular incumbent of a City church was disembowelled, with repulsive publicity, and people began to consider carefully which was the West, or lee, side of the nearest solid building, as they walked about the streets.

When reflection, in the deeper sense, was resumed at six that evening, it went on in minds that were well bruised, weary and sore. People—especially well-to-do people—felt cross with everyone else. They were chafed by everything. They diagnosed hysteria in anybody whose spirits showed more wear and tear than their own, and brutish callousness in people who showed less. They raged at the "damned affectation" of men who made a point of "keeping smiling," and also at the "dastardly defeatism" of men who had always known there would be no luck in this war.

At ten on the next morning, too, the shells resumed their physical and spiritual operations. They did a fair day's work at converting presentable modern architecture into rubble, and turning the nerves of influential Rians into bits of worn fiddle-string. The night that followed was sultry, for the time of year, and this helped to keep people awake and thoughtful. All middle-class bedroom windows were open; through a good many of these some distant lights in the besiegers' lines could be seen twinkling; they looked almost as high as the stars and almost as unlikely to be removed or extinguished by anybody's desire, though this might be strong.

Through open windows, at such a time, there are apt to enter gnats or mosquitoes, and also the other winged and mordant creatures described collectively by Claudio, in the play, as "lawless and uncertain thought." I believe it was during this particular night that a swarm of these little libertines, in search of proselytes, first raised their obsessive wail about the ears of some thousands of Rian men and women who were lying awake in the dark. "Why should you go on enduring it?"—that was the note of the "common sense" midge. Others had subtler modes of solicitation to each person they addressed. "You have done all that man can do," they would whisper to one; "You have fought the good fight and have put a pure soul's trust in your fellows. See what has come of it. Is anything left, even for staunchness like yours, to do, among this crew of slackers?" The buzz that importuned another was—"You are a true man of business—a frank, alert dealer with facts, a skilled taker of means to ends. And all life is business—a nation's life as well as a man's. And the first rule of business? 'Cut losses, and let profits run,' is it not? And do not Ria's losses cry out to be cut before they run the whole length of famine and riot?" The thought that pestered a politician with its hum might be, "Well, you great turner-on and turner-off of the forces that make these grand messes, you that have let out this flood, drain it off now. Oh! blast your pride of consistency and your fine iron will and all your pet graven images of your dear self! Give them up and end this torturing of your dupes before they become your judges and executioners." Or it might merely be, "All a mistake, a mistake—You see it all now—no romance, as you hoped, but a mere humdrum pain. Put it all from you, forget it—war and defeat and vain effort. Just sink back into yourself and your exquisite sense of the beauty and wonder of human life at its best, till this foul hurly-burly around you has settled itself as it may." In so many plausible ways did the heat that was turning milk sour that night help other forces to decompose also the City's will to resist and to win. The heat was increasing all the next day—the fourth day of the Portans' increased and more perturbing shell-fire, the fourth, too, since Hendie had retired from the City. On that fourth night the heat was extreme. It killed sleep and patience; it dulled resolution. Under this torment, ideas that had been mere speculations some twenty-four hours ago, came back as passions—gusts of angry certitude, or of angry astonishment that anyone in the City should think anything else; blind, arrogant fanatics, how could they lie still in their beds all through another night, leaving evil to grow into ten times itself? No, not a night must pass after this with nothing done. Thus did thousands of Rians, tossing sleeplessly on excellent mattresses, screw themselves up to the point of surrender, with all the consciousness of doing something virile, trenchant and robust, and of putting away childish things.

II

Not a word of hope had yet reached the City. Not a gleam of surviving national spirit in all outer Ria had shown itself. Under the fiery sun the next morning the whole wide expanse of the Big Slope, above the enemy's lines, had the dead, empty look that fills the face of a landscape when a haze of heat quivers over it all like the burnt air above a crematorium chimney. You can scarcely believe that under that vibrant fury of heat there can be even a grasshopper hopping and chirping.

Even before the Big Slope was a-swim with that winking glare, things had begun to move in Ria City that morning. A few of the chief men had felt themselves strongly moved to make early calls upon one another. They did it, at first, almost furtively.

But, as soon as they had begun, each found, to his surprise and ' joy, that some other mind had been travelling just the same road as his own. It was like the happy lover's intoxicating discovery that the lady has all the time been wanting him too. The friends of peace had made their proposals timidly, fearing a contemptuous rebuff and almost afraid for their lives. But almost at once they were a band of comrades, a set of superiors to other men, a kind of incorporeal club manned by the best. Soon they could begin to feel that they held the keys of admission to a companionship 'of picked resolute spirits and saviours of the public.

Now that they felt confident, the pioneers were able to shed around them an alluring fragrance of brave initiative or advancedness. Within some six hours of good hard work they actually made it "the done thing" among the "best people" of Ria City to feel that the hour for action had struck and that overtures for peace must be unflinchingly made. By this time they were scarcely canvassers at all. They were more like priests consenting to baptize the jostling throng of converts to the newest fashion in patriotic creeds. For the "best people" in Ria City were like the "best people" everywhere else, and like the best sheep all over the world. It was not man by man that fears or desires invaded them, but as a wind sways a whole patch of tall corn and not just a stalk here and another stalk there.

Only the best people, of course, were consulted at first. You simply can't talk to a half-starving mob about delicate questions of life and death and of honour. Enough that the people were sound at heart— the honest fellows would be sure to follow if properly led and not sacrificed to any super-subtle phantom of national pride.

But what about Burnage? That question had risen at once. For he was a power. He had the Voice. He was prominent in the new "National Cabinet." He had to be thought of. But had he t quite the same prestige as of old? Were not people saying now that if Burnage had stuck to his guns, his original guns, no war would have come and no miseries? And would it be good taste—for, like all the best people, these were great on good taste—to approach, in this matter, one so deeply committed, one who had burnt boats enough to bridge a Hellespont?

No: better, kinder really, not to trouble him with any news of the grand change of wind till the ship's course was already as good as altered to conform to it.

III

Little they knew, those best people. A coming storm of rain might as well have decided not to disturb with any tidings of its advent the bunch of dried sea-weed hanging up to serve as a barometer in the hall. Willy-nilly, the weed will be damp in good time. Nature tells it. Perhaps she told Burnage. Nobody else did, in so many words. But he was aware; his journalist nose snuffed the air, early that day, and smelt change as surely as some sensitive organisms will wake up of a morning, give a slight sniff in their beds and tell you an East wind has come in the night.

"They're breaking," he said in a voice slightly hollow, just meekly and appropriately hollow, as he came into the "chaste" white hotel sitting-room where Rose's vacant mornings were spent since her dismissal.

She did not look up from some little fiddling work she was doing with a needle and silk and a delicate stuff of a faint lilac colour. "Breaking?" she said, with no sign of interest.

"They're crumbling—you can almost hear them," he said, and then stopped, to look at her. She was lovely, as always—even more poignantly lovely because her soft natural colour had failed a little of late, and this touched the lover's heart with a sharp sense of the flower-like impermanence of all the dear world of beauty that she was. Through the very transparent skin of her hands the blue veins looked as pale as the bleached lilac stuff she embroidered. Her linen dress, too, was of a cold beautiful blue, and her lips were a little bloodless. Even on that torrid morning she looked, in the north-facing room, as if the kind warmth of life had suffered discouragement in her.

She did not look up, even now. She said in a cool, trickling voice: "Is David growing so tired of throwing his little smooth stones from the brook?" She spoke as a nurse might do when the children chatter to her about their mighty doings with the sand and she supposes she must say something—any old word or two.

It did not matter much what she said. It was her looks that tormented the love which feareth all things. They almost arraigned him. "Oh! I have ta'en too little thought for this," he could have said. Why, with that transparent blue pallor, Rose might be beginning to die. "It's in the air," he said almost absently, with his mind on her face. "You can feel it. It's every-where—in people's faces, in ways they look at you, in some turn of a phrase in a letter. Something is ready to happen."

"Oh? Happen?" She spoke as if all her concern with these things had ended a long time ago.

"Don't you care, darling?" he asked.

She blazed out in anger at once. "Didn't I? Didn't I try, till they kicked me away? Not that I mind. The outer darkness is quite good enough. It's not stuffy, anyhow. Only, don't ask me to worry about the souls of these worthies."

Suddenly the blaze subsided; her face lost its quick flush; it sank back to its skim-milky paleness and coldness. "Well, well," she said, with a patient and weary show of interest in his cares, "what way, do you say, are weathercocks turning?"

"We meet—the Cabinet, you know—in half an hour. It may possibly be proposed that we ask for an armistice."

"And after—?" Her languid voice seemed to ask why he gave her the trouble of asking. Why not out with this mighty trifle of his without so much' prelude?

He quickened under the spur. "Peace," he said. "That is—utter surrender."

"So? A new lead? And who's to be hero this time?" With a shrug he disclaimed any knowledge. "Grant perhaps. Perhaps Panmure. Possibly even the Bishop."

She laughed a little at the Bishop's name, joylessly. "So you'll hand the lead over to them?" she said.

He scarcely heard the words. He was thinking too hard and too painfully. All his thought was: "She is running down—in the body at least. She can't stand any more of this siege. But she's staunch. She won't ask me to save her."

"You'll oppose them?" she asked, with some slight appearance of wanting to. know.

He did not answer her at once. He was thinking, ". I may be killing her if I do."

"To the 'last gasp'?" she added. "Or is it 'last ditch'? Was it Clemenceau who said that the English would fight against Germany to the last Frenchman? You'll fight against Porto to the last Rian, won't you?"

To-morrow, he thought, her cheeks would be still more trans-parent; the lashes would show still darker against the skin under her eyes; between the joints her fingers would perhaps have fallen in a little. And yet she could be playful—could put herself out of the case and chaff him—oh! quite without rancour— could let him go on enjoying his cheap showy pose—for so it began to look now—of the die-hard, the no-surrenderer of romance. Romance! Faugh!—wasn't it all mad vanity masquerading as honour?— forcing torments and death upon any number of innocent people—soldiers, women, children, Rose herself—using them as spotless sacrifices to be offered on the flashy altars of arrant self-worship? A kind of thought may go on at a magnificent pace if you have the true orator's mind.

CHAPTER XXIV

THE HIGHER COURAGE SETS IN

I

For two days the regular meeting-place of the Rian Cabinet had been lying about in the street, roughly dissected into its elements of stone, steel, plaster and lath. So the Cabinet had requisitioned a first-floor room in Ria's largest hotel—the one in which the Burnages had already found shelter. Cyril had only to enter the lift at his sitting-room door, descend two storeys and walk a few yards, to reach the seat of supreme authority. Thus any emotions with which he started the journey had insufficient time to evaporate before the journey's end.

Of the ten appointed fathers of the country, he was the last to arrive this morning. And, like many late comers, he was received with particular warmth. The others had needed him badly. The Premier had been wounded by a shell on his way to this very meeting: no official Deputy-Premier had been provided by the country's model constitution; and there was not one of the other eight statesmen now present whom some, at least, of the others would not have strongly disliked to see in the chair. Burnage, as the man who had the fewest personal enemies, was pressed on all hands to preside. So he had now to open the day's business.

From saying the right things about the wounded chief—"martyr to duty" and so forth—he went on to the other cares of the hour. There was little need, he supposed, to tell anyone there the bare facts of the case. The daily rations had twice already been cut down. To make the food supply last for ten days more, the rations would have to be cut down again, and that at once, by fifty per cent. A matter perhaps even graver was that the forced stoppage of all the great city industries was filling the streets with perpetual crowds of a dangerous type—hungry, unoccupied, soured, the natural prey of anti-national and anti-social agitators. The Chief Commissioner of Police had just sent to the Home Office a confidential warning that at any moment an organised Communist rising might have to be suppressed. At this news a murmur, almost a wail, of horror came from two or three of the conscript fathers—the ones who had been taken into the Cabinet to appease the outcries of some of the ventriloquists of the Press for a "business Government." This poignant expression of interest in his dark forebodings drew from Burnage a grateful and a hungry look. He had long lived on applause and of late he had been starved of it. He kindled a little as he went on: "I have been doing my best," he said, "to cast my thoughts forward, if only a week. When I do so, I seem to see still the pinched faces that we see round us to-day—only more deeply lined, and more tensely drawn. I seem to feel the despair and bitterness swelling higher and higher in the hearts of husbands and fathers tortured by fear for their dear ones. I cannot, alas, blind myself to the fact that the last hope of any sort of help from without—always tragically small—has now vanished. What, then, remains? Courage."

At that word a look of alarm crossed the faces of a good half of the Cabinet. Burnage saw it with a secret satisfaction—almost secret from himself. He continued, with a most manful air: "Yes—courage. Now, as always, in every question of conduct, for every man or nation, courage holds the solution. Courage is the master-key. Even more fearlessly now than ever before we are bound to cross-examine our inmost selves, to make sure that our courage is true courage, the courage of clear eyes and of undismayable hearts."

By this time all the different kinds of men round the table were looking uncertain, though expectant. No doubt their experience of public life told them, on second thoughts, that there was no practical conclusion which could not be drawn, as easily as any other, from this sort of lofty moral generality. "I know well," he went on, "how attractive the easy and obvious course is. Not to think anything fearlessly out, not to imagine boldly—just to shut our eyes and go on revelling in some darling vision of ourselves as heroes prolonging to fantastic lengths our mere physical resistance. To deaden ourselves with these anodyne drugs to the natural pangs of tenderness and pity for our country's women and children, our own flesh and blood."

The distress now expressed in Burnage's face, as he paused and looked around the table, was genuine. He was in torment for Rose. And he was an artist. Orator, actor, singer—every artist comes to feel sincerely, in a sense and for a time, the emotion he tries to express. Burnage's pause and his look had a manifest meaning: "What I have to say next is, for me, unbearably hard to utter. Take it as said, if you can. If you can't, then your will be done, and not mine."

More of his silent prayer was answered than of its historical original. One stout, bald man gasped, "Sense at last!" and then leant well back in his chair, with his hands in his trouser-pockets, and glared gallantly round at his colleagues, as though to say, "There! Now I've said it. So, crucify me if you like."

He was perfectly safe. The eager light in his eye was cordially answered by several other lucid signals of the same kind.

Burnage read every signal. The moment was like a show of hands to him. The thing was decided. He went on in a chastened, bleached sort of tone, sad and clear and yet resolute, as the feelings of most of his audience required. They had a great need just then to think themselves resolute and unswerving—all public men have to be so extremely unswerving. "Defeat is bitter, God knows," Burnage said, "but if defeat it must be, duty bids us to accept it with an unflinching frankness and manliness."

"Accept!" General Miln almost shouted. He was aghast. No doubt his slowly travelling mind had only just overtaken the others, and seen what they had come round to.

Burnage eyed the horrified man almost tenderly... Burnage bit his upper lip to control its sympathetic quiver while Miln rocked on his chair, all his professional aplomb shattered by misery: "The cur! The dirty dog!" Miln muttered.

They all gazed at the General. Two or three clearly agreed with him. Burnage showed no trace of resentment. He looked to his front, straight into vacancy. His aspect betokened a noble detachment from all trivial private regards; he would give no offence he could help, and he would take none. His seemly bearing during those moments probably gained another convert or two before he next spoke, which he did very gently: "I do not know, gentlemen, what your feeling may be. If—we are—agreed—"

"No!" the General's voice rasped harshly in.

Burnage turned to him, and spoke with warm courtesy. The Minister for War, he said, their honoured Commander-in-Chief, had been the life and soul of a gallant defence. If he would do them the kindness now of speaking his mind with the utmost freedom—There was' a general murmur of assent and encouragement. Miln had to speak. That made him assuredly ineffectual. With no genius for anything, merely a man of honour and courage and some routine diligence, he was at his worst when he had to argue aloud. I suspect that none of his thoughts seemed to him to be over five words in length. "I'm against you," he said.

Burnage's attitude of courteous expectation became even more deferential. He sat and looked like a man settling down to digest an expert's full exposition.

It made Miln more helpless than ever. "No!" he said, "I've got no speech to make. Only, I'm against you. One thing—it's much too soon to know we're beaten. Then there's another. What if some fellows are getting together up there on the hill, to give us a hand? Nice business if they were let down by us here. Why, we'd stink for ever. That's all—I'm against you."

They all waited politely for awhile, in listening attitudes, to let the giftless speaker acquire the gift of speech if he could, and put his plea better. But no miracle happened. So Burnage, after a long, patient pause, said he would like to suggest that by no mere bare majority could anyone there desire to see overridden the judgment of the great soldier who had just spoken. He wished to propose that only on a vote approaching unanimity—say three to one—should so grave a change in public policy be made. Such moderation carried further the disablement of Miln. He looked eagerly round at the other men's faces. A dog might look thus at the human friends whom it believes to be intending to drown him.

Everything worth having was slipping away from him. Still, fair play must be acknowledged. "That's decent," he said to Burnage.

Burnage's proposal was adopted. Then he said it was now his painful duty to make a formal proposal that three representatives of the Rian Government be sent at once to General Delarey, the Portan Commander-in-Chief, with full powers to ask for an armistice, and if possible, to conclude a peace.

'"Not to ' conclude,'" Miln entreated. "For God's sake, not to 'conclude.' Won't you make it 'to treat'? For our man-hoods sake, gentlemen, let us keep up our end, if it's only that far."

"The Commander-in-Chief," Burnage said, "has proposed an amendment. Has it a seconder?" Burnage glanced round the circle of faces. No one spoke. No one raised a hand, though Burnage gave plenty of time. At last, he said, "We vote, then, on the main resolution. Those in favour. . . ."

Six hands were held up. "Against—" Burnage said.

There rose Miln's hand and that of a young Labour man who had been co-opted into the Cabinet in token of the perfect union of all classes for the prosecution of the war.

"The resolution," Burnage tolled out with slow dignity, "has been carried by the required majority. One other point. Is it understood that, in the improbable event of a disagreement between our three plenipotentiaries, a majority of their number shall exercise the full powers entrusted to them as a body?"

There was a general nodding and murmur of assent. Miln and the young Labour man needed more time than there was to work out in their minds the way this provision might tell.

"That is carried," said Burnage, "without opposition. It only remains to appoint our three envoys. I would suggest, first, our most gallant and loyal Commander-in-Chief; secondly, Mr. Grant, our greatest living authority on international law; and, thirdly, Mr. Panmure, whose distinction and fitness are known to you all. Are the names acceptable?"

Another murmur of assent. The compliment to Miln completed his tactical disablement. He did not know enough about his fellow-envoys to be aware that they would make him powerless.

The peace delegation was constituted. Burnage reviewed it before it went on its errand under a white flag. He had to say the right word: "Gentlemen, we know you will do your best for your stricken country. May God lighten your task."

II

The Cabinet had then adjourned. But only to stand by; each Minister was to be near a telephone, ready to hurry back at a call.

Burnage killed time at first by reading and signing many typed letters of routine. When that distraction gave out, he sat at his high window and watched the shadow of a spire lengthening and swinging round as the sun sloped down: it turned the wide, choppy sea of city roofs into the face of a monstrous sun-dial. He looked at it dully for nearly an hour, with wandering glances now and then over the great sun-smitten slope that rose Eastwards. All the slope looked dazed, even now, with the late afternoon heat, battered down by it, swooning under the brute glare. The one visible sign of a life and a will that nothing could drug was a distant leisurely puff of grey smoke. It was periodic. It came into being precisely every seven minutes, swelled, thinned and drifted slowly away from the sylvan spot where one of the enemy's high-velocity guns was plodding, in perfect-seeming security, through its eight-hour day of humdrum homicide and demolition in the sweltering City.

A silence may startle as much as a sound. At the end of Burnage's hour of idle waiting, the Portan gun had just fired one of its shells. It burst in a second-rate suburb of the city. Then the usual seven minutes passed, but no discharge followed. Thirteen minutes passed; then he could almost hear people holding their breath in the street as the last sixty seconds ran out. But, again, no sound came. It was almost as if Big Ben had stopped at Westminster. Peering down, Burnage could see on the face of the City a note of interrogation. People were looking at watches and listening; strangers spoke to one another. "What can it mean?" the whole multitude seemed to be saying—the multitude whom the wise and great had not taken into their confidence.

Burnage guessed, of course. He had done it: the war was over; the defeat was accomplished. "You've got your wish. Now enjoy it"—he heard already the dreary challenge that usually comes to spoil the taste of the consummation of tainted desires. Keeping nervously behind a curtain, he peered down at the common people who did not know yet that, last as well as first, he had compassed their subjugation. Soon the sight of them began to hurt him: he looked away, for relief, at the travelling shadow of the spire, and at the scorched vineyards and gardens enduring with arooped leaves, and, far above them, at the impassive towers and falls of white ice—the whole companionship of stoical forces and things that make the best they may of living in accord with unalterable laws. They held no consolation for him; he was not of their company. He came away from the window and tried to write formal letters.

How slow that news, was in coming! He wrote, or at least he handled a pen, till the shadow thrown by the spire was lost in a shadow more comprehensive. Sunset had come, but no call for him yet. It was astounding. Was it possible that the acting head of the Government of a State, even a conquered State, should become in an hour or two a person whom nobody rang up oh the 'phone to tell him how his dying-country was doing? Never in his adult life had Burnage been wilfully rude, and the rudeness of it pained him.

The bell did ring at last. He fairly jumped to the receiver. Not the right call, though. Only one from his private secretary, now installed on the ground floor. Some one had called and was waiting—had asked first of all for the Commander-in-Chief—then, on hearing that the Commander-in-Chief was not in the City, had asked who was in charge—and, hearing that Mr. Burnage was now the acting Premier, had said that was splendid—the very man—must see him at once—had a message that he must deliver in person into the acting Premier's own hand. The. private secretary's voice sounded sceptical.

Scepticism is highly infectious. "What sort of a man?" Burnage asked.

"Well, a bit queer, sir, in his manner."

"Is he a—sahib?" Burnage inquired.

"He might be—well, a disguised one. He's got up as a peasant." The devoted secretary ventured to add a suggestion that it might be safer if Burnage were not left alone with the visitor.

That settled it; let the caller be shown up alone find at once. The notion of running a little merely physical risk, the off chance of a shot from some crazy crank, was mere refreshment to a mind beset by care and fears so much less simple.

III

Certainly the messenger looked rather queer. Burnage could not have made a guess at his age, when he came in; nor yet at the normal look of his face, it was so bloated and blotched with sun-blisters. The man's upper lip and part of his neck looked grotesquely dropsical or goitred with these water-bugs. Elsewhere the blisters had burst, and the unrelenting sun, with some assistance from insects and dust, had attacked the more delicate skin underneath, and even the raw flesh below that. The whites of the man's eyes were so fantastically bloodshot as to differ little in colour from the rest of his sanguine, frayed and tattered countenance: he looked relatively eyeless.

Burnage was instantly touched with humane concern for the poor devil. He felt-pretty sure the man must have a temperature. That was what the manner meant. Everything about the creature—speech, gesture, emotion—was keyed up a little above normal pitch. He was not delirious, but he was going that way. Burnage gave him the easiest chair. "You've had a very bad time?" Burnage said, kindly.

The man did not answer the question. "So you're old Dobbin's friend—John Willan's friend? Well, he is a great old Dobbin, ain't he?" Merrick's jaunty talk was no more like its natural self than his face was. "Willan!—alive!" There was a kind of horror in Burnage's voice—perhaps a horror at himself, at finding he was not glad, simply glad that his friend was not dead.

"And kicking. J. Willan, C.O. Willan's Force, makers of history on the shortest notice. Haven't I just given you his letter?" Merrick looked bewildered for a moment. Then he got hold again. "Gosh! no, I've not. Why, I'm forgetting whole objec' of journey." He moved a hand uncertainly towards one of his pockets, rummaged in it, found nothing, and then went on to search the other. All the time he apologised for these symptoms of incapacity. "Not drunk, really. Been in the sun a bit—been in the river a bit—little af—fair with a scythe.

Hullo! " He suddenly ceased to rummage and stared at one of the windows. "Which way d' you look here?"

"Due East, that window," said Burnage.

"Gad! you'll get a good sight of it, sir. You deserve to."

"Sight?" Burnage whispered, "of what?"

Merrick's voice shrilled up in triumph. "Sight? Why, the old Light in the East, you know—Star in the East—all in the Prayer Book. Remember, at school?"

The happy, fevered being chanted in exultation:

"Which thou hast prepared, before the face of all people,

To be a light to lighten the Gentiles,
And to be the glory of thy people, Israel."

"All your doing, sir, and old Willan's—it's you've kept the heart in 'em here, else he'd have no one to signal to."

"Signal? My God! Signal!" Burnage gasped.

Merrick stared. "Ain't it all in the letter I gave you?"

"No! No! I've not got it. Look—quick—" Burnage spoke low and furtively. "Some other pocket?—a boot?—in a lining?"

"Got it. You're right every time, sir." Out of the worn lining of one of his coat-sleeves Merrick proceeded to cut, with a rusted knife held in a shaky hand, a thin flat case of oiled silk. He babbled all the time. "

Very sorry, sir—dispatch got damp—been in the river a bit—damn scythe nearly mowed dispatch in two. That's it—now you just read your Valentine—don't mind me. Pm quite all right—I'll sit here good as gold and see the pretty traffic." He had lurched up on to his feet and crossed the room. Now he flopped weakly into a low chair at the room's Eastern window. His elbow on the sill, his chin propped on his hands, he gazed up at the Big Slope and down at the street and its wondering crowd.

To Merrick the moment may well have seemed golden. Crawling mile after mile on his belly, chased like a rat in the scrub for day after day, starved, parched, blistered, bled almost white by the string of whetted scythes in the torrent, he had come through, he had finished his course, he had not failed. At such moments the separate sweets of labour accomplished, danger outfaced and victory won may be gathered up into one heart-filling joy so immense that the fragile vessel of flesh, now all battered and worn thin, may be hard taxed to contain and to carry it. So, perhaps, Merrick's beatitude brought him the nearer now to a collapse.

"Bed is where you have to go," said Burnage. "I'll ring." He did, and then put a hand on Merrick's shoulder, lest Merrick should fall off the chair. Burnage had taken the letter out of its waterproof case, but not read it yet: he held it in his other hand.

While they were thus, he suddenly felt the limp muscles of Merrick's shoulder stiffen convulsively under his hand. Then they went slack again, and Merrick drew his head back from the window and looked up at Burnage with a pitiful expression of distress, like a child whom a strange onset of illness has frightened. "I'm mad," he said. "I was too happy. I've gone mad."

Merrick lay back in the chair, troubled. Below, in the street, a sinister silence had fallen: it was like that of a great public funeral. Only the hoofs of a few walking horses were ringing slowly on the stones.

"I had a sort of mad vision," Merrick said, "frightfully real it seemed, like vile dreams. I thought I saw old Delarey—you know his photo—riding down there, in the street, and Miln with him, and Miln had no sword!"

The shock of his abrupt loss of belief in himself seemed to use up the last kick of Merrick's endurance. "Thank heaven!" thought Burnage, "he's unconscious."

A servant, answering Burnage's ring, appeared in the door-way. "Have this officer taken to hospital, instantly," Burnage directed. The servant ran off for help, while Burnage held up the fainting man's drooping head with genuine tenderness.. He was so rent with sorrow for Merrick that he forgot for the moment everything else, even the letter. He held it unread, absently, while he chafed Merrick's forehead.

The sound of walking hoofs stopped under the window—why, yes, at the hotel's very door. Oh! of course, the hotel was a seat of government now—the conqueror had come, and his cavalry escort was waiting. Burnage heard the pettish stamp of an impatient horse and the jinkety-jink of a chain as the horse tossed up its head in the deep silence.

Almost together there came two knocks at the door. Two stretcher-bearers had come to take Merrick away; and a message was brought to Burnage: General Delarey would be glad to see him at once. Burnage obeyed. He moved now like a man with some of his faculties fully awake, some rather confused, some utterly dormant. To the hand which still held the unread letter from Willan his brain sent, for the present, no fresh commands. So the hand remained closed on the letter.

CHAPTER XXV

A NEAR THING

I

General Delarey had a sound ironical sense of the effectiveness of courtesy on the part of a conqueror. When you take from your enemy every solid good thing he has, you can still enhance the piquancy of the case by conceding to him everything that is quite insubstantial. So Delarey was most civil when Burnage was presented to him. The victor complimented the acting figure-head of the vanquished upon their gallant defence.

He was almost tenderly regretful about the unhappy accident to the Premier.

Delarey was all velvet, too, when he and the Rian Cabinet sat down to 'do business. Without any formal proposal he was propelled in a deferential way towards the presidential chair, his retinue of A.D.C.s and private secretaries flitting and fussing about him like the tugs round an in-coming liner. When he was berthed in the chair the great men of Ria shuffled into other chairs, Burnage on Delarey's right, Miln as far off as possible from the enemy.

Delarey thanked the Rian Government for choosing pleni-potentiaries so distinguished and so amiable as the three gentle-men who had just paid him the honour of a visit; also for its wisdom and humanity in averting needless bloodshed by concluding, through an accredited majority of those admirable agents, an agreement for an unconditional surrender.

The last two words were spoken very slowly and distinctly. So let there be no mistake about that—such was 'the obvious implication of Delarey's tone. There was a choked groan from the one working-class member of the Rian Cabinet, and Miln threw across to this Spartan a rueful gleam of grim sympathy. Delarey's eyes dwelt for a moment on this recalcitrant pair. He said suavely, and yet with just a tinge of urbane menace, "There is, I gather, no dissent from that?"

None that found words, certainly. "I thank you, gentle-men," Delarey said. "One other point—a mere matter of form.! take it as guaranteed by you all that your people and troops are in hand—that no unlawful attempt to renew resistance need be apprehended?"

"Our army does not mutiny," Miln grunted savagely, humours of a military mutiny in Porto had amused Rian officers' messes a few years before.

Burnage listened like a man removed from what was going on. It was like a thing in a book—of interest, but a thing to hear about, not to act in.

Delarey bowed to Miln slightly and said, "I felt sure of it." That finished the preliminaries. Delarey went on at once to say what he had come to say. To avert from both countries all danger of recurrence of war his Government had decided to incorporate the whole of the territories of Ria in the Republic of Porto. On behalf of his Government he offered a welcome to its new citizens. He assured them that they might rely on a measure of freedom fully commensurate with the loyalty which he was convinced that they would display.

Extinction! So it was that. The worst fears of the Rians had not gone so far. There was heard a slight sound—the one you make with the lips when your breath is taken away by some portent.

Delarey only grew blander. "I cannot doubt," he purred, "that, as men of strict honour, you will all"—he looked hard at the young workman and Miln—"abide whole-heartedly by the arbitrament of war, which you invoked."

"Don't say that, sir," the Labour man burst out, earnestly. "It's killing a nation. For God's sake, don't do it, sir." He was dead white and had tears running from his eyes. His manners had no true-bred repose. He spoke as if this were a world in which you need only show that an act is cruel in order to get people not to do it.

Miln hated to beg, still, he could not let that good fellow try single-handed. "Take every gold mine there is if you want 'em." he said. "Take any amount of indemnity. Only, don't ask a man to eat dirt."

"I tell you, sir," the workman pleaded eagerly, "we couldn't make our people stick it. They'd lynch us if we tried to." So much sincere passion is seldom to be seen among any equal number of distinguished public men.

Delarey did not hurry. He let the first cries of pain wear themselves out. As soon as they ceased he said, in his most dulcet way, that he felt the extreme liberality of the General's offers—no doubt authorised by his colleagues. But Porto was not seeking gold-fields. She had no wish to turn out the pockets of Ria. She wanted no more, as she was taking no less, than the security that he had named for her, freedom to live her own life in future without molestation. One gentleman, he said with a distinct increase in the silkiness of his voice, had forecast some trouble, and even danger, for eminent Rians in reconciling their people to the settlement that had been decided upon. Let him feel assured of full protection in the discharge of that duty. An adequate Portan force would at once undertake the maintenance of order throughout the new province.

"Province," most stinging of words, was pronounced by Delarey with a gusto truly ambrosial. The man was like a dilettante artist-executioner pressing a sharp spike softly and delightedly into a bound prisoner's eye. But this time all the Rians kept silence. They were learning servitude.

Delarey had not quite finished. "For the moment—as you have, no doubt, anticipated—martial law will be in force. As an act of grace and an earnest of Portan equity and clemency, I propose to employ as a member of the chief tribunal trying any prisoners under martial law, one of yourselves, chosen by yourselves. If you will have the goodness to give me a name—"

He looked down for a minute or two and wrote on a piece of paper, leaving the dispossessed rulers of Ria to choose their man as they might.

They did not set about it well. They made some show of conferring informally. But they had lost readiness and composure. They were like school-boys essaying a task of self-government under the eyes of a master who does not believe in the thing. They fumbled and groped and they reached no result.

Delarey looked up at last, scanned the embarrassed faces and spoke with an air of coming to their relief. "No name occurs to you, gentlemen? Possibly, then, I cannot do better than put my trust where you have put yours. Mr. Burnage, you will, I think, do me the honour of undertaking this duty." The voice was bland, the manner was honeyed, but somehow the words were an order, the look that went with them a menace, though a covert and delicate one.

Murmured sounds of encouragement reached Burnage's ear, from some of his colleagues. Miln's mutter of "Dirty job—it will suit him," did not quite reach him. So the only external forces at work on him at the moment were pushing him towards acceptance of the task. Within him there was no longer any force that could firmly determine anything. His brain was quite conscious, in a narrow sense, but quelled and inert as if after recent concussion: the will had become almost null and void; thought was no longer a process, coherent and progressive; it had been deadened into a mere stupefied gazing at this and that dim fragment of an old system of things now broken—Rose fading, Ria fallen like Troy, Willan far out of reach, scarcely real, involved in some hopeless adventure obscurely visible through that poor devil's ravings about stars in the East and signals of fire. Adrift, unengined, unballasted, rudderless, waterlogged with all these contending waves of distress, with little of his old self left in action except a vague habitual impulse to play the show part, to make the noble gesture and the grand renunciation and to stand alone in the tragic and terrible breach, he caught the encouraging whispers of his friends. That settled it. He said to Delarey, "I place myself in your hands."

II

The other Rian Ministers let out deep breaths of relief. What each had hated and feared for himself had fallen to somebody else. Delarey hurried them off, with a few oily words, to fag for him. "You will," he Said, "be anxious not to delay in commending your partiotic decision to the good sense of your countrymen." Burnage was rising to go away with the rest, when Delarey touched his arm. "You—stay," he said curtly. It was the first time that he had not troubled to veil his imperiousness. He seemed not to admire Burnage, or like him, so much as most people did. "Stay here, Latta," he said to a field officer of his Staff. To the rest he gave a nod of dismissal.

As the door closed on the others Delarey turned sharply to Burnage. "The thing I want to say to you is—" he began, and then he stopped, with a frown. Burnage was not attending so closely as the vanquished ought to attend to their victors. Dazed and half absent, he had been looking blankly at a folded letter that he held in one hand. Even now, while he turned towards Delarey, he twiddled the thing with nervous fingers while listening imperfectly to the master of his' fate and Ria's. "I beg your pardon," Delarey said, augustly, "I interrupt your reading?"

"No, no," said Burnage eagerly. At first he was only shocked at himself for having been rude. Then, glancing vacantly at his hands, he remembered what letter it was, lost his head, made a panic movement to pocket it quickly, then saw that this move was a blunder, gave it up, and rushed to a different safety device—the first lie he could think of: "Merely a letter of mine, for the post."

No great clairvoyance was needed to read these display advertisements of alarm. Delarey held out a hand. "Permit me," he said, "to have it sent to the post with my own. I fear I may keep you here for some time. I should grieve if I were delaying any correspondence of yours."

The way he uttered the word "correspondence" was not an open challenge; not even an insinuation, and yet it made Burnage shiver. He floundered pitifully in the web that your in-efficient liar weaves so swiftly; he can enmesh himself almost without assistance from the efficient spider. "So many thanks," Burnage said hurriedly, "but it's not stamped."

Delarey took a pen up from the table. He was becoming alarmingly cat-like—a furtive stalker, killing in Velvet, crouching with a purr while it measures the requisite spring. "How charming!" he said. "You give me the pleasure of franking it with my name." Again he held out his hand.

Burnage tottered on from lie to lie, and never a shrewd one.

"My mistake—I beg pardon—merely a note to a neighbour—I'll send it by hafid."

"Ah! You stamp notes when you send them by hand? A prudent precaution!"

At that slight thrust, and quite suddenly, Burnage gave up. He hated lying. Whatever unrealities he hugged to his soul, coarse, obvious mendacity was no method of his. The use of it made him feel dirty, with no gain to show for the dirt. Something that seemed to be like love of truth and an innocent faith in its guidance flooded into him and took control of him, as some of his happiest inspirations had done in old days, when he made speeches. Now, as then, he gave himself up to the god, or whatever it was.

I am the clay—thou art the potter"—that was the feeling, and pow he spoke as a child walks when it is led by the hand. "I fear I have been wandering. Please forgive me. This letter was handed to me almost at the moment when you arrived here."

"And you were sending it on to a friend? Give it to me."

"I have not read it," Burnage said truthfully, as he handed it over.

"By your good leave"—Delarey's politeness was quite contemptuous now. He opened Willan's budget of hopes and great news, read half of it and then, without ceasing to read, said "Map out, Latta—the captured one. Sheet 20 S.E. III. Got it?" He turned to Burnage, "You," he said, "turn on the light."

The twilight was rapidly thickening. Burnage did that humble service.

The Staff Officer whipped a map out of a bulging map-case attached to his belt. "Right, sir," he said. Before Delarey had read Willan through, the map was spread out flat on the table, a compass with a floating dial was lying on it, and the map had been turned till its North coincided with that of the compass. "Map set, sir," Major Latta reported, as Delarey ceased reading.

From the latter the General's eyes went straight to the quivering line that marked East on the compass. It pointed straight at a tall window, the only one on that side of the room, though others looked West— the only one, too, which had its blind drawn. "Up with that blind," the General said. He had a voice that could spur, when he wanted it to.

The Major ran to the window. The catch of the blind had stuck, as is the way of these toys: he could not work it: the blind remained down. Delarey turned on Burnage. "Open it—you!" he snapped. "Hiders can find."

"I do assure you"—Burnage was protesting, but Delarey roared at him: "God damn you, put up the blind."

The acting Premier ran like an errand hoy. To some purpose, too, He knew the tricks of that forward blind no better than Major Latta did. And yet, by some wayward 'fluke, the restive catch ceased from its restiveness at the first fumbling touch of Burnage's hand. The great blind flew up out of sight and hid somewhere close to the ceiling. And in another moment Burnage had tottered back from the window and Delarey had breathed an exultant and venomous "So?"

A window always frames some picture, but seldom a picture quite so pictorial as that window contained. Centred exactly aright in the tall rectangular opening, a huge cross of fire was flashing and twinkling amazingly, deep set in its mystic back-ground of night. Distant lights are, as a rule, merely Spots of dead yellow: these pulsated like stars; eager life and passion seemed to blaze in them, flashing out expression and burning to be understood. Close to the ends of the arms of the Cross, where the feet and hands had been nailed, a few red lights had been placed, to Burnage the glitter of these seemed to stream downwards, as if some invisible figure were bleeding up there in the dark, in the agonies of a new crucifixion.

No mode of brief human appeal can compare with a signal of fire at night in its power to rouse the heart or wring it. The rocket from a foundering ship or an assaulted trench, the running thrill of alarm or joy along chains of hill beacons—what can match these in beauty and poignancy? Instantaneously they will rend or exalt you, set men hastening to look for their deaths, only glad of the chance, or scorch them with a searing sense of some old baseness or indolence, now irreparable. Words as unconsidered as moans of bodily pain rose to Burnage's lips: "My God—they've come!"

Delarey heard it. "They!" he said. "So you knew!"

Off his guard, sick with remorse, far past remembering what he had said and how much he had tried not to say, Burnage babbled out "It's in the letter." '

"Which you had not read," Delarey sneered.

III

To Burnage he said nothing for a while. There was business to see about, first. With Willan's dispatch in one hand, to refer to, Delarey dictated several short orders. He had everything he wanted now—the time of the attack, the exact place of it on the map, the numbers to be reckoned with, the chance of a collusive sally from the City in concert with Willan. While Latta was writing but the first order, Delarey wrote something too. While Latta wrote the second order, Delarey sent sliding along the smooth table to Burnage what he had written himself. "Read and sign," Delarey ordered.

What Burnage read was: "To J. Willan, or person in charge. We have made a genuine surrender. It is total and unconditional. You must immediately disarm." It was no letter that Burnage himself could ever have written to his friend. He tried to, say so. But Delarey. stopped him with "Damn it, sign. Do you want battles for your amusement?" And Burnage scrawled such an approach to his natural signature as his state of nerves would permit.

Delarey turned to Latta. "Simply a matter of getting on with Plan F, as applied to Situation 7. Read out what I've given you." Latta read aloud, clearly and fast.

"Right," said Delarey. "'Phone all that to Hardy. And this"—he gave Latta what Burnage had just signed—"to go at once to the ruffian-in-chief, if findable. Send it by Rian officer—prisoner—one of the early ones—with a white flag. Tell me the time Hardy gets your last word."

The Major went off, at top speed, and then there settled on Delarey, almost as visibly as an alighting dove, the peace that visits efficient modern generals when a battle is just about to begin. By that time their own work is done; the thing is out of their hands; their book has gone, as it Were, to the printer's; they have provided for every emergency, every variation that may diversify the normal course of the imminent game. So they can let their minds play while they await, with an agreeable confidence, the fruit of their inspired labours. They have time to kill flies if they like.

Delarey took a good look at Burnage. "Well," he began, "and so it was a blind—this remarkably early surrender?"

"No!" Burnage, I left it at that. Why say more, when the market value of words spoken by him had gone the way of the old rouble's and the mark's.

Delarey probed him lazily with his eyes. "Not in league with these bandits?" he asked.

"I had not dreamt they existed till—"

"Till I prevailed upon you to unveil them?"

"No—till an hour ago."

"You knew while we sat at this table?"

"I knew nothing. I know nothing now. All I heard was a man half-delirious, raving of rescues and signals of fire—a man who had crept through your lines more dead than alive. He gave me that letter."

"And you didn't read it?"

"No."

"Just held it in your hand, for me to notice?"

"No."

"You meant me not to notice it?"

"I meant nothing. I was past that. I can't explain. I meant no deceit or foul play, but it looks black, I know, and I've no explanation to offer that you would believe. I don't blame you." Delarey considered him curiously. "You do see, then," he said, "that you make some pretty exorbitant calls upon faith?"

"Oh! I know. I can prove nothing now. They're true—all the things I say now—but I know I can't prove them."

"You may. Do you want to? D'you know I have half a mind to believe you? Nothing is too improbable to be true.

All the circumstantial evidence on the earth seems to get mobilized now and again, to do down an innocent man. Your case may be one of these freaks. But it needs to be proved."

Burnage opened his hands in the common gesture of despair.

"What does it matter?" he said. "Better finish me now. I don't care to get off."

"Lord! what egoists you martyrs are! As if it much mattered whether you get off or not! Man, it's your country you've brought under suspicion. It's Ria that you have to get acquitted of plotting a bogus surrender, just to stab us in the back. Well, I'll let you try. I'll not arrest you. I shall let you keep the post I gave you half an hour ago. I'll let you go about now and damp down any riot that breaks out in aid of these ruffians. The straighter you go, the better for Ria. You understand that? She's on probation and your behaviour is what we shall judge her by."

Never, at its best, was Burnage's mind one of the few that seriously weigh conflicting considerations against one another before they send to the tongue or the biceps an order to act. One relevant consideration would rule his mind at one time, and another at another time. It would endure no rival near its throne. And so, if at either time he had to act, the right course would seem beautifully clear to him at the moment. There was just the one thing to do in the world. And just now the one thing to do was to clear his poor country of this foul daub of dishonour. He felt that the whole mess was his fault. Absent-minded, irresolute, shifty, he had brought down upon Ria this cloud of calumny. Now he would atone. Welcome any agony or obloquy, so long as he did that: right up the steep road he would go to the end, with his cross on his back. Oh! his mind was in fine spate now; every thought rushed the same way, with the delicious and delusive clarity and swing of first-rate perorations.

He bowed to Delarey with the proper dignified humility and went off at once to pump the requisite jets of water on the embers of the fire he had lit.

First he went to his room and 'phoned to every friend who seemed likely to help in keeping things quiet. Then he turned off the light and gazed from his high window, like a fire-watcher on his tower, over the perishable city. Nearly all of it lay silent and dark. Only in a poor northern quarter were fitful spurts of smoky flame to be made out, with a noise like cheering: he caught the tune of a stirring war song that all Ria had been roaring three weeks ago under his office window. It came from the slum in which Sprott had certified that everybody had lost heart.

IV

While he listened, the huge cruciform light burst into bright-ness again, after one of its obscurations. An answering roar, as it seemed, rose at once from the place of unrest in the slums. Clearly the people were watching the cross and were drawing from it some sort of excitement. Then the shouts sank and far up the hill-side a new noise began. Three weeks ago the little mountain gun of the Rian army had become a kind of public pet or mascot with all classes of people in the City. Everybody knew its curious crackling detonation and delighted in its mobility. It was to win mountain battles; it would astonish the world, like the old French seventy-fives. And there it was now, the unmistakable voice of a friend raised again and again in the darkness, crying out that it was come at last, that it was trying hard—could they come out and help it? The thing really spoke like a voice—to Burnage the voice of a cock crowing thrice after all his denials; to common men whom blood warmed, and no laboured subtleties had enfeebled, it was the voice of lost friends come back and of hope raised from the dead.

The answering roar from the slums of Ria was terrific. It did not stop, either. The din spread out over the City and lights spread with the din; the central streets below Burnage's window were growing black with tumultuous crowds. While the crack-crack of the little gun held stoutly on, and the fire of many rifles joined in, a drum began to beat in that poorest quarter of the City which had never been quiet.

CHAPTER XXVI

WILLAN ARRIVES

I

No one except Mrs. Case had guessed how useful Clare Browell would be as a nurse. It was as if a Virginia creeper had been judged on its performance as a standard tree in the middle of an empty space. Hardly anyone could guess what it would do if put to a wall. When once Clare got at the work she did it with much the same tranquil, persistent and business-like passion as an ampelopsis climbs.

When the final smash came, on the night of the day peace was signed, the hopeless rising in the poorer quarters of Ria City was squashed in an hour. A few machine-guns did the job. But the attack by a mystery force on the Portan siege lines was only defeated after the hardest fighting of the war. The attack lasted all night; about midnight it looked like succeeding; from then on, the man-power of the assailants wasted So fast that, with no reserves to bring up, the attack became a mere spirited sham or forlorn bluff, a desperate bid for that most fortuitous of fortune's gifts which comes once in a hundred times to the weak who fight on hard without hope. But this was one of the ninety-nine times: At dawn most of the survivors of Ria's last force in the field, now wounded prisoners, were bundled into a roughly improvised hospital in a big city warehouse. Nurses were requisitioned from the existing war hospitals, and Clare was one of the first to offer herself and to be taken.

Her new ward was not very large, but its contents were valued so highly that an armed guard was put at the door, as if it were a Bank of England or the palace of a King. The treasures within were the chief public criminals of the day. There were the ringleaders of the treacherous anti-Portan riot in the City, and also the organisers and leaders of the lawless attack upon the Portan lines outside. These guilty ones were to be nursed back, at any cost, to a state of health in which they could becomingly be hanged, to put the fear of God into this wicked city.

One patient, in particular, was believed to be esteemed above the rest as an eligible stoat for nailing to the barn-door. It was understood that if Number Sixty were to defeat justice by dying of his three serious wounds, a much longer list of other examples might have to be made. Still there was hope for these other lives. The Portan surgeon in charge was skilful and zealous: Clare was a nurse of talent; Number Sixty had a great constitution, and after a couple of weeks spent chiefly in unconsciousness or semi-consciousness, it was pronounced to be—with good luck—only a matter of days till he could sit up in a court and hear himself tried for murder. One eye was clean gone, and an ugly hole left in its place; but an eye-shade of a pleasant colour could easily be used to obviate any growth of maudlin sympathy with the prisoner in court. Another of his wounds caused more anxiety—some affair of internal bleeding. At any moment this might rescue the guilty from the hands of justice. So a still more distinguished Portan surgeon was called in to consult.

With this pundit there came the Portan Provost Marshal. He looked on, grave, sympathetic and unobtrusively eager while Number Sixty's visible wounds were examined once more, and the invisible damage was re-assessed. The eminent surgeon was sanguine. So long as the prisoner might sit down in court ("Oh! that's easily managed," said the Provost Marshal joyfully) and so long as a surgeon and nurse were kept within call ("This seems a capable woman," he added, indicating Clare with a thumb), he saw no reason why the man should not stand his trial the day after to-morrow. Anyhow, the bandage had better come off the remaining eye now to harden it to the light.

II

When the two higher officials had departed, well pleased with the way things were going, Clare settled the bedclothes where they had been disarranged for convenience in estimating the fitness of Number Sixty for the slaughter. Then she took the bandage off the eye which had been only singed and put out of action, not destroyed like the other.

The patient could just see her enough to make nearly sure it was she, but not quite. So he said nothing at first, but followed her about the ward with his one eye. He grew more certain by degrees, as the eye played itself in to the daylight. Whenever she was passing out of his sight as he lay, he lifted his head an inch or two from the pillow, to follow her longer. He heaved it up with a struggle, much as very young children left lying in perambulators lever up their heads, with a mighty straining of the neck, to reconnoitre the world.

The next time she had to do anything for him he said: "You're Miss Browell—I'm sure of it now."
She said, "Yes."

"Mine's Willan. We only met once. But I know your cousin quite well."

"Dick Merrick?"

She was visibly moved at the name. He went on: "He kept us all going, out there. He did everything well.
And he's a great joker. He cheered us all up."

He saw her lip tremble. And she was no lax emotionalist, he could swear. So all was clear now. He went
on: "He did one of the bravest things ever done. We pretty well knew that we should slip up if we
couldn't send word we were coming. There was scarcely a ghost of a chance for a messenger to get
through. But he tried."

"He succeeded," she said.

"Good Lord!—the great fellow!—and I never knew!" Willan's voice was a real ovation for Merrick.

"You know," she said, "what he found here?" Her voice was firm, but Willan could see a kind of wave of
whiteness fleet across her face like the scudding patches of paleness that traverse blown corn.

"I've heard nothing," he said.

"He found we had failed. We had just given in."

He shut his eye, to think hard for a minute. Then he opened it. "Is that why there's a guard at the door?"

"Yes."

"We're for it? No licence to fight? We were disowned?"

She bowed her head a little. His eye closed again while he worked out the line of his thought. At last he
asked her, "Had Burnage been killed?"

"No."

"He couldn't stop this rot?"

"We all failed," she said.

"They just let him stand out alone?"

"We all failed," she repeated in a low voice.

She grieved so sternly for him in his undiscovered loss of a hero that he was awed, only finding her grim
and not knowing why. So they were both silent, till a harsh sound broke in on the taut immobility of
their pain.

Across the room an atrociously wounded Rian had just lost hold on himself, and burst into long screams and keenings of agony, cries uncontrollable as a woman's in labour, or those of some wild creature trying to tear its broken legs out of a trap. In another moment the sound was audibly cutting the strained nerves of men in other beds. One of them half rose and yelled, "Oh! choke him, some one, for the love of Christ!" and then fell helplessly back. Another sobbed loudly, and a little wailing whimper came from a third. There are such moments in a Zoo; a sudden intensification of misery seems to infect all the captive beasts of a neighbourhood, till they roar together in some sort of frantic communion of anguish, as if in the mad hope of touching a heart in their unpitying bars.

The trouble was that the Portan army surgeons had run short of morphia and its beneficent kindred. There were too many Portan wounded alone for the little anesthetic mercy that there was. And the bread of the children was not to be given to dogs till all the children were fed. So Clare had no material means of relief for the poor bundle of shattered bone and torn flesh that had first lost mastery of itself. She went to it, where it wriggled on its rustling mattress of canvas and hay, moved its head back to the pillow, pressed her hands on its forehead and eyes, and spoke the merest commonplaces of sisterly compassion.

Somehow the screaming subsided under her touch, rather like a child's cries when it is taken up and pressed to its mother. First it sank to a moan, and then diminished away into a silent ground-swell of convulsive sobbing. In ten minutes the creature who had done with all hope and joy was once more enduring stoically the torture of continued existence, mysteriously re-convinced that this is best.

When she had made the storm a calm, she came back to sit by Willan. She had been ordered to give to him all of her care that was not absolutely required elsewhere. He fancied her to have altered in the last ten minutes in some infinitesimal way. Perhaps some tiny portion of her had perished—worn down or wasted away in the benign spirit's struggle to staunch that spurting hemorrhage of uncontrol; possibly some faint line, as yet undetectable, had begun to be drawn, which years would yet etch into a wrinkle on an old face minutely engraved, as his mother's had been, with a long history of brave effort, tenderness and grief. He wondered. What was she thinking now of them all, with their war and their wounds, their grand gallantries and their crying? Perhaps as of small children playing with nursery fires and horribly burnt in their pitiful naughtiness. Yes, woman was older than man, in spite of the yarn about Eve; she was not childish; the life that she gave by facing more than war's torments and dangers was no cheap toy in her eyes, to be broken for fun. He thought so hard that at last his thought passed into speech, as if they had been talking over his thoughts all this time. "It isn't all just swank and bunkum, and flash hero stunts and sly medal-hunting. Look at Dick. He just wanted to do what you'd wish. He wasn't sure what it was, but he thought about you all the time."

"Oh! I know," she said sadly. "I knew what he used to wish."

Willan stared at her. "Used to?"

"He died three days ago. It was tetanus. A small wound, not cared for in time."

Willan sank into himself for a moment, shutting his eye while he took in the idea of all that loss of warm sunshine to the world—most of all to this smitten girl.

"I'm sorry, I'm sorry," he said.

Perhaps his tone expressed more than the actual words. "No, no," she said quickly. "Nothing like 'that. He was a dear old friend—that was all. What more could I do? You can't make feelings come. The wind, you know—it 'blows where it listeth.'"

Slowly he took that in too. Clare un-won! Her heart free! He could have no real hope, but he wanted to live.

CHAPTER XXVII

JUSTICE IN FULL BLAST

I

The court-martial sat in the Bankruptcy Court of the late Republic of Ria. General Delarey, with his sound sense of irony, liked the notion of such a congenial venue for the winding up of his assailants' wild-cat enterprise. Besides, the Court was large; plenty of room for Rians to look on at the show and learn a lesson. To make the lesson more impressive, Delarey himself deigned to preside over the Court of three judges, with Major Latta as its other military member.

First they tried a few samples of the mob that had rioted in the slums in sympathy, if not in collusion, with the brigands from Lost Valley. One flagrant sample was Brench. His younger friend Joe was another. In spite of the uniform that they wore and the discipline that it called for, these and eight other Rian soldiers had beyond doubt been well to the fore when a street barricade was thrown up and bloodthirstily defended. So these ten were clear cases for hanging. They all got their sentence together, in one deliverance of the President's, as people of very small means get the Burial Service in England when they are dead, with one parson reading it out for a lot of them and standing equitably equidistant from the open graves. Many people in court were friends of one prisoner or another, and some of them moaned or snivelled as loudly as the soldier ushers would allow: others gazed with stony fortitude at the vanishing figures of their friends. Of the second kind were Joe's father and Mary. Perhaps the beneficent order of this world still seemed to them to need some explanation.

II

Then came the more dangerous bandits. The first man to be tried wore an undistinguished mixture of Rian uniform and mountain homespun. The best things he had on were his boots. He must have been pretty badly wounded, for he was lifted rather than helped into the dock.

The President ran his eye over the caitiff's scarecrow exterior with soldierly distaste for the man who comes on parade dirty. The official Prosecutor had begun to strain visibly in the leash, at sight of the hare, when the President slipped him with a nod. But, eager as this Prosecutor had been, and happy in using his gifts on so big a day, he did not fall into the error of showing, when once he was off, a greyhound's frank passion of desire to compass the death of the scut. With dignified gusto, ruled by good taste, he recited the damning facts. Ria had capitulated sixteen days ago; the war had ended; every acre of the country had become part and parcel of the territory of Porto; from that moment it had been the legal, aye, and the moral duty of every Rian to fulfil the pledge of his own chosen rulers and transfer his allegiance loyally to their successors. But what had happened? Peace had scarcely been signed when an attack had been made on the Portan forces at a moment when they would naturally be assumed to be off their guard. Nothing but the extraordinary perfection, if he might say so, of the precautions presciently taken by the Portan Commander-in-Chief had averted from both countries the calamity of a momentary success for the forces of disorder. As it was, a long night of absolutely wanton bloodshed only ended after the capture of the rebel ringleader, who would shortly come before that court. There might be some pretence put forward that the prisoner did not know the war had ended when he committed the crime. That plea would be dis-posed of by proof that the fact in question had been conveyed to the rebel leader more than an hour before the attack began. The Prosecutor submitted that in view of these facts the part taken by the prisoner in the killing of some hundreds of Portan subjects amounted to wilful murder.

This piece of eloquence certainly gave the effect of a fine strong engine working well within its powers, with lots of reserves to bring up if any unforeseen doubt of the prisoner's fitness for extinction should arise. This handsome effect was immediately improved by contrast with the confusion of the prisoner's mind, presumably the confusion of conscious guilt. For, when invited to plead "Guilty" or "Not Guilty," he answered, "Not guilty o' murder. Why, they was twenty to one. That ain't no murder, twenty to one ain't." A plea of "Not guilty" was charitably entered.

A sergeant of British origin, wearing the highest Portan decoration for courage in the field, was called to prove the offence. At first his speech was all "Yes, sir," and "No, sir." But soon a certain human exuberance began to well out of him pleasantly. Even soldiers are like roses; they cannot all refrain from emitting characteristic perfumes, even in law courts.

Did the prisoner, the Sergeant was asked, take part in an attack at the stated place, date and hour? "He did that, sir." Was the Sergeant absolutely sure the prisoner was the man? "I am that, sir. There's no man but he, bar one, would ha' done it."

"Done what?" The Prosecutor's voice was growing austere.

"What he did, sir. Like this. We 'ad some wire round our guns—the long 'uns, sir, as shelled the City. The enemy "

"Enemy?" said Delarey severely.

"Beg pardon, sir—the rebels seemed dead set on getting at them guns."

"By cutting through the wire?"

"That's right, sir. We'd a Lewis gun in place to enfilade that Northern stretch of wire. Search-light, too, sir, all along the wire. The prisoner come running straight out o' the dark with 'is nippers an' started in, cutting our wire, quite systematic. He 'adn't an earthly, an' us not 'ardly fifty yards off."

"Well?"

"'You're a done man,' thinks I. 'But you're the best man ever I see.' I 'eld our fire 'alf a moment, just to look at 'im. Best man I ever see."

"You were wrong," said the President.

"I was, sir. Saw a better one next minute."

President and Prosecutor exchanged looks of condolence. Pity the fate of clear brains doomed to much converse with the muddleheads of this world. "Perhaps," said the President resignedly, "he had better tell it his own way. Go on, Sergeant."

The Sergeant did. "Then we downed 'im. He wriggled a bit, then 'e stopped and I saw 'e was working again, with one 'and, cuttin' our wire. He couldn't get up, but 'e was working. I was just giving the word to send 'im a stopper when a big orf'cer"

"A rebel leader, do you mean?" said Delarey.

"Beg pardon, sir—a rebel leader comes doublin' out o' the dark, straight to this man, picks 'im up an' orfs again out o' the light with 'im—then outs again, out o' nowhere, an' starts in on our wire 'imself, a treat to see 'im work. Course we downed 'im, but then 'e got up 'alf-way, on to his knees, an' got feeling about in the grass for the nippers 'e'd lost—'e'd got it through the eye an' couldn't see—an' then 'e got it in the guts an' couldn't stir, an' so we brought 'im in at the finish."

"Is this leader here?" the President asked.

The Prosecutor understood that he was.

"Name?" asked Delarey.

The Prosecutor understood that the man was Willan, the actual leader of the whole conspiracy. "Ah!" said Delarey. He glanced quickly round to his right to see a look of blank horror fill the face of Burnage, the second member of the court. Delarey gave this colleague a look with which the colleague was becoming painfully well acquainted. If looks can ever resemble cords, that look was like the cord which pulls up a terrified goat with a horrible jerk in all its frantic rushes hither and thither. It always brought Burnage back to the thought that in his person all Ria was on probation; that hundreds of lives might depend upon his behaviour; that by his success or failure in exhibiting the passionless rigour of upright judgeship it might be decided whether the future of all Rians would be happy or unbearable. While visions of sternly dutiful judges, in history and in fiction, were thronging into Burnage's mind, with their agonies and their glories, their tragedies of mastered private affection and of noble self-exposure to the hatred and contempt of the unthinking, the President spoke in the mellifluous tone of conscious reasonableness which Burnage was learning to dread more than, any other. "How would it be, Mr. Prosecutor, to deal with this alleged ringleader first? For all that we yet know, the rest might turn out to be mere dupes and tools. And, if so, the fact should be at any rate considered as a mitigating element in their cases."

Oh, yes! Mr. Prosecutor was entirely in the President's hands. Should the present prisoner stand down? No; the President would not trouble the present prisoner to move.

III

It had been thought best, in the end, to equip Willan for the trial with a single large green shade that covered his weak left eye as well as the empty right eye-hole. So he had to be led into the dock, where his great stature and obvious strength, his blinkers and his inveterately docile expression were perhaps less reminiscent of the fallen Samson than of a very fine English shire horse wearing more than the usual safeguards against its walking in the ways of its heart and in the sight of its eyes.

Willan's plea of Not Guilty was duly put down, and the Portan Sergeant's recorded evidence was read out. Did the prisoner wish to question the witness? No, only to thank so sporting an enemy. Did the prisoner wish to make any statement? Yes—-that when he ordered the attack to begin he did not know, nor believe, that peace had been made.

"No word to that effect had reached you?" the President asked sweetly.

"A rumour had," the prisoner replied.

"A rumour of what?" the President asked.

"Of a total surrender."

Delarey went on. "You say a 'rumour.' Why a 'rumour'? Was it not true news of a plain fact?"

"I believed it to be an invention.

"Why?"

"From its form."

"What was its form?"

"It purported to be a message signed by a friend of my own."

"Why should that discredit it?"

"I knew the man."

"Was he so unbelievable?"

"No."

"Why, then?"

"I knew him so well that. I knew he could not have sent me that message."

"Really," the President expostulated softly, "you give us somewhat little help in our search for some excuse for your action."

The prisoner had no pat answer ready. So there was a short silence. It was rather a fraught and sinister silence. You might have felt the prisoner's chance ebbing slowly, but palpably. When words began again they seemed rather like the slight lapping sounds of a-tide, fallen half-way and still falling, among the wet green baulks of slimy timber under a sea pier. "Do you mean," the President asked, "that this person was not in a position to send such a message—that he was not entitled to?"

"Oh! he was that, all right. It was just this—that he wasn't the man to do such a thing."

The President repeated Willan's words with an air of perplexed forbearance. "'Not the man to—'?" He held the phrase, as it were, in his hands and turned it over and over, as if he tried to make sense of it. Willan made an effort. "It's this way," he said. "The man had said things, only a few weeks ago, that couldn't possibly have been said by the man who wrote or dictated this letter. I knew he had said them, for I heard him. But I didn't know he'd sent this letter. So the only thing I could make of it was that the letter was a spoof one, just to hold us up till you were a bit better placed for a fight."

"Did you communicate all this," the President asked, "to your followers in this business?"

"No."

"You left them quite in the dark?" Willan did not answer. "You kept them," Delarey resumed, "under the delusion that they were engaged in an act of lawful warfare?" The President's questions were asked slowly, and Willan's answers were not rapidly given. In the deepening silence of the intervals you could hear more and more clearly that lazy cavernous lapping of the ebbing waters among the piles.

"I decided," said Willan, more stiffly than he had said anything yet, "not to circulate any defeatist propaganda among my command."

At this there was a longer pause than usual—one of those pauses in which you may sometimes feel, during a murder case, that a second person is dying, under your eyes.

IV

Delarey turned to the Prosecutor. Would it, he asked with dulcet and leisurely gravity, be worth while to proceed any further against those men whom this prisoner had avowedly misled?

The Prosecutor again declared himself in the hands of the court. The President turned right and left. "Do I interpret correctly," he asked, "the feelings of my colleagues?"

Latta bowed. Burnage tried to say "I concur" as low as possible. Minute by minute he had sought to put off the pang that must visit the blindfolded Willan when he found that among his judges was the friend to whose staunchness he had just testified so strongly. Possibly Willan might never have to know it. There might be no public giving of independent verdicts. But no spoken word, not even an oratorical adept's, can be wholly trusted to leave the lips precisely as it was ordered by the brain. The "I concur" came out with an almost violent fulness of emphasis, and in another moment Willan had pushed up the shade from his eyes and was blinking round the court eagerly.

The last place he searched, with such sight as he had, was the bench. But he reached it at last and saw who was there. Willan said nothing and did not make even a gesture. He just withdrew, in some more than physical way. You might have thought that a glaze had spread over his face, deleting its previous expression, or that some veil of impalpable gauze had drawn itself across his first look of recognition and appeal. Even before he replaced the eye-shade, more of him than his eyes had passed behind an impervious screen, and the court may be said to have seen him—the whole candid, untroubled and unsuspecting nature of him—no more.

The other prisoner in the dock was told to go, and sin no more. As he was helped out, past Willan, he whispered, "Second time, sir, God bless you." Willan wished him luck.

"Is it your wish," the President asked the accused, "to call as a witness the person from whom this letter purported to come?"

"No, sir," said Willan. "I'll leave it."

"Are you aware," the President cooed, "that if the letter were proved to have been unauthorised by him, this would tell in your favour?"

"I'll just leave it, thank you," said Willan.

"Is there anything else that you wish to say to the court, before it gives its decision?"

"Nothing at all. I've had a fair trial. I'll leave it just as it is."

There was another of those hanging pauses. The President said to each of his colleagues in turn a few words that no one else heard. The prisoner sat quite still: his figure had something of the curious stoical look that a horse has when it has to stand in its harness under sudden and heavy rain. In the public gallery a low hum of talk-was, for the moment, suffered to arise. Sprott was there and had seen justice done on his enemy, Brench. He confided to a neighbour his contempt for the want of spirit shown in Willan's abortive attempts at a defence: "Thort 'e'd do a bluff on 'em—thet's wot 'e done. Then 'e chucks it in the strite—more'n 'arf wye 'ome. Call 'im gime!" Then silence was reimposed.

V

The President summed up with an insistent indecisiveness worthy of a professional judge. That court, he said, was sitting as much for the vindication and relief of all honourable Rians as for anything else. A slur had been put upon their good name. Whether that slur should be wiped out or not—whether the crime of Peace Night could now be set down as the mad act of a few fanatics—especially one—or whether it had been the outcome of a treacherous conspiracy between the actual murderers and a great many persons of all ranks within the City—that was, at bottom, what would be indicated to-day. If the crime were only the freak of a knot of hotheads, or of one intriguer who deceived all the rest, justice might, he thought, be satisfied with the exemplary punishment of the obviously and pre-eminently guilty. If, on the other hand, those who had been caught red-handed, leader and all, were only the instruments of a far-reaching plot in which public men of the first rank were implicated, then the court might rightly decline to deal with this case till the whole affair had been sifted thoroughly. The members of the court would now give their judgment in turn. The better to ensure the free and independent exercise of their discretion he would reserve his own judgment till the last. And he would not deliver it at all if it were found that his two colleagues, representing the conscience of Porto and of Ria respectively, were found to be of one mind. Nothing could satisfy him better than that. He would call first upon the colleague sitting on his right.

Burnage had striven excitedly to read whatever underlay the President's sleek and careful words. And he had felt it to be horribly sinister—a threat of some dreadful vengeance on the helpless City if Willan were let off. No! Not if Willan were let off. For Willan wouldn't, in any case, be let off. Whatever Burnage might do, these two Portan soldiers would of course hang Willan: he was a dead man already. No, the vengeance was threatened in case Burnage did not acquiesce in this inevitable death of Willan's. Willan was lost, anyhow! the only thing left to be settled was whether many other precious things should be lost too—whether Ria should remain blacklisted in Delarey's mind as an unrepentant conspirator who would flout evidence and poison-justice to get a confederate off. And if Delarey and his Government did made a Poland of Ria—chain her, torture her, heavens knows what—it would be he, Burnage, who by his vote to-day would have brought this new misery upon her. And why? To save his friend? No, for his friend was past saving. Merely to save himself pain—the egoistic pain of reflecting "Technically, though only technically, I sent my friend to his death."

At this point in the hurry and heat of his feverish thought, all the bewildering calls of this and that duty and desire seemed to simplify themselves into one overwhelming demand for a tragic sacrifice of private affection on the altar of a patriot's duty. Before he had had time or power to scrutinise this impulse further he had said, with the exalted sorrow of a Brutus, "I find the prisoner guilty," Delarey had turned to Latta, and Latta had said "I'm for acquitting him."

Latta's response was so quick that his words seemed to be trying to run after Burnage's, overtake them and hustle them back, away from the horrible terminus of the road they had taken. Overtake them! Bring back the wisp of soiled air that was now twisting up to the sky in some little fatal pattern of fugitive eddies and twirls irreparably given to it by lips and teeth that had meant no harm.! Sensitive and changeful, a bit of a poet, if only a cheap one, Burnage was quite up to feeling now the terrible fixity of some of the most evanescent things: one quick glance the less from Helen's eyes and no Troy might have burned.

VI

Already the whole atmosphere of the place had been changed by the little explosion from Latta's remarkably virile lips. Till Latta spoke, a certain ascendancy had been fastening itself upon every commonplace mind in the court. They had all been drugged by the solemn hush, the slow parade of patience and fairness, the anaesthetic sense, which every individual seemed to have, of being only a very small cog, nut or bolt in a large and august machine which surely must know what it was doing.

"My instructions simply are—"; "My only duty is—"I merely have to put before you this—": like some mystic chant these customary formulas of self-relief from responsibility for any harm that might come to anyone had droned on and on through the whole unctuous rite. Responsibility for an imminent death might possibly be floating somewhere high up in the air among the motes suspended in the sunlight near the windows. But it, too, was well in suspense; "Thou canst not say I did it," had been the practical absolution given to each man by himself.

That drowsy anodyne had bemused even Burnage. He had given his judgment in a trance of fancied helplessness. Now he was awake. Everyone was suddenly awake. The least expected person of all had smashed the imposing spell like a pane of plate-glass. To acquit the accused had become, in one moment, a quite natural course instead of an impossible one.

Delarey, turning to Latta, said low, for him only to hear, "You don't think it's proved?"

"Oh! It's proved all right, sir," Latta whispered. "It's the waste I mind—to hang such a man. You don't get the like of him often."

"Of course he's splendid, but what could you do with him?"

"Give him a good high command, sir."

"But what of the law, my dear boy? No respect for the law?"

"Law, sir? Why, if that's our line here, we might almost as well be a damn civil court."'

The private colloquy ended, and Delarey delivered his judgement. He was sorry, he said, that a deciding voice from him was required. But he must not shirk his duty. He would be rightly thought fantastic if he affected a clemency so extreme that it had not even been found in a colleague whose impulse to practise it in this case must have been incomparably stronger. The prisoner would be hanged at sunrise to-morrow. If the President were to consult his own feelings he would commute the sentence to one of being shot. But to do so would only encourage the popular tendency to idealise vulgar crime .and to confuse brigandage with war, and the practice of felony with the pursuit of the noblest of professions. He hoped sincerely that with the execution of this prisoner it would be possible for punitive measures to end. In this hope the other sentences that had been passed that day would for the moment be suspended, for future revision. But everything would depend on the measure of order maintained in the City and outside it. To the prisoner he need say no more than warn him to try to make his peace with God. To aid him in any such endeavour an eminent Rian divine would be sent to him.

Willan made his bow to the court and Latta returned it. A man of the guard put an arm under Willan's, with notable gentleness, and led him out.

In the relaxation of the judges' room, behind the bench, Delarey could rally his favourite Staff Officer more freely. "You really are too pure and noble for this world," he said, "with your romantic morality. You'd wreck whole civilisations."

The handsome Latta looked rather stiffly at his commander.

"Well, well," said Delarey, "let us hope you will always have somebody like our good Roman friend here to keep you from going too far when the mercy-before-justice fit is upon you." He smiled at Burnage with all the contempt, as the French say, that there is.

CHAPTER XXVIII

WILLAN GROWS IN THE NIGHT

I

Willan was not taken back from the Bankruptcy Court to his hospital. To give his case its full admonitory and deterrent value, it was thought better to house him for the night in a more unmistakable jail. As a means to this moral end, the chief jail of Ria City was a veritable treasure. The Government had built it in a spirit of robust reaction against the namby-pamby sentiment which would allow prisons to lapse into places which prisoners might like. And the ingenious architect seemed to have fairly revelled in giving his employers a masterpiece of frowning detentiveness after their own hearts. Giant Blunderbore, Giant Despair, or any other first-rate penal expert of the old school would have found it a congenial piece of building.

The large cell designed for persons about to be hanged was the choicest fruit of its author's genius. Willan, far as he was from dwarfish, looked like a mouse confined in a bank safe when they immured him in this fortress, with its six-foot walls and its one smallish window. But his inveterate equity allowed that on a hot afternoon like this, with your one eye somewhat bleary, you might be in worse rooms. He was left alone to make this and other reflections till the day cooled down enough for official persons to feel that they could now get to work. At five a civil middle-aged man, quietly well-dressed, came in and weighed him. The visitor was so manifestly anxious not to seem to be the hangman that Willan was moved to join him in hushing up their obvious business relationship. When the man had the figures that he desired, he went away beaming with a happy sense of having tact.

II

But if any recording angel made an entry, to Willan's credit, on account of that small addition by him to the sum of human happiness, he may have had a serious counter-entry to make in the books a few minutes after. Again there was a theatrical grinding and clanging of rusty locks and over-sized bolts; again the cell-door creaked open with a reluctance almost affected. This time it was Bishop Case that came in.

Willan certainly ought to have known better than he did. For one thing he ought to have been joyfully keeping in mind the favour done him in court when Delarey said that a clergyman of distinction would be sent to give him any of the supports of religion that he might desire. Besides, the Bishop was not thrown, or kicked, or hustled into the cell; nor did the Portan soldier-jailer curse him at all, nor even say that the bloody grub would be dished out at six. Still—you know what Willan was: except under the stimulus of active warfare he could not tumble at the first moment to everything that a truly nimble mind would in that time guess or infer. The dull fellow could only think of the tall divine in gaiters as the eloquent warrior-priest of the Burnages' star-lit balcony, a place from which his own mind had for some time refused to detach itself. So he jumped up and said very cordially, "You one of us, sir? Why, I thought it was only me they were hanging."

"We are all one—in Christ," said the Bishop, somewhat austerely. He did not remember the man. It had been dark on the balcony, and Willan not a man of importance.

"And you a top-holer, sir," Willan rejoined, "in all this old business. You bucked the men up. All that seeing 'em off at the station, and telling 'em how they'd got to lay on God's rod—they liked it first-rate, I can tell you. They didn't forget. It made 'em hang on at the fighting."

"My poor brother—" the Bishop began. He went on in the right professional tone. He begged Willan to put away from him at this dreadful hour these memories of earthly strife. Let him think only how soon he must meet God.

"You're right, sir," said Wijlan. "It is a close call. Ten hours, about—and a sleep to come out of that. So don't let me be in your way. You'll have your own packing to do, so to speak, and I have a bit too. But I'm pleased to be hanged with you, sir."

"Me? Hanged!" But there the good Bishop checked his natural indignation. Sheep, he knew, were froward creatures; pastors had to practise infinite patience. In the most temperate terms he adjured the passing sinner not to repel with insolent jests the bearer of God's offer of infinite mercy. The clock of a neighbouring church was just shaking out on the quiet air its six rather melodious strokes from a tower peaceably resting its outline upon the serenest of blue skies. "Listen," the Bishop said, with his noblest delivery. "God, from His own house, is counting out to you the minutes till He shall call you into His presence."

Willan was slowly getting a grip of the case. "Calling me?" he said. "And not you?"

"Think of your soul—not of me!" the Bishop implored with sincere fervour, the proper ardour of the spiritual rescuer being strongly reinforced by an earnest wish that Willan would take some other line. Poor Bishop! But now his trial was over. That farcical key squealed again in the pantomime lock, and the Portan turnkey appeared at the opening door. "Sorry, sir," he said to Case. "Prisoner's supper."

The man. did not say the Bishop must go. But he could easily be taken as meaning it. The Bishop took it so, with some alacrity. "Quite right, my man," he said to the turnkey, in a tone of manly resignation to a painful necessity. "You are doing no more than your duty." Out went the resourceful divine, to disappear from this history.

III

Willan, the wayward rejector of the viands of the spirit, as cooked by Case, applied himself contentedly now to the bread, the cheese and the water that perish. When these were done, he lay back for a while on his bed of two planks, to consider his ways. It seemed very curious, all that department of things—religion, morals, the whole racket about being good. Right and wrong were, in a way, like people dancing quadrilles—sliding across and taking each other's places, or going half-way and bowing and then coming back, or twirling about together indistinguishably in the middle for awhile. At least, so they seemed when the wise and holy and eloquent people told you what you were to think.

The odd part of it was that, barring one case in a thousand, there never was the slightest doubt what a man ought to do. It was only too beastly clear. Every time it was just like the six o'clock getting-up bell in the winter mornings at school. The one thing in doubt was never whether you ought to show a leg when the bell went, but how the devil you were to make yourself do it.

Lying, thieving, loafing, cadging, swanking, boozing, doing the cruel, fooling with women—why, never for a moment could you honestly say you were in the slightest doubt or perplexity when you were up against some inclination to do one of these. You might do it, but not because you were puzzled and thought "It may be a good thing to do." That way humbug lay.

And yet there is that thousandth case—the case of real doubt, where you did have to think mighty hard first, and where you might really go off the rails altogether, and never get back, if you should start by sizing up this and that wrongly. In fact—had he been a bit of a cadger and sorner for most of his life since he grew up, through making one of these far-reaching bloomers? He had had a wonderful time of it—Oh! a life of tit-bits, the pick of adventures, the best of good sport, game after game, and never a dull one—and all the time eating away at the world's jolly good food and lying in its excellent beds— those delicious inventions—and, altogether, using up part of its stock of useful and delectable things, and then bilking it—not bearing a hand, like a game man, in the everlasting job of keeping things going and something in store for bad times.

Of course he had always tried to "fight for the right" and all that, but here, it seemed, was this crowning case of the justest of all just causes, the Tightest of rights, going the way of the rest and turning out to have been only another questionable pretext for the good old game of scrapping, on some scale or other. He thought, with a kind of half-envious affection, of men coming back of an evening from stuffy offices and shops in towns, with the dust white on their boots, and their shabby hats pushed back on hot foreheads, and women carefully cleaning the house while their men were away, and keeping up the whole kindly, rhythmic routine of places where right habit has time to take root and children slowly draw into themselves the power and joy of self-mastery. While he thought, he became more sorry that he was to be hanged. He would have liked to try the plain life. He fancied the right tip must be, not to go for the cake, but to stick to bread till you find out, some day, that it's delicious.

Then he gave a quick little laugh at himself. Pretty cheap, that—first to live the merry life of nips and drams, for all it was worth, and then to turn round and cry up the life of humdrum, just when he was secured against having to live it No, he couldn't put a very good face on his thoughts, and yet he fancied there was something in them; what he wanted was one of those magical people who can make out just what you mean, when you can't do it yourself—put it into fine words too, so that you wonder at yourself for having had such a presentable notion.

To feel this was to think of Burnage, the only master of that delightful craft among Willan's acquaintance. He would like to see Burnage. As to Burnage's latest doings, Willan had simply not arrived at any definite state of mind. It was all a grand puzzle. Ten to one, Burnage had totted up the pros and cons right enough, and had then done the best he could think of, things being in the muck that they were. Certainly Willan had no grand reproaches to utter—no proper sense, indeed, of the dramatic requirements and possibilities of the situation. He did not even suppose that Burnage must be finding it too awkward to come for a last word with an old friend. He thought Burnage was probably too busy. But he did wish that Burnage could come. Then they could have had it all out about this affair of the plain stuff and the dainties. Willan went to sleep wishing for half an hour of Burnage.

IV

The thing was a marvel, a good dream come true, Willan awoke, and lo! Burnage was there.

It was not daylight yet. But day was not far off. Burnage had spent much the greater part of the night in working himself up to come. He had felt sure it would lacerate him thoroughly to see Willan again. And laceration was what he most craved for. He longed for reproaches. To find himself spurned by his old adorer as a false friend, a time-serving wind-bag—that was the only thing that could serve in the slightest degree the purpose of scalding water, soda and soap for his consciously soiled spirit. If only he could be put to even more torture than he deserved, that would be best: perhaps he might feel less horribly overdrawn at the bank if some punishment contritely endured could be atrocious enough to outweigh the monstrous sum of his squanderings of honour.

No doubt he did not put it quite so clearly as that to himself. His mind had always shunned the astringent cold of precision. Still, he went to the prison, at four in the morning, possessed with little else but desire to hold his hand in the flame. Possibly some canny cell of his brain may have seen, before the rest of him knew, that this itch was likely to come. For at the close of the trial—he scarcely knew why, at the time—he had asked Delarey for a pass to the prison, on the chance of his wanting to use it.

Delarey had written out a pass at once. "I think I can trust you," Delarey had said, with his foul, sneering urbanity, "not to change cloaks with the prisoner—the old dodge, you know."

The turnkey went back yawning to his sleep, when he had let Burnage into the fattening-coop, as the turnkeys called Willan's cell. He left a lit candle behind, but even its light and the grinding squeals of the key took time to rouse Willan out of the deep sleep of a healthy man who has just got the better of wounds. He had taken off boots, coat and collar, and lay cool and easy, outside his brown blanket.

It almost shocked Burnage to see Willan so little transformed.

The world was in travail and torment; a nation had fallen; in three hours Willan would have in his mouth the strange taste of death and be facing whatever strange events may come after it; all the air tingled with pain; the earth rocked and burned with it the sombre wings of some vast Passion Music ought to be felt filling the universe with the rustle of their slow beating. The placid sleep of Willan's big body and untumultuous mind jarred upon Burnage like some wrong intonation, marring those tragic harmonies.

When a sound sleeper awakes, there are some conscious moments before the events of yesterday come back to his mind. So Willan awoke to the sight of Burnage's face framed in an oval of candle-light—not the Burnage of yesterday—only the friend of his youth, and an irremovable part of the scenery of many happily remembered days, Willan gave a friendly grin first and said, "You, Cyril? All right?" Then yesterday's doings came flooding back into his brain.

Burnage began, "You know why—?" but his voice came out badly, as if clotted with stickiness.

"Drink of water?" said Willan. Justice had left a tin mug of this on the floor, near his hand, with some bread on a plate of the same. He offered the mug.

Burnage drank, and then started again: "You know why I've come?"

"I know I went asleep wishing you would," Willan said cheerfully.

Somehow it threw Burnage out. It put him off. The dreadful scene that he must act with poor Willan was not going the way that it should. "I owed it to you," he said darkly, "to come. It was I that brought you to this."

"Oh! that's all right," said Willan. "Mind if you sit on the floor? They don't risk a chair with us here." He had sat up himself, on his two planks, and begun to put on his collar, and then stopped. Perhaps they would rather not have the collar on. Burnage sat down on the floor, with his back to the wall. The position is one of extraordinary disadvantage for the delivery of tragic speech. But Burnage was going through with his penitential exercise. "You saw," he resumed, "what I did for you yesterday. I took it out of Latta's power to save you."

"Latta? Latta? Oh! yes, I remember. I liked Latta. But wasn't his law a bit rocky?"

Burnage was not to be checked in that way, in the full swing of his arraignment of himself. He pressed for a conviction. "And not yesterday only," he urged. "You remember a letter of yours—the one Merrick brought?"

"I've heard he got through."

"Yes. He gave me the letter. I gave it to Delarey—into his hands."

"I don't quite see you doing that," said Willan, scarcely knowing what to say. He took it for granted that there must be some other side, some quite-all-right side, to what Cyril had done. To suppose that Cyril could ever be just a story-book villain was merely silly. But Willan didn't want to have it all out. For one thing, he really was a bit pressed for time. Already the window of the-cell was grey with the approach of dawn. And he did want to beat up that other old subject with Cyril, now he had got him—the affair of the plain ways of life and the coloured ones.

But Burnage, by now, was far past taking notice of anything so external to himself as Willan's choice of a topic for his last hour of conversation. Burnage had himself well in the pillory now: nothing would do but to keep on pelting himself for as long as the munitions of hatred and scorn would hold out: the business absorbed him as wholly as simpler egoists are absorbed in their bouts of self-praise. "Oh! I've been a good friend to you—first got you into this trap of a war and then sold you. Oh! yes—sold you, twice over. I only came round to the side of the yellers for war because I believed Bute had bought the Voice over my head and would sack me if I didn't."

"Bute? Man who sold boots?" Willan knew well enough. He only said it in desperation—in the vain hope of impeding the flood of Burnage's self-impeachment.

No use: the torrent swept such pebbles out of its way. "I was bribed—or blackmailed—put it the way you prefer. And then Delarey held up a big stick and I caved in and sold you again. See? Judas only did it once. I've beaten him hollow." What can you do, besides wince, when a friend insists on flinging himself on the ground before your feet and writhing in ecstasies of self-abasement? Willan did not know. And here was his remnant of time running out. The grey window had whitened; a sleepy twittering of birds had begun; a few feet of men hastening early to work could be heard from the streets. The pleasant church chime that had been silenced since midnight regained its voice and struck six as if it liked it. For the first time in his life Willan had a strange feeling that he was, just in one little respect, older than

Cyril. He must make allowance for Cyril. "Bread?" he said, holding out the tin plate, at the next pause in Cyril's revel of self-flagellation.

Burnage declined. You don't eat much, in a condition like his. But you drink. When Willan had eaten his bread and put out a hand for the mug, all the water was gone. It did not matter. Willan was not really thirsty. But Cyril seemed queerly dry. The child couldn't be well. Oh! Willan was becoming much older than Cyril.

In some way, perhaps, the nature of Willan's disquiet on Cyril's account disclosed itself. It was so sort of fear lest Cyril should die of remorse, or live out his life in a cold shadow; it was only a feeling that Cyril had had a poor night, and might have a chill. And somehow Cyril began to perceive it; he saw that Willan was not being overwhelmed with horror at such a tragic fall as his friend's. Willan was failing him, in a sense; he did not come up to the full stature of the authentic sufferer of such a fate as his; he was not doing what some men might have done in his place to help in wringing Burnage's heart as cruelly as it deserved and desired; he was underplaying the whole rending scene; and he had none of the conscious momentousness of the dying; no shred of awesome feyness about him as about Caesar and Duncan and Banquo just before their betrayal consummated itself in their deaths. The tremendous moment had come, but not quite the man for it.

So they sat for a while in a state of pathos, with Burnage's eloquence flagging and none coming to Willan; friendly enough, but each with a criticism of his friend taking shape in his mind, against his will. Both were silent at last, and consciousness of their silence was growing hedge-like between the two, when nature provided an incidental break in the tension by throwing a sudden square of bright yellow high up on the Western wall of the cell. Willan looked up quickly, with the fresh delight of an old-time sun-worshipper, to see the dazzling rim of the cool ball of light just clearing the shadowy highlands of snow above the head of Lost Valley.

Steps were instantly heard from the flagged corridor. Official persons must have been up in good time, ready to take from the fresh lips of dawn the traditional cue for the extinction of the wicked.

This time the head-warder, a Portan Sergeant-Major of fine appearance, came in. He ignored Burnage, saluted Willan with great care, and said: "If you please, sir, the Governor-just coming."

Burnage was sunk in thought of some sort, and Willan had to touch him on the arm. "So long, old son," said Willan. He had to hustle Burnage out of the cell in a gentle, elder-brotherly way. He was now amazingly older than Cyril.

They met at the door the Portan Governor of the prison, a middle-aged Major, full of courtesy. He said he had brought Willan's doctor and nurse from the hospital, just to make sure that the bandages on his wounds were all comfy. Would Willan like to have them in—for as long as he wished? He'd like Willan to feel there was no sort of hurry.

Feeling sure of this good fellow, Willan looked straight at his eyes and asked if the nurse might come in alone. "She's a friend," he explained.

"Lord! Yes," said the Major, "Ten minutes? Twenty? I'll see that no one butts in."

CHAPTER XXIX

JUST IN TIME

I

They had brought in a chair for Willan to sit on, with his head raised, while Clare stood in front of him and adjusted the bandage over his empty eye-socket. That took up one of their minutes. Then he said: "Let's leave the rest. They'll do for to-day. And there's so much to say."

She said "Yes," without any maidenish fencing. These minutes must be his, every second of them, to use as he wished.

"You remember an evening?" he asked.

"On the Burnages' balcony? Yes—every moment of it—every word that was said."

"That's bad for me. I was gassing, no end."

She shook her head hard.

"Mean to say you agreed?" he asked eagerly.

"No," she confessed with an effort. "Not then. But I didn't disagree really. Only—they were so sure, all those others! And I admired one of them so much, it almost hurt—as you did another one, didn't you? And everything was so lovely, just then, and somehow it all seemed to be on their side—the night and the music and stars, and the snow, and the dear, living noise from the town."

"I know, I know," he said. Just didn't he know them, those hopeless odds?

"I missed my chance," she said ruefully. "I didn't help you."

"Yes, yes—immensely."

"No. I said nothing at all."

"One doesn't say kindness and fairness and slowness to judge. One looks 'em, and breathes 'em. One is them. And you were. You were so just that it made me afraid, in a way." For if you'd barred me too, I'd have known that all the others were right."

"Barred you!" He was still sitting and Clare looked down at his face from her height with a kind of benedictive glow warm in her brown eyes. "Do you know something—?" she opened abruptly, and then found it hard, as it seemed, to go on, and then she made an effort and gulped down whatever the obstacle was. "I seem to have lived all my life among people—Oh! nice people of course, but they seemed in a way to have used up the world—they had seen all the grand things and read all the books, and they knew all the wisdom and wit that there is to know—they always knew what would be round the next corner, or over the wall—you see what I mean? But there was something they never had found—or they had lost it."

He gazed up at her, listening and marvelling, eager to hear; and Clare, looking down at his face, gave the uncertain little laugh of some women when they are suddenly moved to affectionate pity by the grave simplicity of a child. I think it is half laughter and half weeping. "That's it," she cried. "They hadn't that. They couldn't wonder—they were so old and they felt so certain that they were in all the great secrets that ever there were. And then you came, like—Oh! no, not like somebody less wise, but like someone just fallen out of a star, on to the earth, with nothing dull to you yet, and all the wonder still in your face, and whenever you looked at a thing you made it new with your eyes."

It was beyond him. No quite unbedevilled creature can easily understand that there is beauty in its own mere unbedevilment. But this much he saw—that, at least in some little degree, he had been in her thoughts, and kindly entertained there—only humanely, no doubt, but to any man of humble mind it is miracle enough to be given such hospitality in the mind of a woman loved without hope. "You thought that of me!" he said in astonishment. "You remembered me!"

Looking straight at his wondering face, the girl threw away, as it were with one sweep of an arm, all the reserves that wise maidens practise with men who have more than some few minutes to live. "I've loved you ever since," she said, with a noble shamelessness. He had not asked for the gift—perhaps might not value it—still she would offer it; if her love could be little more now than a flower on a grave, yet she would have the dead know it lay there, if he cared.

He rose in a moment and hid her eyes on his breast, clasping her tightly and babbling the passionate repetitions of happy lovers, "Oh! my love! My one love! My dear love!"

"You did care?" she murmured from the warm cover her face had found for itself. Like all lovers, she longed to hear the words said, though she knew.

In the cell window a little Alpine landscape was framed. "I found out up there," he said, showing it.

"I was greedy," she said. "I wanted advantages. When you were gone I kept wondering, 'Will he ever let anyone in so close to his heart that she too will be able to look out at things with his eyes that make everything new?' And then I wanted it all for myself and—"

From where she had hid her eyes since her avowal she looked up with a face of appeal to be understood in the ways of her love, whatever they were. But the rest of her words waited unsaid while they kissed. Once, for an instant, he drew his lips back from hers, to say one of the hundreds of things that pressed to be said. Then he gave up the attempt. The things to say were too many, and speech too slow; why waste one of their small remnant of minutes on any way of telling their mutual story that was less fluent than their embraces. So they closed again in a kiss that made time stand still while it lasted: eternity was in their lips and eyes; they were unhurried while they told each other, by the quality of their silent tenderness, what words could not have told—how their love was neither a mere fire in the blood, nor yet a dry skein of unsensuous thought, but a stir of new life in both body and mind, interfused like the words and the air of a great song, each the more glorious for its union with the other. All the life together that might have been theirs had to be lived how, in their kind and intimate thoughts, and they lived it with a will and neither cried out against fate.

One pang stung him to words: "You'll be alone."

She scouted the sad thought. "Oh! no, no, not so much alone as if we hadn't met. And you won't be dead—all of you won't—while I'm living. No one has quite finished living as long as he fills someone's life. You won't even grow old; you'll be young to me always; your face and your brown hair cannot change now."

II

The grind of nailed boots on stone clanged hollowly in the corridor. In another moment the Major's voice was heard raised, giving some minor order. "Good fellow!" said Willan. "He's letting us know." When the door was opened, a good minute later, the prisoner's nurse was putting together her scissors arid lint and so on. Time to go back to her hospital.

Reaching her ward, she went round the windows, as was her custom at dawn, to see that they were all duly open. Through the last she noticed a tall new flagstaff over the great prison. As she looked, a black flag fluttered, jerk by jerk, up to the top of the staff. It stayed there, flapping lazily. A sudden silence followed—so deep that Clare began to hear the light crepitation of the cord as it whipped against the long pole. Then she saw that every one in the street below was standing still and that men were bareheaded. For somehow the rights of Willan's story were known, and Clare was only the chief mourner in a mourning city.

C. E. Montague – A Short Biography

Charles Edward Montague was born in London on New Year's Day, 1867.

Montague was the son of Francis Montague, an Irish Roman Catholic priest from County Tyrone, Ireland, who after falling in love with Rosa McCabe, the daughter of a successful merchant from Drogheda, left the Church, married Rosa and, in 1863, moved to England.

His education was excellent; he attended the City of London School and then went on to university at Balliol College, Oxford.

Whilst at Oxford he achieved, in 1887, a First in Classical Moderations and two years later a Second in Literae Humaniores.

In addition to his time studying Montague, a keen writer, wrote several and well-respected literary reviews for the Manchester Guardian.

In February, 1890, the editor, C. P. Scott, invited him to Manchester for a month's trial at the paper. Montague was obviously an impressive young man and he was soon given a full-time job.

It was here that Montague was to begin his career in earnest; his hard work and talents turning him into a respected leader writer as well as drama critic.

Montague and Scott shared the same political views and between them they turned the Manchester Guardian into a vibrant and campaigning newspaper. Today it would be called a mission statement back then it was stated as "to bring all political action to the same tests as personal conduct".

This quickly led to their support of Irish Home Rule, a divisive issue at the time. Scott was now to take his views in front of the public and stand for Parliament. He was elected to serve between 1895 and 1906 and Montague now became the de facto editor of the paper. Once more the paper ran contrary to government policy and was in opposition to the Boer War which had begun to show many of the latent evils that war was to bring in terms of its brutalising conduct and the use of new technology and new ideas.

The relationship between Montague and Scott also became one of father and son-in-law when Montague married Scott's only daughter, Madeline, at the Unitarian Chapel in Manchester in 1898.

Montague had always had a great interest in literature and theatre and by the turn of the century was applauded as one of England's leading drama critics. Such was their insight and popularity that many of these essays were gathered together and later printed in book form.

As the storm clouds of war gathered over Europe in the summer of 1914 both Montague and Scott argued in the paper against Britain becoming involved in a war on the continent.

However argument was futile. When the Arch Duke was shot the dominos fell one after another. Britain intervened and went to the aid of its Allies. The First World War was now upon them with all its savagery and butchery.

Montague believed that it was important to give full and unequivocal support to the British government now that war was upon the Country. The general feeling that 'it will be all over by Christmas' became a realisation that it would drag on for years and the world now watched the horrific spectacle of trench warfare where tens of thousands were slaughtered for an advance of a few yards.

Montague wrote to Scott: "I have felt for some time, and especially since I have been writing leaders urging people to enlist, a strong wish to do the same myself. I wrote last week to the War Office to ask if there was any chance of getting over the difficulty of my few years over the limit of age, and I was told that although the War Office could not directly break the rule itself, it did not veto exceptions made by those responsible for the raising of new battalions locally."

Those 'few years' were, in fact, decades. Montague was now age forty-seven with a wife and seven children dependent upon him. Although his hair had been grey since his mid-twenties, he made a passable attempt at dying it darker in order to help persuade the army to take him. (or, as H. W. Nevinson put it in his witty and truthful way "Montague is the only man I know whose white hair in a single night turned dark through courage.") On 23rd December, 1914, the Royal Fusiliers accepted him and he joined the Sportsman's Battalion.

His military training was held at Climpson Camp in Nottingham. By November, 1915, Montague had been sent to France.

Upon his arrival on the Western Front, his commanding officer at once questioned the wisdom of having a man in his late forties in the trenches. Montague was sent before the Medical Board on 28th January

1916. He wrote "I went in and found the Colonel-Surgeon, who had barred me a month ago on the ground of my age, again presiding. He looked up at me genially, when I came to the table, and said, "So I hear you want to have another whack of the Germans". I admitted that I did. "How old are you - I mean, your real age?" "Forty-nine, Sir", said I, "but only just". "Sure you're fit?" I said yes. Another doctor at the table said something about my having been there before. "Yes, yes", said the Colonel, "I remember him perfectly. Well, Sergeant, all right", and he marked me a big 'A' on his report. I grinned and saluted and made off. He called after me as I was making for the door, "Sergeant, I believe you'll do better up there than some of the young uns".

Whatever the virtues of his patriotism it did help to bring about a new rule. Three months later it was announced that all men over forty four were to be banned from trench work.

Being a soldier in the trenches was hell on earth. You were either fighting, being shelled by artillery or living cheek by jowl in deep, muddy slits of earth where conditions can only best be described as appalling, the landscape often littered with dead and rotting corpses.

Montague wrote of the conditions to Francis Dodd: "The one thing of which no description given in England any true measure is the universal, ubiquitous muckiness of the whole front. One could hardly have imagined anybody as muddy as everybody is. The rats are pretty well unimaginable too, and, wherever you are, if you have any grub about you that they like, they eat straight through your clothes or haversack to get at it as soon as you are asleep. I had some crumbs of army biscuit in a little calico bag in a greatcoat pocket, and when I awoke they had eaten a big hole through the coat from outside and pulled the bag through it, as if they thought the bag would be useful to carry away the stuff in. But they don't actually try to eat live humans."

The journalist, Philip Gibbs, later recalled: "Prematurely white-haired, he had dyed it when the war began and had enlisted in the ranks. He became a sergeant and then was dragged out of his battalion, made a captain, and appointed as censor to our little group. Extremely courteous, abominably brave - he liked being under shell fire - and a ready smile in his very blue eyes, he seemed unguarded and open. Once he told me that he had declared a kind of moratorium on Christian ethics during the war. It was impossible, he said, to reconcile war with the Christian ideal, but it was necessary to get on with its killing. One could get back to first principles afterwards, and resume one's ideals when the job had been done."

Montague was, as described earlier, a worker, a doer, and was soon promoted to the rank of second lieutenant and with it a transfer to Military Intelligence. For the next two years he had the task of writing propaganda for the British Army and censoring articles written by the five English journalists authorized to write, albeit with 'help' from the censor, on the Western Front.

Another of his duties was to escort important visitors for tours of the trenches. Among his charges were: David Lloyd George, Georges Clemenceau, George Bernard Shaw and H. G. Wells. (It is a bizarre thought now that this could happen but just over 60 years earlier many had picnicked with their wives on the hill-tops as the various battles of the Crimea war unfolded in the valleys below).

But the carnage also re-kindled his own feelings that War in the end solves little. Disillusioned by its scale, futility and bleak prognosis, he wrote a note in his diary in December 1917: "To take part in war cannot, I think, be squared with Christianity. So far the Quakers are right. But I am more sure of my duty of trying to win the war than I am that Christ was right in every part of all that he said, though no one has ever said so much that was right as he did. Therefore I will try, as far as my part goes, to win the war, not pretending meanwhile that I am obeying Christ, and after the war I will try harder than I did before to obey him in all the things in which I am sure he was right. Meanwhile may God give me credit for not seeking to be deceived."

George Bernard Shaw was one of those who Montague took for a tour of the frontline trenches: "At the chateau where the Army entertained the rather mixed lot who were classified as Distinguished Visitors, I met Montague. Finding him just the sort of man I like and get on with, I was glad to learn that he was to be my leader on my excursions. The standing joke about Montague was his craze for being under fire, and his tendency to lead the distinguished visitors, who did not necessarily share this taste into warm corners. Like most standing jokes it was inaccurate, but had something in it.... Both of us felt that, being there, we were wasting our time when we were not within range of the guns. We had come to the theatre to see the play, not to enjoy the intervals between the acts like fashionable people at the opera."

In November 1918 the war was over and Montague could now return home to his wife and family and also to the Manchester Guardian where he would continue to stay until retirement in 1925.

After the end of World War I Montague wrote in a strong anti-war vein; "War hath no fury like a non-combatant." Disenchantment (written in 1922), a collection of newspaper articles about the war, was one of the first prose works to strongly criticise the way the war was fought, and is a pivotal text in the development of literature about the First World War. Disenchantment criticised the British Press' coverage of the war and the conduct of the British generals. Montague accused the latter of being influenced by the "public school ethos" which he condemned as a "gallant robust contempt for "swats" and for all who invented new means to new ends and who trained and used their brains with a will".

Perhaps the paragraph in Disenchantment that most readily captures his overall feeling is: "The freedom of Europe, The war to end war, The overthrow of militarism, The cause of civilization - most people believe so little now in anything or anyone that they would find it hard to understand the simplicity and intensity of faith with which these phrases were once taken among our troops, or the certitude felt by hundreds of thousands of men who are now dead that if they were killed their monument would be a new Europe not soured or soiled with the hates and greeds of the old. So we had failed - had won the fight and lost the prize; the garland of war was withered before it was gained. The lost years, the broken youth, the dead friends, the women's overshadowed lives at home, the agony and bloody sweat - all had gone to darken the stains which most of us had thought to scour out of the world that our children would live in. Many men felt, and said to each other, that they had been fooled."

For Montague the war had been corrosive on his ideals, his faith and his time away from his young family. But it had given him much to write about both for the paper and also for his books which he now hoped to also spend more time working on. Among those to flow from his pen are the novels A Hind Let Loose and Rough Justice as well as collections of short stories, other essays and a travel book.

He finally retired in 1925, and settled down to become a full-time writer in the last years of his life.

C. E. Montague died in Manchester on May 28th, 1928 at the age of 61.

Today Montague is seen as an Edwardian writer who, in his best work, was able to deliver the reality of the situations with their corrosive emotions and doubts. Though undervalued, much of his work has now begun to be again recognised for its honesty and its literary value. A writer with a sharp eye and keen ear and a brain unafraid to think things through and give us the benefit of those thoughts.

His collected papers are archived at John Rylands University.

Montague also wrote some poetry. Much of the conflict between his Christian faith and his soldierly duties are summed up in this poem:-

Unnamed Lines

Yes, of course it was sin
And no Christ would say `Fight
For the right' -
But we had to win.

When the chaplain would bluster and blow
About laying the rod
Of God
On the back of `His foe',

I knew it was all just a form,
And there was no fiery sword,
And the Lord
Was not in the storm.

Yet - to have stood aside
Hoarding my fortunate life
With my wife
While other men died!

Some sort of god, good or bad,
Would have kept me longing in vain
To be slain
As I am, if I had.

Written sometime in 1917

C. E. Montague – A Concise Bibliography

Dramatic Values (1911) Reviews
The Morning's War (1913) Novel
Disenchantment (1922) Essays on the First World War]
Fiery Particles (1923) Short stories (Another Temple Gone/Honours Easy/My Friend the Swan/A propos des Bottes/The First Blood Sweep/In Hanging Garden Gully/All for Peace and Quiet/Two or Three Witnesses/A Trade Report Only
A Hind Let Loose (1924) Novel

The Right Place (1924) Travel writing
Rough Justice (1926) Novel
Right off the Map (1927) Science fiction novel
Action (1928) Short stories (Action/A Cock and Bull Story/Sleep, Gentle Sleep/Judith/In the Ways of his Heart/A Pretty Little Property/The Great Sculling Race/Wodjabet/A Fatalist/Man Afraid/Ted's Leave/The Wisdom of Mrs. Trevanna/Didn't take Care of Himself
A Writer's Notes on His Trade (1930)